"I got the impression t[...] man, but I'm changing my mind. Fast. Because if you think voicing my concerns about Harcourts amounts to nothing more than *insolence,* then you're plain stupid."

"Stupid?" He glared at her, astounded.

"Yes, stupid stupid stupid!" Sylvia repeated, throwing up her hands crossly. "You know full well why I came to London, yet you've done everything humanly possible to make my life as difficult as you can." She shook her head and blew out a sigh. "I'm not a threat to you, Jeremy—I think you're the best man for the job. All I care about is that we get to the bottom of how Thackeray stole our designs. But you don't really care," she spat. "All you think about is your damn pride. I suppose in some way my presence makes you feel belittled. Well, let me tell you something, *Lord* Warmouth. I run a team and I don't like lone wolves. Particularly those that out of sheer pride and idiocy can't see the forest for the trees."

"Rubbish," he bit out, but the distressing truth of her words hit home hard.

"Then tell me you haven't done everything in your power over the past week to make my life impossible," she repeated, arms akimbo.

"Of course I haven't. That's ridiculous," he muttered.

"No, it isn't." Sylvia leaned forward, eyes level with his. "You can't stomach the fact that I'm the CEO and that ultimately, I'm your boss."

Also available from MIRA Books and
FIONA HOOD-STEWART

THE LOST DREAMS
THE STOLEN YEARS
THE JOURNEY HOME

FIONA
HOOD-STEWART

SILENT
W I S H E S

MIRA®

ISBN 1-55166-728-2

SILENT WISHES

Copyright © 2003 by Fiona Hood-Stewart.

All rights reserved. Except for use in any review, the reproduction or
utilization of this work in whole or in part in any form by any electronic,
mechanical or other means, now known or hereafter invented, including
xerography, photocopying and recording, or in any information storage or
retrieval system, is forbidden without the written permission of the publisher,
MIRA Books, 225 Duncan Mill Road, Don Mills, Ontario, Canada M3B 3K9.

All characters in this book have no existence outside the imagination of the
author and have no relation whatsoever to anyone bearing the same name
or names. They are not even distantly inspired by any individual known or
unknown to the author, and all incidents are pure invention.

MIRA and the Star Colophon are trademarks used under license and registered
in Australia, New Zealand, Philippines, United States Patent and Trademark
Office and in other countries.

Visit us at www.mirabooks.com

Printed in U.S.A.

To
Frances Parsley Lynch
my beloved Mater Americana

ACKNOWLEDGMENTS

No book is written alone. Much of the success is owed to those surrounding the author, those who, day after day, follow the bumpy trajectory from the book's conception and birth and through its growing pains. There are many to whom I owe much gratitude for their patience, time and generosity. Unfortunately it would be impossible to name them all.

Thanks to my sons, Sergio and Diego, for being patient with Mom; to John Nash for guiding me day by day through the rough and the smooth; to my patient editor, Miranda Stecyk; to Dianne Moggy, Donna Hayes and Meg Ruley for being such a fabulous team. Many thanks to you all.

There was never yet an uninteresting life.
Such a thing is an impossibility. Inside of
the dullest exterior there is a drama,
a comedy, and a tragedy.
—Mark Twain
"The Refuge of the Derelicts," 1905

1

In the climate-controlled chill of the spacious conference room, the air hung thick with tension as each person gazed in somber amazement at the pictures spread haphazardly on the huge stretch of highly polished mahogany. They stood stiffly, staring, unable to register the enormity of it all. Ira Romano, Harcourts's vice-president of marketing—tall and suave, immaculately dressed, as always, in a beige linen Italian suit—was the first to react. He cleared his throat and muttered an expletive. Hamilton Burke who, in his scruffy jeans and T-shirt, looked more like a graduate student than chief of design for Harcourts USA—one of the largest fine-home and decorating companies in the nation—lowered his face to his hands and let out a sound between a sigh and a groan.

Sylvia Hansen, whose ultimate responsibility this situation was, showed no emotion. It was all happening inside.

When Hamilton had hastily requested a full meeting of the company's top management this afternoon, she knew instinctively that a major disaster had hit.

Now, as he sat up and explained in a raspy monotone that someone, somehow, somewhere, had leaked the plans for the entire spring collection to their major competitor, the full scope of the catastrophe loomed, like a storm on a lake: one minute the sky was blue and clear; the next, dark swirling clouds threatened to mar what up until now had been fairly plain sailing. Straightening the jacket of her black designer suit, Sylvia swallowed imperceptibly, let the information seep in and gave herself exactly one minute to recover as the initial shock of seeing Harcourts's innovative spring collection copied almost piece for piece in the Marchand catalog coalesced into a fermenting and focused rage.

She reached out a fine, manicured hand, randomly picked up one of the photographs, and studied it carefully. Except for a slight modification in the curve of the arm, the black and brushed metal lamp was an exact replica of what had been forecast as one of Harcourts's best-selling items this season.

Worldwide.

Her lips tightened. With an effort, she stopped herself from shredding the damn picture and giving way to rising frustration. Instead, she laid it carefully back on the gleaming surface with a shrug of her slim shoulders that barely hinted at her inner anger, and addressed her staff.

"Well, it's obvious Aimon Thackeray's behind this. With his reputation for destroying the competition, this kind of sleazy tactic has Thackeray's name on it. Any idea who might be responsible for the leak?" She raised a brow and glanced at Ira.

"None," he replied flatly, shaking his dark, silver-streaked head somberly. "Ham and I have been going over and over the design team in London and there's just nobody that comes to mind. First," he enumerated, lifting his tanned hand, "they've all been with us for several years now, and second, it doesn't make sense that any of them would leak info to Marchand, since suspicion would fall right at their door."

"That's right," Hamilton agreed, suddenly coming to life and cocking his head toward the scattered pictures. "If it were one or two items—but shit, man, that's the whole fucking collection they've gotten hold of. It's fucking incredible."

"Ira, have you asked Aaron if there's anything we can do about the situation legally?" Sylvia said, leaning back, tapping her knee with her pen and ignoring Hamilton's language. Then, unable to sit still, she rose and moved to the other end of the long, windowed conference room, which hovered fifty-two stories above Park Avenue.

"He's looking into things as we speak. But frankly, I don't think so. The differences are just subtle enough to justify the similarities. This job was done by an expert. And even if we did fly in with an injunction, what good would it do? They're already out there in the goddamn market, Syl. We'd merely look more foolish than we already do." Ira clenched his fist and pounded the back of one of the sleek chairs that formed a perfect row of chrome and leather along each side of the table. "Whoever did this knew every damn thing there was to know—our trims and options, our timing, our pricing for each item. It's unbelievable." He threw his hands up in a gesture of incomprehension and moved around the table, shaking his head once more. Then he reached for his brief-case on the floor. There were two dull clicks as he opened it.

Sylvia returned thoughtfully to her place at the table and sat down once more. There had to be a solution, a way to thwart Thackeray's unexpected attempt to sabotage her schemes. She barely heard Ira as he sank despondently onto the chair next to her and pulled out a thick sheaf of papers. What she needed now were solutions, not more lamentations over what had taken place. But she was wise enough to know that her loyal, creative co-workers needed to let off steam.

"It's all here." Ira slid the documents toward her. "Their price projections undercut ours, the articles are virtually identical.... Do you realize what this means?" he asked at last, handing her the list.

"That Thackeray may very well have won this round," she answered dryly, flipping through the list, her razor-sharp brain registering each detail while her inner calculator did the math. The enormity of what this could mean to the company battled with her determination to defeat Thackeray, trounce him, show him he'd made a mistake. But how?

The bastard.

In a way, she was to blame. She should have known Aimon Thackeray was up to something, guessed that the huge cash investment he'd made in Marchand was only the beginning. He didn't just want to be in the market—he wanted to dominate it. And knowing Thackeray, he'd try to succeed with his usual slimy methods—by either buying out or destroying the competition.

But Harcourts wasn't for sale. And she sure as hell wasn't going to let it be swallowed up—not on her watch. Not only did she love the company—practically considered herself married to it—she'd fought tooth and nail to get where she was. She'd earned her place, every step of the way, to reach the spot she held today. Her eyes drifted from the papers to the portraits of former CEOs gracing the wall. One day, her picture would hang there, too—the first woman among a line of powerful men. Finally she was where she belonged—at the head of a major multinational corporation—and she wasn't about to let a Neanderthal like Thackeray unseat her.

Flexing one hand impatiently and holding the testimony of Thackeray's malicious intent in the other, Sylvia rose and stepped again to the window. She stared down absently at the traffic, miniature toy cars crawling up and down Park Avenue, people like dots hurrying along the sidewalks, and controlled her seething anger. She knew, of course, what Thackeray thought of her appointment as CEO. He'd made that plain enough at the time. Not a place for a woman, he'd hinted to the press, especially a beautiful woman of just thirty-five who looked as if she should be gracing the cover of *Vogue*. At the time she'd brushed off his snide comments, paid little attention to them. But apparently his opinion didn't stop there, she realized, suppressing her fury. These latest developments proved that he thought her role at Harcourts made the company an easy target, and this little case of corporate theft was his first volley. Well, she vowed, flipping through the document and focusing, eyes narrowed, on the last page of figures, he'd just made the biggest fucking mistake of his life.

Or so she hoped.

A niggling, inexplicable chill crept through her gut. What if he succeeded? What if he was too tricky for her and she floundered, out of her league, as he'd boasted to a reporter from *Fortune?*

Closing her eyes, Sylvia practiced the breathing her yoga teacher had taught her and ousted the gremlins. If she allowed fear, she allowed weakness. And there was room for neither. She'd handle this, just as she'd handled so many other intricate matters that had come her way since she'd assumed the chairmanship of Harcourts over a year ago. What they had to do now, she reasoned, opening her eyes and turning from the window, was find out who was responsible for letting the information fall into enemy hands. Loyalty was as important to Sylvia as the air she breathed. It was outrageous and unforgivable that any member of her staff had betrayed the company. And she would personally annihilate the culprit. Now that Thackeray had finally thrown the first punch—and there was no disputing it was a body blow—she'd have to counter immediately.

"Perhaps," she murmured thoughtfully, addressing Hamilton and Ira, "we could still turn this around."

"How?"

"I'm not sure yet." It wasn't enough to want to turn it around, she had to figure out how. Fast. Ira's next words echoed her doubts.

"It's virtually impossible to do anything. There are thousands of containers being shipped into the stores as we speak. You've seen the numbers, Syl." He gestured at the papers she held. "Marchand made record sales in the last seventy-two hours."

"I know. Which is why we have no choice but to go ahead with the spring launch," she said finally, as the beginning of a palliative measure presented itself.

"What?" he exclaimed, laying his palms flat on the table. "Put an almost identical collection on the market priced a third higher? That's crazy!" He looked away and let out a long breath that expressed more than words how they all felt. "He's trying to blow Harcourts out of the market, and he must really want it bad," he added darkly, wagging his index finger "'Cause he's got to be suffering one hell of a loss."

She nodded. "Profit margins were calculated precisely right for the present market. His pricing is suicidal."

"Whatever Marchand's loss, it's nowhere close to what we'll suffer," Hamilton muttered, giving his scruffy beard a frustrated rub.

"Okay. He wants to cripple us," Sylvia said in a slow clear voice, mentally reviewing matters as she moved closer to the table. It was all falling into place now, the meeting two weeks ago at Cipriani's, when Thackeray had stopped by her table and they'd exchanged a few words. She was surprised he'd done so, after their tiff at dinner the week before, and had even given him some credit for brushing aside the other incident so elegantly. In fact, she realized, she'd been smoke screened. At the time, his comments had struck her as cryptic, but she'd paid little attention. Now his warning about "making sure Harcourts had enough room in the warehouse" made all the sense in the world. Why the hell hadn't she paid more attention? Taken the warning, instead of allowing herself to be duped all too neatly? Perhaps she'd become too secure, too settled. Just because she was now CEO didn't mean she was entirely safe. As this morning's exploit had proved only too clearly. Another chill scuttled up her spine and lodged in her neck. Would she always be vulnerable, no matter how hard she tried, how far she ran, or how high she climbed? Ira's voice droned on, but she could only think of her own susceptibility.

"By the way, Warmouth's been trying to get in touch with you since early this morning."

The mention of Jeremy Warmouth jolted her back to reality. She stiffened and her fingers drummed the table. Ira sent her a curious look from under his groomed silver brows. Sylvia never demonstrated her feelings, however tired or pushed she might be.

"What did he want?" she asked sharply, unable to suppress the irritation that the mere mention of the man's name caused her.

Ira shrugged. "I guess, like all of us, he's concerned."

"So he darn well should be. Harcourts's designs are technically his responsibility," she muttered coldly. "After all, the product designers are based in London. He could be held directly accountable."

"I guess." Ira raised a doubtful brow at Hamilton who shrugged and rolled his eyes.

For a moment, Sylvia pondered the notion of dethroning the man she'd come to view as her archenemy at Harcourts. It still rankled that the insufferably arrogant *Lord* Warmouth, head of Harcourts Europe, had been such a vocal opponent of her appointment. On the few times they'd met, he'd never failed to get her back up. He was conceited, condescending and insufferably British.

Remembering their last run-in, when he'd sandbagged one of her proposals with the ridiculous comment that such things just weren't "done" in the U.K., she was sorely tempted to use their predicament to undercut him with the board. For fifteen delicious seconds she toyed with the possibility. Then her ever-present sense of fair play got the better of her. This fiasco was no more Jeremy Warmouth's fault than it was hers. And, however tempting the prospect, she did not have the right to lay the blame at his door. Besides, much as she'd love to point out that all this had happened on his turf, she wasn't the gloating type. This wasn't about how she felt about him personally, she reminded herself. This was about Harcourts's future. And however much he annoyed her, his competence as president of the European division of the company was undisputed.

"I think he's truly extremely upset, but he sounded perfectly calm—you know that icy English manner of his. We hardly spoke. He wants to talk to you personally."

"Right." She nodded.

"I still can't believe one of the team would have leaked the designs," Hamilton muttered from the window where he stood etched against the New York skyline. "They're all great people. I know them," he insisted, shoving his right hand into the depths of his baggy pocket. "I mean *really* know them." His easy-going features strained in an uncharacteristic expression of pained disbelief. It was as if he'd been personally struck by a shell and was still reeling. Sylvia nodded then looked away, touched by how loyal the members of her close staff were.

Or so she'd believed.

"I know it sucks, Ham. But there's no point in our obsessing about it. What we need now are facts." She sighed. "I'd better go call London," she added, smoothing her black jacket once more with unusually nervous fingers. Knowing her staff was watching, she straightened her shoulders and walked confidently through a side door into her adjacent corner office.

She closed the door quietly, Hamilton's words echoing in her ears. "This isn't just a few designs we're talking about, it's the whole fucking collection that bastard's gotten hold of, down to the last fucking box of matches."

She walked over to the wide leather chair and stared at it as she dropped the papers on her slick designer desk, fingering the buttery soft leather. She swallowed nervously and closed her eyes. There'd been a time, years ago, when the only leather she'd touched was her stepfather's belt—his favored method of keeping her in line. Even then, she'd dared to dream of being in a better place, of being in control of her life and her destiny. By the time she'd fled Arkansas, she'd known where she wanted to be—in business and at the top. Looking around her spacious, beautifully furnished office, she still found it hard to believe she'd finally made it.

Neither could she have dreamed she'd be in the CEO's chair so soon. She sank into it, forcing her shoulders back, laid her palms on the desk and took a deep breath. Now that it was hers, she had no intention of giving it up. And no one, no demons—past or present—would be permitted to get in her way.

She channeled her thoughts back to the disaster and an uneasy cold sweat broke out under the fine gabardine suit. Something as big as this could finish her off if she didn't handle it just right. Her heart plummeted, and for a brief moment she saw herself back on the other side of the tracks where she'd started out. It didn't take much to bring back the smell of rotting trash, cold winters and summers with no air-conditioning. She shivered. That was the least of it. But she wouldn't allow herself to fall into the trap of thinking about her past. Her behavioral psychologist had taught her ways to manage the fears that occasionally haunted her, popping out of nowhere like Scud missiles. She must, at all cost, avoid her old thought patterns. Instead, she rationalized, repulsing the dark memories and pulling herself abruptly together, she must focus, concentrate. She had work to do, a plot to unmask, an enemy that must, at all costs, be defeated.

She swung back and forth in the chair and toyed with a pencil, picturing Thackeray and the perpetual smirk on his bronzed face. She knew he must be reveling in what he believed to have scored. But not for long, she vowed.

Leaning forward, she lifted the receiver off the shiny chrome telephone, pressed the speed dial for the London office. Soon she heard the purr of the double ring on Jeremy Warmouth's private line and waited, replaying the scene in the restaurant with Thackeray over and over. He'd handed her a clue that she'd totally missed. If only she'd listened properly. Her instincts were obviously blunted, she reflected, disgusted.

She glanced blindly past the sheaf of papers on the minimalist teak desk chosen with such care, the chill impossible to ignore. This incident could wipe them out. Not completely, of course—Harcourts was too big and too solid a firm to be taken down by one failed collection—but the quarter's results would be shot to hell in what was already a shaky market, unless urgent measures were taken. The board would get jittery. That could result in serious consequences.

Where the hell was Warmouth? She cradled the phone in her left hand and doodled aimlessly on a legal pad, irritated. Why wasn't he answering his phone? Probably lunching at his damn club or having cocktails down the road at Buckingham Palace. Ha! The one time she needed him and he wasn't there.

Sylvia tweaked her smooth blond hair behind her ear and listened a moment longer. The monotonous double ring grated in her ear and she slammed down the receiver. Didn't they have voice mail, for Christ's sake?

Thackeray was counting, she was certain, on this incident to undermine the board's confidence in her. Cold anger spiked as she dissected his tactics. Create a snowball effect. Lose the confidence of the shareholders, and make her look so fucking incompetent that they would want her replaced. He probably figured they'd be glad when he came to the table with a perfectly fair and decent proposal. He was too smooth an operator to have come forward before, and would make sure his timing was exactly right. He knew the board would stand behind her if he made a hostile bid.

Staving off her growing fear, Sylvia glanced again at the phone, glad now that Warmouth hadn't answered. She was in no mood to talk, and needed time to think straight and get all her ducks in a row. To not mess up.

She closed her eyes tight, determined to find the answer. After that, she'd get out there and kick some serious butt.

2

Chewing thoughtfully on the end of his Cuban cigar, Jeremy Warmouth glanced impatiently at his thin gold Patek Philippe watch, inherited—like so much in his life—from his uncle, the late Earl of Warmouth. In a few minutes, Sylvia Hansen would be walking through that door. And he was no closer to having an explanation for the Marchand fiasco than when she'd called him three days ago.

He turned impatiently and glanced in the gilt-framed mirror. Was the dark gray, pinstriped suit he'd elected to wear too formal? He stared at himself, annoyed. It was quite unimportant. What the hell did it matter which suit he wore, or that he'd discarded three other Hermes ties before deciding on the yellow one? Perfectly ridiculous.

His lips thinned and his brows creased. It infuriated him that she'd decided to suddenly descend upon the London office—*his* territory—to look into matters herself, as though he was incapable of dealing with the situation. What made it increasingly irritating was knowing she had every right to do so, and he could do nothing to stop her.

How the hell could a blunder of such magnitude have occurred in his organization? he asked himself for the umpteenth time. He'd been over the list of suspects again and again, had grilled Reggie Rathbone, his right hand and the head of design, and every other member of his staff over and over, but nothing tallied. Hell, he couldn't even come up with a motive—why would any of the designers, all of whom were highly paid and apparently satisfied employees, want to sandbag their own work? It didn't make sense. Yet the truth must be faced: there was a traitor among them and, ultimately, as head of the division where the conspiracy had evidently been born, he was responsible.

Raised to revere trust and fair play, Jeremy had given the team members an unprecedented amount of autonomy, and up till now, they'd rewarded his loyalty with designs that were the talk of the industry. Now one or more of them had used that freedom to pass proprietary information to Harcourts's toughest competitor: Marchand. He felt bitterly betrayed. He'd barely slept the past few nights, tossing and turning in his flat in Cadogan Gardens, trying desperately to answer the question, Why?

As if that weren't bad enough, he'd had Harriet Hunter—the oldest and most trustworthy member of his staff—bugging him half the morning, harping on about what a disgrace the whole matter was for Harcourts, and making ominous pronouncements about what Dexter Ward—the chairman who had made the company famous—would do were he still alive. As if Jeremy didn't know.

And now, to top it all off, he had Sylvia Hansen to contend with.

The prospect was more unsettling than he cared to admit. His brows creased and he puffed intently on the Montecristo, making certain the cigar didn't go out. Knowing the woman, she'd probably spent the whole of her transatlantic flight sharpening the knives she planned to plant in his back.

He stretched his tall form, crossed the paneled office, with its built-in bookcases and muted leather furniture, and stared gloomily at the rain trickling relentlessly down the high, ancient windowpanes. Then a thought occurred to him and the nasty weather provided some small degree of satisfaction. Sylvia hated rain. Just as she hated British tradition, England and afternoon tea. He toyed with the idea of inviting her to tea at Fortnum & Mason, conveniently situated just across St. James's on the corner of Jermyn Street and Duke Street. He'd suggest they walk there in the rain, and make sure she got properly sodden. Serve her right for interfering.

Then he pulled himself up with a start and ran a hand through his thick brown hair, embarrassed to find himself plotting such adolescent revenge. But she could have at least given him a chance to investigate things on his own, couldn't she? he reflected resentfully. But no. As usual, here she was, poking her bloody oar in where it was least wanted, as though only *she* knew how to take care of business. He ground his teeth vengefully on the innocent cigar and ended up with bits of tobacco sticking to his tongue.

Twenty minutes later he was still at the window, still glaring at the rain, trying desperately to be reasonable and not begrudge Sylvia's arrival, when the large black company Mercedes drew up. Quickly he turned and glanced in the gilt-framed mirror that hung above the fireplace, straightened his tie, and glanced at himself. He suddenly wished his hair didn't have that damn wave in it, though why anything so inconsequential should come to mind at a time like this was beyond him. He stood to a full six feet two. Adopting a calm expression that disguised his inner misgivings, he elected to forget that he never quite knew how to deal with Sylvia.

He might not like her style but neither did he underestimate her professional ability. Now, as he awaited her entrance, a half smile escaped him. *Admit it, old man, she's a force to be dealt with.* He moved away from the mirror and pondered, ear attuned to the sounds outside in the hall. Her business skills were unquestionably impressive. There were even times when he wondered why he'd been so adamantly set against her becoming CEO, when he knew perfectly well Brad Ward, Sylvia's predecessor, had made an excellent choice. It was just… He shook his head, perplexed. It had nothing to do with her professional skills or the fact that she was a woman—of course not. It was her manner, that impossibly brash, forthright way of dealing with things, that stuck in his gullet.

All too soon he heard feminine voices exchanging greetings in the hall. Old Harriet Hunter's raspy Benson & Hedges monotone a sharp contrast to Sylvia's lilting American twang. He sat down quickly behind the huge mahogany partners desk and pretended to be busy. Why did the woman make him nervous, for Christ's sake? It was absurd, and must immediately be got under control.

When the knock finally came he uttered a bored, "Come in," and continued writing for a full fifteen seconds before looking up. When he knew she'd been standing just long enough to begin feeling ill at ease, he rose and smiled graciously, struck despite himself by how stunning and vibrant she appeared, how blue her eyes shone, and how glowingly healthy and creamy her skin looked despite the past few days' worries and a transatlantic flight.

"Hello, Sylvia, do come in. Miss Hunter, ask Finch to serve the sherry, will you?" Jeremy marshaled his thoughts, annoyed with himself for even noticing her appearance, and spoke in a cool yet welcoming tone.

"Hi, Jeremy." Sylvia glided across the room and accepted the seat he offered on the well-worn leather couch, her shapely, stockinged legs crossing with confident elegance.

Smiling graciously, she deposited a large black leather designer purse next to her and registered everything about him. The fifteen seconds were not lost on her. So this was how he wanted to play it. Very well. The fact was that he aggravated her, and she couldn't quite put her finger on exactly why. The upper-crust British superciliousness, she supposed, and his rejection of her candidacy as CEO—that still rankled. Still, she could not help but recognize what an exceptionally handsome man he was. Tall, well-built—probably worked out at least three times a week—his hair brown and slightly wavy, which was rather cute. He had an attractive golf tan. She glanced disparagingly at the windows, draped in heavy, dull-green brocade, and wondered how you picked up a tan in a climate like this. But of course you didn't. You went to the Algarve, or Lyford Cay, or Palm Beach, or some other place with a fancy name.

She wondered all at once if he was going to marry that skinny stick of a woman he'd once introduced her to—the Honorable Clarissa something-or-other. Reggie had told her the two had been dating for years. Not only had the woman been too pale and too thin, she was clearly the type who broke out in a rash whenever circumstances forced her to mingle with the hoi polloi. For a moment Sylvia forgot the serious nature of their meeting, overcome by a sudden desire to giggle. But she kept a straight face and answered Jeremy's innocuous questions, watching how nonchalantly he sat, one leg flung carelessly over the other, as they waited for the tedious ritual of the sherry to be over.

The trouble was that you could never tell what Jeremy was thinking. Did he resent her sudden arrival? Not by a twitch had he demonstrated anything but bland politeness. His vague half smile looked as if it had been surgically set in place. She smothered a sigh. Much as she'd love to unsettle the man, she was determined to stick to the decision she'd made back in New York: she would seek cooperation. This was no time for cat-and-mouse games, much as she would enjoy crossing swords with him. Right now, she needed everyone bright-eyed, bushy-tailed and rowing in the same boat.

But would he want that?

For a chilling moment she asked herself if Jeremy could possibly be in league with Thackeray—after all, he'd made it obvious right from the beginning that he resented her role at Harcourts. Perhaps he and Thackeray had decided to take her down together. Her mouth went suddenly dry. She swallowed and leaned back into the ancient sofa gripped by panic, the cold sweat that always hit when fear struck, breaking out under her white cotton shirt. It took a brief moment to regroup, to realize that she was being paranoid; he might act like a stuffed shirt, but he was also as straight as they come. Jeremy's next words confirmed this sentiment and slowly the alarm subsided.

"I don't know who's responsible for this mess," he remarked, frowning. "I assure you we'll get to the bottom of it and root out the culprits. I'm very sorry it's happened on my watch," he added, tone clipped and unemotional. "And I hold myself ultimately responsible. I can't think who it can possibly be. Reggie and I have talked with everyone on the design team, and have reviewed anyone from outside who might have had access. Frankly, we still haven't come up with a damn thing. Still, there was no need for you to go to the trouble of coming over. I could have handled the situation perfectly well on my own."

There was a perceptible edge to his voice, but Sylvia pretended not to notice. She merely nodded, surprised at his candor. "It's a tough one," she agreed slowly. "This is Aimon Thackeray's way of telling us he's out to take over."

"Bastard," Jeremy muttered between his teeth.

Sylvia glanced at him. It was the first time she'd seen him display any emotion. His muttered oath and dark expression left her strangely reassured. So he wasn't an enemy after all. That was one positive among the many negatives she'd had to deal with over the past few days. Not that she could let down her guard. He might still try to use this state of affairs to turn the board against her. But then, she could do the same to him, she reflected as uneasy silence settled between them. In fact, she reassured herself, *she* was in the stronger position.

The embarrassing silence was broken by a polite knock followed by the ancient white-haired butler, Finch, carefully balancing a silver salver with the sherry decanter, a selection of small glasses and a crystal bowl filled with a blend of mixed nuts that Sylvia already knew to be tasteless. She'd wanted to mention the nuts on a previous visit but had changed her mind, not daring to after Harriet Hunter pointed out proudly that the same brand had been used by Harcourts for the past fifty years. A veritable institution. Obviously, change was not a welcome word in the St. James's Place agenda.

Finch bowed politely, Sylvia smiled graciously, murmured formalities were exchanged, the sherry served and the nuts placed reverently on the glass table—the one concession to modern living—between them. Sylvia eyed them askance. She hadn't felt like eating on the trip over, but now a pang of hunger hit and she yearned to sink her teeth into a large, juicy, medium-rare burger and fries. Her mouth watered. Jeremy raised his glass. She raised hers and sipped sedately. She disliked sherry, but was damned if she'd give him the satisfaction of knowing it. She even went so far as to finger a dry, unsalted cashew.

Two minutes later, another brief knock announced Reggie and her face broke into a grin. She liked the short, rotund, balding Reggie Rathbone. There was something open and pleasant about him. Too bad his agreeable nature hadn't rubbed off on Jeremy, she reflected, eyeing the two men.

"The whole thing's a bloody cock-up," Reggie exclaimed, accepting a glass of sherry from Jeremy and plunking himself onto a faded ottoman, elbows leaning heavily on his thighs, his sandy, bushy brows knit.

"Any ideas about who might be involved?" Sylvia asked, feeling more at ease now that he'd joined them.

"Not a clue. We've interviewed all the design team—I felt like scum doing it, since I know them so well—and dragged in a detective from a private agency. We didn't want to call in the Yard," he explained. "Too much risk of this leaking out."

"The yard?" Sylvia quirked a brow.

"Scotland Yard."

"Of course, so stupid of me." She waved a hand, furious at herself. This was no time to be giving Jeremy opportunities to belittle her.

"Bad enough as it is," Jeremy agreed dryly, staring into his glass, apparently oblivious of her blunder, "we must keep this whole thing under wraps and take some rapid counteraction, or our stock'll start dropping. The market's in a rotten enough state as it is." He cast a dark glance her way and Sylvia got the impression she was being accused.

"Bloody awful timing," Reggie conceded.

"This would have amounted to a disaster at any time," she retorted crisply. "As for countermeasures,

I've decided to go ahead with all the deliveries.'' She looked at them, waiting for a reaction. ''I've also given orders to cut the initial prices by fifty percent.''

''What? Fifty percent?'' Jeremy exclaimed. He got up and faced her, arms folded against his chest. ''That's absurd. Madness. We'll take a hell of a hit.''

''I'm aware of that,'' she answered coldly, ''but at least we'll be priced lower than Marchand.''

''Wonderful.'' He eyed her witheringly. ''You might at least have taken some professional advice before barreling ahead like a—'' He stopped himself, clamping his mouth tight shut.

''I'm working on an aggressive marketing campaign to draw customers into our stores,'' Sylvia continued evenly, keeping a hold on her temper. ''Worst case scenario, we'll have a worldwide blowout sale.''

''Good God, you'll ruin us,'' he muttered, draining his glass.

''Actually, Sylvia, that's not a bad idea,'' Reggie said enthusiastically. ''It's probably the only thing we can do at this stage. And even though it will mean a loss, we'll save face and ride out the worst of it,'' he added approvingly while Jeremy stood by in silent fury.

Ignoring him, Sylvia opened the briefcase she'd deposited on the floor and handed them each a document.

''I've already had some figures drawn up. Not good, I'm afraid, but better than the alternative.''

Jeremy glanced at the printout scathingly.

''Phew!'' Reggie whistled, reviewing the document.

''This is ridiculous,'' Jeremy dismissed, flipping

the pages. "We can't possibly sustain such decreased earnings. Our whole market position will be badly affected."

"Any other bright ideas?" she asked sweetly, cocking her head.

"I'm working on them."

"Great. Once you come up with 'em, send me an e-mail! In the meantime, since circumstances demand we act *now,* not next month, we'll go forward with this." The words were out before she could stop them. Immediately she regretted the impulse, annoyed with herself. Hadn't she sworn she wouldn't let him get to her?

Reggie's eyes flitted uncomfortably from one to the other. He was used to the tension that reigned whenever these two were in a room together, but still. It permeated the place. And today was worse than usual. He cleared his throat, thinking fast about how to redirect the discussion. "I think Sylvia has the right idea. Her plan will stave off the worst of the damage. Harcourts is sound enough to take a few bashes. What really concerns me," he continued, scowling, "is what's going on inside our own offices, damn it. It's intolerable to have deceit of this kind under our very noses."

"You're right," she agreed, nodding. "We simply must find out who's responsible. It can't be gotten away with."

"Do you think Thackeray has any other moves up his sleeve?" Jeremy sat down behind his desk and, steepling his fingers, addressed Sylvia in his usual neutral voice.

"I don't know. I can't be certain, but I think possibly."

"This strikes me as the initial step in a complex strategy, rather than a single episode. More like the first significant move in a game of chess."

"Could be," Sylvia agreed. Jeremy's words exactly described her own fears. Despite her newfound control, the nervous tension that had been her constant companion over the past week hovered dangerously.

"What do you think of Thackeray?" he asked, eyeing her curiously. "After all, you know him quite well personally, don't you?" He sent her a piercing glance, as though she was hiding something.

Despite her annoyance at his insinuation, Sylvia felt a dull flush rise to her cheeks. "I've met him on occasion. He's a tough guy who came out of nowhere and made it too big too fast."

"Yes, but you know the man," Jeremy insisted, never taking his eyes off her.

"Yes, I know the man," she answered, exasperated. "I consider him a lowlife, a reprobate and a criminal, and I don't want anything to do with him."

"Well, that's putting it bluntly!" Reggie looked at her, surprised.

"Sounds about right," Jeremy replied. "Which makes one wonder why you were dining with him three weeks ago at a restaurant."

The insinuation and suppressed wrath in his voice left her taken aback. "I—what damn business is it of yours whom I dine with?" she retorted furiously, wondering how he'd found out about the last-minute dinner meeting.

"It becomes my business when events such as these occur and my division could take the blame." His tone was smooth and calculated, eyes icy and unforgiving. For a moment, Sylvia nearly forgot all her good intentions not to dump responsibility at his door and be done with it. Then grudgingly she realized that, under the circumstances, dining with Thackeray must look suspicious, and pulled herself together.

"I dined with Aimon Thackeray because I was networking," she said deliberately, mustering her dignity. "Believe it or not, it's considered good policy to be on talking terms with one's competition."

"Really? Then why did you flounce out of Aureole's in a towering rage?" Jeremy asked, tone conversational as he leaned back in the deep leather chair, twiddling his pen between his fingertips, and eyeing her as though she were an erring adolescent.

"I did not *flounce*—and how do you know what I do and don't do? Do you keep spies in Manhattan?" She slammed her empty sherry glass down, furious at his domineering manner. How dare he accuse her?

"Not at all. I have friends who happened to be dining there on the same evening and found the scene intriguing, that's all." He shrugged, slipped the pen into his breast pocket and leaned forward, sending her a penetrating glance tinged with enough satisfaction to leave her seething. "You must admit the meeting does seem somewhat…coincidental."

"I don't owe you any explanations."

"Of course not. You're my boss. Who am I to question you?" He leaned back again, crossed one leg over the other and coolly observed her.

Stay calm, she ordered, gritting her teeth and suppressing her fury, knowing he was trying to provoke her. She did not need to explain herself, would not be dictated to by this man. Yet something compelled her to justify. "If you must know, Thackeray had the gall to suggest I get into bed with him, in more ways than one," she retorted, mustering every ounce of control. "He made a none-too-veiled suggestion that together we could control Harcourts hands down. That's why I 'flounced' out. Satisfied?" She sent him a smoldering look over the cashews.

Jeremy raised a satirical eyebrow.

Reggie cleared his throat, followed by an embarrassed cough. "Always difficult to maneuver in enemy territory," he muttered sympathetically.

"I agree with your instincts," Sylvia continued, sending him a grateful smile and ignoring Jeremy's sardonic expression, "that he's throwing up smoke screens to conceal a bigger agenda."

"Such as?" Jeremy queried.

"Such as taking over Harcourts," she said bluntly. "He's finally shaken his reputation as a corporate raider and doesn't want to mess with his new image, but my gut's telling me—"

"We can't base business strategies on *gut* feelings," Jeremy retorted witheringly.

"Why not? Some of the best strategies are built on just that," she countered swiftly, sitting up straighter on the couch and meeting his hooded eyes dead on. "I know you're a CPA—"

"Chartered accountant, actually," he murmured.

"Whatever." She waved a disparaging hand.

"They're one and the same thing. A bean counter. No imagination."

"Really?" Jeremy's tone went quiet and dangerous. "Perhaps you feel this particular situation needs artistic flair? I hear you're remarkably proficient at…is it interior decorating?"

"Well, I wish I was since we're a decorating company—it would come in mighty handy," she retorted. "You seem to see and hear a hell of a lot." Sylvia took a deep breath, determined not to get any more riled than he'd already left her. She counted silently to ten, resolving not to let him get the better of her. But, boy, she would have given a lot to wipe that amused smirk from his mouth.

"I didn't come here to argue," she said finally, voice as cool as his. "I came here in a spirit of mutual cooperation." Then, shrugging in a dismissive manner that she hoped showed she would not lower herself to his level, she addressed Reggie with a smile. "I think I'll go to the hotel now and get my stuff unpacked. We can meet again later. By the way, I'll need an office." With a swing of her silky blond hair she faced her nemesis once more. "I thought about borrowing yours, Jeremy, but I've decided I need something a little less gloomy."

"Of course," he replied stiffly, "Miss Hunter will arrange it." She couldn't resist peeking for his reaction but he didn't so much as blink.

"Absolutely," Reggie concurred heartily. He jumped up solicitously and smiled. Jeremy followed suit at a more leisurely pace. "You must be tired. I'll pop over with you to the Stafford, Sylvia." Reggie bustled about, helping her with her briefcase. "Have your things been dropped off? We can walk. The hotel is around the corner.''

Sylvia glanced ruefully at the pouring rain, then down at her Prada pumps. ''Sure thing. Got an umbrella?'' she asked gamely.

She shook hands formally with Jeremy, noting his obvious truculence. She was tempted to pull rank, show him just who was in charge around here, but knew it would serve no purpose. They had to work together for the common good of Harcourts and its future. Their personal feelings about each other were neither here nor there.

She was about to leave, but something held her back. She hesitated, refusing to start on the wrong footing this time around. Determined to give it one last attempt, Sylvia racked her brain for something to say to break the ice. But he made things so damn difficult. Taking a breath, she faced Jeremy straight on and, smiling brightly, went with the truth. ''I know you feel bad about what happened here, but please don't think that I'm laying this mess all at your door. It could just as easily have happened in New York. I'm sure that, working together, we'll come up with solutions. I know I need your help, and I hope that you'll accept mine.'' She turned quickly before he could answer, and left the room, followed by Reggie.

Jeremy stood stunned in the middle of the room, staring at the closed door, painfully aware that he'd just been bested.

The woman was a bloody menace and a bane to his existence. Yet she was honest and forthright, too. *That* he had to acknowledge. But how dare she come hurtling into his domain and imply that what had happened here wasn't his direct responsibility? As if he wasn't man enough to shoulder it. Who the hell did she think she was, interfering, telling him how to run his part of the business? And letting him know in that high-handed, insufferable manner that henceforth *she* planned to run things. It was humiliating, unthinkable, intolerable! And must be dealt with immediately.

Damn, damn, damn.

Picking up his reading glasses, he flopped down behind his desk once more and dwelled sulkily on her dinner with Thackeray. Networking, indeed. Hobnobbing with the enemy was more like. But despite his angry outburst, he had no doubt that what she'd said was the truth. However annoying the woman might be, she was a force to be reckoned with. As Thackeray had apparently found out, hopefully to his cost, he observed grimly.

He stared at the papers before him. He'd meant to pop over to Boodle's for a bite of lunch but he seemed to have lost his appetite. Focusing on the business at hand, he pressed the button of the intercom. "Miss Hunter, could you pop in here a minute, please?" Just because Sylvia was technically his boss didn't mean he'd let her get the upper hand. He didn't care how many schmoozy little speeches she made about cooperating and working together. He didn't need her help to get to the bottom of matters on his own turf. And the sooner she realized that her presence here was utterly superfluous, the better off they'd all be.

"They have a jolly D salad with melted goat cheese on it. The boys are all French," Reggie remarked, referring to the smiling young waiters in their green jackets standing behind the bar.

"What's jolly D?" Sylvia glanced at the menu curiously, wishing Reggie would speak plain English.

"Sorry. Abbreviation for jolly decent." Reggie smiled apologetically then pointed to the item on the menu.

They were pleasantly ensconced in a cozy corner of the American Bar of the Stafford Hotel. For the first time since landing at Heathrow, Sylvia allowed herself to relax. At first she'd wondered about the hotel, having always stayed at Claridge's on previous trips. But when Miss Hunter had pointed out that the Stafford was very pleasant and just around the corner from the office, staying here seemed to make sense. Her first impression had been doubtful. Dreadfully British and chintzy. The suite was British traditional, with a canopied bed and more of the requisite chintz. But the bathroom was modern and marble; the television had cable, CNN and Bloomberg. Plus, under present circumstances, she might need to spend long hours at her desk. The convenience of being able to pop around the corner for a breather and not have to wait for the car or sit stuck in London traffic could be a major advantage.

Now she sat with Reggie under a colorful array of old ties, weathered baseball caps and flags hanging from the ceiling. The walls were plastered with photographs of the America's Cup, cartoons and horse racing, the shelves filled with trophies and odds and ends picked up over the years by the famous bartender, Charles.

"I'm going for the goat cheese salad," Reggie remarked after ordering a glass of the house champagne. It was Pol Roger. She recalled Brad Ward, her ex-fiancé, telling her the brand was Winston Churchill's favorite. That struck her as a good omen.

"I think I'll go for the burger," she remarked, eyeing a large man with a mid-Western twang, dressed in a pink polo shirt, seated opposite tucking into a large, juicy hamburger and fries.

"Quite right. Best burger in the West End," Reggie agreed, signaling one of the waiters. "Just thought you might be worried about slimming or something. So many women are." He grinned. "But I suppose you don't have to worry about that sort of thing. I've stopped worrying myself," he added, patting his large belly with a resigned grin. "I waged the battle of the bulge for too long and have now given up. Nothing to be done but enjoy and accept the consequences."

Sylvia laughed and let go of some tension. Reggie was a sweetheart as well as competent. Why couldn't Jeremy loosen up and be like this? It would make life so very much easier.

By the time she'd consumed her burger, comfortably served on a lap tray, she and Reggie had their teeth well into the problems besieging Harcourts.

"This has all made for a hell of a rotten atmosphere in the office," he said mournfully. "I mean everyone, like it or not, is suspicious of one another, yet we all know the culprit can't be any of us."

"I know. It's horrible. And exactly what Thackeray intended. I'd bet he's determined to cause as much internal strife as possible." She eyed her champagne flute, then muttered sarcastically, "I hope *Lord* Warmouth is willing to roll up the sleeves on those custom shirts of his, because we've got a dirty fight up ahead of us.''

''Oh, he will. Don't worry. Or underestimate him. I've known Jeremy a long time, and believe me, there's more to the man than you'd ever guess—and no better person to have in your corner.'' He paused, his face serious and set. Then he stabbed his fork into his salad with renewed determination. ''As for what he thinks? I'd say he's bloody livid. Just doesn't harp on about it. Jeremy's a man of action, not words. He wants results.''

''We could use some right now,'' Sylvia agreed dryly, wiping her mouth on a large linen napkin. ''Have you ever met Thackeray?'' she asked.

''Never had that pleasure,'' Reggie muttered.

''He's a tough, relentless, mean son of a bitch.''

''Sounds like the kind of chap you'd want with, rather than against, you.''

''Frankly, he's someone you'd rather did not exist,'' she replied. ''I've seen him ruthlessly take down three companies. He has no mercy. The head of the last outfit he went after committed suicide.''

''Good God.'' Reggie held his fork in midair, clearly shocked.

''Exactly.'' She sent him a meaningful look. ''I just hope Jeremy is truly aware of what we're up against.''

''I hope so, too,'' Reggie agreed wholeheartedly, pushing away his tray.

Evidently the food no longer tasted quite so jolly D, Sylvia observed, finishing off the champagne in one quick gulp and preparing to leave. ''Don't worry, Reggie. We'll outsmart him. Now, get all your de-

signs together, along with the Marchand catalogs and
any other material we can lay our hands on. The New
York team is working 24/7. There should be e-mails
and a couple of faxes in shortly. We'll go over them
one by one, see if we can't pick up some legal loop-
holes. Aaron, the head of our legal department,
doesn't think there are any, but still, we'd better make
sure.''

"Jeremy feels that to sue might further expose our
position.''

"He may very well be right,'' she concurred grudgingly. "But we'll check anyhow.''

"Of course. And Syl—''

"Yes?'' She sent him a questioning glance.

"Don't let Jeremy get to you.'' He patted her arm
in a friendly manner.

"I won't,'' she muttered grimly. "I simply don't
understand why he resents my presence so much.''

"I can't explain that, either.'' Reggie gave a puz-
zled frown. "It's been baffling me for a while. Jer's
normally such an easygoing, pleasant chap. I've
known him forever. We went to Harrow together, you
know. Not one to take a miff.'' Reggie shook his head
and raised his hands uncomprehendingly. "Oh, well.
No use conjecturing.''

"None at all,'' she agreed. Then, thanking him for
lunch, she got up, smoothed her dress and smiled. "I
guess I'll see you at the office later.''

"Absolutely.'' With a warm wave, Reggie opened
a large black umbrella and waddled off between the
empty wrought-iron tables tightly grouped on the
small patio terrace that led to a cobbled courtyard.

Sylvia made her way upstairs to her suite, smothering a yawn. Jet lag loomed as she opened the heavy door. She surveyed the conservative sitting room, as far removed from her minimalist Upper East Side condo as could be, and grimaced. Definitely not her taste. Too old-fashioned. But comfortable and cozy all the same. Frankly she had priorities other than interiors right now.

She sat on the sofa, kicked off her shoes and flipped on CNN, curling her legs under her. She watched for a few minutes, mind wandering, then turned and reached for her purse. She hesitated briefly before taking out her wallet and eyeing it for a long moment. Then she slid her fingers carefully between two expired credit cards and drew out a tiny photograph.

For a while she stared at it, eyes watering, and ran her fingers along the photo's withered edges. Then, just as carefully, she replaced it and returned the wallet to her purse. Suddenly exhausted, she sank back into the cushions, stretched her legs out, closed her eyes and blanked out the memory. It was a while since she'd looked at the picture. Why now? she wondered, stifling another yawn.

Then Thackeray's expression when she'd last seen him came to mind and she shuddered, bewildered. Nothing made sense. And she was just too damn tired.

Why was the world such a tough place? she wondered. Why did the bullies—people like Thackeray, and a couple of others she could mention—so often win? It was unfair. But as she'd learned, to her cost, life was rarely fair.

She opened her eyes and focused on the TV screen, determined to shake off the doldrums. She'd take a quick nap, then head back to the office and set the ball rolling. There was no time to waste. No way would she allow Thackeray to get the better of her. For a moment she thought again of Jeremy and his reluctance to give her a break. Then she shrugged and leaned further into the cushions.

Let 'em come. She'd deal with them one by one, whatever it cost.

3

Aimon Thackeray lounged in a deep wicker recliner. The veranda of the mansion he'd acquired two years earlier after capitalizing on an exceptionally good stock option—a well-deserved present to himself for his fortieth birthday—stretched wide and comfortable. The house, built shortly before the Civil War, crawled with history. General Lee had even spent a night here. That gave it cachet. Not that he needed cachet anymore—power was a far more desirable commodity.

Pensive, Thackeray reread the fax he held in his left hand. The sun dipped behind the sloping hills and a slight breeze picked up. Looking up, he stared thoughtfully past the stables and the man-made lake that had cost him almost two million—including the black swans from Western Australia—and gazed across the Shenandoah Valley.

Things over at Harcourts weren't falling into place *quite* as he'd anticipated. His lips tightened. He hadn't expected that bitch, Sylvia Hansen, to counter his first move so quickly. A blowout sale running simultaneously around the world, accompanied by a huge PR campaign, was fucking brilliant. How the hell had she pulled it off?

His teeth ground the fat Cuban cigar he'd had produced for him personally in Pinar del Rio, then pulled it out of his mouth. After dipping it absently in the brandy snifter next to him, he lit it and sat forward. A slow grin dawned. Frankly, he was glad the slut had decided to fight back. Her resistance now would only make the victory sweeter when she finally bent to his will.

And bend she would, he vowed, remembering their disastrous dinner in New York. His lips tightened and he took a long drag, replaying the scene in his mind. The bitch had the gall to walk out on him at Aureole on a Friday night when the place was packed. People were probably still snickering about him, if the smirks and murmured comments that had followed him out the door were anything to go by.

She would pay for that. He'd teach her she was no match for Aimon Thackeray. Stupid woman hadn't realized that letting him fuck her would have made all this so much easier. If she'd spread her legs without a fuss, he might have considered leaving her in her present position for a while. She'd proved herself an able administrator, and his plans for Harcourts required stability at the top. Plus, it wouldn't have done him any harm to be seen shacking up with a woman of her social caliber, beauty and class.

Too bad that it hadn't worked out. Too bad she'd tried to outmaneuver him. Too bad she'd have to learn the hard way.

He took another long, thoughtful puff, watched the smoke spiral into the evening shadows, then exhaled slowly, following the movements of the wiry, lean horse trainer he'd imported from Ireland as he took Blue Chip, his favorite racehorse, through his paces in the riding ring. But his mind wasn't on horses or the Kentucky Derby. All he could think about was Sylvia's fucking global sale that had blown a hole through his plan to cripple Harcourts's new collection. Instead, it was the Marchand copies that were piling up in the warehouses, costing him a bloody fortune.

He consoled himself with the reminder that his Harcourts efforts were nothing more than a cover for other far more profitable venues, but it galled him that Sylvia had so effectively thrown down the gauntlet. Clearly she intended to fight. So be it, he thought with a grim smile. Of course, the bitch would expect him to use conventional weapons. She'd carefully plot her strategy, never realizing—until it was too late—that the battle was being fought on a very different plane, and that she'd already lost the war.

He sucked in his cheeks and visualized her. Sylvia was one hot little number. He'd bet she was an animal under that elegant facade of hers, although she played the role of sophisticated New York power broker to perfection. He frowned. Was it real or just a facade? Instinctively he knew Sylvia wore her position at Harcourts like a coat of armor.

The frown deepened. Was she shielding something? And if so, what? he wondered, eyes narrowing as he stared thoughtfully into the darkening Virginia sky. On the surface she had it all: position, money, beauty, credibility. Okay, Brad Ward had married someone else, but he sensed that didn't bother her much. It was something else, something elusive in her manner that spoke of past secrets, something that told him there was a vein of vulnerability that, if pinpointed, he could exploit. He chewed his lip and savored the thought, then downed a long gulp of brandy.

A slow, mean smile lit the curves of his tanned face. Now that he thought of it, he'd never heard Sylvia mention where she was born, or who her family was. She came across as an Upper East Sider, but that sexy voice of hers had a tinge of the South just below the surface. And while she certainly had enough class to fill an eighteen-wheeler, that didn't necessarily mean much. Class, as he well knew, could be acquired. At a price.

Stubbing out the cigar in a large enamel ashtray that already contained two cigarette butts, Thackeray gazed fondly at the chestnut thoroughbred trotting in the ring. The same instinct that told him Sylvia might have an Achilles' heel told him he had a winner.

He got up and moved toward the white stone balustrade, fingers rhythmically drumming one of the sixteen neoclassical columns that surrounded the mansion. Everyone had a past, a skeleton stashed in the closet. You just had to dig deep enough. Maybe Sylvia was all WASP and his search would be worthless. But something told him otherwise. And the prospect of bringing her to her knees was simply too tempting to pass up.

As he turned back across the veranda, stepped past the huge classical urns filled with tropical ferns and through the French doors to the study, Thackeray experienced a feral rush, almost sexual in its intensity, the same rush he felt tracking elk in Idaho. It took time and patience to circle his prey, but once he had them cornered, he got a guaranteed hard-on when he went in for the kill.

A week of fruitless investigations, strained interviews with staff and persistent probing from the private detective had uncovered little, but had left Harcourts's London offices in a state of frayed tempers and general unease. The only positive discovery was that they'd narrowed down the period during which the designs had likely been pilfered.

"They clearly were stolen before final fabrication in our factories in Colombia," Sylvia observed.

"Oh? What makes you think that?" Jeremy, seated on the opposite side of her desk and looking far too at ease for her taste, sent her a skeptical glance. Good thing she was learning to get a grip on her temper, Sylvia reflected before answering in a measured tone.

"Because of these." She smiled sweetly and slid some photographs and the Marchand catalog over the desk. "If you compare carefully, you'll see that none of the Marchand designs reflect any of the small but significant last-minute changes; the designs that Reggie finalized with Bernardo at the factory."

"She's absolutely right," Reggie exclaimed as he and Jeremy pored over the photographs closely, matching them to the Marchand catalog. "For the most part, the changes were made in the ethnic pottery line and textile collections. Sylvia's right. Marchand's products appear to be based on the earlier designs."

Jeremy stared at the photos, brows creased, furious for not having caught the detail himself.

"That's quite observant of you," he remarked grudgingly. Damn. He had to admit her methodical persistence and determination to get to the bottom of the problem were impressive as hell. Still, the fact that she'd come up with what he and Reggie should have seen themselves did not improve his mood. "This also means we may well have been working this whole affair from the wrong angle," he remarked.

"Absolutely." She nodded. "Given the time line, the designs must have been robbed from the Cartagena factory days before completion."

"That changes everything," Reggie agreed, placing the photos back on the desk. "It's dreadful, of course, but I must say, it's a relief to know the leak didn't happen here."

"We can only assume that it didn't, and it's still too early to make assumptions," Jeremy murmured.

"Any idea who, in our Cartagena operations, might be responsible?" Sylvia asked.

"Not the foggiest, I'm afraid." Reggie shook his head. "Bernardo Villalba's a good chap. Plus, he's been a Harcourts director for several years, wealthy in his own right."

"Well, until we've got a better handle on the situation, we mustn't say anything about it to our team here," Sylvia declared.

"That seems a bit hard. Morale's pretty low as it is."

"I know, but we must be sure of our facts before we hand out any more info. We need to know if there were any break-ins, any unusual occurrences at the factory. And if there were, why no one bothered to report them to us.''

''Pretty easy to go around casting aspersions,'' Jeremy remarked coolly. ''For all we know, the leak may have nothing to do with the factory. The designs could have been tampered with at the Miami office, before they even reached Colombia. Didn't you talk to one of the chaps over there about some changes?'' He glanced at Reggie.

''Nobody's casting any aspersions,'' Sylvia cut in, her tone measured, ''but it's clear we've reached a dead end here in London. It would seem we've been barking up the wrong tree. We must get Bernardo moving on this right away. Whether the leak came from Miami or Cartagena, it must be stopped immediately.''

''That,'' Jeremy said with a withering look across the desk, ''is stating the obvious.''

''These changes were pretty obvious, too, but I didn't see you spotting them,'' she retorted, her tone matching his.

Reggie got up and cleared his throat. ''Now, now. No bickering, you two, I'll see to this right away.'' He moved toward the door, and Jeremy followed suit.

Sylvia barely glanced in their direction as the two men left her office. Frustration welled within her, like a pot on the boil with the lid ready to pop.

When the door finally closed behind them, she dropped her pen, slumped in her chair and sighed. The strain of the past week had gotten to her. Thank God it looked as if the worldwide sale would be a success, she reflected, tapping her foot on the side of the heavy mahogany desk in the office that was serving as hers. The initial feedback from stores showed exceptional results. The ploy had worked and would considerably help to reduce the overall damage.

She glanced around the gloomy office with stifled claustrophobia. She'd been touched when eighty-five-year-old Major Whitehead, the eldest member of the board, had come personally down from Shropshire for their initial board meeting, then risen gallantly to the occasion and offered her his rarely used office. Given that the room had been his private domain for the last forty years, the gesture was particularly gracious and had helped her feel a little less like the interloper Jeremy was clearly bent on labeling her.

But she still couldn't get comfortable, trapped in this alien world of ancient books piled high on dusty shelves, yellowing photographs of the khaki-attired major holding a rifle next to a slain tiger in India, tarnished sports trophies and medals in glass cases. And of course, Jeremy's general attitude didn't help. The only bright note was the lovely bouquet of delphiniums Reggie had sent to welcome her. She smiled briefly. The flowers, in a huge Waterford vase, were now gracing the half-moon table in the corner. She'd thought of moving them to the lowboy where she could see them better, but Miss Hunter had pointed out that the half moon was the officially recognized spot for floral arrangements in this particular office. Sylvia wondered what would happen if she placed them elsewhere. Would the building come down? Would Dexter Ward's ghost come back to haunt her? Lord, how she longed for New York, for her sleek, up-to-the-minute office and her minimalist apartment on the Upper East Side. Most especially, she yearned for distance from Jeremy Warmouth.

With a sigh Sylvia rolled her shoulders, sat straighter and glanced resolutely at the screen of her laptop. No use longing for what couldn't be. Right now she was needed here, despite Jeremy's insistence to the contrary. And here she planned to remain until matters were satisfactorily settled. At least she could take comfort in the fact that Thackeray must be stewing. Of course, he'd be keeping close tabs on Harcourts's movements, and by now he'd know about the sale. Knowing that she'd won this round generated a gleam of satisfaction. Perhaps he'd get the message, realize he'd chosen the wrong target and leave her and her company alone.

But even in that best-case scenario, she'd still be stuck with Jeremy, she acknowledged ruefully. Despite her hopes that he'd back down and cooperate, it seemed they couldn't get through a single day without "bickering," as Reggie had so aptly put it. The constant tension was wearing her down. Why couldn't he understand that her only reason for being here was to help, not hinder?

She glanced at her agenda, then grimaced at the engraved invitation lying next to it. It was from Brad and Charlotte Ward, inviting her to their daughter Freya's christening next weekend. She was deeply touched that her ex-fiancé and his wife had asked her to be godmother to their firstborn daughter. She just wished that the christening didn't entail a trip to the Isle of Skye, the thought of which brought shudders. After all, her previous visit to Strathaird Castle last year hadn't exactly been pleasant. Would returning there bring back bad memories?

On reflection, she thought not. That was all in the past. Brad and she were much better off as close friends than they would have been as husband and wife, and she'd grown fond of Charlotte and the rest of the MacLeod clan. In fact, she looked forward to seeing them again.

The only hitch was the man they'd chosen for the child's godfather—Jeremy Warmouth.

The thought of having to share the corporate plane with him to fly up north inspired nothing but weariness. She was sick of quarreling, sick of his grudging cooperation. Frankly, she failed to understand how such an intelligent man—for that couldn't be denied—seemed incapable of realizing what to everyone else was obvious: that only by working together would they solve this complex matter. He cooperated with her reluctantly, as though he believed she must have some secondary agenda. The trials of dealing with male ego, she reflected bitterly. Why did he believe that he alone was capable of finding answers? What did it matter who discovered the truth, as long as the situation was brought under control?

Sylvia fingered the invitation, then pushed back her sleek blond hair from the shoulders of her steel-gray Max Mara dress. Maybe she was making too big a deal out of it. Traveling with Warmouth for a couple of hours in a plane couldn't be *that* bad and, once there, Strathaird was large enough to get lost in. After the harrowing week she'd had, perhaps the time away would even do her good.

But would taking time off right now be wise? She

had no doubt that Aimon Thackeray was hot on her trail, busy planning his next move. Her earlier thoughts were wishful thinking. He wasn't one to quit the fight so quickly. She stared at the neat, well-stocked bookshelves. Instead of leather-bound first editions, she visualized Thackeray's handsome, tough, bronzed face. The other question bothering her was how badly did he want Harcourts? Was it his prime target or had this turned into a personal vendetta? Since the unfortunate dinner at Aureole, she had the nasty feeling it had become personal. She shifted positions, crossing her knees, disturbed that Thackeray had acquired such a wealth of information from inside the company. It signified that a deep fault line ran close beneath the surface, menacing Harcourts's stability.

Realizing there was nothing more she could do at present to alter matters, Sylvia thought, instead of what to buy the baby for the christening. Was there some particular present a godmother was supposed to give? Some erstwhile British tradition of which she was unaware? No one had ever asked her to be a godmother before and she found it strangely awe-inspiring. Perhaps a piece of jewelry from Cartier, or a silver mug from Tiffany? She must find out exactly what was appropriate. Maybe she'd ask her new personal shopper at Harrods. She wondered what Jeremy was going to give the baby. Not that she would ever lower herself by asking him. Still, it would look too ridiculous if they turned up with the same gift.

By midafternoon Friday, Sylvia was headed to Heathrow airport in Harcourts's black Mercedes.

Since the company plane, the Gulfstream V, was being serviced, she was flying commercial. She'd wanted to fly on her own but, unfortunately, Miss Hunter had booked both her and Jeremy on the same flight. She'd thought of protesting, then decided she was being juvenile. Surely she could handle a few hours in his company. At least Jeremy was heading to the airport by himself, which allowed her a few moments of peace. She leaned back in the soft leather and stared out at the heavy traffic, at the cars maneuvering among roadwork in Knightsbridge, commuters leaving town early for the weekend and shoppers hailing black cabs. The car crawled along Cromwell Road, past the Victoria and Albert Museum, and rows of dreary terraced houses before heading over the flybridge and on to the M4.

Sylvia thought of her godchild and the gift now carefully stowed in her large Kelley purse. She'd finally decided on an exquisite heart-shaped tennis bracelet from Cartier on the principle that diamonds were a girl's best friend and that you could never begin collecting them too soon. Her goddaughter would be privileged from the word go. No striving to subsist for Freya Sylvia MacLeod, thank God. This little girl would never know the pains and fears that had peppered her own early existence. Hastily shelving the unwelcome memories, Sylvia concentrated on the baby, wondering what she would look like. Since both Brad and Charlotte were gorgeous, little Freya was sure to be a beauty, she thought, smiling. For an instant, she swallowed a sharp pang of envy and regret. Then the airport appeared and she concentrated on identifying the departures terminal.

She was taking only her Vuitton garment bag and her tote, which she figured would prevent Jeremy from making snide remarks about too much luggage when they boarded the chopper to Skye.

The sudden reminder of the upcoming helicopter ride made her stomach lurch. God, she hated helicopters.

As the car moved up the ramp to the terminal, she ignored her quickened pulse rate and schooled herself not to think about the ride. At least it would be short. Before she knew it, she would be at Strathaird. After all, she'd made the trip several times before, without incident, so what was she worried about? Still, nothing could suppress the lurking panic that gripped her each time she was obliged to ride in a chopper.

After checking in for the Glasgow flight, Sylvia headed upstairs to the British Airways lounge. She spotted Jeremy immediately, his tall, handsome frame lounging in a bright red chair, the top of his head peeking above *The Economist*. She hesitated, admiring the bright red and blue chairs, the chrome and light wood furnishings and the well-stocked granite bar facing huge windows that overlooked the busy tarmac. A number of planes were readying for take-off, others landing. Jeremy still hadn't noticed her and for a brief moment Sylvia was tempted to sit behind a large palm tree well out of sight in the far corner. But that would be childish and impolite and only add fuel to the fire, she realized, reluctantly making her way to where he sat, one gray flannel leg crossed casually over the opposite knee, absorbed in the article he was reading.

"Hi." She deposited her luggage in a chair and peered over the tip of his newspaper.

Jeremy rose formally and they smiled perfunctorily at one another.

"Coffee?" he asked politely.

"Thanks." She sat down, unintentionally displaying a shapely stretch of smooth stocking, as she crossed her legs.

Jeremy noticed, swallowed, and then turned smartly toward the long bar laid out with coffee, drinks and snacks for the travelers. Trust the woman to dress as if she were headed to a fashion show. Who in the name of all that was sensible would wear a white skirt and rain jacket to go to the Highlands of Scotland? She even had a Burberry bag and umbrella to match. Probably thought it gave her a "Scottish touch," he decided, trying desperately to find her ridiculous and deny the knee-jerk he'd felt when he'd seen her.

He returned with the coffee and sat down opposite, determined not to stare at her or the alluring expanse of leg. She was always beautifully dressed, but somehow at the office he didn't notice her the same way. Here, surrounded by businessmen returning north for the weekend who were unable to take their eyes off her and kept casting him envious glances while pretending to read *The Times* and *The Spectator,* it became harder to continue ignoring the fact that Sylvia was not only exceptionally bright—that much had become clear in the past two weeks—but she was also stunning.

He cleared his throat and made a brief comment about the weather, which was looking good. The forecast for Glasgow wasn't bad, either. After that, he and Sylvia retired behind their respective newspapers until the flight was called.

On arrival in Glasgow, Jeremy and Sylvia walked straight across a stretch of tarmac to the chopper hangar. A fresh westerly breeze blew clouds like gamboling sheep across the clear blue sky; and after an uneasy glance upward, Sylvia let out a relieved sigh, grateful for the fair weather. It helped to squelch the threatening jitters.

At the hangar, she stood aside and let Jeremy deal with business. Everything appeared to have been efficiently prearranged. She smiled politely at the young man behind the desk and an older guy in oily blue overalls, and waited for the pilot to appear. Perhaps he was already in one of the three choppers sitting outside. Raising a hand to shade her eyes, she glanced at each of them, wondering which one would be theirs. She liked to look at the chopper and send it good vibes before boarding. She even prayed at take-off.

"Okay. All set." Picking up her garment bag with his briefcase, Jeremy gave her a brisk smile and headed toward the first chopper, a Hughey that glistened, sparkling and new.

"Where's our pilot?" Sylvia asked, surprised to see the chopper empty. Usually by this stage, the engines were turning and the pilot waiting, staring intently at the instrumentation.

"I thought I'd fly us up myself and keep the chopper there during our stay. Might be amusing to make a hop over to Egg or one of the other islands," Jeremy said, reaching up to open the door.

Sylvia stopped dead in her tracks. "*You're* planning to fly this thing?"

He turned. Seeing her look of horror, he replied haughtily, "I have a license. It's current, in case you're worried."

"But we can't go by ourselves. You can't fly that thing. How do I know it's safe?" Sylvia burbled, clutching her handbag nervously. "I can't get in there with you."

"Why on earth not?" Jeremy asked bluntly.

"I just can't."

"That's ridiculous. I know as much about choppers as any pilot you'll find here. In fact, probably quite a lot more. I flew with the RAF."

"I know. I'm sure— I didn't mean to insult you, it's just that I—" She cut herself off. Realizing she must appear ridiculous, she made a desperate effort to pull herself together. He had a license, had even flown with the air force, and she would do anything rather than let him see just how frightened she was. With a weak smile, Sylvia stepped forward and summoned her courage. "You're right. Let's get going."

"Okay." Jeremy raised a quizzical brow, then placed the tote with the other baggage in the back.

Sylvia took his hand and allowed him to help her climb into the chopper. The sight of the instruments made her grab nervously for her seat belt. A familiar chill seeped through her bloodstream, which she tried desperately to ignore. No way, she swore to herself, was she going to admit to this man climbing aboard so confidently that she was scared witless.

"At least the weather seems fine," she remarked

in a tight voice. Then, before she could stop herself, she added, "You're *sure* you're a qualified pilot?"

"They'd hardly rent me the chopper if I wasn't," Jeremy replied with a dismissive laugh.

"I guess that's okay, then," she murmured with another nervous smile.

"Your confidence in me, both in the office and in the air, is mind-boggling," he muttered sardonically as he turned on the ignition.

"I didn't mean—" The engines whirred and the propeller picked up speed. Sylvia closed her mouth and eyes and put on her earphones.

"You doing okay?" Jeremy's voice came through the phones.

"Great," she lied.

"Right. Then we're off." After that he paid no attention to her, talking to the tower and concentrating on takeoff. Sylvia glanced at him surreptitiously, anxiously checking his every movement. He seemed in control and she leaned back, relieved, trying desperately to relax.

Minutes later they were airborne. She twisted the diamond ring on her finger and forced her pulse rate back down, hating that she still reacted like this after all these years. It was absurd. *There's no need to be scared,* she repeated like a silent mantra, *no need at all. You've never had a problem. Why would you this time?* A sudden memory of the chopper dipping wildly into the Ozarks made her shut her eyes as tight as she could and wish she was anywhere but here.

Now that the takeoff had been handled smoothly, Jeremy's thoughts returned to Sylvia. He knew the route well, enjoyed the lush Scottish countryside below, and usually took the flight time to wind down. But not today. The woman next to him sat wired like a time bomb ready to explode. What was wrong with her? he wondered, taking a sidelong glance. She wasn't her usual composed, cool self. Her hands clasped and unclasped, and he could tell she was making a sustained effort to control her breathing. For a moment he thought of asking her if anything was wrong. Then, fearing a rebuff, he stayed silent. She obviously had no desire to get more personal and neither did he. No point in changing the status quo just because they were out of the office. Still, it was hard not to wonder what she was truly like beneath that sleek, impenetrable unbreakable surface.

Still desperately trying to mask her fear, Sylvia forced herself to stay in control. It was like this every time. You'd think she would have gotten over her fear, that flying in a chopper would be routine by now. But it wasn't. Gut clenched, she listened carefully for the right sounds from the engine, still spying warily from the corner of her eye as Jeremy expertly maneuvered the controls.

"Tower says we may hit a patch of bad weather after Loch Lomond as we head into the Highlands," he remarked. "Nothing serious."

"Sure," she replied vaguely, so distracted she hadn't even heard the transmission. Lord, she dreaded bad weather. So far so good, she thought, searching the sky. Surely the forecast was a mistake. There was no sign of any clouds. The sun was out, the sky blue, and the snowcapped tip of Ben Nevis shone in the distance as they crossed Loch Lomond.

"Have a snooze," Jeremy suggested after pointing out a couple of landmarks.

"Mmm-hmm."

He'd removed his jacket and tie and looked younger and more relaxed behind his Ray-Ban sunglasses. He obviously enjoyed flying. Learning that he'd been a chopper pilot in the air force had come as a surprise; she wouldn't have thought of him as a military man. What other revelations did his past contain? she wondered. There was something so annoyingly enigmatic about Jeremy. He seemed so lazily laid-back, yet right below the surface was a steely strength she'd been privy to time and again. A stubborn streak, too. She'd tested his intelligence several times on several levels over the past few weeks and had realized very quickly she was pitted against an impressive mind. So much for his laid-back exterior.

Determined to distract herself, Sylvia began wondering about Clarissa, Jeremy's thin upper-crust girlfriend. Why hadn't Miss Hoity-Toity joined them on the trip? From what Sylvia remembered of her, Clarissa hadn't seemed the type to dismiss an invitation to a castle, no matter how remote.

She was about to ask him, when an ominous rumble made her jerk up straight and stare ahead. Dark purple clouds loomed and a sheath of rain blurred the horizon. A sudden flash of lightning left her trembling.

"Oh my God."

"Just a bit of a storm, nothing to worry about." Jeremy downplayed the scene. But she noted that his concentration had changed and her heart chilled.

"Can't you do something to avoid it?"

"Looks as if we're too late to miss it. Never mind. Should be over shortly. Hang tight."

The chopper lurched as the pressure changed abruptly. Sylvia held on to her seat and forced the scream back into her throat. *Not this, please, dear God, not this way.* As they flew into the eye of the storm her eyes glazed. Suddenly she was back in the Ozarks, the mountain looming just feet ahead as the chopper dived. She could hear raucous laughter, smell heavy alcohol-laden breath. Control shredded and she screamed.

"It's all right, don't worry," Jeremy shouted above the noise, looking at her with surprised concern.

"Do something," Sylvia screamed once more, hysteria reaching new levels as the chopper lurched and another streak of lightning ripped the sky.

"I'm doing everything I bloody well can. You're not helping by screeching," he shouted back, gripping the controls. The chopper dipped and Sylvia cried out in terror.

"For God's sake shut up," Jeremy yelled back.

Pressing her hands together, Sylvia closed her eyes and prayed every prayer she'd ever learned at the Pulaski Convent School for Girls.

After what seemed like hours they finally outrode the storm. Peering nervously out the helicopter's windshield, she could see neat green fields and heather-covered moors below, but no sign of civilization.

"Please land," she begged, a cold sweat pouring off her forehead.

"We'll be fine now that we're beyond the storm," Jeremy argued, taking a glance in her direction. What he saw left him cold. "Christ, Sylvia, it wasn't that bad. You've been in choppers before. I promise you, another pilot wouldn't have done anything differently."

"Just get this goddamn thing onto the ground," she muttered through clenched teeth, "or I'll fire you."

For an instant their eyes locked in a battle of wills. Jeremy hesitated, straining mightily to control his temper. The woman was totally irrational. How dare she threaten him? He didn't need this damn job—hell, he was being made offers all the time. It went against all his principles to let her blackmail him. But a stubborn streak said this time he would have it out with her. On the ground.

"Very well," he said tersely.

The sudden plunge made Sylvia scream again and he steadied the chopper, determined not to let his temper get the better of him. Even though she might not be worth the effort, he was still a gentleman, and however far she pushed him he wasn't about to forget it.

A few minutes later the chopper came to a standstill. Rain had begun again, beating down relentlessly, making it hard to see more than a few feet ahead. They seemed to have landed in a void, with nothing— no houses, no farms, not even any sheep—in sight. But being on the ground was all that mattered. Sylvia sank back against the seat and closed her eyes, limp with relief.

"Happy now?" Jeremy threw her a fulminating look.

"Yes. Thank you," she added weakly, the haze of panic slowly clearing.

"What for? Obeying madam's orders? Did you give me any choice?"

Gradually she regrouped, sat straighter and stared out the window to the bleak scenery beyond. They were on a Scottish moor in the middle of nowhere and Jeremy was furious.

Seeing his livid expression, she felt her face flush a dull red. "I'm sorry...I reacted badly," she muttered.

"That's the understatement of the year. What do you propose we do now?"

"Get out of this wretched thing," she said immediately. Even sitting here with the wind blasting them left her feeling insecure.

"You must be flaming mad. Haven't you seen the weather? In case you hadn't noticed, it's raining. Rather hard."

"Look, just leave me alone," she retorted, nerves frayed to a thread. "I'll go by myself. You go on to Skye if you want, but I'm staying." She began fiddling nervously with the door catch. "Shit," she exclaimed. "I can't get this darn thing to open."

He leaned across her, unlocked the door and opened it. A blast of rain and wind made her draw back.

"Have fun," he remarked contemptuously.

Slowly, Sylvia straightened, then turned and stretched into the back of the chopper for her tote. "I'm leaving the garment bag. I'll just take this."

"You're not seriously thinking of getting out and walking to God-knows-where, in this?" Jeremy pointed out the windshield, leaned past her and pulled the door closed.

"I am. I'm not flying another foot in this contraption. If you want to go, then—" She was near tears and could bear it no longer. Anything, even blistering wind and rain, would be better than this.

"But there might be nothing for miles. I have no idea where we've landed and won't until the rain stops. Christ, you could die out there."

"Frankly, I don't give a shit," Sylvia retorted, "I want out." She knew she was being totally unreasonable but she was beyond the point of caring what Jeremy thought of her.

"You really mean it, don't you?" Jeremy leaned back and looked at her as if seeing her for the first time.

She nodded silently. A few seconds elapsed.

"You're absolutely stark raving mad, but if you're determined to go, I suppose I'd better come with you. We'll leave the stuff here and come back for it later. Maybe we'll get lucky and find a barn or something to take shelter in. Here, grab this." He handed her the umbrella. "Won't do much good but it's better than nothing."

"You don't have to come."

"Like hell I don't," Jeremy retorted. "I can hardly go before the board and explain that I managed to misplace our CEO." Jeremy stared at her sardonically, then seeing her expression checked himself, struck by her pallor, the true fear he read in her eyes. The storm was bad, but it was nothing that merited the almost desperate look on her face. "Come on," he said in a lighter tone. "Let's go before I change my mind."

"There's no need to be so pissed about it," she

remarked, retrieving some of her old resolve. "You're the one who got us into this mess in the first place. If we'd flown with a local pilot, I'll bet he would've avoided the storm and—"

"If you don't want me to strangle you here and now, I recommend we end this conversation immediately and get moving." The words were said in a quiet, deliberate tone that left no room for argument. Sylvia opened her mouth, saw flint flashing in Jeremy's green eyes, and shut it again. Turning from him, she pushed the door open and tumbled onto the sodden moor, heedless of her black patent-leather Prada shoes. Slowly she stumbled across the heather-covered moor, her legs so weak she could barely walk.

Jeremy caught up with her and took her arm, "Steady as she goes," he said in a soothing voice, forcing her to lean on him as they struggled through the driving wind and rain in no specific direction.

"Wait a minute. This is ridiculous." Jeremy stopped to take his bearings. "Let me see if I can make anything out. Do you see something over there?" He pointed with one hand while screening his eyes from the downpour. "Looks like a hamlet or something. Over there."

Aware of her sodden feet and the undergrowth ripping her stockings, Sylvia eagerly followed the direction of his pointing finger. "I think you're right," she agreed, her voice hopeful. "It looks like *something* on the horizon."

"Come on, then. I could do with a drink after all this." Jeremy grabbed Sylvia's arm once more and guided her as best he could through the gorse and bracken, his one objective to get them out of the drenching rain.

Sylvia followed his lead, glad of his support. She looked as if she'd been doing battle with the devil himself, with her hair stuck like rats' tails about her head, and her white raincoat filthy, but she didn't care. All she wanted was to reach a safe haven, a place as far away from the chopper as possible. The feel of Jeremy's strong arm gave her courage as she stared, eyes narrowed, trying to decipher what lay ahead.

Thank God.

"Look." She pointed, shaking Jeremy's arm excitedly, tears and rain mingling as a small huddle of houses became visible about half a mile to the left. There was definitely a hamlet, a farm, whatever, up ahead. She walked faster, tripped on a tuft of earth and would have fallen had Jeremy not held her up.

"Steady on, old girl," he said in a soothing voice. "Hold on tight to my arm."

She clung to his strong biceps, following him blindly as he forged ahead, tramping through the rain and tangled gorse with the ease of a veteran. Occasionally he asked her if she was doing okay; otherwise there was nothing but the rustle and howl of the wind and the odd thunderclap in the distance.

After another fifteen minutes battling weather, they passed a large Celtic cross engraved with the names of those who'd perished in both World Wars. The hamlet boasted one cobblestone street, bordered by neat hedgerows, small white cottages, some tiled, others thatched, featuring miniature windswept gardens and brightly painted front doors.

Jeremy headed purposefully toward an ancient, low-roofed whitewashed establishment with crooked, dark window frames and a large oak door. The wrought-iron sign hanging proudly outside read, The Laird and Dog.

"That must be the local pub," he muttered, passing a hand through his drenched hair, relieved. Now that sanctuary lay only steps away he glanced again at Sylvia's pallid countenance, still ravaged by vestiges of terror. She hadn't struck him as the sort of woman who'd be a bit bothered by a smidgen of rain and a storm. Which proved you should never judge by appearances, he decided, still perplexed. Was there another side to her he'd never suspected? He eyed her, truly worried as she climbed heavily up the steps, a disheveled figure whose bent shoulders and dripping hair little resembled the high-powered corporate figure of an hour earlier.

It occurred to him that he should be laughing at all this, at her, at her insane histrionics. Instead, he felt sincerely sorry for her and desperate to get her warm and dry before she caught a chill.

Inside, the pub was warm and cheery. Dark red walls covered with bright-colored snapshots, honorary certificates and yellowing sepia photographs spoke of sentiment and permanence. Bells of all shapes and sizes hung from the beamed ceiling. Dark wooden tables were surrounded by chairs and welcoming benches piled high with a colorful array of tartan cushions. Several locals sat nursing whiskeys at the bar, behind which a burly fellow with a shock of curly red hair stood wiping glasses. His bright blue eyes echoed the color of his striped blue-and-white waist-coat and watched their approach.

Evidently the landlord, the man was immediately sympathetic. "Caught in the storm, were ye? A bad 'en it was and nae finished yet. Comes from the Loch, ye ken," he added as an explanation.

"I wonder if you have anything dry my friend could put on," Jeremy asked, indicating Sylvia.

"If ye wait two ticks I'll call the wife." A loud shout echoed into the back regions of the pub. Then, with a broad grin, the landlord told them his name was Jamie MacFaddon and plunked down a couple of crystal tumblers with two fingers of amber single malt in each. "Have a wee dram and ye'll nae suffer any harm," he said with a wink as his wife, a plump red-head with an open face, came scuttling in from the kitchen, wiping her hands on a bright floral apron.

"What the deil are ye calling me in here for, man, when I'm about to put ma scones in the oven?" she exclaimed, arms akimbo. Then, seeing Sylvia, her eyes widened. "Och, ye pur wee lassie. Caught in the storm, were ye? Come along wi' me and we'll get ye all dry in a jiffy." Clucking like a mother hen, she swooped Sylvia out the door and up narrow stairs to a bedroom. Shivering, Sylvia sank gratefully into a worn armchair while the landlady switched on an electric fire.

"Th-thank you." She tried to smile but her teeth chattered. "It's so-o kind of you. We got caught in th-the st-storm."

"Aye." She nodded kindly. "What ye need is a gud hot bath and a toddy. Dinna worry. We'll have ye all sorted out. I'll tell Jamie to find something fer yer husband to wear, too.''

Before Sylvia could explain that Jeremy was not her husband, the woman entered the bathroom and turned on the taps of a gigantic old-fashioned bathtub.

''There ye go,'' she said with a broad smile. ''Ma name's Maggie. If there's anything else I can do fer ye just give me a wee call.'' Maggie gave her another broad freckled smile then turned to an ancient armoire standing against the wall. She rummaged a while then returned triumphant. ''I dinna ken if ye'll fit into these.'' She laughed good-naturedly, lifting up a large pair of pink sweats and a top. ''They may fall off ye. I was a wee bit slimmer when I bought them in Disneyland, but still, never like you,'' she added with a rumbling laugh. ''But dinna heed, dearie, ye'd look lovely whatever ye wore.''

''Thank you,'' Sylvia murmured weakly, eyeing Minnie Mouse on a candy-pink background, unable to conjure up a response.

''I'll leave ye to it now. You come along doon when yer ready. I'll go see te yer husband.''

''He's not my—'' But the door had closed behind Maggie. Sylvia sank down on the wooden toilet seat gazing at the rising steam and bubbles. Maggie had added something fragrant from a bright green bottle sitting on the side of the tub and the bath smelled delightfully warm and welcoming. After peeling off her wet clothes, she dipped a toe gingerly into the deliciously hot water then turned the taps off.

''Aaah.'' Sylvia let out something between a moan and a delighted sigh and, closing her eyes, sank in farther. It was sheer heaven. Better than anything she could remember. As the warmth seeped into her chilled limbs, she slowly relaxed and took stock of her situation. Thanks only to herself, she was stuck in a pub in the middle of the Scottish moors, in a hamlet God knows how many miles from Lord knows where, and downstairs Jeremy Warmouth awaited, probably furious at her for having caused so much drama. She trailed her fingers thoughtfully through the bubbles, trying to convince herself that he'd been irresponsible. It had been stupid of him to have made the flight, hadn't it?

By the time Sylvia got out of the bath, dried herself, donned the landlady's bright pink tracksuit and brushed her hair, she'd worked up a fine temper. After all, any seasoned pilot, particularly an air force pilot, should have taken special precautions regarding the weather conditions. If storms zipped in from nowhere on the loch, lake or whatever the damn thing was, then it was his responsibility to know that, too.

Donning a floppy pair of inelegant but warm carpet slippers that Maggie had left for her by the bed, and trying not to think how lowering it was to have a picture of Minnie Mouse emblazoned across her chest, she shuffled out into the corridor with every intention of telling Jeremy in very explicit terms exactly what she thought of him. The small inner voice that insisted blame might be better placed at her own door was studiously ignored.

Head high, she made her way down the narrow wooden stairs, determined to purge her soul. Maggie was waiting for her at the bottom.

"Feeling better?" she asked.

"Wonderful. Thank you so much for everything."

Some of Sylvia's righteous anger diminished at the kindness she was being shown by complete strangers.

"Come into the sitting room," Maggie invited, leading her into a warm, cozy living room with a blazing fire.

"There. You sit yersel' doon and I'll get ye a toddy."

"I really think I've had enough whiskey," Sylvia demurred.

"Och, ye canna have too much o' that!" the other woman exclaimed with a deep rumbling laugh that filled the room. "Dinna ye worry. You just let Maggie take care of ye and nae harm'll come te ye." She winked and left the room.

Sylvia gave up. It was impossible to stay cross for long when people around her were so cheerful. The frown turned into a smile. Sighing, she sank onto the couch and pulled the tartan throw her hostess had offered more closely about her shoulders. It felt so good to be dry and warm and safe that she almost forgot her grudge against Jeremy. Where was he? she wondered, curling her feet beneath her. Had he had a bath as well? Or maybe he'd gone to secure the chopper. She glanced through the lace curtains and stifled a yawn. The rain had lessened but a heavy gray mist and drizzle plugged relentlessly. For a moment she feared he might want to resume the journey, but quickly pushed the idea aside, turning instead to stare into the flames. Her head sank drowsily onto a soft, worn cushion and slowly her eyes closed.

Entering the sitting room fifteen minutes later, Jeremy discovered her curled under the blanket on the sofa. All he could see was her face and a ponytail peeking out from beneath a bright, patterned throw. He stood a while, staring down at her sleeping form, the hard glimmer in his green eyes softening. Quietly he tiptoed over to where she lay and pulled the slipping blanket back over her. It was hard to stay angry with her when he'd read on her face the intense fear she'd experienced. Watching her lying peacefully before the fire, he found it nigh impossible to reconcile this fresh-faced, almost childlike creature with the same woman he'd been doing battle with—well, not quite battle, but they'd certainly been at odds—for the past two and a half weeks. With her hair scooped up and her face devoid of makeup, she looked as vulnerable and innocent as a little girl, certainly nothing like the sexy fashion plate who'd attracted all those masculine stares in the airport several hours earlier, or the observant sleuth seeking solutions to their problem at Harcourts.

He shook his head and frowned. At the time, her hysterical reaction in the chopper and her silly threats had left him infuriated, but given how formidable Sylvia was in most arenas, the fact that riding in a chopper had so unnerved her clearly pointed to some kind of trauma in her past. She seemed powerless against the panic. But then, he'd known seasoned pilots who'd refused to fly after a bad airborne experience.

He toyed with the thought, his curiosity peaked. He'd decided to leave Harcourts and its predicament behind in London. Nothing could be done over the weekend, and both he and Sylvia would be better off taking some distance from it. Now he wondered if there was some deeper reason for her odd behavior.

Had she been in a crash? Who was Sylvia Hansen? Perhaps being alone with her in this isolated corner of the planet might be a good time to find out.

Up until now he'd made little effort to discover anything about her. And his approach, he admitted, a trifle ashamed, had certainly not helped.

Then he shivered, realized that he was still soaked from seeing to the helicopter and needed a change of clothes. Closing the door softly behind him, he climbed the stairs to seek out the landlady.

"We'll need two rooms," he remarked to Maggie, seeing her at the top of the stairs carrying a pile of sheets.

"Oh! I've only the one room, I'm afraid." She cast him a curious look. "Are ye two no married?"

"No, no." Jeremy gave a deprecating laugh. "Just business associates."

"Aaah!" Maggie gave a slow, knowing nod, then dumped the sheets on an old oak chest and raised her hands. "I'm sorry about the room. Can ye no share fer the one night?"

"Good God, no," he muttered. "That's out of the question. I can sleep downstairs on the sofa," he added quickly. "That is, if you don't mind."

"I dinna mind, but I've nae notion how comfy it may be," she said doubtfully, preceding him into the bedroom.

"Don't worry, Mrs. MacFaddon, I'll be fine. I'd be grateful for a hot bath though."

"Of course ye would. Now ye get out of those nasty wet things or ye'll catch yer death, young man. The bath's in there," she said, pointing in the direction of a half-open door in the flowery-wallpapered room. "The towels on the hot pipe are clean. Now, here's a tracksuit of Jamie's that should fit you."

"You really are too kind, Mrs. MacFaddon," Jeremy murmured, trying to sound grateful and conceal his horror at the bright orange tracksuit laid out on the bed. A logo on the left-hand breast read Torremolinos.

"Och away," she laughed and pulled the curtains closed, making the room suddenly welcoming and warm. "It should fit ye just and there's a pair of Jamie's slippers there fer ye, too." With that, she sent him another broad smile and left.

Jeremy peeled off his sodden slacks and blazer and deposited them in a forlorn pile with his shirt, socks and underwear in the corner of the room. Wrapping a towel around his waist, he entered the bathroom and stared at the huge old tub. The faint, floral scent of Sylvia's perfume lingered disturbingly in the room. He thought about the fact that she'd been in this same room, naked and languorous in this same bath, and tried to marshal his earlier anger, remembering the utter fury he'd experienced when she'd threatened to fire him for not kowtowing to her commands. But all he felt now was sympathy and a powerful desire to protect her.

He shook his head at himself in the mirror. It was foolish to believe that Sylvia had suddenly transformed from corporate lioness into swooning maiden. "Sucker," he muttered, grimacing at his reflection. Then, turning thankfully toward the steaming tub, he concentrated on warming up.

4

She woke to the soft distant strains of a single soulful bagpipe and the smell of damp fur, and felt so snug, content and rested that it took her a few seconds to remember exactly where she was. Then it all came back in a rush, the chopper, the perilous landing on the moor and the rain-soaked arrival at the inn.

Still huddled under the warm tartan rug, Sylvia pulled her knees up under her chin and stared at the low-beamed ceiling, feeling strangely peaceful, as though the world had stopped rotating and had framed her in a specific moment in time. There was something soothing about the room, its worn flowered-cotton curtains, the old couch covered with faded chintz throws and cushions, the crackling flames in the grate. Things that before had got on her nerves, but that in this instance made her feel cozy and secure.

A soft snore made her look down. At the foot of the sofa a large, furry, damp gray dog lay stretched before the hearth. For an instant she cringed. She'd always recoiled from dogs. A dog required such things as looking after and grooming. They could bite.

She eyed it uneasily for a while. But the animal appeared harmless, and when it shifted and grunted contentedly, a slow grin touched her lips. Tentatively she reached down to stroke it. When it didn't leap up and snap at her, she let out a sigh, and gathering courage, continued to knead the space between its ears, wondering where Jeremy was and what had become of the chopper. She caressed the dog and reflected. It was embarrassing to remember how she'd behaved, knowing she'd been hysterical. It made her vulnerable, and the last person on earth she would have chosen to appear vulnerable before was Jeremy Warmouth.

Voices in the hallway made her regroup, something she found surprisingly hard to do, lulled as she was by the warm and languid atmosphere. She watched warily as the door opened.

"Ah, you're awake." Jeremy walked in and Sylvia reluctantly braced herself for the inevitable confrontation. But when he stepped farther into the room, her jaw dropped and she burst out laughing.

"Oh my God, is that really you?" she asked of the figure clad in the Day-Glo orange tracksuit. Aside from the fact it was obviously a garment Jeremy wouldn't normally have been caught dead in, the tracksuit's shoulders were too broad and the legs too short. He looked decidedly like something out of a bad comic book. Noting the dull blush under his tan, she smiled and rose to her feet. "Don't feel bad," she said sympathetically. "Look at me." She waved the arms of the baggy candy-pink sweatshirt flopping over her hands. "I look like a pink version of the scarecrow in the *Wizard of Oz,* and let's not forget Miss Minnie. I didn't even wear this stuff when I was a kid."

"Certainly, neither of us will make the best-dressed lists this year," he ventured, a slow grin hovering as he joined her by the fire.

"That's for sure," she agreed, surprised at how different he looked when he grinned.

Almost human.

They stood, smiled a little too brightly, then sat down.

"What happened to the chopper?" Sylvia asked quickly, curling once more on the sofa and glancing out the window. The rain had stopped and a soft violet haze rose from the moor. She could hear birds through the half-open window, muted voices from the pub and the sound of a heavy tractor making its way home. London and New York and the buzz of busy streets seemed a world away.

"A couple of chaps from the village helped me secure it for the night. It'll be fine." Jeremy leaned back in the sagging armchair and eyed Sylvia warily.

"That's good. I guess we'd better call Strathaird," she said a trifle sheepishly. She felt ridiculous for having caused so much trouble. The storm probably wasn't nearly as bad as she'd made it out to be, and the MacLeod family would be awaiting them for dinner. This was all so embarrassing.

"Already taken care of. I talked to Brad earlier. They quite understand."

"Great. Thanks for handling that," she added, truly grateful.

"Not a problem," he replied gruffly, reaching down to stroke the dog between the ears. "Big fellow, isn't he?"

"Yeah. Nothing seems to disturb him."

"He wasn't here when I looked in earlier."

"You came in?" Her head shot up, horrified at the idea of him catching her unawares.

"Yes. You were curled up snug as a bug, fast asleep. Probably did you a world of good."

Sylvia swallowed hard. "I— Look, I'm really sorry about all the fuss earlier and…and what I said to you in the chopper…it was out of line."

The hand stroking the dog halted. He looked up, eyes narrowed. "That's all right," he answered slowly. "If I'd known you were so frightened of helicopters I would have found an alternative mode of transportation." She seemed ill at ease and quite unlike the Sylvia he'd become accustomed to.

"It's true I don't like choppers," she acknowledged, "But I fly in them all the time," she added hastily. She was obviously trying very hard to gloss over the matter, but he wasn't convinced. Clearly, the whole episode had affected her deeply.

"Did you have a bad experience in a chopper?" he asked quietly. When her expression closed once more, he continued quickly, "I've had a couple of experiences of my own that have left their marks." He leaned back again, flung one leg casually across the other and smiled while his mind worked overtime. "Every damn time I get into a biplane I think my heart's going to drop out."

"Oh?"

"An accident with my father when I was a kid. We

nearly didn't make it.'' His jaw tightened. She murmured sympathetically, knowing exactly how it felt.

Jeremy waited, hoping she might volunteer some information, sensing that she needed to do so. But she remained silent.

''Well, I suppose we'd better see what they've got for dinner,'' he remarked. ''Great smells coming from the kitchen when I passed by just now. We're lucky to have fallen on such nice landlords, I might add.''

''We sure are,'' Sylvia agreed wholeheartedly, glad of the neutral theme of conversation.

''Tell you what, I'll go see what wine the house has to offer and get us a glass. What would suit you, red or white?''

''Red would be fine. Thanks. In the meantime, I guess I should try calling Ira and Ham. What time is it in New York?'' She glanced anxiously at her gold Cartier watch. ''Christ, I've missed the morning meeting. I said I'd phone in, and—''

''Sylvia, why don't you forget it for tonight? Just put your feet up for once and relax. Harcourts won't go bust because you take some time to yourself,'' he added, seeing her stiffen. ''Here, have a look at a magazine or something.'' He shoved an old copy of *Vogue* at her, left behind by a former guest.

''Thanks, but I don't read that kind of thing,'' she said witheringly, laying it aside. ''I don't have time.''

''Maybe you should make time. You might find it does you good to do something frivolous.''

''Look, it's nice of you to bother, but I don't need to be entertained, okay? I'm perfectly able to relax without you telling me how I should go about it.''

''Fine, sorry, far be it from me to contradict you,''

he said, raising his hands and retreating toward the door. "I'll be back in a minute. Meanwhile, I'll wager a bet with you."

"A bet? What kind of bet?" She eyed him suspiciously.

"I'll give you twenty to one you can't sit still and read a silly magazine for ten minutes." He came back across the room, eyes alight with a challenging grin that left them greener than usual.

"That's absurd." Sylvia protested, flinging the magazine aside.

"You think so? I don't know. It's worth a try. Don't you ever do anything fun? Like shop or go to the hairdresser, I don't know...the things women do."

"Of course I go to the hairdresser," she snapped. "I go to Uribe in New York. They have me in and out in exactly thirty-five minutes."

"There. You see? That's what I meant. How about spending a morning having yourself pampered at a spa or—"

"Do you really believe I have time for that kind of nonsense? Get real. How do you think I run this company? Or maybe that's exactly what you'd like," she added, eyes narrowing, "to be able to portray me to the board as some dumb blond bimbo who spends her days lounging around the beauty salon, instead of looking after Harcourts's interests."

"That wasn't what I meant at all—"

"Oh? Then what exactly did you mean?" she challenged. "That women secretly lust for mindless days at the spa while macho men like you put their noses to the grindstone? And if spas are so relaxing, when's the last time you went to one? Anytime in, oh, the last century?''

"Forget it." His face closed once more and he looked like the Jeremy she knew. "I'm merely suggesting you try and enjoy life a little, instead of spending your days registering every damn thing on that BlackBerry pager of yours. You're wound tighter than a drum—as our little chopper ride illustrated rather definitively."

He was standing behind the sofa. She turned and faced him square on. "I don't see what business that is of yours. I'll organize my life in the manner I please. What's it to you? What do you care?"

Too late she read the suppressed anger.

"I care very much when delayed stress means that the passenger I'm flying loses control and almost causes a bloody accident," he retorted deliberately. "Are you aware, Sylvia, of just how close we came to crashing because of your absurd behavior? I don't care how you manage your life except when it affects my own survival. If you can't handle your neuroses, then don't fly. And," he added in a low harsh tone, eyes boring into hers and lips tight with anger, "don't ever blackmail me again."

"I didn't blackmail you, I merely said I—"

"You know damn well what you said, and believe me when I tell you it's the last time I'll tolerate your insolence."

"Insolence?" Sylvia jumped up and faced him again over the worn sofa covers. "Insolence, by definition, is something that subordinates exhibit when they lack respect for their bosses," she hissed.

"You have a bloody nerve. If your interference in

my office doesn't amount to insolence, then I don't know what does.''

''Really? Well, I'd like to remind you that the word hardly fits our situation. We're dealing in crisis control. If those designs were stolen from the factory, then we need to know that ASAP. All I'm doing is seeking answers, not trying to put a spoke in your ego-winding wheel. I got the impression that you were an intelligent man, but I'm changing my mind. Fast. Because if you think voicing my concerns about Harcourts amounts to nothing more than *insolence,* then you're plain stupid.''

''Stupid?'' He glared at her, astounded.

''Yes, stupid stupid stupid!'' she repeated, throwing up her hands crossly. ''You know full well why I came to London, yet you've done everything humanly possible to make my life as difficult as you can.'' She shook her head and blew out a sigh. ''Christ, I'm not a threat to you, Jeremy—I think you're the best man for the job. All I care about is that we get to the bottom of how Thackeray stole our designs. But you don't really care,'' she spat. ''All you think about is your damn pride. I suppose in some way my presence makes you feel belittled. Well, let me tell you something, *Lord* Warmouth, I run a team and I don't like lone wolves. Particularly those that out of sheer pride and idiocy can't see the forest for the trees.''

''Rubbish,'' he bit back, but the distressing truth of her words hit home hard.

''Then tell me you haven't done everything in your power over the past week to make my life impossible,'' she repeated, arms akimbo.

"Of course I haven't. That's ridiculous," he muttered.

"No, it isn't." Sylvia leaned forward, eyes on par with his. "You can't stomach the fact that I'm the CEO and that ultimately, I'm your boss. You made *that* abundantly clear when you actively lobbied against me," she added, her voice laced with sarcasm, all the emotion of the helicopter ride welling within her. "Still, I was stupid enough to believe that with time we could overcome all that." She spun back toward the fire, determined to conquer the tears that for some inexplicable reason were suddenly choking her throat. She couldn't understand why this man made her so angry, so hurt, so... She stared into the flames, shoulders heaving.

"I may have not been keen on the idea of your assuming the chairmanship," he admitted stiffly, taken aback by her emotional reaction, "but it had nothing to do with you personally."

"Oh? Then what exactly did it have to do with?" She whirled around again, hands planted on her hips, eyes hot with pent-up anger.

"I didn't think you were up to the job," he responded tightly, taking a step back, as though distancing himself. "You have since proved me wrong."

Her eyebrows arched and she crossed her arms protectively over her chest, controlling the hurt anger.

"My mistake," he continued, sounding unbelievably polite and reserved once more. "You're doing an excellent job. Now, if you'll excuse me, I shall go and investigate the wine situation."

Sylvia stared as the door closed after him, trying to control her tumultuous feelings.

The nerve of the man. How dare he think she wasn't capable? She plopped down among the cushions with a thump and clenched her fists. All that British arrogance and self-confidence, all that aristocratic superciliousness! Even as he excused himself he'd managed to keep his damn composure in place. She let out an angry huff and wished she could smother his handsome face in a bucket of composure. Then she picked up the magazine and flipped nervously through it. How dare he? How could he?

The old collie, who appeared indifferent to quarrels, shifted, let out a lazy grunt and snuggled closer to the grate. Sylvia continued to flick the pages nervously and stared over the dog's head at the dying embers, mentally reliving the argument. God, how the man must loathe her. He'd accused her of blackmail!

Which, she realized belatedly, heat rushing to her cheeks, was exactly what her words had amounted to.

And then he'd actually apologized.

Considering his pride, that couldn't have been easy. But he was probably just being polite in his stiff-necked British way.

Unable to stay still, she rose and paced the sitting room, restless as a caged leopard. She felt hemmed in, cooped up with him here. How the hell were they going to get through an evening together at this rate? She was darned if she'd eat with him. But what could she do without appearing ridiculous? Sit at the other side of the pub and cry in her coffee?

Flopping down again, she flipped irritably through the magazine pages. The man goaded her, pushed the limits of her patience. Not able to read a magazine, indeed! Like she was some kind of moron. His words implied that she wasn't feminine, that she—

Oh, blast him! Trust him to believe all women should spend their days at hairdressers, reading garbage. She stared scathingly at the glossy coverage of a charity ball, admitting that she quite liked being featured there herself. But that was for a different purpose. She needed the exposure. It was good for Harcourts. She turned the page, distracted by a couple of familiar names and faces.

Then her eyes froze on a photo of Aimon Thackeray, his rugged good looks and ever-present smirk jumping from the page. It was uncanny the way he seemed to be staring straight at her. Her spine stiffened and she threw the magazine aside. Here, in this remote part of the world, where mists swirled on heather-wrapped moors, it was easy to forget that this man had declared himself her enemy. Would he give up easily now that she'd won the first round?

Somehow, she didn't think so.

5

Although the prospect of dining with Jeremy should have been enough to turn her off food, Sylvia went down to dinner very hungry. She moved warily across the pub toward the corner table where Jeremy was already seated in his borrowed clothes, hoping he'd at least try to make dinner tolerable. He rose when he noticed her approach, and she eyed her companion with wary amusement.

Even if he proved to be his usual odious self, she decided, biting back a giggle, at least she'd get to enjoy his obvious discomfort at having to wear such ridiculous clothes. What she wouldn't do for a camera. Just as she was happily formulating a sarcastic remark, she remembered her own outfit wasn't any more flattering.

The pub was filling up nicely, she thought as she made her way among the tables. This must be where the locals assembled, she decided, glad there was zero chance that she'd run into anyone she knew. She'd learned earlier from an old man with extraordinarily blue eyes, very thick white hair, topped by a tartan

tammy, that they'd landed by the village of Clachnabrochan, situated in a remote spot between Dunoon
and Oban.

"Rarely get anyone from the outside," he'd remarked, obviously considering this to be a blessing.
"Nae many folks find us here. A gud thing, too," he
confided, nodding wisely over his dram. "The young
folks want away to the city, but 'am fer always tellin'
them they'll regret it. What does Glasgow have," he
asked reasonably, "that Clachnabrochan canna offer?"

Sylvia could think of a number of things, including
shops, e-mail, phone lines that worked and central
heating. But she'd murmured sympathetically. For an
hour she'd shivered in the hall, wishing she was by
the fire, trying in vain to reach Ira on her cell phone.
That was when she'd come in search of a landline
and come across Geordie MacPhife who, shaking his
incredible white head, told her the wind must have
blown the line down and that Alistair Feeny, who
knew how to fix it, was pacing the corridor of the
nearest hospital three hours away, where his wife was
having her firstborn. Sighing, Sylvia had eyed the
inn's ancient rotary phone with suspicion. She
doubted it worked even under the best of conditions.

Bracing herself for sarcasm, she reached the table.

"Hi," she offered now in a neutral voice, aware
that it would be hard to remain distant and detached
when they both looked so bizarre.

The table angled intimately into a wood-paneled
nook. Had she been with any other man, she might
have considered the setting romantic. Maggie had set
the table with pressed white linen. A breadbasket

filled with whole-grain rolls and deliciously scented soda bread made her mouth water. A small enamel pitcher spilled over with wildflowers, and the flickering light from a single beeswax candle made for a warm, friendly atmosphere.

Sitting stiffly on the edge of her corner of the bench, Sylvia eased herself as far from Jeremy as the seating arrangement would allow.

"Did you manage to get through to Ira?" he asked politely as he picked up a bottle of red wine. "Can I pour you a glass? It's actually a surprisingly fine vintage."

"Thanks." At this point, she'd have downed straight whiskey if it would help her get through what was sure to be a drawn-out evening.

"As for Ira, unfortunately not," she continued in a cool tone. He was acting as though the earlier quarrel hadn't taken place. Fine. If he could, then so could she.

"Well, at least we've found a comfortable place to wait out the storm. This is an excellent year," Jeremy commented cheerfully, twisting the bottle expertly as he finished pouring, "Lynch Bage, 1982. An exceptional Pauillac. It's had a little time to breathe." He twisted the bottle for her to read the label.

"I like Bordeaux, particularly the Pauillacs," she remarked, relenting some as she glanced at the label, glad she'd attended that wine seminar in Napa last year.

Jeremy placed the bottle on the table and raised his glass. To her surprise, he sent her a speculative smile.

"Sylvia, why don't we call a truce and start over. Let's forget Harcourts for tonight and relax. Why not drink to the health of our goddaughter? After all, she's the reason we're here.''

"To Freya," she agreed, raising her glass and taking a first sip, amazed at how smoothly the wine glided over her tongue. Clearly this was a special vintage, and she couldn't for the life of her figure out how Jeremy had acquired it in a remote hamlet such as Clachnabrochan.

"Where on earth did you find such a bottle as this?" she asked, curiosity winning the day. "The Laird and Dog doesn't strike me as a place that bothers with a vintage-wine list.''

"No," he agreed, a grin hovering over his tanned features, "I came across it by pure chance with Jamie in the cellar. Good chap, Jamie," he added, eyeing his glass thoughtfully. "He got an excellent deal on a couple of cases from a wine merchant a few years ago. Then he forgot about them. Excellent, isn't it?''

"Superb." Sylvia took another appreciative sip. "What's on the menu?"

"Potted shrimp."

"Ah." Another one of those British delicacies that up until now she'd avoided like the plague.

But when the plates were set before them and she gingerly placed some of the pale, pinky-brown concoction on a slice of thin, brown, buttered bread, Sylvia found it to be delicious.

"Not bad," she remarked between bites.

"You've never had potted shrimp?"

He really should smile more often, she reflected, taken aback by how green his eyes lit up and how his teeth flashed white against his tan.

"Frankly, I always thought they were kind of weird-looking."

"You have a point," he agreed, eyeing his plate thoughtfully. "Which proves one should not be put off by appearances." She pretended not to catch the innuendo. "Have you ever eaten haggis?"

"Good God, no. And I've no intention of doing so."

"Pity—" Jeremy gave a worried shake of his head "—it's our next course. Maggie asked me if I thought you would enjoy a typical Scottish dish and I said yes. I'm dreadfully sorry. Too late to change the order, I'm afraid." He sighed and sent her a contrite glance.

"You have to be kidding! You mean haggis is all they have to eat here? No sandwiches, nothing?"

"Sorry," he said apologetically. "It's entirely my fault. I should have known better than to think you'd want to try a local delicacy." He shook his head worried.

Just as she was about to resign herself to an evening of chips and a hard-boiled egg, Sylvia caught the mischievous twinkle in his eyes. She laid down her glass, eyes narrowed.

"Dreadfully sorry," he repeated, hands raised regretfully. "If I'd known, I would have—"

"Liar!" she accused, laughing. "You're no more likely to eat haggis than I am."

"Forgive me. I couldn't resist," he murmured contritely. "You rise too well to the bait."

"No kidding." She shuddered. "Anything related to sheep intestines does tend to set my senses on full defensive alert."

"Don't worry, no sheep's innards on the menu, I give you my solemn promise. Just shepherd's pie."

Sylvia leaned back against the cushions, her shoulders shaking. "Well, thank God for that. I try to be sensitive to local customs, but haggis..." She shuddered once more. "That really would have done me in." The tension had lessened, she realized thankfully. Perhaps if they kept on neutral ground, they could actually spend a relatively civilized evening in each other's company. And the sooner they got used to doing so, the better it would be, she reflected, relishing the last of the potted shrimp. After all, the present corporate structure might stay in place for years.

"As for Ira," she said, remembering his initial question, "I tried dialing him for almost an hour, but that gentleman sitting on the bar stool over there—" she lowered her voice and nodded in the direction of the bar "—the one with the very blue eyes and the tammy, he told me the phone lines are down. Do you think that by tomorrow we'll be able to reach New York? My cell's not working."

He hesitated a moment, then looked straight at her. "Don't take this the wrong way, Sylvia," he said, "but as I pointed out earlier, Harcourts will survive without you for a day or two. And don't even bother with your mobile—I don't think there's a cell tower within fifty miles of this place. Which means," he continued with a growing grin, "that you have no choice but to take a break from business for a while. Here, have another glass of wine."

"Easy for you to say," she remarked tartly. "What'll we do if Thackeray launches another offensive while we're out of touch? What if—"

''The answer to that is nothing. Because right now there's not a damn thing we *can* do about it if he does.'' He shrugged. ''So what earthly point is there sitting here worrying about it? Besides, I'm sure he learned his lesson. Your idea of the massive sale was rather brilliant,'' he conceded, a smile flirting around his lips. ''Congratulations.''

She glanced at him warily across the empty plates, searching for any cynical twist to his mouth, or the patronizingly curved brow she'd gotten used to in the past two and a half weeks. But to her surprise, his expression was one of undisguised admiration, making her cheeks flush. She took a quick sip of wine to cover her embarrassment. ''Thanks,'' she muttered. He was being inordinately pleasant tonight, and it was hard to believe this was the same man she'd crossed swords with on an almost hourly basis back in London.

''Hey, you've earned yourself a break,'' he said, slipping a hand over hers and giving it a friendly squeeze. ''Here, have some of this home-baked bread. Add lots of butter. And don't you dare do a cholesterol count,'' he said sternly, placing a large dollop of rich yellow butter on her side plate. ''Now, go on, eat. I won't have you wasting away. You've been looking a bit peaky the last few days.''

''Yes, sir,'' she responded, hiding her astonishment that he'd even noticed such a thing. She'd never seen this side of Jeremy, never believed he could be so relaxed, charming and amusing.

''Now—'' he leaned forward ''—let me tell you the latest office gossip.''

"Gossip? In that mausoleum?" It was out before she could think.

"Good Lord, yes. The place is rife with it. You must know we Brits thrive on gossip."

"Well, I don't really see what there is to gossip about. Did Major Whitehead have a convulsion over dressed crab at his club?" she asked, quirking a well-defined brow.

"Now, now, don't be mean. Old Whitehead's not a bad fellow. Very respected officer in his day, I'll have you know."

"I didn't intend to be mean—in fact, he's been very kind to me lending his office and all—" Seeing his laughing eyes, she broke off again and placed the bread back on the plate, realizing he was teasing her once more. "Why don't you just tell me the latest rumors and stop letting me make a fool of myself," she laughed.

"You never do that," he said, turning suddenly serious. "I shouldn't think you've ever made a fool of yourself or made a wrong move since you were in nappies."

"Nappies?"

"Diapers," he explained.

"You'd be surprised," she muttered. Then, not wanting to bring the convivial atmosphere to a close, she continued, "You changed the subject. Fill me in on the gossip."

"Right," Jeremy said breezily, wondering what he could make up to distract her and keep the flow of conversation light. It was uncommonly pleasant to be dining here, satisfying to know he'd been right in his earlier assumption that perhaps there was a side of her he'd never guessed existed. Watching as she spread the butter sparingly on the bread and took a bite, he continued, tone conspiratorial, as if imparting state secrets, "Did you know that Miss Hunter is part owner of a new racehorse?"

"You're kidding me," she exclaimed, genuinely surprised. The thought of the prim Miss Hunter, with her horn-rimmed glasses, white chignon, threadbare tweeds and twinsets, even setting foot on a racetrack was outlandish. Actually, she found it hard to visualize the old curmudgeon anywhere but behind the large desk that dominated the entrance of Harcourts Europe. "It can't be true," she said decisively. "You must have gotten it wrong."

"I swear it's true. Reggie got it firsthand from Finch," he added smugly. "As you can see, my sources are impeccable."

"Wow! I can't imagine her caring about anything but her phones and that notepad and pen she wields all day, much less letting anyone see her urging on her horse from the stands." Sylvia shook her head and let out a giggle. "I mean, Miss Hunter's kind of like an institution, isn't she? I was terrified of her. Still am, I guess," she added, grimacing.

"You're not alone," he said with feeling. "The woman's a world-class harridan. Even Major White-head trembles before her."

"You know, you're right," she agreed between bites. "The other day I heard her tell the Major he shouldn't be having three lumps of sugar in his tea, that it was bad for his blood sugar, and do you know that he just meekly agreed? Not one protest. I even heard him tell Finch that in future he'd have only one lump.''

"Which just goes to prove my point." Jeremy flashed her a triumphant smirk as Maggie placed the steaming shepherd's pie down on the mat between them.

"Eat while it's hot," she recommended before swooping down on the next table, where an elderly couple was studying a menu they most likely knew by heart.

"Go on, tell me more about Miss Hunter," Sylvia prompted, serving herself a dainty portion of shepherd's pie and placing the serving spoon carefully back in the dish.

"Only if you eat properly. Here…" Jeremy lifted the spoon and scooped up an enormous helping of pie, which he deposited firmly on her plate.

"But that's far too much," she protested. "I'll never be able to—"

"Eat, or forgo the knowledge I am about to impart," he ordered with a menacing scowl. She shook her head and laughed despite his high-handed manner.

"Okay, you win. I eat, you tell. So Miss Hunter races horses? You mean she goes to Ascot and stuff like that?"

"Absolutely. She's been going for years. The Major got her approved for the Royal Enclosure several years ago. You won't see Harriet Hunter around the office during Ascot week," he said, shaking his head decisively. "She's off hobnobbing with the royals. Looked smarter than the queen last year."

"Wow! Who would have believed it?" Sylvia savored the shepherd's pie, absorbed by the image of

Miss Hunter in a frothy pink hat shrieking encouragement to her horse. "She seems so prim and proper in those old tweed skirts that it's hard to imagine her any other way."

"I'm sure the skirts are as old as she is. But that's because she spends all her money betting on the races. You know, when I joined Harcourts five years ago, I managed to avoid her for a whole month, then I gave up. There wasn't a place I could hide in that she couldn't track me down. I'd swear that woman's part bloodhound." The last was murmured in a low, husky voice she was finding increasingly sexy.

Sipping more wine, she observed him. "What did you do before you joined Harcourts?" she asked suddenly, mellowed by the Pauillac and the conversation, and curious all at once about his background.

"Oh, this and that. After Oxford I went into the air force for a while," he replied vaguely. "I was obsessed with flying."

"But on your résumé it says you went to Yale," she remembered.

"That was later. After I sobered up and decided it was time to take life seriously. I did a Ph.D. That's where I really got to know Brad."

"Brad never mentioned you were at Yale with him," she remarked, surprised. Then the strains of a fiddle began, and she gazed beyond him at the busy tables. It was like a tableau, she reflected, poising her fork and seeping in the atmosphere. The fiddler struck up a jolly reel in the corner, and Maggie bustled between her customers, throwing out a smile, exchanging good-humored abuse and jotting down orders that she relayed to her husband, manning the bar.

Jeremy sent Sylvia a sidelong look, marveling at the mellow light in her eyes. In that awful borrowed sweat suit, she was still shockingly beautiful but less dauntingly sophisticated. Approachable for the first time, he reflected. Perhaps the chopper incident wasn't so bad after all. At least it seemed to have broken the ice between them—ice that he was largely responsible for, he acknowledged. It was shaming to admit that he'd been stubborn and blockheaded. In fact, his ungentlemanly manner toward this woman, who had done nothing but her job, was reprehensible and totally incompatible with his principles and up-bringing.

He wondered suddenly if she regretted the broken engagement from Brad. Seeing her so relaxed, sipping her wine and watching the crowd contentedly, it was easy to forget that this trip to Skye couldn't be simple for her. After all, she and Brad had been together for, what, almost five years? He felt a sudden rush of sympathy, even as he tried to remind himself that this was Sylvia Hansen, the tough corporate ace. But in the muted light, the flickering candle lending a soft glimmer to, what he had to confess now that he'd taken a proper look, were exceptionally lovely eyes, it was easy to believe this was a different person from the business Amazon whom he faced every day. Indeed, this delightfully feminine creature was proving to be excellent company.

He'd always wondered what Brad saw in her. Now he was beginning to understand. It was surprising she hadn't found another man to replace Brad in her life. But then, she was so committed to Harcourts she probably didn't have the time, he reasoned, wondering all at once why the notion pleased him.

As he continued to observe her in friendly silence, he thought of their earlier heated exchange. It was embarrassing to admit, but Sylvia was right. He had treated her with marked condescension over the past two and a half weeks, rather like a child whom one tolerated, but just barely. The thought left him ill at ease. Sylvia might get on his nerves, might be a pain in the butt at times, but the truth was, he knew very well that her motives were totally sincere. If anyone had Harcourts's interests at heart, it was she. The disturbing fact was he just hadn't given her a chance.

"This shepherd's pie's the best," Sylvia exclaimed, savoring each mouthful. "And that tune's lovely, isn't it?" Her smile softened as she gestured toward the fiddler, joined now by a handsome dark Gael with eyes as bright as old Geordie's. Seated on a low wooden stool, he accompanied the fiddler with a squeeze box and drummed his foot.

"Yes." Jeremy cleared his throat, struck by the wistfulness in her expression. "Quite jolly, these Scottish tunes."

"Yeah." She looked away and the mellow expression disappeared. "Say, how come Clarissa didn't join you on this trip?" she asked, deciding it was time to satisfy her curiosity as to the whereabouts of Jeremy's girlfriend. Reggie had assured her the two were all but engaged.

"She had a previous family commitment in Northumberland that would have been bad manners to cancel," he answered easily.

Very smooth, Sylvia reflected, noting the lack of

concern in his voice—as if he was actually rather happy not to have her along. What was it that attracted a woman like Clarissa to Jeremy? she wondered. Apart from the obvious—that he was a smart, good-looking, presumably wealthy guy.

Years of working corporate boardrooms—as well as the ordeals of her own youth—had made Sylvia a rare judge of character. And the one time she'd met Jeremy's girlfriend, Clarissa had struck her as calculating and strangely cold—a woman who wouldn't do anything unless it benefited her. Which suggested that no matter how compelling Jeremy might be, it wasn't the man himself that interested Clarissa.

To put it bluntly, Sylvia considered, studying Jeremy as he tapped his foot to the fiddler's music, people like Clarissa ruthlessly weeded from their lives anyone who couldn't enhance their own status. Jeremy was a definite catch, of course, for he had a title, and she doubted that a woman of Clarissa's ilk and temperament would settle for anything less. That, and a *very* secure existence at some posh country home.

"You've been dating for a while, haven't you?" she ventured casually.

"Six years."

"Wow! So when's the wedding?" she asked with an air of polite interest, hoping Jeremy wouldn't consider her sudden questions out of line.

"Our relationship hasn't progressed to that point," he said stiffly.

"Well, Clarissa must be a very understanding sort," she replied doubtfully, "because where I come from, she's only a year away from becoming your common-law wife."

"My wi—" Jeremy's spluttered, coughing.

"Sorry," Sylvia interjected softly. "I didn't mean to shock you. Of course, you'd have to have been living together all that time for the legal obligation to kick in, depending on what state you lived in, of course," she reassured him.

"You Yanks," he replied, waving the notion aside with a quick humorless laugh. "So obsessed with putting labels and legal terms on every damn thing. We just haven't got around to talking about that sort of commitment yet, that's all."

"In six years?" she murmured.

He took a long sip of wine and Sylvia hid a smile when he sent an irritated glance toward the television, stuck high up in a corner. A soap opera of some sort was playing, despite the other activities taking place in the pub.

"I wish they'd turn that damn thing off."

Seeing he wanted to change the subject, Sylvia decided to humor him. "I guess people here like following the soaps," she remarked, glancing up at the television. Contrary to American soaps, where everything was glitz and glamour, British soaps seemed to center around pubs, grocery stores and Laundromats. "These shows always seem so...dowdy," she commented.

The tenseness around Jeremy's mouth eased and he laughed. "No kidding. *Coronation Street* has been running for twenty-odd years on the same old set. I suppose it must be a hell of a lot cheaper to produce than *Dallas* or *Dynasty*."

"I guess." But it still struck her as weird that people would be interested in the humdrum little dramas of small-town living. Heck, she'd lived that herself and it had *not* been an existence worth memorializing on television.

"Landlord should be pleased with us," Jeremy murmured, taking a sidelong glance at the bar. "I think we've managed to attract quite a crowd." She followed his look, amused to see he was right. They were definitely the focus of numerous curious gazes from the locals.

Perched on worn, red velvet stools, elbows leaning heavily upon the stained, scarred and weathered wood counter that had witnessed the laughter and tears of many generations, the pub's customers seemed like characters out of a history book.

"I wonder if life today is all that different from when this place first opened," she murmured thoughtfully, raising her eyes to his, trying to imagine what it must have been like to live here in another era. Scotland always had this effect on her, making her remember that there were places where past and present coexisted. During her last stay in Skye, this thought had driven her half-nuts, but tonight for some reason it relaxed her, helped her step away from the worries of the real world.

"They work the land, I suppose, then come in here for a dram and some gossip, just like their forefathers." Jeremy sipped and glanced about the room. "The young folk probably leave for the towns, of course, but I should think that those who stay have lives similar to their ancestors'."

"I guess," she said, agreeably mellowed. Strange how, an hour ago, she'd sat down with the expectation that dinner would deteriorate into yet another fight between them. Instead, here they were, chatting cozily, and the evening had turned into an uncommonly pleasant interlude, one she would never have expected. Perhaps Jeremy was right. They needed to let go of the predicament at Harcourts for the weekend. Maybe it would give them a better perspective. And if they just avoided any controversial subjects, maybe they could continue to be, well, friends, as they'd been tonight. Sylvia found the thought alluring, wishing wistfully that it could be so.

Which was crazy, and unrealistic. The minute they hit the London offices on Monday, everything would likely be the same as they'd left off. But Jeremy was being so darn nice tonight. Nicer than she'd ever known him. Than she ever imagined he could possibly be. The man was decidedly charming when he set his mind to it, she reflected, warily revising her former impression as she laughed at the punch line of a well-told joke. Though her hardened business self had misgivings, knowing he was probably just feeling guilty about this afternoon's events, the woman in her couldn't help but thaw. Nor could she deny the hovering twinge of attraction.

By the time Maggie replaced their empty plates of shepherd's pie with two large portions of sticky toffee pudding, Sylvia was in stitches listening to another entertaining yarn.

"Maggie, I beg of you, no more," she pleaded while the delicious scent of warm toffee filled her nostrils. "Thank God I'm only staying here one night or I'd be waddling out of here."

"Damn good stuff," Jeremy agreed, tucking into his pudding. "Come on, Syl—" he grinned "—you don't have to worry about weight. You'd look fabulous whatever you weighed.''

Her spoon stopped in midair and she stared at him, taken aback. Jeremy had never, *ever* called her Syl, much less paid her a direct compliment.

''I have to admit,'' she replied slowly, covering her confusion, ''that this is the most wickedly delicious dessert I've ever had, and worth every calorie. As for that pie—I simply must get the recipe out of Maggie before we leave tomorrow.''

''You cook?'' Now it was his turn to look surprised.

''Sure. Have a problem with that?'' she challenged, her usual defenses slamming back into place.

''Not at all. You just never struck me as the cooking type.''

''Why, because I don't run around in an apron with a cute little logo stuck on the pocket?'' she inquired, cocking her head, searching for any overt signs of mockery.

''No,'' he responded, eyeing her in a speculative way that left her strangely breathless. ''Merely that I'm used to seeing you in the boardroom, not slaving over the stove, that's all. Tell you what,'' he added, popping another mouthful of pudding in his mouth. ''Next time I'm in New York you can invite me to dinner and I'll tell you how your domestic skills are shaping up.''

''You'll—'' She was about to fly off the handle, when she caught the mischievous gleam in his eyes and realized she'd almost fallen for his teasing once again. ''Well, thank you, kind sir!'' she murmured, flapping her eyelashes and adopting a sweet southern drawl, disguising the fact that she was drawn to this relaxed, amiable and amusing side of Jeremy. "You're too kind. May a' really have the privilege of feeding you? The prospect just makes ma' little ol' homemaker heart flutter."

"Scared?" he taunted, a wolfish grin spreading. "I promise I won't tell if it's ghastly."

"Done deal." She gave him a thumbs-up, then finished off the last of her pudding. "Guess I'll have to dig up my recipe for braised crow. That's a specialty where I come from," she laughed.

"And where would that be?" he asked, suddenly curious.

"Nowhere in particular. Just a joke," she replied hastily.

He laughed, but the way her eyes had shuttered so quickly hadn't escaped him. He pushed his plate away regretfully and didn't pursue the subject. "I'm afraid I've reached my limit. How about coffee in the sitting room by the fire?"

"Why not?" She turned brightly to Maggie as she reached their table. "This was a glorious meal," she exclaimed. "You put a lot of New York chefs to shame." Sylvia groaned appreciatively and rose from the cushioned bench.

"Excellent cuisine, Mrs. MacFaddon," Jeremy agreed while Maggie, wreathed in smiles, promised to bring them coffee.

They crossed the dark-beamed hallway and Jeremy gallantly opened the door of the sitting room for her. Sylvia passed through, feeling completely at ease despite the dreadful sweats and slippers. There was something in the way he'd handled things tonight, from the moment they'd sat down to the manner in which he opened the door for her, that left her feeling special and feminine and—*What is the matter with you, Sylvia Hansen? This type of thinking will get you nowhere.* She forced herself to take stock of the room, instead.

"This is cozy," she remarked, glancing at the low crooked beams, the flowered curtains and the old sofa. The faded throws and cushions sagged comfortably, welcoming and mellow in the lamplight. The door creaked ajar and Dougal, the large collie that had kept her company that afternoon, loped across the carpet. Paying little attention to the new guests, he lowered himself once more before the rekindled fire and, head drooping on his paws, fell promptly asleep.

"He seems to spend most of his time like that," Sylvia remarked.

"That's because he's old. At least twelve or thirteen, I'd guess." Jeremy leaned down and patted him gently.

"Do you like dogs? I guess you must, since you're a Brit. Let me guess, you like nothing more than wandering around your country estate with your beloved corgis in tow," she observed, tongue in cheek.

"Actually, they're bloodhounds. The corgis are my aunt's. She lives there."

"Sorry," she laughed, settling among the cushions.

"You're excused," he murmured, keeping the tone light. "Actually, I keep a spaniel at the flat. I walk him in St. James's Park in the evenings. You should join me sometime. Early evening can be very pleasant."

Sylvia suddenly pictured him walking the dog in

front of Buckingham Palace, having to clean up any little messes the dog might make, and grinned. "Funny, I wouldn't have pictured you as an animal person."

"No, well, neither would I—I mean, imagine you as an animal person," he added in an explanatory tone. He sat up and raked his right hand through his hair. "Do you keep a dog?"

"Me? Good gracious, no. I couldn't deal with a dog." She glanced at Dougal's tangled coat and winced. "Just imagine having all that hair all over the apartment. My decorator would have me shot. No," she said with a firm shake of her silky blond head. "I definitely couldn't handle it."

"I'd think you could handle anything. But in the event you *chose* to, you certainly could get some service to deal with the mess. I thought New York had services for everything."

"True," she murmured upon reflection, tilting her head, the idea of a dog suddenly appealing. A nonhairy, nonmessy one, of course. Perhaps one of those wrinkly sausage ones like those owned by Mrs. Harmond the Fourth, who lived on the floor below her. "Maybe if I could find someone who'd keep it fed and cared for," she decided.

"Lucky dog," he said dryly, flopping into the opposite armchair. "What's the point in having one if you don't play with it and walk it yourself?"

She shrugged impatiently. "Look, I don't know. It was just an idea. I'm not a dog person, okay?"

"Fine." He raised his hands, drew back, then leaned toward the fire, added a log and neatly changed the subject. "I think we should leave about eleven tomorrow morning, weather permitting."

"Uh-huh." The mention of tomorrow morning and the chopper brought on a tinge of suppressed panic.

"How about a game of Scrabble?" Jeremy suggested, seeing the box lying on a shelf near the fireplace.

"Good idea," she answered quickly. That would surely be better than avoiding the controversial subjects that would inevitably surface if they went on talking too long. Miss Hunter's racing habits and dogs were safe. But God only knew what would happen if they ventured onto one of the many flash points that seemed to exist between them. And she didn't want another argument. If she was *completely* truthful, she didn't want their comfortable intimacy to end, even if it was only a temporary illusion.

Jeremy retrieved the game, then crossed the room and, tipping open the box, spread the board on the well-worn green baize surface of the card table in the far corner. They sat opposite one another. Sylvia mounted her letters painstakingly on the slight wooden stand and studied them with a frown. She'd been a Scrabble champion in eighth grade.

Jeremy did the same. But his eyes were on her, not the letters. There was intensity about everything she undertook, be it work or a simple board game.

And it fascinated him. The way she focused all her attention so completely on whatever she was doing. While he arranged his own letter blocks, he studied her long, slim, manicured fingers caressing the letters and felt an odd twinge in his gut.

After several minutes of play, most of it spent ignoring her delicate, alluring scent, he leaned forward. "You'd be better to place that C there." He pointed. Their fingers touched as Jeremy reached over, guiding her hand firmly to a double-letter score. For a moment his hand rested over hers.

An electric charge sparked up her arm. She looked up and their eyes locked. Pulling swiftly away, Sylvia stared blindly at the little white blocks, their black letters swimming before her eyes. For an instant she'd felt something surreal, a dreamy vortex of intense sensation, as if they'd stepped out of time.

What on earth was wrong with her? Why was she having ridiculous thoughts this evening? Just because the man had decided to turn on the charm for her benefit shouldn't leave her mooning like an adolescent. Deciding she must be seriously overtired from the chopper ride and the storm, she concentrated on the letters. Suddenly a slow smile dawned as a word formed before her. "I have a great one," she said triumphantly as he finished his turn.

"Okay, let's see."

Placing each letter carefully on the board Sylvia added *sensual* to the word *con*. "That's ten letters plus a double letter on the N," she pointed out smugly.

"So it is. How about this," he countered, neatly popping an E and an X onto the middle S in *consensual*. "Triple letter on the X, I'm afraid," he murmured apologetically, eyes brimming with laughter.

"Well, of all the—" Sylvia burst out, then lifting her arms she fell back in her chair and gave way to laughter. "I give up. You win. I'm too tired to go on.

I think it's time I went to bed. You going to retire, too?"

"Uh, yes. In a little. You go on up. I'll put the game away. How about a nightcap before you go?"

"I don't think I will—" she rose and yawned "—but thanks anyway."

He followed suit. "It's been a very pleasant evening. I hope you sleep well. And don't worry about tomorrow. The weather forecast is excellent."

"Great." She gave a tight little smile and smothered the rush of fear. "I guess I'll get going then and see you in the morning. Give me your room number and I'll make sure we both get wake-up calls."

Jeremy shifted uncomfortably. "Actually, I don't have one." He hadn't intended to tell her about the lack of accommodation.

"What do you mean? Do they only have one room?" She looked at him, horrified.

"Yes. And you're in it, I'm afraid. This is a pub, after all, not a full-fledged inn or B and B. But don't worry, I'll camp out down here, quite the thing." He pointed to the sagging couch.

"What? You're going to sleep on that lumpy sofa?"

"Believe me, it's a Stearns & Foster mattress compared to some of the places I've slept in the past."

Sylvia sent the sofa another doubtful glance. "Are you sure?"

"Absolutely. Don't give it a thought." Slipping his hand under her arm, he walked her firmly toward the door. She felt bad leaving him for her comfortable bed upstairs, and tried hard to remind herself that it was his fault—well, mostly his fault—that they were stuck here in the first place.

When they reached the door, he laid a hand on the brass knob and smiled. "Sleep tight and don't let the bedbugs bite, as you say in the States."

"Are you *really* sure you'll be okay?" Sylvia gazed uncomfortably over his shoulder at the sofa.

"One hundred percent certain. Now, off with you, young lady, you need your sleep."

She looked up, smiled, then nearly fainted when he dropped a chaste peck on her cheek. Head spinning, she moved hastily out the door, made her way swiftly across the dimly lit hallway and up the stairs to her room, unable to explain why it bothered her so much that Jeremy was going to spend the night on the sofa, when a few hours earlier she would most likely have relished the possibility.

Shaking her head, she entered her room and closed the door firmly behind her, determined not to let anything, much less Jeremy's misfortunes, disturb her sleep.

6

As she'd feared, Sylvia spent a large portion of the night waking and wondering. Just the thought of getting aboard the chopper in a few hours left her stomach queasy. She felt like a prisoner living her last hours. Long before dawn she gave up trying to sleep and, frazzled and tired, climbed out of bed to pour herself a glass of water, determined to get her panic under control.

Had Jeremy been able to sleep on the sagging sofa? she wondered, filling the glass from the single tap at the sink. She was suddenly tempted to go downstairs and take a look.

But that was impossible. It was none of her business what kind of night he'd spent. She glanced out of the window at the inky, star-trailed night. A full moon lit up the sky like a great lightbulb, defining the outline of the roofs of the small village. All was quiet, the only sound piercing the silence the distant hooting of an owl. The storm appeared to have cleared completely.

She drew the curtains shut again in the hopes the

darkness would help her sleep and thought of Jeremy, huddled on the uneven cushions below. Then she gave an irritated yawn. It was his own fault that he was spending a miserable night on the couch, after all. Maybe it was concern for her own safety that prompted her unwarranted solicitude, she justified, clambering back between the sheets. If he didn't sleep right, he might not be as alert as he should on the flight tomorrow. The chopper ride up would be fine, she reassured herself, for the night was clear and tomorrow would be a bright sunny day. No need to worry. And, despite her panicked accusations, she had to admit, Jeremy had proved himself a competent pilot.

Still, it was impossible to repulse the constant visions that leaped around in her head like jeering leprechauns. For several years she'd managed to relegate the nightmarish memories to a remote corner of her brain, and this uneasy compromise had offered her a certain measure of peace. But ever since Thackeray had set Harcourts—and herself—in his crosshairs, many of her long-forgotten vulnerabilities had resurfaced, clear and disturbing as ever.

Yesterday's fiasco had provided ample evidence of that. She'd known she was exaggerating the gravity of the situation, but couldn't have stopped herself if she'd tried. She hadn't had a panic attack in years. Knowing Jeremy had seen her at her most vulnerable left her uneasy and depressed. For all she knew, his pleasant behavior last night was nothing but a ruse. Maybe he was searching for her Achilles' heel. Maybe, like Thackeray, he was counting on charm to plot her downfall.

Admonishing herself to stop being paranoid, Sylvia pulled the thin comforter up to her chin and closed her eyes tight. She felt suddenly very alone, like a small child trying to hide from the monsters in the closet. She'd grown too confident, believed she'd finally buried her personal demons, yet they'd been lurking in the nearby shadows waiting for the right opportunity to pounce.

She felt suddenly desperate. What if she couldn't control it? What if it got worse? Fears could get out of proportion and make her lose her perspective, as she had at the beginning of her career. Despite all those hours with therapists, all their assurances, she hadn't licked her problems. Dr. Hirshbaum's confident declaration that she was cured had proved to be a lie. You were never cured, could never let go of the past completely, she reflected bitterly, punching her pillow. You could excise the cancer, but the scars remained, and as the earlier episode proved, the illness could come back when least expected.

Since Thackeray, the nightmares had resurged. Several times she'd woken up screaming, oppressed by a face from the past that still terrified her in the darkest hours.

After another half hour of tossing and turning, of pulling the pillow closer, then throwing it to the floor, she gave in and groped for her sleeping pills.

Four hours later, Sylvia stepped into the passage, washed and dressed in her own clothes, which Maggie had kindly laundered. Although she still felt groggy from her restless night, she knew her carefully burnished armor was safely back in place. Thank God for travel-size cosmetics kits.

As she walked through the hall she hesitated outside the sitting-room door, but it was firmly closed and all was quiet. With a shrug she crossed the hallway and entered the empty pub. Sitting down at last night's table, she glanced hopefully at the kitchen. She'd give her left arm for a large cup of strong black coffee.

A few seconds later the swing door opened wide and Maggie passed through carrying a huge tray filled with everything from scrambled eggs and bacon to oat cakes and homemade marmalade.

"Did ye have a gud sleep?" she asked brightly, heaving the tray onto the next table.

"Fine," Sylvia lied, smile bright.

"Then ye'll be wantin' yer breakfast, nae doubt. Here." She placed the scrambled eggs and bacon before her and Sylvia hadn't the heart to refuse. Mercifully, a pot of steaming coffee followed and she sighed, relieved.

As she was about to take the first longed-for sip, Jeremy entered. She looked up and smiled. With a terse good morning, he sat down on the bench in the nook next to her.

The table might be the same, but the atmosphere and the man weren't. This was a very different Jeremy from the man who, for whatever reason, had tried to charm her out of her doldrums on the previous evening. She felt oddly disappointed. Dressed once more in his blazer, his expression closed, he looked uncommonly like his old disagreeable self.

Sylvia murmured, "good morning," and let out a

sigh. Thank God she hadn't succumbed to her feelings of sympathy for him during the night. Swallowing a long sip of coffee, she sent him a sidelong look, admonishing herself for being a fool. Why should she have expected things to be different between them? It was clear he'd merely been acting out of self-interest—probably trying to get her to divulge something in a moment of weakness he could use against her.

Determined to match his mood, she sipped her coffee in stony silence, and spread a piece of toast with butter and marmalade, watching in disgust as Jeremy heaped bacon, eggs, toast and black pudding onto his plate. Black pudding at any time was revolting, but in the morning and before flying, it was too much.

"We'll be off in half an hour," Jeremy stated after several minutes of silent munching. "I'll give you a shout when I go to retrieve the chopper. If you stand at the end of the road just off the moor, I can pick you up."

With that, he wiped his mouth on a large white napkin, folded it and laid it by his plate. "See you in a little."

"Have a great day, too," she muttered at his retreating back. The man was like his country's weather—fine one minute, gray and gloomy the next. Well, that was okay by her. There was no need for words. They'd said all they had to yesterday. Now all she wanted was to reach Strathaird, where, thank God, there was enough space to lose him.

As she was finishing her coffee, Jeremy popped his head around the door. "I'm off." He glanced at his watch. "It's nine forty-eight. I'll see you there in twenty minutes precisely.'' Then he disappeared, leaving her fuming. Who the hell did he think he was to be issuing curt orders, as if she was his servant, instead of his boss?

Pulling herself together, Sylvia thanked Jamie and asked the landlord what she owed.

''His Lordship took care o' that,'' Jamie said with a bright grin while beckoning to Maggie, who came promptly out of the kitchen, wiping her hands on her large apron.

His Lordship. Ha! What a perfect way of describing him. The ultimate British, aristocratic snob. No doubt he liked the locals knowing he'd been born with a title—assuming he hadn't bought it off the Internet, she thought scathingly. Recognizing that her own foul mood was hardly Maggie's fault, she made an effort to smile graciously, thanking the landlady for her kindness and promising to send her a postcard when she reached New York.

They stood on the steps and waved her off down the cobbled street. Sylvia admired the brightly-colored window boxes on the whitewashed cottages, raised her face to the shining sun and desperately tried to feel upbeat. After all, there wasn't a cloud in sight.

At the end of the street, she turned the corner and headed down the road, when an all-too-familiar buzz made her gut clench. She looked up. Her mouth went suddenly dry and her head spun when she saw the chopper readying to land a few hundred feet away. Sylvia swayed, swamped by a wave of dizziness. Her eyes riveted, and she watched the machine land on the edge of the moor. Jeremy, Ray Bans and earphones in place, was motioning to her.

Taking a long, deep breath, Sylvia steadied herself. She could do this. Of course she could do this. All she needed to do was take that first step forward and everything would be all right. Once she was in the chopper, the rest would be a breeze.

Gritting her teeth, she instructed her body to move. But nothing happened. Her feet, which should have followed orders, remained firmly glued to the ancient stones. Oh God, this couldn't be happening, not now, not with him. Desperate, Sylvia gazed, horrified, at Jeremy waving impatiently from inside the chopper, gripped by humiliation. She couldn't allow this to happen, couldn't let nerves and fear overcome her. She had to make it, had to do this.

But she couldn't.

For a terrible moment Sylvia's legs buckled and her head reeled. Please, dear God, no, she pleaded, desperately seeking somewhere to lean on. She couldn't faint here, in the middle of the street. Then, before she could restrain them, hot tears rushed to her eyes. Her shoulders shook and her body trembled. It was hopeless. She let out a despairing moan, smacked her hand over her mouth to stop the rising yell of anguish and, spinning around, stumbled back up the narrow cobbled street, around the corner and toward the pub. Sobbing breathlessly, she hurtled up the steps and burst open the door.

"What on earth?" Maggie, who'd been setting the tables for lunch, wheeled around and gazed at her in amazement.

"I c-can't," Sylvia sobbed, shaking her head wildly, "I won't, I—" She leaned against the wall, body heaving, knees shaking as Maggie hurried toward her and engulfed her in a bear hug.

"Now, now, there's nothing tae worry about, dearie," she comforted in a motherly tone, pulling Sylvia's head onto her ample shoulder. Sighing, Sylvia gave way and wept, shedding the pent-up tears she'd been holding for longer than she cared to remember.

Several minutes passed while Sylvia cried her heart out and Maggie soothed. Then the door behind them opened.

He'd been astounded when he'd seen her turn and run. Then concern got the better of him. Switching off the helicopter's engines, he'd hurried after her up the street. What could have happened? He knew she was afraid of choppers—that much had been made clear yesterday—but such a dire reaction spoke of much deeper, more serious motives. Worried, he'd rushed into the pub and stopped in his tracks at the sight of her weeping in Maggie's strong arms. Catching the woman's eye, he indicated with a firm nod that he would take over. After a moment's hesitation, Maggie gingerly let go of her charge and allowed Jeremy to slip his own arms around her.

"I can't, I w-won't," Sylvia continued muttering between muffled sobs. "I won't let him—even if he tries to force me I w-won't let him…" The words trailed into an anguished wail. Appalled, Jeremy held her tightly in his arms.

"Shush, now," he soothed, gently stroking her hair. "I promise I won't force you to do anything you don't want," he affirmed, slipping his hand behind her neck and massaging it gently, crooning soft words in her ear, wishing he could help her. But she seemed barely aware of him.

"I won't go back," she muttered hoarsely.

"Won't go back where?" he murmured gently, removing a large white handkerchief from his pocket. "Let it out, Syl, let whatever it is that's eating you go." Pulling back slightly, he raised her chin. "Don't cry anymore," he murmured softly, gazing down into her tear-stained face, "I promise I won't make you go anywhere." He wiped her wet face with gentle dabs, then patted her eyes, the fear he read in them making his heart lurch, for he'd seen that look before. This woman, he realized, shocked, had lived through something dreadful. Clearly, the chopper reminded her of some appalling event she was still too frightened to talk about. With a rush of compassion he took her trembling hands in his and drew them to his lips, kissing her fingers one by one. "It'll be all right," he repeated, listening to her ragged breathing, "I won't let anything hurt you, I promise. Trust me."

Her eyes flickered in response, then her shoulders sagged and he felt her go limp in his arms. Drawing her close, he was about to set her down in the nearest chair, when she raised those lovely, tortured eyes to his as though begging him for something. Instinctively, Jeremy dropped a soft kiss on her lips. It was a tender, spontaneous gesture, designed to soothe. But the visceral reaction that followed made it impossible to pull away. This couldn't be happening, he assured himself. This woman needed him, he must not take advantage of a situation. But Sylvia's eyes, brimming with emotion, left him unable to do more than stare into them, like a rabbit trapped in headlights.

"Syl," he muttered. "I didn't mean—"

For a long moment they stared at one another, then, mesmerized, Jeremy brought his lips down on hers again, feeling her body cleaving to his. His hands mussed her hair while his lips ravaged, amazed when he felt a needy response. Somewhere in the back of his mind he knew he must be mad. But as their tongues met and fire erupted, he didn't care.

The kiss deepened. Instead of surprise, Sylvia glowed with sudden relief, and a warm, delicious heat coursed through her. The haunting images gave way to hot arrows of passion. For an instant, she tried to rationalize, stop the craziness, rally her senses and take control. But only for a moment. For his lips devouring, hands deliciously working her neck, and the feel of his body pressed hard against hers left no room to think.

Nor did she want to.

Holding him tightly, she let out a ragged sigh, shivered when he groaned, succumbed when he pressed his hand into the small of her back and gave way when at last he plundered.

7

A dark, fiery sunset etched the Ozarks in a purple-bluish haze. Pretty in its own way, Aimon Thackeray conceded, casting a sideways glance out the window of the Cessna he was flying. Personally, he preferred the Blue Ridge Mountains. Closer to civilization and the world he'd built around himself. This reminded him a little too much of the backwater where he'd spent his own childhood. Thank God he'd had the balls to get out.

Fayetteville loomed ahead. He could distinguish the tower of the single airstrip and the large hangar in the distance. The report lying on the seat beside him mentioned the hangar. Apparently it was an air museum, Fayetteville's claim to fame. The report had also furnished him with a number of other interesting items. Like the fact that Sylvia Hansen—or rather, Sylvia Kutchevsky, as the report suggested—wasn't exactly who she claimed to be.

His instincts about her were right after all. A thin ripple of a smile lit up his lean, weathered features. *Tsk, tsk, Sylvia, one really needs to be a bit more*

careful about guarding one's e-mail. A good sleuth—
and he only hired the best—had quite easily tracked
down her true identity.

Thackeray concentrated his attention on talking to
the tower. Landing permission was granted and he
maneuvered the throttle carefully into position. These
were the moments he loved, the times when he soared
above it all, felt the rush of power seize him. *He* was
in control. If he felt like it, he could glide her down
as smoothly as a dove, or alternatively, he could ram
the plane into that damn red-roofed hangar over there.

If *he* felt like it.

What mattered was that *he* had the choice. It was
choice that gave him power: to create and to nurture,
or to manipulate and, if things got in his way, destroy.

Destroying Sylvia had become something of an obsession, he acknowledged, one that if he wasn't careful could overwhelm his usual objectivity. Forget that
he'd already decided over a year ago, when she was
named CEO, that Harcourts would be his for the picking, since it provided him with the perfect mechanism
for laundering the money he made in some of his less
legitimate transactions. That was only part of where
he wanted to go. He'd always viewed Harcourts, with
its long-standing, lily-white reputation, as the ideal
cover. When the IRS went looking for fraud, traditional porcelain and household-goods companies
weren't even on the radar. Which is why his own
company, Marchand, had proved so useful. Still, a
merger and the growth it would afford were the best
cover possible.

And now, after her spectacular performance at Aureole, he reflected, his eye twitching involuntarily,

even if it turned out that Harcourts no longer suited his purposes, he'd discover a way to take it down simply because Sylvia Hansen was at its helm. He'd never forgive that bitch for the incident at the restaurant, the public humiliation, for suggesting before all those fucking society queens that he wasn't fit to lick her boots. That was unforgivable and must be punished. No woman should be allowed to get away with that.

Despite his anger, he landed the plane smoothly on the tarmac, slowed, and steered the controls toward the main parking area scattered with a couple of private jets and a commercial Boeing. Following the ground control, he came to a standstill at the indicated spot and saluted the man military style—a technique he'd learned gave others an automatic impression of authority. Then, switching off communications, he prepared to disembark.

Picking up his garment bag, his sleek black Italian briefcase, a fishing rod wrapped in a used, blue canvas cover and the report, he jumped out of the aircraft and made his way toward the building.

"Howdy." He waved amiably to two mechanics in brown overalls slowly heading toward one of the other aircraft. He'd traveled in light jeans, a pale yellow polo shirt and a navy sweater thrown lightly over his shoulders. Casual and inconspicuous, like a tourist on his way to one of the lodges for a weekend's fishing. In fact, he'd made reservations. And maybe he would take in a day's fishing. His face broke into a mean grin. Big-game fishing was what he was after. And one hell of a slippery fish. But if he wasn't mistaken, the bait was about to be hooked.

Entering the small building, he headed to a desk where a middle-aged man in a white shirt, dark tie and thick glasses sat hunched over paperwork. He looked official.

"Hiya."

"Howdy. You the pilot of the Cessna?"

"That's right. Okay if I leave her there overnight? Might even be a couple of days." He patted his rod and glanced at the sun sinking quickly behind the mountain range. "Looks like the weather may cooperate for once."

"Sure thing." The man smiled and signed off. "You headin' up to fish?"

"Yep. Gonna take in a couple of days' fishin'. Kind of felt like stoppin' off for a bite to eat before I head on up, though. Didn't have time before I left Dallas. Any suggestions? Somebody mentioned a place called Smokey's Hole?"

"They did, did they?" The man eyed him curiously. "It's hardly on the tourist circuit."

"Yep. Told me they've got catfish as good as anything you'd find down in the Delta and the best ribs this side of Texas." He grinned winningly.

"'S'right." The man nodded, pleased. "Make a left when you leave the rental-car lot and head on till you pass the air museum. That's the wood hangar at the end of the road with the red roof."

"I saw it as I was flying in. Impressive."

"You interested in old planes?" The man rubbed his glasses and cocked an eyebrow with the relish of one about to impart a state secret.

"Sure thing."

"Then you go see the museum. One of the best in the country," he declared proudly.

"I'll certainly make a point of it. But about Smokey's Hole...?"

"Just keep on going till you reach the main road. It's a log cabin on the right-hand side, after the strip mall. There's a big sign up top says Smokey's Hole. Can't miss it," he said. "And them spare ribs is well worth it."

"Thanks." Thackeray smiled, accepted the papers the man handed him, then followed the car-rental signs.

Fifteen minutes later, he was driving a two-year-old Ford along the road bordering the airport. Normally he wouldn't be caught dead in this domestic piece of shit, but for the present it suited the part he intended to play. His luggage was stowed in the trunk and the report lay reassuringly next to him. He pulled in to a rest stop and flipped through the document until he found what he wanted, skimming quickly over the lines.

Don Murphy. Retired helicopter engineer. 'Nam veteran. Although he wasn't a qualified pilot, he'd served as one on several special missions when the pilots he'd been flying with were shot down. Previously married to Leila Kutchevsky, deceased November 1990. Mother of one daughter, disappeared, presumed dead, June 1982.

Thackeray smirked, left the report open on his knee and drove slowly on. It might be a dead end, might give him nothing, but his gut told him it could be the key to Pandora's tightly closed and oh-so-seductive box. According to his source, a Sylvia Kutchevsky, whose age and description corresponded to Sylvia's, had disappeared without a trace. It might be a coincidence, but it wasn't a common name. And certainly worth a few hours spent at Smokey's Hole where, the report told him, Don Murphy hung out most nights, steeped in a sour mash stupor.

All the more reason to get there early. He wanted the man coherent. Drunk enough to talk, but coherent.

He drove slowly, mind filled with Harcourts, the use he intended it for, and Sylvia. Damn, she was a hot little number. Which made it all the more surprising that she was proving herself such a worthy adversary. Not that she'd win, of course. But the fact she was putting up a fight would make her eventual fall all the more enjoyable, and the fact that she hadn't already crumbled had fueled his genuine curiosity. Who the hell was Sylvia Hansen? Given what he suspected of her background, it was clear the confidant corporate-ice-princess act was a sham.

So where did she get off turning him down, when her blood ran just as hick-country red as his own? His lips twitched nervously. He detested being crossed. Worse, humiliated. He'd made a rule of systematically eliminating anybody or anything who tried to block his path or belittle him. His fingers clenched the wheel, knuckles white. He would get Sylvia, grind her into the ground, and then wipe her off the map. And the information contained in the little report on the passenger seat might well contain the seeds of her downfall.

He hugged the next bend, eyes narrowed, peering carefully at the signs. Ah, there was the strip mall. He drove on slowly a few hundred yards and finally

saw a tin roof sagging over a drooping sign. Big bub-
bly letters that had once been bright blue, but had
faded to gray, read Smokey's Hole. As though con-
firming its name, wisps of smoke coughed from an
old chimney and merged with the early-evening haze
as he drew up and parked the Ford between a rusty
Chevy truck that had lost its original paint and a
brand-new four-wheel-drive pickup. The place looked
run-down, but the smell of roasted ribs and charcoal
was unmistakable.

Slipping the report into the glove compartment,
Thackeray sniffed the air appreciatively. A slab of
spare ribs wouldn't do him a mite of harm.

He locked the car and headed toward the double
saloon door. He could hear voices, the odd shout of
laughter. He opened the door and stood for a moment.
The place was dark and dingy. Fishing flies hung
from the ceiling and rods and photographs plastered
the walls. Two TVs blared in each corner. On one
screen, the Atlanta Braves were losing to the New
York Giants; on the other, Coach Riley of the Miami
Heat was giving an interview.

Thackeray moved across the sawdust and peanut
shells littering the plank-wood floor and headed to the
bar. Several men in checked flannel shirts and baseball caps sat in various degrees of stupor. One nursed
a beer can. His free hand gesticulated, commenting
on the game. His neighbor slouched, arm leaning
heavily on the counter, and stared into his glass. They
looked as if they'd been there a while—like their
whole lives, Thackeray thought cynically.

From behind the bar, a heavy-built strawberry
blonde of uncertain age gave him a long, speculative

look. She sported a tight red T-shirt with Ozarks stretched over her voluminous breast. The Z on the strained cotton was barely visible.

Thackeray approached, sat casually down on one of the scuffed Naugahyde bar stools and smiled at her.

"Howdy."

"Hi. What can I get y'all?" When her mouth opened, he noticed her yellowing teeth, chewing a piece of bright pink bubblegum.

"I'll have a Bud and a slab of your best ribs," he said, giving her the once-over.

She seemed not at all perturbed. With a knowing look and a swing of her wide hips she turned, grabbed a can of Budweiser from the refrigerator, and sent it skidding toward him down the bar. He caught it, grinning. The chilled can breathed a gratifying white frost. He popped it open, threw his head back and took a long satisfying chug while observing the men to his right and left, wondering which, if any, was Don Murphy. Could it be the little wizened fellow at the far end of the bar chewing peanuts? Or the heavy-bellied individual to his right, head sagging on his chest, whose voice slurred when he addressed the older man next to him?

He decided to ask the blonde, who stood eyeing him suggestively from across the counter.

"Know anyone here called Don Murphy?" he asked casually.

"Y'askin' me, hon?"

"Yeah." He smiled again and tried not to stare at her teeth. They offended him.

"What would a cute city boy like you be wantin' with Don Murphy?" she asked, leaning forward,

breasts touching the counter as she pulled out a Marl-
boro from a squished package in her pant pocket.

Thackeray searched in vain for matches or a lighter,
but found none. "Sorry," he said, sending her a be-
guiling grin that he hoped might break the ice, "I
don't smoke."

"Doesn't matter, honey. What you be wantin' with
Don?" The question was posed with barely disguised
hostility. The other two men stopped talking, the older
one looking at him suspiciously, and the slouched one
sitting straighter and peering at him through bleary,
unfriendly eyes.

"I have a message for him. Thought I'd deliver it
in person. I was told he comes in here from time to
time."

"You ain't from the *po*lice or nuthin', are you?"
she asked, lowering her voice and glancing from left
to right.

"Lordy, no. I'm a friend of a friend of his, that's
all. Old pal from the war days. When I told him I
was coming this way for a couple of days' fishing, he
told me to look up his old buddy Don Murphy. They
were in 'Nam together."

"That figures." The older man to his right indicated to the blonde that he wanted another beer.
"Don's always mutterin' on about that there war. Figure it was the best time of his life. Finally got to fly
them choppers over there. I know, I was there. No
one gave a goddamn whether or not you was a real
pilot out there. 'S'long as you could fly the damn
things, it was good enough." He gave a crack of
coarse laughter that ended in a heavy cough.

"Let me buy you a beer." Thackeray moved his stool a tad closer. "What's your friend drinking?"

"Billy Bob? He be drinkin' sour mash like he always does."

"Then give him another one." He motioned to the waitress and cast the man a quick conspiratorial glance that said, *I don't know her name, help me out.*

"Myrna. Her daddy was in love with Myrna Loy," the man added knowingly.

"Ah." Thackeray nodded. "Say, Myrna, how about another round?"

"Sure. But tell me sumpin'—who are you and why are you lookin' for Don?"

"Well, it's a long story." Thackeray pondered whether or not to lie about his name, then remembered he'd made the reservation at the lodge. Everybody knew everything about everyone in a place like this. Lying would only come back to bite him.

"Name's Louis," he said, using his middle name, which he rarely if ever used, and stretching out his right hand.

"Good to meet ya." The two men nodded, then one gestured to the others at the bar. "He's Bert and this here's Ernie."

"You're kidding. Like Bert and Ernie from the kiddie show?"

"'S'right. That's what they calls us around these parts, Bert an' Ernie." The man gave Thackeray a toothless grin as Myrna plonked the round of drinks before them and the door swung open.

"Well, here's a piece of luck," Bert exclaimed. "There's your man right there. Say, Don." He raised his voice above the din of the TVs and beckoned, "Get your ass over here. You got a visitor."

Thackeray put down the beer can and studied the thin figure dressed in a dingy pair of stonewashed jeans and a bomber jacket staring at him from across the dimly lit saloon. He was tallish, had probably been good-looking in his youth. Now he looked craggy, tough and belligerent.

Thackeray hesitated, immediately on his guard. This was a tough customer, not like the beer-bellied louts sitting to his right. Slowly the man made his way toward the bar. He didn't look at Thackeray, merely propped himself next to Bert. Myrna placed a glass before him with the automatic gesture of one who does this every day of her life. Don lifted it, sniffed, then sipped. Slowly he turned, leaning his elbow on the bar in a manner that told Thackeray better than words that he was trespassing on his turf.

"What d'ya want?" he asked, twisting the glass slowly while his other hand delved in his left pocket from which he extracted a cigarette.

"I wanted a word with you." No use wrapping it in clean linen—either the guy would play ball or he wouldn't. Clearly, it was no use beating around the bush with this customer. Better to go straight to the point and see what his reaction was. If Sylvia was in fact his stepdaughter and he believed her to be dead, he might be glad of news. On the other hand, he might not. Either way, Thackeray knew he'd elicit some kind of reaction.

"I've got a message for you from a friend from way back when."

"Oh?" Don swirled the ice cubes in his mash with his index finger. "And who would that be?"

"Perhaps you'd like to sit down over there? It's kinda hard to talk above the noise."

He saw the other man's eyes narrow. Silently they left the bar and sat in the far corner at one of the old wooden tables where hunting knives had whittled the names of several generations.

"Sylvia told me I could find you here." Thackeray waited, watching for a reaction. When he read shock and recognition he let out the breath he'd been holding.

Bull's-eye.

He took care to conceal his triumph. His gut hadn't failed him. God, how he loved it when things went just the way he'd planned them. This time, he'd planned for a home run, and he'd gotten one. Now it was all a question of tactics.

"Sylvia?" Don eyed him cautiously and straightened his shoulders. "What does she want?"

"Nothing. I guess that after letting you guys believe she was dead for so long, she didn't have the guts to face you herself. Y'know how it is—" he shrugged and sipped "—time goes by, you make it out there in the big world, but when it comes down to it, family's what counts."

"Bull crap. What'd she tell ya?" Don took a long drag from the half-smoked cigarette, his eyes two narrow blue slits peering from behind a film of smoke.

"Nothing much. We're friends, and well—" he raised his hands and smiled engagingly "—I told her I was coming out here for a couple of days' fishing. At first she looked kind of sad. I asked her what was up and she said her folks were from Arkansas, said her stepdad lived here in Fayetteville.''

''Hmm.'' Don nodded, sucked in his cheeks. ''What's she up to nowadays?''

''Syl? She's done good. Made it big-time. She's CEO of a big international company in New York.''

''Son uv'a bitch.'' Don shook his head and drank long and deep. ''She always said that one day she'd make it. Never believed her, of course. Guess she fucked her way up there, huh? Isn't that how all them bitches make it to the top?''

''Not entirely. She's a smart cookie. Of course, a great butt and tits like hers never did a girl any harm.'' He grinned and their eyes met.

''She sure teased some cocks around here,'' Don agreed with a lascivious grin. ''Say, she got money?'' he asked suddenly.

Gotcha. Thackeray felt his pulse rate quicken.

''She makes a good living.'' No use letting this prick think she had too much. He could read the signs, the calculating glitter in the other man's eyes. Much better for Don to think his best chance for cash was staring him right in the face.

Then Don Murphy looked at him speculatively. ''What do you want?'' he asked suddenly, taking another long suck on his cigarette. ''You didn't come here to pass the time of day. And don't snow me with no bullshit about Sylvia wantin' to connect with her family. She ain't family. Never was, never will be. A goddamn pain in the ass was all she ever was and she got what she deserved. So why'd you come here?''

Taking a deep breath, Thackeray plunged in. ''I want to know about her past.''

"Why?"

"I have my reasons."

"What if I tell you about her past, what'll I get out of it?"

"Ten grand," he answered promptly.

Don leaned back and scratched his chin thoughtfully. "You wanna pay me ten grand to tell you about Sylvia's past?"

"That's right." He leaned forward, anticipation leaving his mouth dry.

"Seems to me this information's mighty important to you," Don pronounced slowly, chewing the butt of a new cigarette.

"Could be. I dunno yet." Thackeray shrugged, tried to look indifferent, knew he could barely hide the excitement and that the price was about to go up.

"How about twenty-five?"

"Not worth it, I'm afraid." He drained the beer can and made as though to rise.

"Wait."

"Yes?" He watched as doubt and greed battled. He had a whole file on Don Murphy. The man owed twelve grand in gaming debts and was overdue on his mortgage payments. He was about to be evicted. "How about we call it around twenty and you don't hold anything back?" he said quietly.

There was a moment's tense silence, then greed won and Don nodded. He looked at Thackeray straight on, a cruel grin spreading over his unshaven face. "It's a done deal, mister. Oh boy, have you got a deal. I hope you take that goddamn piece of shit and fuck her over so badly she ain't got nuthin' left to poke.''

"Believe me,'' Thackeray muttered fervently as he prepared to listen, ''I have every intention of doing just that.''

8

She'd never found Monday mornings daunting before. In fact, quite the opposite. Back in New York, she'd welcomed them, eager to trade the city's languorous, laid-back Sunday-afternoon atmosphere for the fast-paced, tense excitement that permeated the rest of the week.

But this Monday, Sylvia trudged reluctantly into Major Whitehead's office. The weekend at Strathaird had been spent avoiding Jeremy, trying to pretend that what had occurred between them hadn't happened, and it had taken its toll. At least she'd finally met her goddaughter, which had made it all worthwhile. Baby Freya was the cutest little girl on the face of the planet. On this, at least, she and Jeremy agreed. Seeing Brad and Charlotte happier than ever had made her realize that Brad was right to have chosen Strathaird and the life of a Scottish laird over Harcourts. He was still the company's nonexecutive chairman, but you could tell where his heart lay.

Placing her briefcase carefully to one side of her office chair, she sat down and glanced at the pile of papers on her desk, wondering if any progress had been made in discovering who was responsible for leaking the spring collection designs. Every time she thought about it her blood boiled. There had been no call from Reggie over the weekend, so she supposed nothing new had occurred. She let out a huff, determined to get to the bottom of it.

A few tentative rays of sunshine had brightened her brief walk from the Stafford hotel, but here in the gloomy darkness you could barely tell the time of day. With a sigh she pushed her hair behind her ears, switched on the desk lamp and reached for the stack of paperwork. Perhaps concentrating on the real world would keep her mind from constantly wandering back to the startling turn of events in Clachnabrochan.

Half an hour later Sylvia threw down her pen. It was no use. However hard she tried to forget, those magical moments with Jeremy simply would not fade. Leaning back in her chair, she closed her eyes and indulged her determined subconscious. The kiss had been electrifying, but thank God, after the initial shock of his lips causing havoc with her being, she'd torn herself reluctantly from his arms. And, instead of dragging her back into them, what had he done? She clenched her fingers at the thought. He'd offered a stiff apology, and with an inclination of the head, had left the room. Just like that. As if moments earlier they hadn't been close to—

Sylvia shook her head and sat up, determined to regain control. At the time she'd been too stunned to react. Jeremy had arranged for a car to drive her the rest of the way to Skye. Then he'd taken a clipped, polite leave and left her dazed in the middle of the empty pub, wondering if she'd dreamed the whole thing up.

All weekend they'd studiously avoided one another, shunning all but obligatory contact. They'd made it through the christening, been *extremely* polite and pleasant to one another, cracking the required jokes and making very sure no one picked up any signals that things between them weren't quite what they appeared.

Not that one could have guessed anything from Jeremy's bland demeanor and relentless good humor, she observed sourly. It was most unflattering that any man could remain so completely unaffected by what—by her standards—had been a pretty amazing kiss. Chemistry, she figured, was a tricky son of a bitch, something you didn't choose. It hit when you least expected and too often—this being a prime example—with the wrong person. Jeremy Warmouth, she reflected, certainly qualified as the last person on earth she would have considered.

Sylvia turned, absently switched on her computer and bit her lip, wondering how she was going to defuse the situation if the utterly undemonstrative Jeremy refused to even acknowledge its existence? The situation was highly irritating. Not by the merest twitch of an eyelid had he indicated that he had been in any way affected by their physical contact.

"Aagh!" she let out crossly. There was nothing worse than being righteously annoyed, yet with your curiosity whetted. Logging on to her e-mail, she let out another angry huff. Either the man was one heck of an actor or he had ice running through his aristo-

cratic blood system, for she could have sworn he'd
felt the same unfettered longings she had.

She flipped through her messages, answered a couple, then, still unable to apply herself to the task, rose
and paced the office. This was ridiculous and inex-
cusable. Not since preadolescence had she spent precious time analyzing kisses. But how on earth was
she going to sit opposite him in half an hour, pretending everything was business as usual, when all
she wanted was to take him to task?

The thought made her pause. She stopped short and
leaned against the old mantel, a chill running down
her spine. Could the kiss—well, more than just a kiss,
let's face it—and the pleasant behavior over dinner
be part of a strategy to weaken her on the professional
front?

For a moment she wished desperately she could
believe that, since having Jeremy as her enemy had
been a hell of a lot easier than this present ambiguity.

She squeezed her fingers around the voluptuous
belly of Major Whitehead's ivory Buddha and took a
deep breath. She would show nothing. Absolutely
nothing. Let him keep that emotionless, imperturbable
British mask he wore so well. Let him hide behind it,
pretend he didn't care, she'd match him tit for tat. But
however hard he tried to pretend otherwise, the un-
dercurrents were there, coursing between them,
whether they liked it or not.

It was too bad that of all people, the cold-blooded
Jeremy Warmouth had to hit her like an inside curveball. Hell, if he had been a fellow New Yorker she
might have taken the initiative, suggested they meet
to discuss the matter. In an adult manner, they would

both have recognized the attraction and sought a proper course of action: a mind-boggling round of sex that would cleanse both their systems. Or after further analysis, they might have concluded that it was preferable not to engage in anything that might lead to emotional and destabilizing factors within the structure of Harcourts.

She shrugged and rolled her eyes. It was all perfectly simple.

Or should have been.

She had her pick of men in New York, didn't she? Invitations pouring in 24/7. Of course, she consistently refused them because she didn't have time to date. Her work at Harcourts kept her too busy. Perhaps that was the problem, she realized suddenly, grabbing at any jutting straw. Her defenses were down. Well, she'd just build them back up, she concluded with a sniff, replacing the Buddha in its former position on the mantelpiece, causing a flurry of dust to flutter down into the unused grate.

Satisfied that she'd finally identified her problem, Sylvia settled behind the desk and reached once more for the morning's work. Nothing, she resolved firmly, hitting the enter button with more zest than she'd intended, would deviate her from her task. Of that she was determined.

To describe his emotions as "in turmoil" was putting it mildly, Jeremy reflected, stifling a yawn as he settled bleary-eyed behind his desk. The two strong espressos he'd consumed at the tube station had done little to alleviate the tension and fatigue besetting him since Clachnabrochan.

He glanced at the day's agenda that Miss Hunter had placed neatly on his desk. *Oh Lord.* Aunt Margaret was in town and would be descending upon him shortly. A tired smile tweaked his lips. At least that would make for a change. If anyone could drag him out of his present funk, it was Aunt Margaret.

He checked the rest of his appointments, wondering if any calls had come in yet from Colombia concerning the problem uppermost in his mind, then realized, glancing at the carriage clock on the mantelpiece, that his meeting with Reggie and Sylvia was in exactly five minutes. Stretching his legs under the huge partners desk, he stared blindly at the innocuous painting on the paneling opposite and wondered how he was going to fare.

His unexpected reaction to Sylvia had left him floored. Okay, she was an attractive female—that he'd never denied. But to be so completely swept off his feet was something he'd never experienced before. Or not since his very early teenage days when anything remotely resembling sex had left him dizzy. What was more amazing still was that he'd spent a large portion of the weekend knowing he'd behaved like a cad, trying to avoid her, and wishing it would happen all over again. Which, of course, was absurd and unthinkable.

He sighed and loosened his tie, the unanticipated rush of desire he'd experienced in Sylvia's arms a pointed reminder of the stale gridlock his personal life was right now. Last night had been a sharp reminder. Studying Clarissa from across the dinner table at Hugh Spalding's house in Eaton Square, he'd had ample opportunity to weigh exactly how bored he'd become. Was he jaded or just fed up with accompanying Clarissa in her narrow world of stringent social rules. When he'd pointed out that he'd just returned from Scotland and hadn't been consulted about the dinner arrangement, suggesting that they have a quiet evening at home instead, she'd been horrified. "Crying off" after the caterer had set the head count and the seating arrangements simply wasn't done, she'd reminded him in the same tone he remembered his nanny using.

He'd always assumed that someday, in an obscure remote future, he and Clarissa would eventually marry. In their years of dating, she'd time and again proved herself a suitable candidate for the role of countess. But just recently—and he refused to accept it had anything to do with a certain someone's arrival—he'd begun to wonder if he could stomach her as a wife.

Clarissa was solid British stock, he reminded himself. But compared to Sylvia, she seemed bland and rather soulless. Sylvia was frustratingly emotional, to be sure, impossibly forthright and unbearably challenging, all that was considered unacceptable. But she was vivid, compelling and full of life. Clarissa, he reflected dourly, hadn't had a spontaneous emotion since she was in leading strings.

Sipping coffee in Hugh's high-ceilinged drawing room, he'd listened to her affected laugh. Before, he'd found it mildly irritating, now it grated on his nerves. Clarissa was never one to flaunt her attributes, believing it a mark of poor breeding, but the garment she wore left him wondering if she'd raided the bazaar at Wetherton village church where, as the daugh-

ter of Wetherton Hall, she'd spent the weekend helping her mother organize the yearly fete. A more
flagrant contrast to Sylvia, who had looked beautiful,
sexy and desirable even with makeup pouring down
her face, would have been hard to find.

Ashamed at his train of thought, Jeremy had
pleaded exhaustion and they'd left early, each to their
own flat. Clarissa had pursed her lips and eyed him
askance but hadn't demurred, simply said she would
return Horace, his spaniel, on the morrow. Her restrained peck on his cheek left him cold.

On reaching his Knightsbridge flat he'd flopped
into bed, thankful for the time alone. His head ached
and he needed to think, to adjust to this unexpected
turn of events. He felt thoroughly ashamed of himself.
Ashamed of having used Clarissa as a convenient and
socially acceptable dinner companion all these years
and consequently creating in her certain expectations
that he now realized he had no intention of fulfilling.

He'd flipped through TV channels, disgusted by his
mind wandering constantly back to Sylvia. He wondered how she was faring in her suite at the Stafford.
He'd held out the hope that they'd be together on the
flight back to London, but she'd made alternative
travel arrangements. Obviously, she believed what
had taken place between them was a one-time aber-
ration and intended to ignore it.

Crossly he'd switched off the television and made
himself a cup of coffee in the ultramodern kitchen
he'd installed in the flat. The soothing hiss of the
espresso machine had not diminished his impatience.
Mainly with himself, but also with Sylvia's blatant

indifference. For a moment he was tempted to jump in the Jag, head over there and remind her.

From the moment their lips met he'd been bowled over. Jeremy frowned. He was amazed at his own reaction. He'd had no intention of having any physical contact with her—the thought hadn't even crossed his mind. Up to that moment, their relationship had been a series of uptight, strained corporate meetings and one semi-agreeable evening where both were on their best behavior. So why had his lips so naturally sought hers and felt so damn right there?

Now, seated at his desk, he made a conscious effort to forget the feel of her mouth, the smooth curves of her body melding into his, and reached for the brief lying before him. In less than three minutes, he had to conduct a platonic business relationship with the woman and he'd better have his act together.

The phone rang and he answered it automatically, then grimaced—as much in self-recrimination as irritation—when Clarissa's high-pitched, officious voice grated down the line.

"We're meeting the Erskine-Smiths for drinks at the Turf Club at seven," she reminded him. "It's Monday, so I suppose you'll be sleeping *chez moi* as usual? No point in dropping off Horace in that case, is there? I'll get Mrs. Blackburn to walk him in the park at some point. Perhaps you should consider leaving him down at Warmouth this weekend, dearest. A dog in town when you barely have time to walk the poor creature seems rather cruel, don't you think?"

"I'll see about it," he muttered, hit by the daunting prospect of sleeping in the same bed with Clarissa. Not that anything would happen if he didn't want it to, he reassured himself—Clarissa thought it unlady-like to take the initiative in such things, and wasn't very interested in any case. Again the memory of Sylvia's vibrant body melting in his arms, her surprised spontaneous response, left him shifting uncomfortably in his chair, unable to control the inevitable reaction caused by this train of thought. He reminded himself that she was about to be sitting right here, on that very chair on the other side of the desk, expecting his full concentration. Hopefully, she'd have no idea what he was actually concentrating on.

"Jeremy, have you been listening to one word of what I've been saying?" Clarissa demanded.

"Of course. Sorry. I'm a bit rushed just now. I have a meeting in a couple of minutes. We have a particularly delicate issue to handle. Do you mind if I call you back later? I'm lunching with Aunt Margaret."

"All right." Clarissa sent a long-suffering sigh down the phone and Jeremy hung up, relieved, turning his full attention into squelching the anticipation caused by the thought of seeing Sylvia, dressed in one of those clean-cut, neutral-colored dresses whose strict subtle lines left him guessing what lay below.

Ridiculous. Yet his eyes remained glued expectantly on the door. He could already picture her, legs elegantly crossed, skirt just above the knee, glasses perched on the end of her nose while her hair fell forward and she tweaked it back in that efficient, repressed manner that he'd found singularly irritating, but that he now recognized as terribly sexy.

Who'd he been trying to fool?

Jeremy chided himself once again for letting Clarissa so insinuate herself into his life. For taking the easy way out simply because that had seemed the appropriate thing to do. Being heir to one of the oldest earldoms in the country carried a price. It was up to him, the family always reminded him—at first delicately and then, as the years sped by, less tactfully— to produce an heir to carry on the Warmouth line. There had been many passing women in his life but no one he couldn't live without. He supposed he'd lighted on Clarissa as the best candidate.

What a gloomy thought. It made him reevaluate himself and he didn't like the result. The arrangement spelled of mediocrity. Of convenience, of continuity and, if truth be told, boredom. Clarissa was well born and would fit perfectly into the aristocratic world in which they'd both moved since birth, of that he had no doubt. She conveniently turned a blind eye when, more than occasionally, he strayed and, he reflected cynically, he had little illusion as to why she gave him such freedom, picturing Mrs. Wetherton, her mother—a pretty exact version of what Clarissa would become in a few years—giving her daughter sage advice: "Don't worry, dear, they all fall by the wayside from time to time, it's inevitable. The best thing to do is weather it and remember that *you,* not *she*, are destined to become the countess of Warmouth."

He suddenly imagined Sylvia listening to such a speech and couldn't help a broad grin. He had no doubt that under similar circumstances she'd track him down and tell him in no uncertain terms where he could shove his bloody title.

A knock on the door brought him tumbling out of his reverie and he straightened his jacket and tie.

"Morning." Reggie popped his balding head around the door, flashing a bright, pink-cheeked smile.

"Morning," he grunted.

"In a bad mood, are we?" Reggie sighed.

"Shut up," Jeremy growled.

Reggie nodded sagely. "Got out of bed on the wrong side? Oh well." He drew up a chair and plunked a pile of papers on the desk. "I'll bet it's nothing that a good old tussle with the CEO can't sort out. Seen her yet this morning?"

"No," he answered curtly, annoyed by Reggie's good-humored comment.

"Don't worry, she'll be along in a minute. I've been narrowing down the odds. Sylvia's absolutely right about the time frame. The collection can only have been stolen after January fifteenth. I finally managed to reach Bernardo in Colombia. The lines are bloody awful. Took me hours to get through."

"What did he say?"

"Wouldn't let me talk. Said he'd call me this morning from another line." He raised his eyebrows. "Sounded damn odd, if you ask me."

"Very odd." Jeremy frowned, his senses suddenly alert. "Tell Miss Hunter to make sure there's a secure line."

"I already have."

"Let's hope Bernardo can shed some light on this mess," Jeremy muttered. Something very suspicious was going on and he didn't like it. That Thackeray was at the root of it he had no doubt. But there was something more, something he couldn't lay his finger on but that he sensed. He rose, wandered across to the window overlooking St. James's Place, and fiddled with the curtain cord. The sun was out. For a crazy, fanciful moment he wished he could chuck the damn meeting and ask Sylvia to go for a walk in the park, sit on deck chairs and watch the ducks puttering back and forth under the bridge. The thought was incredibly appealing.

Reggie sent him a curious look from across the room.

"The whole thing's bloody awkward. Sylvia's being rather decent about our lack of progress, though, don't you think?"

"Hmm," Jeremy agreed, then turned abruptly when he heard a knock on the door. Reggie rose and moved to open it. "Come in, come in, my dear, we were waiting for you. Have a nice stay in Scotland? Weather all right? Lovely up there when the sun's shining, bloody awful when it rains." He smiled at her and pulled out one of the burgundy leather chairs.

Jeremy nodded politely, trying to steady his pulse, which had missed a beat when she stepped into the room.

"Good morning."

"Good morning." Their eyes met briefly before she turned pointedly to Reggie.

"We were discussing the robbery, as usual," Reggie said, glancing quickly from one to the other.

"Reggie finally got hold of Bernardo in Cartagena."

"Good. What did he say?" She sat down neatly, crossed her legs and pulled out her memo pad, eyeing Reggie with a focused, expectant look that had *I want results* written all over it.

"Nothing much so far. He wants to phone us from a secure line. He's meant to be ringing at any moment."

"Sounds like he may have something important to report," Jeremy added.

"That seems pretty obvious," she remarked dryly. She forced herself to disregard the tightness in her throat. Why, she wondered vaguely, had she never observed how his well-worked-out shoulder muscles rippled under his tailor-made jacket, how disturbingly attractive the man was?

She concentrated, instead, on her notepad. It was all she could do to keep her mind focused on the issue at hand. "I think there's more to this than meets the eye," she said, to break the silence, knowing they expected something. "Thackeray's following some sort of game plan. He knew he had to get to someone inside Harcourts, and presumably our Colombian operations proved easier to infiltrate than those here. Still, I don't think we should totally rule out the possibility of the theft having occurred here, either. Is there anyone you can think of who is going through a difficult time in their private life, someone who for a reason beyond their control might have—even against their better judgment—been willing to help Thackeray?"

"You mean, succumbed to blackmail?" Reggie said, shocked.

"That's right, Reggie."

"Look, this isn't New York," Jeremy muttered tersely.

"This is England," Reggie agreed, puffing out his

pink cheeks. "There's still some sort of decorum, even though it's dwindled over the past few years."

"I'm aware that this is England, Reggie," Sylvia replied, striving for patience. "That here everything is supposed to be highly civilized and aboveboard. But, hey, you know what? We've got a situation and no answers. So why not try looking for some? Even if they don't fall precisely into the slot they're supposed to." She glanced at Jeremy. "You guys need to understand once and for all that Thackeray does not play by the same rules. He's not a gentleman. We're dealing with a tough son of a bitch who doesn't give a flying fuck what the rules are."

"Quite so, of course." Reggie cleared his throat and glanced at Jeremy, who'd posed his elbows thoughtfully on the desk and steepled his fingers.

"You could very well be right," he said finally, the rich timbre of his voice leaving her suddenly breathless. "But on analysis, who could Thackeray have blackmailed here? Major Whitehead? Miss Hunter?" He grinned despite the gravity of the situation. "Can't you just see Thackeray trying to blackmail old Whitehead and the Major swiping his Malacca cane at Thackeray's head? Great scene, I have to admit, but hardly realistic."

"No," she conceded, a smile hovering. "I don't think the Major would be an ideal candidate." God, his eyes held that same mischievous twinkle that reminded her all too clearly of Clachnabrochan. "I know it sounds absurd to think of our resident paragons being blackmailed into doing something of this nature, but I've run out of ideas."

The intercom buzzed. "Mr. Villalba is on the line

for Mr. Rathbone,'' Miss Hunter's crisp voice pronounced over the intercom. "And Lady Margaret is here to see you, my lord."

"I'll take it in my office." Reggie rose quickly and made for the door.

"Oh Lord, I'd forgotten Aunt Margaret was dropping by," Jeremy muttered. Then he turned back to the intercom. "Send her on in. I'm afraid my aunt arrived rather early," he said apologetically. "Would you mind if we continue this meeting—"

Before Sylvia could reply, the door was thrust open by Finch, and a large, brightly clad elderly woman wafted into the office, followed by two snuffling, low-bellied dogs. Sylvia, who'd been about to protest about the interruption of the meeting at this crucial moment, rose instinctively and tried not to stare. The woman wore a cerulean-blue dress and coat, a velvet beret perched at a jaunty angle on her soft, white, permed hair. An enormous diamond brooch—probably the largest Sylvia had ever seen out of a display case—took up most of her lapel.

"Jeremy, dear boy, I'm afraid I'm rather early." Before he had a chance to speak, she raised her crinkled peach-soft cheek for him to kiss and a whiff of lavender permeated the room. "Traffic can be so appalling at this hour, so I thought I'd better make haste. I'm most annoyed with the mayor. I feel very strongly that something should be done about him. You should use your position in the House of Lords to protest, my boy. Don't you agree?" she added, turning toward Sylvia while removing her white gloves, as if she already knew her well.

Caught by surprise, Sylvia murmured incoherently,

and instinctively sought guidance from Jeremy, who winked.

"Dreadful, Aunt, I quite agree. Let me take your coat."

"Thank you. And for goodness' sake, open a window, it's dreadfully stuffy in here. Your lovely guest must be positively wilting," she murmured sympathetically, eyeing Sylvia curiously.

"Aunt Margaret, this is Sylvia Hansen from New York," Jeremy announced in stentorian tones. "She's Harcourts's CEO."

"Really? How fascinating. So *you* are Sylvia," Lady Margaret murmured thoughtfully. "Jeremy, don't just stand there like a landed fish, introduce us properly." She moved forward smiling and extended her bejeweled hand and, allowing her nephew no time to perform the necessary introductions, barreled ahead. "I'm Jeremy's Aunt Margaret, the dowager countess of Warmouth. What a pleasure, after having heard so much about you, to finally meet you."

"Heard about me?" Sylvia, her hand encased in Lady Margaret's, found it impossible to hide her surprise.

"Of course. I've been hearing your praises sung for ages." Her face broke into a conspiratorial smile and her gray-penciled eyebrows creased. "I have to say, I don't know if it was very sensible of Bradley to drop you for Charlotte," she murmured, ignoring Jeremy's gestures.

Sylvia caught her breath, taken aback. Then, catching Jeremy's horrified expression, she squelched a gurgle of laughter. "I think breaking the engagement was very much the right thing for both of us," she answered easily. "Brad and I are great friends, and always will be. You'd be surprised how quickly we went back to being just good pals after we broke up. Gave us both a moment's reflection. Plus, now I have a godchild." Normally, Sylvia might have found the woman's interest rude and invasive, but Lady Margaret was both amusing and straightforward and she sensed no malice in her words. It was impossible not to be caught up in the dowager countess's whirlwind and diverted by Jeremy's obvious embarrassment.

"Well, you may be right about Brad," Lady Margaret conceded with a nod. "Charlotte's a complete airhead, of course, but wonderful at what she does, isn't she? You know, successful women fascinate me. You see, it is my firm opinion," she continued with barely a pause, "and I have no qualms in voicing it, as Jeremy well knows, that making it to the top in the world of business is a *very* arduous task, indeed." She nodded sagely, soft cheeks wobbling. "And for a woman, doubly so. Just think, my dear, of all the mediocre imbeciles who, merely because they happen to have been born with an extra appendage to their physique, are considered naturally competent." She laid a featherlight hand on Sylvia's arm. "It always strikes me that *any* woman who has made it to the top must possess *vastly* superior qualities than the best man around, or she never would have stood a chance." Unable to resist, Sylvia cast Jeremy a sidelong glance, and saw to her surprise that his eyes were brimming with fond amusement. "Now tell me, my dear," Lady Margaret continued, looping her arm through Sylvia's, "how long are you over here for?"

"I don't quite know yet. It depends on a number of things."

"Doesn't it always?" Lady Margaret murmured sympathetically. "Jeremy, dearest, tell Finch to bring us some coffee," she ordered. "And not that dreadful hogwash that Harvey Whitehead insists on. I told Dexter fifty years ago he must do something about the coffee in this place but he never listened. We even quarreled about it the week before he died, poor old Dex." She sighed. "Now let's sit down, shall we, and have a comfortable chat." She drew Sylvia toward the fireplace and onto the deep leather sofa while Jeremy obeyed orders and got on the phone.

"Now, my dear, tell me all about yourself." Lady Margaret, having settled comfortably into the well-worn leather, tilted her head inquiringly with the look of one ready to enjoy a prolonged conversation. Sylvia wondered anxiously what had transpired on the phone with Colombia, but her manners forbade her from escaping. Neither did she want to. Lady Margaret was the first person to make her feel appreciated since her arrival in England.

"Where are you from in America? It is such an *extraordinarily* fascinating place. The late earl and I used to love it. You must lead the most *interesting* existence, flitting back and forth on private jets. Dreadfully exciting." Lady Margaret's sincere interest made Sylvia relax and she smiled. Out of the corner of her eye she watched Jeremy laying down the phone and supposed he was keeping tabs on the situation.

"Aunt, might I remind you that Sylvia is a very

busy executive?'' he said in a pained voice, moving before the fireplace.

"I'm very well aware of that, dear boy. But everyone needs elevenses. Ah, Finch," Lady Margaret turned toward the opening door. "You managed some espresso, I hope?"

"Yes, my lady." Finch answered, voice laced with impending doom.

"Wonderful. Thank you, Jeremy," she said, settling into the cushions and patting him on the cheek as he placed the cup before her. She ignored Finch, who eyed the scene with patent disapproval.

"Pay no heed to him," Lady Margaret whispered to Sylvia as she passed the cream. "He's an old stuffed shirt."

"A biscotti, m'lady?" Finch's censorious tone barely masked his outraged feelings.

"Good gracious, no. I'd not have a tooth left in my mouth if I bit into one of those. I'll have a digestive biscuit if you please, Finch."

"Very well, m'lady."

"Dreadful old bore, isn't he?" She sighed as the door closed behind the butler. "But, of course, it would be impossible to go on without him. Rather like Miss Hunter, I suppose."

"The proverbial battle-ax," Jeremy agreed.

"Not entirely," his aunt replied, raising a finger. "Do you know, I can remember a time when Harriet Hunter was quite popular with the lads? She used to be rather attractive in her youth."

"Miss Hunter?" Jeremy and Sylvia voiced in tandem.

"Yes." Lady Margaret tilted her head, remember-

ing. "She had this rather—how can I describe it—
sexy sort of blond hairdo." She gestured descriptively
with her glittering free hand. "It was rather dashing
in wartime. But then, we all looked rather different
then in our uniforms and one thing and another. Oh,
well. Time and tide wait for no man. Nothing to be
done about it, is there?"

As the questions were purely rhetorical, Sylvia
merely smiled, as amused by Jeremy's efforts to deal
with his overpowering relation as by Lady Margaret
herself.

After half an hour of hilarious nonstop monologue,
the dowager countess finally rose. The dogs scuffled
around her, glad to be leaving.

"I shall be off, then. Jeremy, are we lunching?"

"Yes. Wilton's at one."

"Perfect. I have to pop over to Fortnum's for some
chutney. Oh, and that wretched Augusta Rowland's
granddaughter is getting married. It goes against the
grain, but I suppose I shall be obliged to buy the child
a wedding present. Though after the way Augusta
conducted herself with your uncle the last time they
met, I feel seriously inclined not to." She sniffed and
Reggie, who had just stepped back in the office,
handed her an umbrella.

"Aunt, that occurred twenty-five years ago," Jeremy pointed out. "And it was never *proved* that they
had a fling," he said, tongue in cheek.

"Much you know about it. Fling, indeed. Had I
believed *that* to be the case, your uncle would have
had a much earlier demise, I can assure you. As for
the present, what a waste. A dreadfully dull girl—the
granddaughter, I mean—" She explained for Sylvia's

benefit. "I was quite surprised to know she actually walked off with a French marquis. But then, he didn't seem terribly bright, either, which would explain it. Oh, well." Lady Margaret shook her head, as though deploring the ways of the world, and pulled on her gloves. "It has been a *great* pleasure meeting you, Sylvia." She paused and smiled and her eyes lit up. "I have just had a splendid notion. You shall come and spend the weekend at Warmouth!" she exclaimed, enchanted at the thought. "Clarissa's invited herself down again," she added with the tiniest deprecating sniff, "but Arabella will be there, which will be very merry. Her latest boyfriend, some Spaniard or other—he may be an Argentinean polo player, I can't quite recall—will be there as well."

"That's very kind, but I don't think—"

"Oh, but I absolutely *insist.*" She squeezed Sylvia's hand warmly. "You'll be the breath of fresh air that will make the whole gathering bearable," she murmured, then turned to her nephew. "Jeremy, I shall leave it up to you to make the arrangements. Don't forget to phone Hubble and advise what time you'll all be arriving."

"Aunt, Sylvia doesn't necessarily *want* to go to the country for the weekend," Jeremy observed, sending her a pointed look.

"Not want to go to the country for the weekend? Really, Jeremy. You do come up with the most absurd ideas. She'll love Sussex. Plus, a beautiful woman like her must look lovely set in a garden among delphiniums and hydrangeas. You do like gardens, don't you?"

"I guess…"

"Of course you do." Lady Margaret beamed. "Well, that's all settled then. Don't you think she'd look irresistible framed by hyacinths, Reggie?"

"Absolutely," he waxed gallantly, winking at Sylvia.

Lady Margaret waved to them and tugged the dogs' leash. "Come along, children, no dawdling. Tootaloo. Jeremy, I shall see you at one, precisely."

The door closed and Jeremy collapsed, groaning, behind the desk. "I might have known. Sorry to have imposed that on you, Sylvia. Aunt Margaret is impossible. Please don't feel obliged to go to Warmouth for the weekend. She's devilishly good at bending people to her will."

"On the contrary, I think she's great," Sylvia laughed.

"She can be rather fun in small doses," he admitted. "But I don't want her bullying you. You probably have other plans for the weekend." He sent her a questioning glance. The more he thought about it, the more the idea of having her at Warmouth pleased him. Still, he didn't want to look obvious, much less keen.

Sylvia hesitated, tempted to refuse. Then curiosity and something more, which she disregarded, won. "I don't have anything set for the weekend."

"Well, if you're sure you wouldn't mind indulging an old lady..."

"It was kind of her to invite me. I appreciate it. I think I might just take her up on the invitation." Sylvia sent him a bright professional smile. "A weekend in the country would do me good," she added. "Unless of course you'd rather I didn't come?" she queried innocently. The chance to test his *sang froid* too tempting to resist.

"I wasn't trying to put you off," he replied stiffly.

"Thank you. I'm not. I found your aunt delightful. Who, by the way, is Arabella?"

"Arabella is my very much younger sister, who is in a fair way to following in her aunt's footsteps if she's not careful."

"What does she do?"

"She's taking a master's degree," Jeremy muttered, twiddling his pen.

"Oh! Nice. In what?"

"Nightclubbing," he responded with a hollow laugh. "If we had any sense, we'd pit her against Thackeray," he added with grim humor. "She'd take care of him. Wouldn't know what had landed on him."

The mention of Thackeray caused Sylvia to become grave. "What did Bernardo have to say?" she asked Reggie.

"He's horrified at what's occurred and will investigate immediately. I got the feeling there's something not too pleasant going on, but it's all so damn vague." Reggie shook his head disapprovingly and tut-tutted. "He mentioned the Miami office several times. Apparently *incidents* have been occurring there."

"What incidents?" Jeremy frowned.

"He wouldn't say, but suspects there may be a link. Talked of a suspicious character—some Cuban chap known to be from Miami—who's been in contact with one of the factory foremen, Ronaldo something or other."

Jeremy frowned. The name sounded oddly familiar.

"No surname?"

"No."

"Nothing we can link?"

"Not yet, I'm afraid," Reggie replied regretfully. "Bernardo didn't seem keen to talk over the phone. But he said he'd be back in touch as soon as he had something concrete to report."

"Let's hope he's quick about it." Jeremy murmured dryly. "Miami," he mused, drumming the pen on the desk again. He was certain he'd heard the name Ronaldo before, and was annoyed that he couldn't immediately place it.

"The Colombians have access to the Miami office," Sylvia remarked thoughtfully.

"Just Bernardo. Nobody else."

"It might not have been too hard for another party to get access though, might it?" she queried.

After a pause, Jeremy got up and leaned on the edge of the desk. "Nothing's impossible in Miami. A well-paid henchman could very easily pick the lock or take a wax copy and have keys reproduced, I imagine. That office is basically a drop-off. But there's an updated computer, a state-of-the-art printer, scanner and a fax machine. Which opens up a whole new can of worms."

"It certainly does," Reggie corroborated, nodding in agreement. "I have full confidence in Bernardo, though. He's a good chap. We knew him at Harrow," he reassured Sylvia.

"Which does not make him watertight," she snapped, unable to contain her annoyance at this immediate assumption that because a man had attended the same school, he was automatically above suspicion. Christ, she could think of a number of old classmates who were presently guests of the federal penitentiary system.

"Quite." Reggie cleared his throat and glanced uncomfortably at Jeremy, who raised an eyebrow but made no comment. "Bernardo made it clear he didn't want to rush things, in case he scares off any suspects."

"Let's hope he comes up with something fast." Sylvia rose, picked up her papers, adjusting them neatly, all business and efficiency once more.

After she and Reggie left, Jeremy remained seated, still trying to identify the name that had sounded so familiar. Then, knowing it was little use—it would probably come to him in the middle of the night—he indulged in a moment of masculine self-congratulation. Sylvia had actually agreed to come to Warmouth. After the pithy remarks she'd made at Strathaird about castles and grand houses in general, her response had surprised him. Was she, like he, intrigued by what might happen if they spent more time together outside the office? Recalling his earlier conversation with Clarissa, he groaned as he realized she would be at Warmouth this weekend, as well.

Torn between anticipation and concern, Jeremy jotted down notes that included florists, foie gras and a special delivery of caviar. The four-hundred-year-old cellars at Warmouth were well stocked with the finest wine and champagne. Still, he'd call Hubble, the butler, and make sure all was exactly as it should be.

It couldn't hurt to stack the deck in his favor.

9

*"**P**uta mierda!"* Ricky Rico threw his glittering new cell phone across the room, where it landed next to his diamond-studded Rolex among a pile of black leather and Gortex strewn randomly over an electric-blue daybed. It stood incongruously on the white marble floor under an art deco mirror that Tania, the blond Russian bitch at a store on South Beach, had insisted he buy. It was that or not fuck her. And she was hot. Real damn hot. So damn hot, Ricky had laid down ten fucking grand on the goddamn mirror. He stared at it moodily, passed a hand over his dark, unshaven chin and muttered to himself. She'd been worth it, he conceded, dragging himself out of the black satin sheets that his sister Elsa said made him look like an even uglier motherfucker than he already was.

In the bathroom he took a piss then stared at the mirror. *"Come mierda,"* he hissed at the pockmarked image staring back at him. "You run like a bitch in heat every time that Gringo opens his big mouth." He leaned heavily on the marble basin and spat contemptuously at the gold-leaf taps. He'd wanted all this so badly, hadn't he? The fucking penthouse on the beach, the bitches, the Beamer.

And now he had it all. He even snorted top-quality Colombian coke whenever he wanted. So what was the big deal? What did it matter that he pissed in his pants every time the Gringo called wanting something. He, Ricky Rico, as he liked to be called, delivered, didn't he?

Half an hour later, dressed and shaved, a heavy diamond cross swinging against his black Versace T-shirt, Ricky steered the shiny Black M3 onto I-95, and cruised past the high-rise buildings of downtown and Brickell. On Thirty-second Avenue he made a right.

Very quickly the neighborhood went down-market. The houses became smaller and more squalid, the streets dirtier and the people sloppier. Men in worn shorts and undershirts played dominoes by the side of the road. Stressed-out Latino women screamed at kids and at each other.

Ricky let out an oath. He hated coming back, hated being reminded of his origins. When he opened the car window he met a blast of heat and humidity laced with black beans and *chicharrones*—fried pork chips. The neighborhood smelled poor and he despised it.

He drove for a while in the maze of back streets, one-story houses with barred windows and front doors. Some home owners tried to disguise the fact that they lived in fear, training the odd hibiscus or clematis up the walls to conceal the bars. Some of them remembered a time back in their villages in Cuba when they'd owned real gardens and life had seemed sweet. Even sweeter in retrospect, Ricky reflected angrily. It annoyed him that they rattled on about the past, all day every day, those glorious, sundrenched days they claimed were so much better than the present, when in reality it had sucked just as much.

. He avoided coming back unless he had to. But when he did, navigating the anonymous streets was a sort of compulsion. It reminded him why he remained at the Gringo's beck and call and why, right now, he was headed to Calle Ocho to find a fucking taxidermist. At first he'd thought a taxidermist must be the owner of a fleet of taxis, which had surprised him as he knew everyone in the area. Then fucking Hernandez, that prick lawyer—who thought that because he had some fancy law degree from up north he could lord it over the rest of them—had explained the guy was an animal stuffer.

Who the fuck would take a job doing that? He swerved into the street, ignoring the stares of passersby and the kids gaping at his sleek black car. His nose twitched and he sniffed uncomfortably. He hadn't snorted today. Maybe he should take a quick blow from his stash in the glove compartment. Glancing in the rearview mirror he groaned. Fucking cop car, goddamn it.

He slowed, peering at the numbers on the buildings. Then, slamming on the breaks, he veered into a run-down parking lot next to a Nicaraguan supermarket where they wouldn't mess with him. The owner owed him big-time. He waved to Juanito, the old man with the wooden leg and the dirty patch over his eye and too many stories about the Bay of Pigs, sitting on a rickety stool sipping a *colada*—syrupy black coffee—in a tiny white plastic cup, supposedly checking the lot. Ricky grinned, flashed his new gold tooth and parked just badly enough to show the Nica, who would be watching from his high-barred window, that he was in charge.

Getting out of the car, he slammed the door and hailed the old man.

"¿Cómo andas, compadre?" He patted the old man on the shoulder and slipped a hundred-dollar bill into the breast pocket of his worn *guayabeira*—the traditional short-sleeved, straight white cotton shirt worn back home. When the time came to get his money back from the Nica, the old man—who was a cousin of his sister's father-in-law and, like his own family, hailed from the province of Oriente—might prove useful. *"Díme,"* he said. "Where do I find the animal stuffer?"

"Tony Lopez?"

"Yeah, that's the motherfucker I'm lookin' for."

"Over there. Second floor." The old man pointed with his stick to a building across the street.

"Gracias, viejo. I'll be seeing you." He grinned again, glanced in the direction of the supermarket then headed across the street.

What the fuck could the Gringo want a stuffed beast for? he wondered, wishing he'd snorted at least *one* row before leaving the apartment. And shit, why did he, Ricky Rico, care? All that mattered was the motherfucker paid, wasn't it? Or rather Hernandez, the ass-licker, did. No, *Meester* Aimon Thackeray wouldn't soil his fingers with shit like him. At least, not so far. And it was hard cash and no questions asked.

He entered the building. Pink paint peeled off the walls. Above the elevator, a hand-painted cardboard sign hung with *Quebrado* written on it. Annoyed at the broken elevator, Ricky climbed the stairs impatiently. Like everything else in the area, they stank of *frijoles, tamales* and *picadillo*—all the things he loved and hated and would never escape, whatever part of town he moved to. He stared angrily at the beat-up front doors on the landing. A solitary lamp hung from the ceiling by wires, shedding barely enough light for him to read the dingy nameplates. Finally he found it: Lopez. He pressed hard on the bell and waited. Soon, shuffling footsteps approached. He shifted uncomfortably, glancing over his shoulder, then the door, locked with a chain from the inside, inched warily open. A pair of guarded brown eyes stared at him from under wrinkled lids.

"El Pájaro?" Ricky inquired.

The white head nodded slowly. The chain grated. Once it was undone, Ricky stepped inside.

"Maybe it's not such a great idea, after all." Sylvia sent Reggie an uneasy glance across Major Whitehead's vast mahogany desk and doodled on her legal pad. She'd had second thoughts about Monday's impulsive decision to go down to Warmouth. Being in close quarters with Jeremy was probably not advisable.

"I don't see why not. Warmouth's a charming spot. You'll love it."

"Hmm." All her earlier enthusiasm for spending a

weekend at Warmouth had vanished in the face of the humbling realization that she couldn't trust herself not to seek a repeat of what had transpired at Clachnabrochan. That, and the increasingly unsettling suspicion that Thackeray was on the move, planning something big. That he'd strike if she let her guard down.

"I promise you'll be enchanted." Reggie smiled and his face creased. "Plus, you need a break, old girl. Can't keep burning the midnight oil or you'll fizzle out. Just like that. Pop!" He clicked his fingers and frowned. "I think you should go down·and enjoy it. Lady M's a laugh and Arabella's good fun. You won't regret it." He took a good look at her, seated rigidly behind her desk, her hair tweaked behind her ears, her reading glasses perched halfway down her nose, her pen poised. No wonder Jer was so keen on her—not that he'd admitted it, of course, but it was glaringly obvious to anyone who had known him as long as Reggie had. They'd skewer him for saying it, but in his opinion these two would do splendidly well together—despite the fact they quarreled like cat and dog.

"Well?" he urged.

"I still think maybe I should just stay here. I have a ton of things to finish. Bernardo's news is still too vague to take action, and—"

"Rot and rubbish. I won't hear another word. You're off and that's it. Of course, it'll be a bit of a shock for poor old Jer— I think he'd counted on you begging off, and now he'll be obliged to take you, like it or not." He rose, tongue in cheek, and waited.

"So he would, wouldn't he?" Her gaze narrowed and her head tilted thoughtfully. "Maybe you're right. Maybe I do need a break.'' She laid down the pen and jumped to her feet, pacing restlessly. ''Another day in this dark, drafty office and I'll need to be committed, that's for sure. I think I'll just pop over and tell him right now.''

''That's the ticket,'' Reggie encouraged approvingly. He held the door for her then followed, a grin stretching from ear to ear.

''Of course I'd love for you to see Warmouth. But you mustn't feel *obliged* to come down,'' Jeremy insisted.

''I don't feel obliged,'' Sylvia responded, wondering why Jeremy, usually subtle, was being so obvious in his hope that she'd change her mind about visiting his aunt's home. On Monday he'd sounded keen. Now, if the idea weren't so absurd, she'd swear he was scared of her—or that he was testing her reasons for wanting to go. Then she remembered Reggie's words and, swallowing any last doubts about whether spending a weekend in his company was a good idea, she continued blithely, ''Besides, I'm actually looking forward to it. I've never been to a real English country house.''

''All right,'' he muttered. From his resigned expression, she'd never have guessed he was battling sudden delight that she was actually going.

Jeremy busied himself with the notes he'd taken during his last meeting and eyed her thoughtfully. ''You know, if Bernardo Villalba doesn't come up with something concrete by the middle of next week I think we should consider a trip over there.''

Sylvia nodded. ''I'd been thinking the same thing

myself. I don't care how many top-of-the-line schools he attended, I still think I'll need to take a hand in this myself.''

''Hmm.'' Jeremy sent her a quick glance but said nothing. He had no intention of allowing her to go to the end of the street by herself, let alone Miami or Colombia. But he remained silent. There would be time enough to expound on his theories once they had more info to supplement the news he'd already received through unofficial sources. And he was not about to reveal that right now.

The week had been a long one and right now Colombia seemed far away. Sleep had eluded Sylvia for the past few nights and it was all she could do to think straight, permanently on guard waiting for the other shoe to drop. Thackeray worried her far more than some one-time scam in South America. He was busy planning something big—she was sure of it— and the tension of wondering and not knowing was exhausting. Her eyes wandered over Jeremy's shoulder to the window. Should she just confront Thackeray and see if he came clean? But what if, by some perverted twist, that was precisely what he was expecting her to do? Then she'd be serving herself and Harcourts to him on a platter.

And that was unthinkable.

Reggie was right, she reflected, watching Jeremy come to terms with her announcement, she needed a break. Lady Margaret's amusing personality would be a welcome distraction. She shifted, swallowed and suddenly realized Jeremy had been speaking for several minutes. She tried to look attentive and succeeded in missing her cue.

"Pardon me, but have you heard a word of what I've just said?" he asked, frowning. Sylvia seemed miles away, which was unlike her.

"Of course," she scoffed. "You said I wouldn't want to spend the weekend at your aunt's home."

"That was five full minutes ago," he pointed out patiently.

"Oh. I'm sorry." She sat up straighter, masking her embarrassment. "Would you mind repeating the question?"

"Nothing," he muttered, feeling for a cigar.

"He was asking if you'd like to drive down with him to Warmouth," Reggie, who'd just walked in, chipped in helpfully, earning a dark look from Jeremy as he lit the cigar.

"I'll be leaving tomorrow at about four to avoid the weekend traffic. If you like, I can give you a lift down," he muttered coldly.

"Fine. Thanks, if you're sure it's still all right with your aunt." *Don't sound so enthusiastic about it,* she felt like saying.

"Well, of course it's fine. She's welcome to invite anyone she wants, and she's excited you're coming."

"Great. Like you really have a say in the matter," she murmured to herself.

"What was that?" Jeremy loomed over her menacingly.

"Nothing." She looked up innocently and their eyes met. "You said four, right?"

He leaned against the desk, eyed her suspiciously, then nodded, his eyes never leaving hers. For a moment she held his gaze, then looked quickly away, the reminder of the last time he'd looked at her in just that manner more than she wanted to deal with right now.

Sylvia got up, suddenly breathless. "I have to go now. I'm going to the theater tonight." She had no idea if she would like English operetta, but knew anything would be better than sitting in her suite, churning over her worries in her mind all evening.

"What are you going to see?" Reggie asked conversationally.

"*The Mikado,* at the Savoy."

Jeremy raised an amused, appraising brow. "I would have thought Gilbert & Sullivan would be far too *British* for you."

"I'm willing to give it a try," she retorted with a defensive toss of her blond head.

"It's had excellent reviews," Reggie remarked quickly, heaving his large form out of the leather chair. "You should have fun."

Jeremy sent her a curious look and frowned. Her slight pallor and the dark rings forming under her eyes hadn't gone unnoticed. It crossed his mind that he too had enjoyed little sleep since the events in Clachnabrochan, and for a moment he wondered why she'd decided to come to Warmouth. There had been no recurrence of their romantic interlude, and no allusion to it. Not so much as the bat of an eyelid had shown, she had any memory of the event.

But he remembered. All too well and all too damn often. Despite every effort to forget.

The thought of seeing her in his ancestral home left him strangely disturbed. Instinctively he knew he'd be forced to examine the emotions her presence provoked. His earlier confidence that she'd perhaps enjoyed their kiss had been shaken by her resolutely cool manner all week and he had no intention of making himself the object of ridicule. Still, short of being downright rude, he couldn't stop her from accepting his aunt's invitation. He'd just have to arrange matters so that they were never alone, was even relieved now that Clarissa was coming down on the ten-thirty on Saturday morning. Clarissa, he reflected cynically, would be sure to see to that they were always chaperoned.

Particularly after last night's conversation on the subject of marriage.

Jeremy shifted uncomfortably. He'd felt like a cad telling Clarissa that he didn't have any intention of entering the matrimonial state anytime in the near future, but the fact had to be faced. Surprisingly she'd had little reaction. After a short silence, she'd smiled briefly and asked him if he'd like more bread and butter pudding, which he thoroughly disliked and had only eaten out of good manners. When he'd tried to stay on the subject of marriage and expound further, she'd dismissed his words with a wave. Was it really not as important to her as he'd believed or was she just playing for time?

He sighed, picked up his briefcase and prepared to leave for the day. Women were an enigma. The thirty-five-year-old Clarissa, whom he'd been dating for years, seemed unconcerned that he'd told her quite plainly that he had no desire to get married. And Sylvia, whom he'd decided it was preferable to avoid, was insisting on coming to Warmouth.

It was too complex by far. Give him Harcourts, with all its intrigues and hassles, any day of the year.

* * *

"I'm sorry. I'm afraid this is going to be rather a squeeze." Jeremy cast Sylvia an apologetic glance as they stood next to the Jaguar.

"It's all my fault," Clarissa purred. "I should have stuck to my original plan and popped down on the train tomorrow morning. So silly of me to muck things up. But it's only an hour and a half, after all. You don't mind, do you, Sylvia?" Clarissa held a wriggling King Charles spaniel on her knee. She patted him on the head, leaned over the driver seat of Jeremy's Jaguar, and smiled at Sylvia in a manner that told her quite clearly she had no intention of budging from the front passenger seat.

They were in front of the Stafford Hotel. Jeremy was badly parked on the curb between two cabs while the bellboy slipped Sylvia's bag into the virtually nonexistent space in the back of the vehicle.

"I'm sorry," Jeremy repeated in a low tone. "I'm afraid this all happened at the last minute. Clarissa decided to come down earlier than expected, and I—"

"You don't have to make excuses, that's fine." Sylvia threw him a bright smile and prepared to climb into the diminutive rear of the car.

"Thanks," he murmured gratefully, watching with embarrassment as she crawled in and made herself as comfortable as she could. When she grinned at him, he grinned back. She was being a jolly good sport about Clarissa's sudden decision to accompany them to Warmouth, he conceded, especially since it promised to make her journey as uncomfortable as possible.

"Would you mind *awfully* taking Horace on your knee?" The "Dishonorable C," as Sylvia liked to think of Clarissa, twisted her neck and handed over the puppy. "He gets dreadfully carsick in the front and yaps the whole way."

"Clarissa, she can't fit the damn dog in the back, there's no room," Jeremy protested as they turned left up St. James's toward Piccadilly.

"I hardly think you want Horace vomiting all over the car, but far be it from me to quibble." Clarissa let out a long, suffering sigh, raised her aristocratic nose and turned toward the window.

"It's really not a problem," Sylvia said, undaunted. "Come here, Horace." She leaned forward as the puppy leaped happily from Clarissa's lap onto hers. "Hey," she laughed, letting him climb over her and find a comfortable spot to settle. "Not so fast, big boy." She stroked his ears and grinned. "You are the cutest dog I've ever seen. Is this the one you keep here in London? The one you walk in the park?" she asked Jeremy as their eyes met in the rearview mirror.

"You mean the one *I* walk in the park," Clarissa replied sweetly before he could answer. "I've told Jeremy time and again that keeping a puppy in town is utterly cruel. Poor little thing. Won't you consider leaving him down in the country, Jeremy darling? Though, of course," she added quickly, "you know best." She let out a measured sigh and Sylvia couldn't help but notice Jeremy's reaction—a hot rush of irritation that he tried quickly to conceal. She gave him top marks for forbearance.

"Do you own a dog, Sylvia?" Clarissa asked, adjusting her seat so that Sylvia barely had room to wiggle her toes.

"Actually, I don't. But seeing this one makes me wonder if I shouldn't change my mind."

"Really?" Jeremy's eyes met hers once more in what was fast becoming a rearview-mirror dialogue. "The other day when we talked about it you didn't sound keen."

"I thought all you talked about was this appalling mess Harcourts is in," Clarissa remarked rather stridently.

"It's a lady's privilege to change her mind," Sylvia replied demurely, exchanging a smile with Jeremy and ignoring Clarissa's comment. There was stony silence from the forward passenger seat. Then suddenly Clarissa spoke, her voice filling the vehicle.

"I strongly disapprove of people owning pets when they don't have time for them," she pronounced as though issuing a royal decree.

"That's why I don't have one. I've never wanted the responsibility." Absentmindedly Sylvia stroked Horace, enjoying the warmth of the dog's belly and his swift heartbeat on her lap. It was comforting and real.

"That's hardly surprising," Clarissa said with a deprecating laugh, as if explaining matters to a three-year-old. "It's not your fault, of course, but you in the States haven't been around long enough to understand the duties that come with privilege, have you? Here in Britain, those of us raised in the proper manner—with all the right standards, that is—know what is expected of us from the time we're in leading strings.'' Clarissa cast Jeremy a pointed sidelong glance that spoke volumes.

Sylvia digested this bizarre comment, recognizing the intended insult, and wondered why Clarissa, who clearly seemed to view her as some kind of threat, was being so unsubtle about it. "Well," she replied slowly, determined to keep the conversation cordial, "the only standards I care about meeting are my own, and that's why I avoid pets. Guess I'm just not capable of walking a dog and running a multinational corporation at the same time. Maybe you could show me how?" she asked sweetly.

Jeremy shot her an approving grin. With a surprisingly undignified snort, Clarissa turned her face to the window and stopped speaking, forcing Sylvia to wonder what on earth Jeremy saw in the Dishonorable C. Not that the woman wasn't attractive—she doubted Jeremy would settle for anything less—but while her skin was gorgeous, her sourpuss expression ruined the overall effect. Plus, she wore a shapeless, midcalf, cotton, flower-print skirt with a pink top and matching cardigan. Her pale hair was pulled back with a comb and topped by a hair band. The whole effect spoke of a tight-assed, intolerant nature. *Better you than me, baby,* she reflected with a sigh, watching Jeremy as he concentrated on maneuvering in traffic.

Settling as comfortably as she could, she patted the dog, which snuggled closer. She'd never been so close to an animal, never wanted that proximity to anybody or anything. But over the course of the ensuing drive, a strategic alliance was formed with Horace, who, bless his little heart, let out a low but menacing growl every time Clarissa's heronlike neck twisted in their direction. Eyeing his master with a grin, Sylvia decided it was pretty clear the dog had better taste.

The first views of Warmouth—seen, as Clarissa made a point of informing her, from the "Porte de Guillaume," the cornerstone of which dated to William the Conqueror—was unforgettable. Perfectly tended velvet grass bordered the driveway that stretched endlessly toward a huge, square Elizabethan manor emerging from among oaks and beeches, in perfect harmony with the English countryside.

Despite her cramped position and the one leg that had gone numb, thanks to Clarissa's pushed-back seat, Sylvia peered at the beautiful, melancholy architectural splendor.

"Wow," she exclaimed, unable to withhold her amazement.

"Like it?" Jeremy caught her eye again in the mirror. There was excited anticipation in his glance, as though he too loved this view and needed to share it.

"It's incredible," she murmured, shifting enough to allow Horace to scramble off her knee. "I thought Strathaird was impressive, but this...this is..." She searched for the word. "Magnificent—without seeming like a monument," she added decisively.

"Warmouth's been in the family since 1066," Clarissa informed her, tone instructive. "The first lodge was built in what now constitutes the inner courtyard. The manor house's history is far too long for me to explain to you now but, of course if you'd like, at some point later I'll show you over the place."

"Thanks," Sylvia replied, trying to pepper her an-

swer with an enthusiasm she was far from feeling.
Personally, she'd far prefer having the owner, Lady
Margaret, or even Jeremy, show her around. The prospect of having to accompany Clarissa as she harped
on about the grandeur and superiority of the Warmouths left her decidedly flat. Still, anything, she reminded herself, would help to keep her mind off
Thackeray's scheming.

As the car glided past magnificent flower beds,
gravel crunching under the tires, she wondered where
Thackeray was right now and what he was up to.
Then, determined not to dwell on what she'd vowed
to put aside for the weekend, she took stock of her
impressive surroundings.

Once the car came to a halt, Jeremy helped her
climb out and she stretched her cramped limbs thankfully.

"Sorry about that," he murmured apologetically.

"That's okay. I'm fine." Sylvia turned and gazed
up the ancient steps at the gray stone facade, the mul-
tipaned windows, the shrubbery, the sprawling trees
that must be hundreds of years old and the lawns
stretching toward a glistening lake, struck by the
peace and permanence. It was as though nothing
could ever disturb the prevailing calm, she reflected,
closing her eyes for a brief moment and breathing in
the warm late-afternoon air, the fresh-cut grass mixed
with a scent she couldn't define but recognized from
Charlotte MacLeod's cottage garden in Skye. She
glanced around her once more, the place bringing
home to her just how different her world and Jeremy's
truly were.

Sylvia suddenly recalled her own family home; the

broken-down chain-link fence, the trash rotting in the yard, her mother's voice complaining from the depths of a dirty, unkempt kitchen, her stepfather's grease-stained undershirts and the ever-present smell of alcohol. She shut her eyes and, slamming down an iron curtain, forced the haunting images to fade.

"Everything okay?"

Jeremy stood next to her, a slight frown creasing his forehead.

"It's wonderful," she exclaimed, reopening her eyes to the beauty of Warmouth, glad now that she'd come. This place felt a million miles away from the real world, from her past, from Harcourts and its present troubles.

Loud barking and a scuffle at the front door made them turn in time to see the butler open the door for Lady Margaret. She stood at the top of the stone steps and waved enthusiastically, her large figure dressed in a brightly patterned cotton dress, head sporting a large, ornately trimmed straw hat. "Hel-looo," she called, the warmth of her welcome chasing away any former doubts. Sylvia couldn't help but grin.

As Lady Margaret waited for them to ascend the well-worn stone steps, Horace hurtled across the lawn and into the fields beyond. The three corgis milling about Lady Margaret's feet waddled down the steps to join in the pursuit, albeit at a more sedate pace.

Sylvia stretched out her hand. "Hello, Lady Margaret. This is simply magnificent."

"Isn't it? I'm *so* pleased you could come, dear child. I'm just hóping the weather will hold for to-morrow's alfresco luncheon. Oh, hello, Clarissa."

Was it her imagination, or did she detect a cool

note in Lady Margaret's tone when she addressed the Dishonorable C?

"I do hope you'll enjoy your stay," Clarissa chipped in, as though she, and not Lady Margaret, were the hostess.

"I'm sure I will." Sylvia stared around her once more, unable to hide her wonder. "It must be incredible to own a place like this so close to London."

"Absolutely. Jeremy's a lucky boy, isn't he?" Clarissa purred.

"Jeremy?"

"Why, of course," Clarissa sent her a knowing smile. "Didn't you know that *he* is the owner of War-mouth? I thought everybody knew that. Of course there will have to be changes further down the line when—" She cut off, glancing at Lady Margaret handing out instructions to the butler, then leaned in Sylvia's direction. "Lady M still carries on the old regime, but once Jeremy and I are married and have the place to ourselves, things will be different. Oh gosh, where have those wretched dogs got to?"

She turned, raised her hand to ward off the waning rays of sun hovering over the lake and peered at the horizon, while Sylvia absorbed the astounding information that Jeremy, the man she'd summarily threatened to fire in the chopper, was the owner of what had to be one of the most incredible properties in the United Kingdom. And Clarissa's comment made her take sudden stock of her own situation. If the pair were truly engaged to be married, what was Jeremy playing at?

With a sharp jolt, Sylvia fought a stab of shame. Of all people, she knew what it felt like to have her fiancé attracted to another woman. She had no business encouraging Jeremy. He was her employee—despite the immense power and wealth he apparently wielded—and, unless Clarissa was lying, unofficially engaged.

As she brooded on these matters, Jeremy came up behind his aunt and gave her a warm hug before proceeding to carry Sylvia's bag inside, despite Hubble's protests.

"My lord, you must allow me," the silver-haired butler said, drawing himself up to his full height.

"Oh, bugger off, Hub." He grinned. "Grab Clarissa's stuff, will you? And show her up to her room. I'll take Miss Hansen to hers."

"Very well, my lord, as you wish." Hubble bowed disapprovingly.

"Where have you put her?" Jeremy asked.

"In the Tudor Room, of course, sir," he replied with a dignified sniff.

"Of course. Come this way, Sylvia, and I'll show you up."

"Tudor Room?" she asked, following him up the red-carpeted staircase through an immense galleried hall showcasing works of art.

"Each of the rooms is named after a different period in the house's history. Some Tudor monarch slept in the room you'll be staying in, but I can't remember which one. You'll have to ask Clarissa. She seems to know more about the place than any of us."

"Really?" Eyeing a spectacular painting she was sure was a Titian, Sylvia wasn't surprised at Clarissa's expertise. As she gazed at the walls plastered with Italian masterpieces, fine tapestries and enough treasures to fill a museum, she had no doubt of Clarissa's interest. The puzzle of why a snob like Clarissa was interested in marrying Jeremy was falling quickly into place.

"That—" Jeremy pointed as they marched up the dramatic staircase "—was the First Earl of Warmouth. Some people say we look alike." Looking up at the forbidding countenance, he grimaced. "I prefer not to think so."

"Well—" Sylvia tilted her head, determined not to show how shaken she was at learning he was the proprietor, then glanced up at him "—they may have a point. There are times—when you're angry, for example—that you have that same rather forbidding expression. I think it's the mouth." Her eyes narrowed. "I can definitely see a resemblance. In fact, the closer I look, the more I—"

"All right." He put up his hand like a traffic cop and laughed. "I asked for that." He grinned, then turned and continued climbing the stairs. "I'll take you through the house later. The staterooms have some very fine works of art you mustn't miss."

"Jeremy…" Clarissa's high-pitched staccato echoed from the hall.

He hesitated, then casting her a conspiratorial sidelong glance, continued up the wide flight of stairs, quickening his pace.

Sylvia followed him in flustered silence, then stopped when they finally reached the Tudor bedroom.

"Why do you intend to marry Clarissa if she gets on your nerves so much?" she blurted out, needing an answer, catching her breath as they entered the vast, high-ceilinged chamber. Despite her discomfort, she let out a long sigh of delight.

"What makes you believe that I plan to marry Clarissa?" Jeremy asked, taken aback. Laying Sylvia's suitcase on the end of the canopied bed, his eyes narrowed.

"I…just something she said that gave me the impression…" Her voice trailed off, embarrassed. Why had she opened her big mouth?

"Impressions can be misleading," he remarked dryly. "I am partly to blame for Clarissa thinking that someday we might—well, it's neither here nor there. But I've let things run too loosely for too long. Convenience, I suppose." He shrugged uncomfortably and stared at the carpet, shoved his hands in the pockets of his beige cords. "And for the record," he added, as though compelled, "I've made it very plain to Clarissa that I have no intention of marrying anyone anytime soon. Unfortunately, I can't alter what she chooses to believe."

"It's really none of my business," Sylvia countered, flushing, realizing she'd overstepped the line. "This room is perfectly glorious." She spun around, hastily changing the subject back onto neutral terrain.

"I'm glad you like it. I'll leave you to settle in. Drinks will be served at seven in the drawing room."

"Right." Sylvia fumbled with her handbag and sent him a bright smile. "Thanks."

"Right." Jeremy hovered near the door for a moment, as though about to say something. Then he apparently thought better of it and with a quick salute he left, the door closing carefully behind him.

Dropping her handbag on the nearest chair, Sylvia

shuddered. How could she have been so crass as to ask him outright what his intentions with Clarissa were? Why did she even care?

She took stock of the room—a far stretch from Strathaird, she thought with relief, remembering with a shudder all that dull, worn-out chintz and the brown water pouring out of the taps that Brad and Charlotte, too busy making moon-eyes at one another, hadn't bothered to modernize yet. Staying at Strathaird was daunting, and she bore it with reluctant resignation, only because of her great affection for them both and her new godchild.

But this room, or rather suite—Lord, it was so huge—was a different story altogether. It had plainly been recently redecorated. And not in the hodgepodge manner she'd grown accustomed to seeing in British houses. A skilled decorator had obviously been to work. The four-poster bed was majestic, the fabrics luxuriant, silky and incredible, the sofas next to the fire plumped high with velvet cushions that reminded her of a palazzo she'd once visited in Venice. Tall windows overlooked the park and the lawn that stretched in a gentle incline toward the lake where ducks glided serenely among the water lilies. Even though the house—castle? whatever—was ancient, there was nothing musty or depressing about it. Rather it had a fresh, vibrant quality that left her charmed.

She noted an enormous arrangement of delphiniums massed on a side table and smiled. Her hosts had seen to every attention. Was it Jeremy or Lady Margaret, she wondered, peering past the rich, flowing, terra-cotta silk drapes into the park. The sun shone a deep crimson, stretching into evening over the hazy marshland beyond as a flurry of geese soared, flying low across the marshes into the sunset. Sylvia sighed and finally began to relax. It was this she needed. A place where she could pretend, at least for a while, that nothing had changed, that the solid stone wall she'd built to protect her fragile world remained intact, and that the ominous winds swirling about her and Harcourts would somehow pass her by.

10

Sylvia's design preference usually ran to modern, clean and minimalist. But now, after a sybaritic soak in a Floris-scented bubble-filled whirlpool bath in her vast honey-beige marble bathroom, she decided old-world luxury definitely had its pluses.

Wrapped in a plush monogrammed robe, Sylvia settled on a supremely comfortable chaise lounge and marveled anew at the splendor surrounding her. Warmouth Manor was the sum of all she'd learned to admire in museums over the past year come alive in the context of a home. It was impressive yet touchable. Grandiose yet approachable. No dowdiness or threadbare gentility here, she remarked, fondling the heavy russet silk of her bedroom curtains looped in rich tassels on heavy bronze hooks.

Warmouth filled her with a sense of serenity and comfort. And yet there was something dynamic about it, too, she reflected, rising and moving to the center of the high-ceilinged room as dusk cast shadows over the neoclassical frieze, the cream-painted walls and bright etchings. This monument to the past was a vi-

brant testament of how the best of yesterday and today could be combined to create a home that exuded
understated refinement and elegance. Was this Jeremy's influence? If so, he'd done a hell of a job.

Looking again through the open window edged in
voile curtains that pooled onto the thick-pile cream
carpet, Sylvia leaned on the windowsill and absorbed
the scene before her. Evening hovered over the
marshes, the night air filled with English-country
scents—damp earth, wildflowers, herbs and roses—
and she breathed deeply. One lone bright star shone
in an indigo sky, announcing a clear night. A night
for lovers, she reflected ruefully, tilting her face up
and sighing. A good thing she was only staying the
weekend, she acknowledged, or she'd turn soppy in
this enchanted environment. Taking a last glance, she
realized how much she loved evening, its subtle
changes, the anticipation of night just around the corner.

Glancing at her watch, she decided to dress and go
on her own minitour. It was early still and too tempting not to wander. She stretched and rolled her shoulders. The bath had left her relaxed and inquisitive.
Not that she intended to snoop, but as she donned the
pearl-gray and silver chiffon Versace evening dress,
Sylvia's curiosity concerning the house grew. She
sorely wished she'd paid attention to all Brad had told
her about Jeremy in the past. But then, she realized,
brushing her hair and slipping on her jewelry, she
hadn't been interested. Hadn't been his boss, she cor-
rected, swallowing.

Letting out the long breath she'd been holding, Sylvia opened the door, peeked down the corridor and

set out on a personal tour, determined to investigate the house and perhaps learn more about Jeremy and his background. A better understanding of what made the man tick could only be to her advantage, she reasoned.

She slipped into the wide, red-carpeted passage and came face-to-face with a bronze equine bust, obviously Italian Renaissance, perched on a marble pedestal. Sylvia stared at it, struck by the perfection of each sculpted muscle. Then she moved on, contemplating, assimilating the full extent of all that Jeremy possessed. To own all this, Warmouth Manor, the land, the art—God, all the status and security it obviously carried. Yet he'd never spoken of it, never let on.

She'd known he had a title, of course, but most aristocrats these days had little else. She'd assumed that Jeremy, like so many of his class, had been compelled to seek a lucrative activity, his family's ancestral lands and fortunes a distant memory. But that was obviously far from the truth. Jeremy, she mused, intrigued, could do anything he chose.

Chose being the operative word.

He didn't *need* to work, didn't *need* to take shit from her or anyone. So why did he? She recalled her hysterical commands in the chopper and winced. He'd had every right to be angry. Furious, even. But never, for one single moment, had he allowed his feelings to interfere with what he had to do. She wrinkled her nose and wandered farther down the passage. Like those she'd noted on her way up, the paintings here were magnificent. She trailed by them in silent awe, taking pleasure in guessing the names of the artists,

willing to swear that one was a Tintoretto, another
from the school of Caravaggio; others she failed to
recognize. They glowed richly in tiny pools of soft
halogen. Even though it was just paint, she raised her
hand, tempted to touch the lush luminous silks and
velvets depicted in the masterpieces that seemed so
real and congenial, almost familiar in this private context.

This, Sylvia decided, admiring a small Jacobean
tapestry protected under glass, represented true
wealth. To live in the midst of all this art, wake up
for breakfast surrounded by what others had to queue
for in museums around the world—that was class. It
was entirely probable that some of these works had
been commissioned by Jeremy's ancestors, taken
years to complete, each piece thought out, appreciated, anticipated and enjoyed over long periods of
time. *This,* she reflected, could not be acquired.

She thought suddenly of Thackeray. However hard
he tried, he'd never come close. This insight caused
a certain measure of satisfaction as she moved along
the corridor, catching sight of a Scottish rural scene
several paintings away that reminded her of Strathaird. She frowned. Both Warmouth and Strathaird
were ancient estates and, in a way, they should be
similar. Yet they were entirely different. In fact, she
realized, all that linked them was age. Strathaird was
all about warring clans, rugged bearded clansmen
claiming their territorial rights, and that gray, churning North Sea wielding its grim relentless power.
Warmouth, on the other hand, reflected centuries of
acquired culture and knowledge, generations of art
lovers, connoisseurs who'd compiled a unique and

wonderful assortment of treasures, creating a magical and refined enclave.

What struck her most was the prolonged sense of continuity. From the different periods surrounding her, she realized that generation after generation must have contributed to make Warmouth what it was today. Was Jeremy adding to it, too? she wondered, listening to the grave chime of the three-hundred-year-old clock in the hall below announcing the half hour.

Few things intimidated her. But knowing the proprietor to all this was the man she carelessly ordered around on a daily basis left Sylvia awestruck. Not that it mattered, she argued, pulling herself together and looking straight toward the large oak double doors at the end of the passage. Everybody came from somewhere. Some just got there quicker than others and had the wisdom to preserve and prosper, to add with taste and refinement to what they'd already acquired.

She ignored a twinge of regret. She was not going to let herself dwell on any feelings of inferiority. Her own status was hard-won, not inherited. And just as good. Still, she was glad she hadn't waited for a guided tour, knowing it would be easier to take all this in on her own terms. Besides, this might be her only chance to enjoy Warmouth without Clarissa breathing down her neck.

As she approached the double doors, she was determined to look at the place critically. Okay, it had an aura, an enchantment all its own, but it probably also had many drawbacks. British property taxes must be crushing, she figured, making some quick estimates as she reached the landing.

For a moment she hesitated, bathed in the soft muted aureole of light coming from the yellow, silk-shaded wall sconce. Then, squinting sideways, she glimpsed a door to her left. It stood invitingly ajar. Would they think her crass for roaming on her own like this? Surely there couldn't be any harm in just looking?

Instinctively she moved toward the door. Then, pushing it farther, she gasped. The room—or gallery, rather—was immense and reminded her in a more subdued, English manner, of Versailles. Paintings and mirrors glistened under delicate three-tiered crystal chandeliers. She could almost see her reflection in the gleaming inlaid parquet floor. Holding her breath, Sylvia stepped gingerly onto it, high heels resonating as she gazed about her in frank admiration. She experienced another triumphant thrill as she recognized Constable and Gainsborough. Her time spent reading and learning about art and antiques—in an uncharacteristic move away from modernism—had not been wasted, she reflected, satisfied, taking on the challenge each painting offered. By the time she reached the end of the gallery she'd scored sixteen out of twenty. Not bad. Still, she'd have to keep on reading and visit more exhibitions to make sure next time she hit them all.

This was an amazing collection, probably one of the finest private collections in the country, she reflected with awe, wondering what lay in the alcove straight ahead. She faltered, then with a shrug went ahead. She'd come this far, so she might as well go the full gamut.

As she ventured farther, a delighted smile spread

over her face. Boy, this was very different from everything she'd seen up until now. Even the lighting changed. Here, spotlights beamed softly, illuminating an astonishing modern collection. She grinned at the Fauves, enjoying Vlaminck's bright colors slashing in sharp contrasts, wondering about this amazing collection, so different from all the rest. Warmouth didn't strike her as modern. In fact, everything about the place spelled tradition. Yet she recognized the hand of a master collector of contemporary art.

She turned slowly. On the opposite wall, Berthe Morisot's impressionist palette was reflected dreamily in muted pastels. Sylvia let out a sigh. There was a small Miró in the corner, a Giacometti bronze on an acrylic pedestal and a de Staël dominated part of a plain white wall to her right. And there, at the very end, looming like a glorious altarpiece, hung a huge Chagall.

For a while she stood perfectly still, head cocked, absorbing the myriad of seemingly separate sketches that formed an intangible whole.

"Like it?"

"Oh!" She spun around. She'd been so absorbed she hadn't heard Jeremy enter. Now he stood in the archway casually observing her, sleek in black-tie and holding two champagne flutes. Crossing the alcove to where she stood, he handed her one.

"I had a funny feeling I might find you here." He smiled down at her. "For some reason people seem to drift in here. How do you like it?" he asked, pointing to the Chagall. "It's my latest acquisition."

"*You* collect these?" She tried to conceal her shock.

"Yes. My contribution to enriching the Warmouth collection."

"The Chagall's incredible," she said, absorbing the news that her supposed "subordinate" was not only the proprietor of one of the nation's finest art collections, but also a serious collector in his own right. She gulped a quick sip of champagne and cleared her throat. "It's truly amazing."

"I think so, too. That's why I felt the collection needed it."

"When I look at a Chagall, I feel like I'm wandering off into a story." She tilted her head and stared at the masterpiece.

"Funny you should say that," he mused, eyes narrowing as he contemplated the painting. "That's exactly what I felt when I first saw this one."

"And so you picked it up just like that!" She snapped her fingers and laughed.

"Yes. Once I make up my mind I want something, I set out to acquire it. Still, I consider myself to have been very lucky." He watched her with new intensity, his eyes turning suddenly greener.

"Must be nice to have the means to *be* so lucky," she murmured wryly, wondering whether to mention that she knew Warmouth was not his aunt's.

"It is. I've been lucky in more ways than one."

"It would certainly seem so."

"It's extremely satisfying to own a masterpiece."

As he turned to study the painting, she realized with a jolt that there was much more to his gaze than just the satisfaction of ownership. He derived intense pleasure from the painting itself, and it showed. She swallowed as she tried to assimilate yet another side of the man. Each new revelation—including his earlier comments regarding his intentions toward Clarissa—was another curveball, wrecking havoc with her carefully considered decision to ignore him, to discount how he made her feel. Evidently, Clachnabrochan had been only the beginning, she realized dryly; her preconceptions about Jeremy Warmouth were in for a sustained assault. And that didn't bode well for her peace of mind.

Determined to escape the sudden memory of his lips, hot and demanding on hers, she gulped too quickly and spluttered.

"You okay?" Jeremy slipped a solicitous hand on her arm.

"Fine," she choked, staring hard at the Miró in a desperate attempt to straighten out the muddle Jeremy was causing. Damn him for popping one surprise on her after another. As if she didn't have enough on her plate. All at once she was annoyed with herself for being so intrigued by the man, the house, the art, the works. Heck, he was just a guy like any other, wasn't he?

"Are you interested in art?" he asked, his hand still gently touching her forearm.

"Sure. Lately more and more so," she replied, stealing another look and realizing ruefully that no, he was not just any other guy. There was much more to him than that handsome, devil-may-care look he sported. And tonight, he seemed somehow different, more relaxed, as though here in his ancestral home, he was somehow complete. And it had nothing to do with his chestnut hair glistening under the gleam of the crystal-laden chandeliers, or that golden tan that glowed smoother and darker in contrast to those green eyes.

Pulling herself up with a jolt, Sylvia retrieved her arm. She'd barely listened to what he was saying. How ridiculous to be acting like a gooey-eyed teenager. She was a woman of the world, the CEO of a multinational company, she reminded herself severely. Surely *she* of all people knew that corporate relationships never worked? Plus, she had a strict and fast rule about such things. Okay, there'd been Brad, but that was different.

Eyes narrowing, she concentrated determinedly on the art.

"You look dreadfully intense," he murmured, leaning back casually against a small drum table in the center of the alcove. "Not worrying too much about Harcourts, are you?" The concern in his voice left her weak at the knees.

"No. I'm fine—I mean, of course I am. Worried, I mean." She stopped, frustrated. "Look, I don't want to talk about it, okay?" Hoping her show of irritation concealed her turbulent emotions, she gestured. "Hey, we came here to relax, take the weekend off. Monday we'll make some decisions."

He nodded, a crooked smile hovering at the edges of his mouth. "We?" he queried.

"Yes, *we*. Have a problem with that?"

"Not at all. Just not used to it, that's all," he murmured, tongue in cheek.

"Good. Then let's save it for Monday, shall we?"

"Certainly. But before we close the subject, I think it's important that you know I got a call from Bernardo just before leaving the office this afternoon."

Their eyes met. She waited impatiently and experienced a moment's amazement when she saw, to her annoyance, that he was deciding just how much to tell her.

"What did Bernardo say?" she demanded as he swirled his champagne thoughtfully.

"Not much."

"Jeremy, do I have to remind you that I'm not a little girl? That I run this company?"

"How could I possibly forget?" he muttered with a dry laugh. "Bernardo said there was a break-in at one of the factories several weeks ago, around the time we estimate the designs must have been stolen. He's following up with the police and the security services and will keep us informed. It may be a clue, it may not be."

"Oh." Sylvia's shoulders sagged. "You should have told me immediately."

"I didn't want to worry you," he responded quietly, eyes resting intimately on her. "You've looked a bit tired lately."

"Tired or not, Harcourts is still my responsibility."

"Of course." He inclined his head and she shifted, wishing that his gaze didn't leave her feeling powerless and ineffectual and ashamed of her sharp words, as though she should be saying *thank-you*, instead of establishing her position. Sylvia stared mutely at the Berthe Morisot, determined not to be overwhelmed either by her surroundings or by Jeremy's ability to render her distressingly vulnerable.

"This painting is perfectly lovely," she exclaimed, painfully aware that she must bring some normalcy back to the conversation ASAP. "This isn't in the usual style of what I admire, but it's charming."

"Exceptional, isn't it? I picked it up last year at a Sotheby's sale in Paris. I'm particularly fond of this painting. I suppose it doesn't fit that well amongst the others, but I still haven't found another spot to hang it."

"What about in your apartment in London?" She let out a deep breath, hoping her voice didn't sound stilted. He looked utterly comfortable, as though unaware that moments earlier the air had been thick with tension. And let's face it, she admonished, desire.

"Odd you should mention my flat." He looked her over curiously. "I was looking at the wall above the dining table just last night and thinking that might be the right place to hang the Morisot."

Their eyes met. Another electric current coursed wildly. And to her horror Sylvia experienced an inexplicable rush of pleasure. She took a hasty, guarded step back, creating distance.

"Maybe I'll take the painting back to town and give it a shot," Jeremy continued, apparently unaware of her inner turmoil. "You could come over for dinner some night and give me an honest opinion," he added, looking toward her again with that smile she was beginning to fear. "You could rate my cooking skills, too. Give you some leverage for when I go to New York." He grinned.

"As long as it's not anything weird, no kidneys or livers or anything like that. You might decide to try a haggis recipe out on me after all."

Laughing softly, he twisted her shoulders about until she faced him. "I promise I'll never try anything out on you that you don't want," he murmured gently, his lips and glinting eyes only millimeters away. "And I'm afraid I have to be honest. My cooking skills are minimal and consist of Mrs. Brown, my daily housekeeper, picking up something at the Harvey Nick's food hall."

"That sounds pretty safe," she muttered, wishing she had the willpower to pull away. But his hands, roaming up and down her arm in a gentle, comforting movement, were delightfully soothing, making her long to lean into him, unbend, and feel the touch of his lips again.

"Ah! There you are."

They looked up as one. Jeremy's head twisted and Sylvia took a quick step back, pulse floundering. Clarissa stood in the doorway. She wore a long, flowery dress of indeterminate style. Her body language was stiff and Sylvia wondered if Clarissa noticed how close they'd been standing.

"Ah! I see you've discovered our little gallery, Sylvia. Quite amusing, isn't it?" Jeremy winced as Clarissa made her way across the room, the harsh thud of her one-inch heels sending a hollow echo through the alcove. "I see the two of you are already drinking. How sensible," she remarked with an affected laugh that held little humor. "I suppose I should pop down and get something, too." She glanced at the flute in Sylvia's hand, then at Jeremy, then turned her attention to the Chagall and frowned. "I really can't say that I *like* that painting," she remarked, staring critically at it. "I suppose he's terribly good and all that. Not that I know much about his work. It always strikes me as rather overrated. But then that's just me,'' she trilled deprecatingly. ''Personally, if I were expanding the collection, I'd concentrate on English landscapes. But, of course, you know best,'' she added, patting Jeremy's arm possessively.

''Since my ancestors stocked up pretty heavily on English landscapes, I thought it was time for a change,'' he remarked blandly.

''Of course they did, darling. They *knew* what to acquire.''

''They collected the contemporary art of their day,'' he answered, annoyed. ''I'm just carrying on the Warmouth tradition and adding my two cents'.'' His eyes met Sylvia's.

Clarissa trilled once more as Jeremy stepped from her grasp. ''Darling, I wish you wouldn't try to sound so dreadfully American,'' she remarked, dripping honey. ''As for the paintings, I'm sure you know exactly what you're doing. And, after all, it's *your* collection and *your* money. Far be it from *me* to criticize. If my taste runs to the traditional, well, so be it.'' Clarissa shrugged and smiled too brightly.

Trying to do a salvage operation of his temper, Sylvia reckoned, noting the tightening muscles around Jeremy's mouth. Working with him closely made it possible for her to recognize the barely visible signs of rising irritation.

''Do you really dislike all these paintings that much?'' she asked Clarissa innocently, gesturing toward the walls of the alcove. ''Personally, I think they're superb. I'd give my right arm to own even half of one. But then, I love modern art. In fact—'' she turned toward Jeremy, smiling more graciously than she'd meant to "—I think we should consider founding a modern art collection at Harcourts."

"You do?" His face, tense for the past few minutes, relaxed.

"Yes. I got interested in art after Charlotte and I organized the Sylvain de Rothberg retrospective at the Met. Every time I went there, I'd find myself wandering into different parts of the museum."

"You mean you had no previous exposure to art?" Clarissa's right eyebrow flew up in horrified astonishment.

"I didn't have much opportunity to study it," Sylvia countered, refusing to let Clarissa's obvious disdain touch her. "But there's already a fine basis to start a collection at Harcourts."

"Absolutely," Jeremy waxed enthusiastically, sending a withering look Clarissa's way. "The Singer Sergeants, the Whistler and the other American art in the New York office that Brad's great-grandfather acquired would make an excellent beginning."

"Not to mention Dex's Braque and the three Picassos," Sylvia added. "But I think it should all be part of a foundation. Brad and I talked about it once, but then I guess there was so much going on we didn't pursue it."

"It's a terrific idea." Jeremy grinned broadly, reached over and clinked glasses with her. "We'll mention it to Brad and Charlotte next time we see them. I'm sure they'll love the idea."

"Well," Clarissa declared tartly, "perhaps when you've finished taking the art world by storm, you'll consider joining the others for drinks. It's dreadfully rude to be powwowing about hypothetical art collections up here when we should be socializing in the drawing room.'' She glanced again at the paintings, sniffed, and then turned on her heel.

"Of course." Jeremy inclined his head and straightened his jacket, motioning to Sylvia to go ahead. "My sister, Arabella, should have arrived. I wonder who she's brought along this time?" he added with a sigh. "It may still be the Argentinean polo player, but he's had a pretty good inning, so I doubt it. Knowing Ara, she's probably moved on to new pastures."

"Are you worried about her?" Sylvia asked perceptively.

"Sometimes. She seems at a loose end. Doesn't settle to anything." He held the door and she passed through. "I think she misses our mother. They were very close." Confiding in Sylvia was not what he'd intended, but he was surprised how natural it felt.

"It's hard having a sibling to look after. Brad has his twin brothers to care for. Of course, they're almost like his own kids."

"How did you deal with that? Do you miss the twins?" he asked, suddenly curious.

"I see them quite a bit back in New York. Of course, now they'll be going to school in Switzerland." There was a sad look in her eyes.

"A good decision, don't you think?"

"Sure. They'll be closer to Brad, now that he's fixed at Strathaird. With Charlotte and her daughter Genny, they have a real family again. But I'll miss 'em."

"Do you mind about the broken engagement?" he asked suddenly, stopping in the middle of the passage, knowing he shouldn't have asked. But he needed to know.

"No." She shook her head firmly and smiled up at him. "Not at all. Brad and I led a well-synchronized, hugely busy existence that became a habit."

"Didn't you love him?"

"Yes. I think I did. But…I don't know how to say this…we didn't have time to be…I guess you'd call it *in* love. We worked too hard, our schedules didn't coincide. Heck, a number of things." She raised her hand, dropped it and finished with an embarrassed laugh.

"I see." Jeremy slipped an arm lightly around her shoulders and frowned. Sylvia had never struck him as a woman who'd cheerfully take on caring for twin boys, yet she had. And done a great job, according to the reports he'd heard. Perhaps if he'd paid more attention to such details, instead of consistently contesting her, he would have been better prepared for the real person.

Still, the knowledge that the broken engagement to Brad wasn't an issue for her anymore left him feeling strangely upbeat, and as they approached the landing he found himself smiling. He hoped she'd enjoy the weekend, take the time to relax, let go of some of the tension caused by the troubles of the past weeks. He took a sidelong glance as they prepared to descend the imposing staircase. The truth was, he was dying to know more about the woman underneath the armor, the one he'd held in his arms and kissed so passionately and whose presence, despite every worthy intention, left him with the same pounding desire he'd experienced on the Scottish moors.

11

Stalking ahead, Clarissa was already crossing the hall by the time Sylvia and Jeremy reached the top of the impressive staircase. In a courtly gesture, he offered her his arm and smiled.

Feeling for all the world as if she was walking through the pages of a fairy tale, Sylvia accepted, not quite believing that this was happening. Could this really be once-white-trash Sylvia from Arkansas gliding down the stairs and across the gloriously illuminated marble hall of an historic mansion on the arm of an English earl she'd spent the better part of a year loathing?

As they approached the last steps, she swallowed. Get a grip, she commanded herself. But she felt strangely dreamy, young, exhilarated and upbeat. Even the lurking worries assailing her at Harcourts seemed to have diminished. Ridiculous, of course, to crave the impossible, but she couldn't help wishing the moment would carry on and on, that she could capture its magical quality and cork it up in a bottle. This house, with its indefinable uniqueness, had captivated her—as had its owner. How had she failed to appreciate his subtle, urbane charm? He was so different from the man she'd believed him to be, from the hard-edged competitor at the office who'd seemed intent only on setting obstacles in her path. Different again from the one who'd cared for her so gallantly on the Scottish moors, despite her appalling behavior. In anyone else, she'd find such unpredictability troubling; in Jeremy, she was learning to admire the many facets of his complex nature, a nature that refused to be constrained within the black-and-white box she'd built for him. Behind the impenetrable businessman was the guy who kept cool in a crisis while maintaining his ripe sense of humor. And along with his tough and cynical side—not necessarily a bad thing out there in the corporate war zone—was a characteristic more important than all the rest: he'd proved trustworthy and reliable.

From behind the closed drawing-room door she could hear the sound of muffled laughter, the rise and fall of chitchatting voices, the clink of fine crystal. She took a long deep breath.

"Ready?" Jeremy asked, smiling reassuringly as though he could read her lurking qualms.

"Sure." She smiled back and watched him reach confidently for the door handle. Tonight he truly was lord of the manor, making her feel welcome and wanted, beautiful and distinct. Jeremy had obviously inherited all the panache and charm that went with his name and position.

Sylvia was shocked to find his courtliness extraordinarily appealing. For there was no false pride or snobbery in his manner. In fact, there was nothing stuck-up or pretentious about Lady Margaret or the MacLeods, either, now she came to think about it. As she was fast learning, the truly well-bred—those who didn't have to pretend they were any better than anyone else—were delightful. The only one living up to her resolutely low expectations was Clarissa.

"Ah, there you are." Lady Margaret, clad in bright red silk, another huge diamond brooch spreading its glistening leaves over her left breast, rested her champagne glass on a side table as they entered the long, high-ceilinged, Adam-green and acanthus-leaf-plastered drawing room. Several people were assembled, some chatting near the fireplace, where a fire crackled gently, and others seated by the vast bow window that overlooked the park and lake. Reggie waved and Sylvia smiled. Major Whitehead, immaculately attired in a dinner jacket and whiskey tumbler in hand, hastened over to greet her.

"Good evening, m'dear. So nice to see you here. Glad you were able to come. Good idea of Margaret's to have invited you." He nodded and harrumphed. "Having a pleasant time, I trust?"

"Very pleasant, thank you," she answered, surprised at the warm welcome she was receiving. "You look very smart tonight, Major."

The Major beamed and harrumphed. "Just part of the old battle gear, m'dear. Wore it the evening Mountbatten handed over, you know. If this dinner jacket could speak, it would have many a tale to tell."

"I'll bet." Sylvia grinned, delighted to see a twinkle in the Major's eye.

"Now, now," he said, the roguish gleam belying

his stern tone as he steered her toward Lady Margaret, "don't get me started on my stories."

"I'll bet you have a few." She pressed his arm lightly and turned to Reggie, who had reached her side.

"Beautiful spot, isn't it?" he remarked with a broad smile. "Very fine landscapes we have here in Sussex. I live only a few miles south of here. Splendid part of the country."

"Quite so, dear boy, quite so," the Major agreed enthusiastically. "Now look here, Jeremy m'boy, you must take her to visit Arundel and the gardens at Petworth. Jolly well worth the visit, I assure you," he said, turning back to Sylvia, his red cheeks and white bushy eyebrows moving expressively. "Not that the ones here at Warmouth aren't a very fine specimen of the classic English garden," he added, glancing hastily in Lady Margaret's direction. "Margaret will scold me if she hears me telling you to visit elsewhere," he added with a wink. "But Arundel's well worth it. Ah, she's calling." Excusing himself, the Major bustled to Lady Margaret's side.

"You're looking ravishing tonight," Reggie said, beaming. "Lovely dress. Makes you look all sort of...different." He cleared his throat.

"Thank you." She smiled, caught Jeremy's appreciative grin and turned.

"Come over here, Sylvia, dear," Lady Margaret beckoned, "and meet Hugh Pevsner."

A thin, blond, pink-cheeked young man in his late thirties, clad in a dinner jacket, shook hands and mumbled politely.

"Lord Pevsner is our neighbor. And this," Lady

Margaret announced, her face breaking into a fond smile, "is my niece, Arabella." She beckoned to a tall, red-haired, sylphlike creature, floating toward them in a diaphanous dress.

Her bone structure was exquisite, her eyes huge and dark with long black lashes that needed little mascara to help them. Her skin looked smooth as alabaster. When she stretched out long fine fingers, Sylvia noticed Hugh blush a fiery red. It figured that every male would be in love with her, she reflected in amazed amusement, the girl was the loveliest creature she'd ever beheld. But Arabella's firm handshake belied the etherealness of her figure.

"Hi," she greeted her in a friendly, curious manner and grinned. "I'm Ara, Jeremy's sister. I suppose you're the obnoxious Sylvia."

"Ara, for God's sake, shut up." Jeremy moved up behind her and tugged her hair in a brotherly fashion.

"So that's how he describes me, is it?" Sylvia sent Jeremy a dark look over her shoulder.

"That was *before* I had the chance to appreciate your finer qualities," he replied smoothly, eyes gleaming. "As for you," he added, addressing his sister menacingly, "you talk too much."

"Ouch! That hurt." Arabella exclaimed indignantly, rubbing her head and making a face at her brother. "Did you see what he did?" she asked Sylvia in an injured tone, eyes bubbling with mischief.

It was impossible not to be captivated by this extraordinary family and their home. And hard not to feel a pang of regret for all she'd never known and never allowed herself to want, for fear that *want* might end up as *need*. And that was a word she'd eliminated from her vocabulary a long time ago. To need anything or anyone was a weakness she couldn't permit.

She watched as Arabella and Jeremy quarreled playfully.

"Oh, do stop bickering, the two of you." Clarissa joined the group, letting out a weary, superior sigh. "Can't you behave like adults for once?"

Arabella made a face at Clarissa's stiff back before spinning on her heel, and Sylvia barely suppressed a laugh. She watched, amused, as the girl slipped her arm through that of a young man standing silently next to her. Ebony locks, burning black eyes, a proud stance and a gold earring made him quite a figure.

"This—" Arabella announced, twirling around "—is Alfonso. He's from Seville. He's a toreador," she added, gazing into his face adoringly.

"Olé!" Jeremy muttered in a soft undertone, leaving Sylvia fighting to keep a straight face.

"Delighted to meet you," Sylvia said.

The Spaniard flashed a dashing smile, bowed, then swooped her hand lightly to his lips and murmured something incomprehensible.

"Sylvia, dear, do come and sit next to me," Lady Margaret patted the brocade sofa invitingly. Smiling at the toreador, Sylvia excused herself and made her way to Lady Margaret's side.

"Sit down," she insisted. Then, raising the monocle that hung on a gold chain around her neck, she surveyed the young man from a critical distance.

"A toreador," she remarked, pursing her lips. "Well, well. One wonders what it'll be next. A very handsome fellow, of course, but I can't understand a word he says. I find it somewhat trying, though with those looks I suppose it doesn't matter. Perhaps he's better at stirring bulls than conversation.'' She let out a gusty sigh. ''I suppose we must look on the bright side. It's probably good for Arabella's Spanish, don't you think? Nothing like pillow talk to improve one's language skills, is there?''

''Uh, I haven't had much personal experience in the matter.''

''Really?'' Lady Margaret turned, full of frank interest, then frowned. ''You know, now I come to think of it, neither do I. The late earl and I were madly in love, you see. There was never anyone else.'' She gazed mistily toward the fire. ''Not that I minded, mark you. In those days one didn't really think much about having affairs or that sort of thing.'' A wistful mischievous smile hovered at the corners of her mouth. ''Though, I do seem to recall a most *attractive* young officer who once made what was considered in those days to be a most indecent proposition. Roderick—that was the late earl—was in absolute *hoots* about it for a week!'' She chortled, raised her monocle once more and scanned the room. ''Tell me, what do you think of Clarissa?''

''I've had very little contact with her,'' Sylvia answered diplomatically.

''I'd keep it that way.'' Lady Margaret nodded sagely. ''I can't think why Jeremy doesn't get rid of her. She's been on his heels like a hound after grouse for ages, counting on the fact that he'll need an heir rather sooner than later.'' Her bejeweled hands dropped into her lap. ''He simply must get married and have a child, you know. But I have to admit,'' she said, lowering her voice, "that although she's dreadfully suitable, I find it hard to actually *like* Clarissa, let alone picture her with a baby. The mere thought of it is frankly horrifying." Her face crinkled into soft, mischievous creases. "Her mother was exactly the same," she remarked, touching the elaborate white wave above her forehead. "If you could see her, you'd understand my qualms. Henrietta Wetherton is a dreadful old battle-ax." She shook her head, lips pursed. "Someone once said she had a Plantagenet face, in which case I assume the Plantagenets must have been a pretty fearsome lot. Personally I would have thought a cast-iron frying pan would have been a better analogy."

Struggling mightily to contain the bubble of laughter that had been present since she'd entered the drawing room, Sylvia sipped her champagne and observed. As in the other rooms she'd visited, the antiques here were magnificent. Clarissa, one arm crossed protectively over her breast, stood next to a French late-eighteenth-century desk, conversing with Major Whitehead and young Hugh, while Arabella and Jeremy were not far away, teasing one another relentlessly under the serene, uncomprehending gaze of Alfonso the toreador. Lady Margaret kept up a hilarious monologue that covered most of the individuals in the room and a number of opinions, ranging from Clarissa's mother's impossible nature to the queen's latest outfits.

Astonished, Sylvia realized she was enjoying every minute. Well, she'd wanted a diversion, she acknowledged with a grin, and it sure looked as if the evening was shaping up to be very amusing indeed.

* * *

Seated at the head of the table, Jeremy bit into roast partridge, quite satisfied with the seating arrangements he'd seen to earlier with Hubble. Sylvia was seated to his right, old Lady Pevsner to his left, while Clarissa was placed at a strategic distance at the far end of the table, next to Hugh Pevsner. The only drawback was the toreador on Clarissa's left, who did nothing but flash wicked smiles at Arabella between mouthfuls of fowl, and made no attempt at conversation, leaving Clarissa free to stare attentively in his direction.

Jeremy conversed politely with the wraithlike Lady Pevsner. She picked delicately at the miniature portion of partridge on the Wedgwood dinner plate and expounded upon her desire to see Hugh "properly settled." Jeremy answered in noncommittal murmurs, deeply conscious of Sylvia's presence next to him. Everything about her, he reflected, agreeing once more with Lady Pevsner's views on the local county council, seemed enhanced tonight. The evening was particularly pleasurable simply because of her presence in his home. Even listening to Lady Pevsner— a bore at best—was bearable knowing Sylvia was at his side. He was glad she'd come, amazed at how quickly the relationship had gone from hostile to…what, he asked himself suddenly. What exactly did their relationship consist of right now? A month ago he'd been convinced she was nothing but an unpleasant curse he was obliged to endure from time to time, a part of corporate life. Now he was wondering how to spend the better part of the weekend with her without Clarissa clinging like a damn leech.

He glanced uncomfortably down the table. It was his own fault for allowing Clarissa to turn into a habit. She followed him around as if it was her right. He wondered if the previous evening's conversation and his announcement that he had no intention of marrying right now had sunk in. Judging by her reaction, he doubted it. The patronizing manner in which she'd patted his arm, as though he were a wayward child needing to be brought back to the fold, told its own tale. Apparently their conversation wasn't enough to daunt her. Something was going to have to be done about the Clarissa situation. Fast.

"No more partridge?" he asked when Hubble had passed the dish for the second time and Sylvia refused.

"I couldn't. Thanks. It was delicious."

"Quite right, m'dear," the Major approved. "Better to leave some room for pudding. I assume it's Pierre's famous chocolate mousse?" he inquired, a hopeful gleam in his eye.

"It is," Jeremy assured him. "Pierre," he added in a low aside for Sylvia's benefit, "is our cook. He's been with the family for over twenty-five years. His chocolate mousse is renowned throughout the country."

"Wow," Sylvia laughed and looked suitably impressed.

"You don't believe me?" He sent her a challenging grin. "I assure you that Pierre's reputation works like magic. If we want to lure some famous guest away from another event, Aunt Margaret simply mentions, very casually en passant, that Pierre's chocolate mousse will be on the menu."

Their eyes, overflowing with laughter, met and held. She was having a better time than she would ever have imagined possible. She had feared the weekend might be stuffy and dull and insufferably snobby. But except for Clarissa, there was not a tad of snobbery. As for Jeremy, she reflected, watching him maneuver the conversation with Lady Pevsner with the savoir faire of a seasoned diplomat, she got the impression he ran his household exactly as he did Harcourts Europe, in a firm, disciplined and quiet manner that required only a look or a slight gesture to indicate his desires to the well-trained staff.

Despite a lingering inclination to try to find something amiss, Sylvia was not only impressed but happy for the first time in weeks. She'd laughed more in this one evening than in all of her stay in the U.K. It felt almost treacherous to be so lighthearted when, for all she knew, Thackeray was plotting a major coup and Harcourts's future might be on the line.

"Everything all right? Not worrying, are you?" Jeremy's hand slipped over hers. His eyes, so full of sudden understanding, made her own water.

"I was just thinking—" she murmured.

"Don't." He squeezed her fingers warningly. "This weekend, as you pointed out earlier, is for R and R."

"I'm trying."

"I know. But try a bit harder." He winked and drew his hand away as Hubble presented the dish of dark, thick, rich creamy chocolate mousse that left her mouth watering. About to dip her fork into her dessert, she hesitated and then decided to broach the one matter still bothering her.

"Why didn't you tell me before that this was your home and not your aunt's?" she asked, gauging his reaction.

"I thought you knew. Anyway, it *was* hers, until I inherited it when my uncle died."

"You mean you kicked your aunt out of her house?" She sent him a shocked glance and her shoulders stiffened.

"Of course I did *not*, as you so crudely put it, kick my aunt out of anywhere," Jeremy exclaimed in a low exasperated tone.

"Calm down. I just asked."

"No you didn't, you implied—"

"Now, now, no quarrelling, children," Reggie admonished. "Lady Margaret resides at the dower house. A perfectly normal arrangement, I assure you, and the reason such a place was built in the first place," he reassured Sylvia.

"Which," Jeremy added with feeling, "is a dashed sight more convenient and manageable than Warmouth itself. She lives there by choice," he muttered, sending Sylvia a fulminating glance. "I personally would have preferred that she stay on in the manor."

"*Excuse* me. Sorry I mentioned it." She popped a forkful of mousse in her mouth—definitely the best she'd ever tasted—peeked at Reggie and rolled her eyes. "It just sounded like that man in *Pride and Prejudice*—what was his name?" She winked.

"Mr. Collins?" Reggie grinned, then disappeared behind a voluminous monogrammed linen napkin.

"This is *not* a Jane Austen novel, and I am not some outdated country squire. I can't think of a more inappropriate comparison," Jeremy muttered through gritted teeth, staring down at them haughtily from the head of the table.

"Oh, take a damper," Reggie laughed. "She's teasing, for goodness' sakes."

"Actually you do a great lord of the manor." Sylvia tilted her head and eyed him.

"Oh, shut up," he growled, lips twitching. "How I stand the two of you all week is beyond me."

"Poor Jeremy. You must be a masochist wanting us here at the weekend, too."

"That," he countered triumphantly, "was Aunt Margaret's idea."

"Touché," she murmured, unable to restrain the growing gurgle of laughter.

"I really don't see why my owning Warmouth should upset you," Jeremy added lightly. "Why didn't you mention it when we were in the gallery earlier on?"

"I dunno." She gave an embarrassed shrug. It was impossible to explain that having her subordinate transform from the not-too-well-off aristocrat she'd imagined into a powerhouse had left her strangely intimidated. Not that she was about to admit that to Jeremy.

The dialogue and intimacy taking place at the opposite end of the long Georgian table were not lost on Clarissa who, scowling, made a desperate attempt to see past the well-polished sterling, glistening crystal and fellow guests to follow the conversation. Why were they laughing? Even from her perch in Siberia, Jeremy's hand posed on Sylvia's had not escaped her. *She* should be the one sitting at his side. Obviously, she decided huffily, she was going to have to do something about the American intruder at once. The fact that the woman was technically Jeremy's boss was a joke; clearly, her real agenda was to steal him away. This whole nonsense about some corporate theft was plainly fabricated, a pathetic excuse to lure him to her side and remain in London for an extended stay.

And Jeremy, damn him, looked as though he'd welcome the prospect with open arms. She'd never had any trouble managing his other little flirtations—she'd outlasted them all. But this one, she sensed uncomfortably, was different. She glanced at Lady Margaret, expounding on the advantages of horse or sheep's dung for her rose beds with Hugh Pevsner, and sighed. She'd get no help in that quarter, she reflected sourly. Lady Margaret was not a fan of hers, though after all the trouble Clarissa had taken to ingratiate herself, it was a mystery why not.

Clarissa tapped her manicured nails against the table's gleaming surface and took in every detail of Sylvia's being, from the top of her wretchedly lovely blond head to the waist of her ridiculously flimsy evening gown that in her opinion was far too revealing. Surprising that any of the men were eating at all. Her décolletage was disgustingly well cut, altogether too low and alluring, and made Clarissa wish she could snap her fingers and have Sylvia swept into a twister like Dorothy in the *Wizard of Oz* and carried back to Kansas or where it was she belonged.

She picked crossly at her mousse and tried not to show her feelings, smiled perfunctorily at the Major when he asked for the sugar. Why had Lady Margaret asked Sylvia down here in the first place? It was utterly preposterous. When *she* was mistress of Warmouth, Clarissa decided, she'd put an end to the old lady's interfering.

Hugh Pevsner turned in her direction and she plastered on a smile, sipped her claret and pretended to listen intently to his theories on haymaking, her mind bent on contriving ways to neutralize the transatlantic threat.

"Let's play billiards. Alfonso's dreadfully good," Arabella exclaimed as coffee was finally removed from the drawing room and the replete assembly sat around the fire enjoying after-dinner drinks.

"Good idea," Jeremy agreed, glancing at Alfonso. Sylvia smiled inwardly. He was weighing the man up, wondering if he was a worthwhile adversary. Clarissa looked over suspiciously from the sofa, where she and Hugh Pevsner were discussing the best manner in which to run an English estate.

"Off you go, children, and amuse yourselves," Lady Margaret said, rising. "I myself shall retire. Hugh, you're not a billiards man, I know. Never mind. You and Clarissa can stay here and chat. I'm sure she's as fascinated as I am by your theories on haymaking. Most interesting, if I may say so."

Very neat, Sylvia recognized, as Hugh flushed a bright crimson and fiddled with his bow tie, looking pleased. Clarissa mustered a weak smile that didn't reach her eyes.

After the Major and Lady Margaret took their leave and Hugh and Clarissa returned to their conversation, the rest of them headed across the hall to the billiards room. It was all walnut paneling, hunting prints and fine leather. A professional-size snooker table dominated the room. A single fly buzzed, caught in a pool of light glowing close to the green baize cloth.

Alfonso removed the jacket of his tux. Deftly he trapped the fly in his long olive fingers and smiled. There was something swift and deadly about the movement. All at once Sylvia pictured him in the ring, clad in bright satin, sword aiming the final blow to the bull's neck and wondered if Jeremy might have underestimated his opponent's skills at the snooker table.

"*Vamos?*" Alfonso sent Jeremy a challenging look.

He nodded and gestured to the cues stashed evenly against the wall, offering him and Reggie first choice. Sylvia and Arabella retired to the open window, leaned against the sill and sipped champagne.

As she'd expected, Alfonso turned out to be an ace.

Sylvia watched the three men thoughtfully. Jeremy stood back from the table chalking his cue, tux jacket discarded, eyes narrowed, a cigar clenched between his teeth, while Alfonso aimed at the ball with the satisfied air of one who knows he has the upper hand. It banked loudly in the pocket he'd selected.

"Ouch," Arabella whispered, giggling. "Jeremy considers himself rather a pro. Won't do his ego any harm to get hammered for once. I think I'll put on some music and liven up the atmosphere." Arabella jumped from her perch next to Sylvia on the window ledge and flipped open a panel in the wall. A state-of-the-art sound system lit up. She flicked a switch and the room resounded with salsa music.

"Damn, Ara, that music puts me off," Reggie complained, brows creased as he aimed.

As though by instinct, Alfonso dropped his cue on the floor, scooped Arabella into his arms and spun her about the room to the fast Latin rhythm.

Jeremy opened his mouth to protest that the game wasn't over, then with a shrug laid his own cue against the wall and reached for Sylvia, plucking her off the ledge, encircling her and sweeping her into the dance. Before she could catch her breath, they were spinning around the billiards table, bodies molded as they moved in perfect sync. Throwing back her head, she closed her eyes in sheer delight, near-drunk with a careless pleasure she'd never known, a sensation so intensely liberating she thought her legs would give way beneath her.

Next thing she knew, they were twirling out the French doors and onto the stone terrace that stretched toward the lawn. When the song came to an exuberant end, Jeremy stopped twirling and stood still. Holding her shoulders, he gazed through the twilight into her eyes. A new tune—a merengue this time—drifted out through the open doors. A light breeze caressing her cheek carried night scents, as though the garden had opened its arms and let go every secret.

Sylvia's pulse raced and she stepped back, dragged her fingers through her hair, and tried to regain her balance.

"Why do you work at Harcourts, Jeremy?" she blabbered breathlessly, taking refuge in words, afraid of what any more quiet might bring. She made a sweeping gesture that included the park, the house, the crescent moon reflected in the lake. "You don't need to. You have everything."

"Wrong." He stood next to her and stared out over the lawn. "I love Warmouth, would probably sacrifice a lot for it if it came to the crunch. But I need a life."

"Surely, owning something like this, you can have whatever kind of life you want."

"Wrong again. For all its treasures, Warmouth involves a tremendous amount of work and responsibility."

"But why sit in an office being paid a salary and taking flak from me?" She gave an embarrassed shrug.

"Maybe I like taking flak from you," he murmured.

"Yeah, right! Up until a few weeks ago you thought of me as a female version of King Kong."

"Now, we can't exaggerate," he admonished with mock seriousness. "I've never had any grievance about your looks. I always thought you were a very good-looking woman."

"Thanks. You're too generous."

"Not at all."

"That still doesn't answer my question about why you've stayed on at Harcourts. Look at Brad. When he realized all Strathaird was going to demand of him, he made a choice."

"Luckily for him, that choice included the woman he loved. I would have thought that you, of all people, would understand that I need to live my own life, in the way *I* choose. When my uncle died I knew I couldn't bury myself here. I wasn't ready to be swallowed up by the place."

"And do you think you ever will be? Ready, I mean, to welcome what fate has dealt you?" she asked curiously, understanding what he was saying better than he could possibly know. His last words revealed more about him than he probably cared to show.

And she liked what she saw.

Liked that he hadn't allowed destiny to dictate how he'd live his life. Liked that somehow he managed responsibilities as huge as Warmouth, *and* Harcourts, *and* his private life, and seemed to have them all smoothly on track.

"Actually, Warmouth's run as a corporation, which helps considerably," he remarked, reaching into his pocket for a new cigar. "I have a management team that runs the place, a competent house staff, and have found ways to write off a lot of expenses in taxes." He flicked his lighter, protecting the flame with his palm. "I know that sounds crass, and probably a number of people—including Clarissa—think I'm a traitor to my class for doing things in this manner. But frankly, it's the only way it'll work."

"But what about all that personal contact with the tenants? All the things Brad got landed with at Strathaird? Don't they expect that from you here, too?"

"Partly. But things are run a bit differently in Sussex. And I'm terribly lucky to have Aunt Margaret. She spends most of her time down here and has carried on with the lady of the manor duties, so to speak."

"But won't you have to take them on one day?"

"I suppose someday I will. But not yet. If I—" *If*

If offer card is missing write to: The Best of the Best, 3010 Walden Ave., P.O. Box 1867, Buffalo NY 14240-1867

NO POSTAGE
NECESSARY
IF MAILED
IN THE
UNITED STATES

BUSINESS REPLY MAIL
FIRST-CLASS MAIL   PERMIT NO. 717-003   BUFFALO, NY

POSTAGE WILL BE PAID BY ADDRESSEE

THE BEST OF THE BEST
3010 WALDEN AVE
PO BOX 1867
BUFFALO NY 14240-9952

MIRA® BOOKS,

The Best of the Best™

The Brightest Stars in Fiction, presents

Superb collector's editions of the very best books by some of today's best-known authors!

2 FREE BOOKS

and a

FREE GIFT!

YES! I have scratched off the gold star to reveal my prize. Please send me the 2 FREE *"The Best of the Best"* books and FREE gift for which I qualify. I understand that I am under no obligation to purchase anything further, as explained on the back of this card.

▲ *Scratch off the gold star to reveal your prize!*

385 MDL DRST   185 MDL DRSP

FIRST NAME	LAST NAME

ADDRESS

APT.#	CITY

STATE/PROV.	ZIP/POSTAL CODE

Visit us online at
www.mirabooks.com

DETACH AND MAIL CARD TODAY!

® and ™ are trademarks of Harlequin Enterprises Limited ©2002 MIRA BOOKS

I were married to the right woman, things would be very different, he'd been about to say.

They were standing a foot apart at the top of the shallow stone steps leading down to the lawn. Sylvia could distinguish neatly trimmed topiary hedges in the shadows and wondered what lay beyond. Flower beds filled with hollyhocks and delphiniums bordering well-tended gravel paths, she imagined. When Jeremy's arm slipped lightly about her shoulders she didn't pull away, and experienced the same rush of desire she had in Clachnabrochan. For a moment she forgot where they were, that Clarissa was in the drawing room next door, and all the good reasons that made it foolish to allow anything to transpire between them. On an impulse she turned and lifted her face to his. It had to happen, she realized, closing her eyes. Nothing could stop it. It was crazy and made no sense, but as his arms tightened around her she knew the one thing they both longed for was the touch of one another's lips.

His mouth came down on hers, hard and fast, a stunning confirmation of all she'd refused to acknowledge. His arms slid around her waist and hers about his neck. She could feel the hard length of his body pressed to her, the undisguised desire, hot and restless as her own. She dragged her fingers through his thick hair, moaned softly as his tongue played with hers, and shafts of unadulterated pleasure shivered through her. When his hand slipped to her breast she gasped as his thumb grazed gently through the flimsy evening gown, leaving her limp with longing.

Then the soft strains of music floating from inside the billiards room came to an abrupt halt.

"What on earth is going on?" Clarissa stood high-lighted in the casement, holding back the curtain like a sergeant major on a surprise inspection of her troops. She peered suspiciously into the darkness, Hugh Pevsner hovering next to her.

Jeremy stepped back and dragged his hand through his hair. He'd forgotten about Clarissa.

"Is that you, darling?" she inquired.

"Yes," he said, an edge to his voice.

"What a rotten thing to do," Arabella exclaimed crossly in the background. Then she appeared next to Clarissa, arms akimbo. "How dare you barge in here and spoil everything?"

"*Calma, niña,*" Alfonso murmured soothingly be-hind her, apparently used to dealing with fiery tempers.

"Ah! Still talking shop, I suppose. Really Jeremy, you should give poor Sylvia a rest," Clarissa contin-ued, ignoring Arabella. Taking charge, she stepped into the pool of light shed by the wrought-iron lan-terns, and held out her hand. "Now, come with me, Sylvia," she said in the tone of a headmistress dic-tating to a rebellious group of fifth-graders, "and I'll make sure you have everything you need for the night."

Still flustered, Sylvia walked into the light, catch-ing the quick angry look that Arabella exchanged with her brother. It read: who the hell does she think she is and why don't you bloody well do something about it?

"You needn't bother about me, Clarissa."

"Are you sure?" Clarissa's solicitous tone was at odds with her glittering anger.

"Everything's perfect, thank you." Sylvia pulled herself together, smiled graciously and avoided Jeremy's eyes. "I think I'll say good-night now. It's been a long day."

Jeremy stepped up behind her, laying a light hand on her arm. "See you in the morning then...and thanks for the dance."

She glanced at him and flushed, and her pulse missed a beat. Why did he have to look at her in just that way?

"Don't bother to rush down in the morning," Arabella said, throwing Clarissa another challenging glance. "We all wander in to breakfast whenever we feel like it." Then she leaned over and dropped a peck on Sylvia's cheek. "Good night. Sorry about the obnoxious interruption," she said, loud enough for her adversary to hear.

Not knowing what to answer, Sylvia made a hasty retreat back through the billiards room, uncomfortably aware of Clarissa's small gray eyes drilling holes into her back.

12

Once he'd passed Fort Lauderdale, the sedate driving on I-95 quickly deteriorated. Cadillacs and lumbering Suburbans gave way to swerving missiles, weaving their way in and out of lanes. Blaring hip-hop and merengue music pounded from boosted speakers of passing vehicles, making his car reverberate despite the tightly closed windows and the air-conditioning on full blast.

As Thackeray approached Miami, the traffic slowed to an impatient tail-on-tail dribble. His only satisfaction was that the opposite lane had come to a complete standstill. He glanced as the gold-chained driver of an orange Camaro squeezed beside him, an inch clear of the flashy bumper of a wide four-wheel-drive blocking his view. He could just distinguish the high-rise buildings of downtown, the sun a red fiery ball lingering to the west over Coral Gables.

Sending a dirty glance at his neighbor, jerking in rhythmic oblivion to the blasting merengue, Thackeray leaned forward and turned on the radio. After flipping through several Latin stations, where whiny voices gabbled in fast Cuban Spanish, he found a station he liked and with another forbidding glance at the orange Camaro turned it up loud. Not that he disliked the Latin mambos—the hot sizzle and fast-paced nights at the clubs on South Beach suited him fine. But right now he was pissed. That idiot he'd hired was a fucking moron. Thackeray decided he'd better take care of business himself. At least this way he'd meet the men on the job—Hernandez, whom he already knew, and Rico—personally. He could not afford to mess up.

What bothered him, too, was that after everything Don Murphy had revealed during their long exchange at Smokey's Hole, he'd have expected Sylvia to show signs of crumbling by now. It just didn't make sense that a woman with all her baggage could stand the threat of exposure. And yet she had; in fact, she'd engineered that fucking sale that had Marchand's books—at least, the ones he showed the auditors—bleeding red. Almost two weeks had gone by, but she'd made no effort to communicate with him. That left him antsy. She had to know he was the mastermind behind the stolen designs, had to guess he had leverage over her. So what the hell was the bitch made of? Fucking steel?

Maybe she was testing him, seeing how much he knew. He let out a short harsh laugh and watched the Camaro try to squeeze into his lane. She'd find out soon enough, he thought grimly, and then he'd own her.

At that moment the traffic began moving faster. The Camaro revved its engine and burst ahead of him, a cloud of pollution emanating from the rickety exhaust pipe. God, it pissed him off that he'd had to come down here himself. It was all Sylvia's fault and all the more reason for the bitch to pay, he muttered, pressing his foot on the accelerator. He glanced at the time. At this rate he should be at the Delano on Collins Avenue in about forty minutes. The thought of a drink in the trendy art deco bar made his mouth water. He grinned, leaned back and relaxed. He was meeting someone who had a special package for him, and he would very much enjoy the delivery.

As the cars shot past him he wondered if Sylvia would still feel like playing hardball once she got his little gift? He doubted it. A slow evil smirk covered his face. His London source said she'd been there two full weeks and had faxed him a copy of her schedule; she'd be returning from her swanky country weekend, relaxed and renewed—the perfect time to welcome her back with an unexpected souvenir. Once she'd opened it and seen the contents, she'd know the game had changed. She'd feel real fear, sense for the first time all she stood to lose. And maybe, just maybe, she'd realize she should have accepted his generous offer after all. The thought of her sheer panic gave him a hard-on. Too bad his first offer wasn't on the table anymore—at least, not unless she groveled. His eyes narrowed and the grin broadened.

Time to show the bitch just who was in charge.

Sylvia woke up refreshed and lay for a while, basking lazily in the huge four-poster bed of her palatial room at Warmouth, pretending nothing existed but the scent of lavender sheets and the cooing of doves from under the ancient eaves overshadowing her window.

Soft rays of early-morning sun bathed the bed drapes, playing on the satin bedspread.

Sylvia let out a warm, contented sigh. A dog barked somewhere in the depths of the house, and the putter of a lawn mower drifted through the open window. Tranquillity such as she'd rarely experienced permeated the room.

She could get used to this, she reflected, sitting up and stretching. She hopped out of bed, thinking back to the previous evening and how it had ended, and grimaced. Clarissa's sudden arrival was perhaps for the best, she reflected. Jeremy was turning out to be very different from the man she'd imagined. It was strange to have found so much common ground after dedicating such a considerable amount of time to thwarting him. And being thwarted, she reminded herself, stretching again at the long window casement and staring out over the park. What must it be like to grow up amidst so much wealth, knowing that everything, even your most outlandish wishes, were within reach? Did one become easily bored? she wondered, lips breaking into a delighted smile at the perfection of the manicured green lawns.

Did Jeremy wake up each morning and experience a similar joy? Or did he just look at the white and magenta hydrangeas contrasting with the emerald grass and think of garden maintenance? Had Arabella had a hand in designing the carefully trimmed topiary hedges she'd glimpsed in last night's shadows? Or did her eyes, too, glaze over the garden, knowing its every bed? Maybe they took the greenery for granted and didn't bother to think about them at all.

Sylvia sighed and stared down at the flower beds

overflowing with very English flowers whose names she didn't know, but whose scent, mixed with raw damp earth, drifted up as she lifted her face toward the sun.

A light haze lurked over the lake, where a sedate duck, followed by a trail of motley ducklings, went about her business. Several white butterflies announced heat later in the day.

She inhaled deeply, stretched her arms above her head, then stopped in midaction. "This is unreal," she murmured, watching a chestnut horse come cantering out of the woodland through the morning haze, caught in the mellow sunbeams hovering over the marshes. At the rider's command, the horse slowed to a dignified trot and drew closer. With a jolt Sylvia recognized the perfectly seated rider in beige britches and gleaming high boots.

Tempering the hot rush of heat that coursed through her, she lolled against the windowsill and watched Jeremy reach the gravel path bordering the lake. He works for you, she reminded herself. *You* are his boss, so stop drooling.

With a gusty sigh she forced her eyes away from the pleasant sight of him dismounting and headed toward the bathroom, last night's embrace still too vivid for comfort. Either she and Jeremy hit the sack ASAP and got this lust out of their systems, or she must police herself more closely. As it was, matters could go seriously wrong. She was far too attracted to him. As, she suspected with some amazement, he was to her.

Mutual attraction had advantages and disadvantages, but that didn't change the fact that, in the end, it either burned out or it burned you. And another thing, she reminded herself severely, enough of this mythologizing of Warmouth Manor, mooning over it as though it were a perfect little paradise. It was probably riddled with problems. *Take it for what it is—a splendid idyll—but realize you don't belong here and never will.*

With a firm shake of her blond head she reached for her toothbrush and, turning on the taps, told herself that she mustn't allow Jeremy to kiss her again, however much she wanted him to. The best thing to do was to find an opportunity for a rational, adult conversation in which she would lay forth all the facts. The thought appealed, and as she rinsed her mouth out she expanded upon it. She would point out the obvious attraction that existed between them, she decided, washing her face, and then explain all the very valid reasons why it was impossible to continue the kind of behavior they'd displayed on the two occasions they'd been alone in proximity. But even as she worked the Mason Pierson brush through her hair, the feel of his lips lingered disturbingly and she sighed.

It would take a lot of convincing, beginning with herself.

Lady Margaret had told her breakfast was served from 7:00 a.m. onward and Arabella had urged her not to rush. Sylvia took her at her word. It was nine-thirty by the time she ventured downstairs and entered the breakfast room. There she found Jeremy's sister, draped in a diaphanous silk kimono, a glossy magazine spread next to her on the embroidered white tablecloth, and a cup of tea balanced daintily in her long tapered fingers. She might have walked straight out of *Gosford Park.*

"Hello!" Arabella looked up and smiled invitingly. "You must be famished. Sorry about the breakup of the party last night. Clarissa can be such an absolute bitch. I couldn't believe she had the nerve to barge in like that!"

"That's fine."

"I'll bet she thinks Jeremy'll marry her one day and that then she'll be able to order us all around. Serve her right when he doesn't. She clings to him like a leech. Anybody else would have got the message aeons ago. But not her." She paused dramatically and rolled her eyes. "Could you possibly imagine having her as a sister-in-law?" She made an impressive grimace and dropped the cup in the saucer with a shudder. "The mere thought sends shivers up my spine."

Sylvia sat down with a noncommittal murmur. Judging by Arabella's and Lady Margaret's comments the previous evening, Clarissa's ratings definitely needed a boost if she planned to stay in the running.

"I'm so glad we've finally met," Arabella continued, passing down the coffeepot, barely masking her curiosity. "Jeremy made you sound perfectly horrid, which of course meant you'd be wonderful—and you are. But *please* don't do everything he says or let him boss you about," she begged, "or he'll become more odious than he already is. Not that I don't adore him," she added, gesturing for Sylvia to take toast from the small silver rack perched invitingly among the floral-patterned English porcelain, silver butter dishes, crystal sugar bowls and homemade jams that littered the table. A woven silver breadbasket piled high with a variety of delicious-smelling rolls stood in the center.

Amused at Arabella's assessment of her brother, Sylvia reached for the toast.

Arabella observed her critically. "Those trousers and that shirt you're wearing look fantastic. Not that they would suit me, of course—I look better in droopy things. Still, it must be nice to look terribly chic the whole time, *and* be dreadfully intelligent and successful to boot," she said wistfully.

"Hey, don't let's get carried away," Sylvia answered, laughing as she placed a crisp linen napkin on her knee and wondering what on earth *she* had that Arabella could possibly want. After all, the woman had everything she'd ever need poured into her lap since the day she was born.

"I'm not getting carried away. But I mean, look at you." Jeremy's sister gestured as though what she was saying was so obvious a small child could recognize it. "You could be a model or something like that, but I know—because Jer's told me—just how smart you are," she said smugly. "It must be dreadfully nice to be *so* perfect." She let out a breezy sigh and slowly spread butter onto half a roll.

The idea that she could be anybody's paradigm was so ridiculous that for a moment Sylvia remained speechless. Then, realizing Arabella knew nothing of her disastrous past and saw only what was before her, she decided to take the comment in the spirit it was offered and smothered a laugh. "I thought you said your brother found me…what was it?'' She raised an eyebrow at Arabella and reached for the jam.

''Oh, that was ages ago,'' Arabella said dismissively, waving long delicate fingers. ''Before you came over. Milk?'' she inquired graciously.

''Please.'' Sylvia extended her cup for Arabella to pour.

''Eggs and all that are on the sideboard,'' she said with a grin, ''but I'll bet you don't eat any.''

''Hey, you're talking to a Southern girl—a good breakfast is one of the things we hold as our birthright. Though in general I do try to stay low on cholesterol.''

''You mean you're not worried about putting on weight?''

''That, too,'' Sylvia conceded, eyeing her roll with a sudden qualm. ''But I try to find a healthy balance.''

''Ah! You see? Another example of your brilliance. I, on the other hand, eat whatever I feel like and damn the consequences. Of course, I used to be anorexic. I had to spend three months in a clinic.''

Sylvia stared down at her hands, stunned that Arabella could share such a secret so readily. She herself would face down wild horses before allowing light on her own darkest truths. Still, Arabella wouldn't have mentioned such a thing without expecting a response, would she? It was becoming abundantly clear why this beautiful, fragile woman caused Jeremy such considerable concern.

Sylvia cast about, trying to find the right words. ''That can't have been much fun,'' she said finally, hoping she'd hit the correct note as she spread strawberry jam on whole-grain toast and wondered why it was that wealth, titles and anorexia seemed to go hand in hand. "If you don't mind my asking, what do you think drove you to it?"

"What, the anorexia?"

"Yeah."

"Gosh, I don't know. Life in general, I suppose. I was bored and dreadfully depressed, popped too many pills, that sort of thing. My boyfriend turned out to be a complete sleazeball." She shrugged. "I suppose in a way it was something to do. Something I could be good at."

Or maybe a plea for some much-needed attention? Sylvia wondered sadly, suddenly seeing Arabella in a new light. Beneath that stunning, sophisticated front, there lay a waiflike quality and something undefinably vulnerable. But she didn't get the impression the girl was spineless. In fact, based on last night's performance, quite the opposite. So what was wrong? What caused someone to react in the manner she was describing? Could it be the result of finding herself adrift in society without much of a rudder?

"Do you study?" she asked, remembering Lady Margaret's remark the other day in the office and deciding it might be time to steer the conversation onto less emotional ground.

"Not really. I've done this and that, taken lots of courses. Let's see," she said, ticking them off on her fingers, "interior decorating, batik, fine arts and Cordon Bleu cooking. That sort of thing."

"Cool. What can you make?" Sylvia asked, hoping to elicit some enthusiasm.

"Dinner reservations," Arabella muttered gloomily. "I seem to spend most of my time ringing up restaurants, clubs and hairdressers for my friends who are in town and need a hand to get into the right places. Usually they're not members and I am. Some of my girlfriends have a terrible time deciding what to buy for their latest house or flat or villa in St. Barthes, so I make up their minds for them.'' She shrugged. ''Nobody seems to have a clue what they really want. I'm a pro at figuring that out—it's just myself I have problems with.''

Sylvia stared across the table, an idea burgeoning. She'd be willing to bet top dollar the girl's main problem was a lack of direction. It impressed her that Arabella seemed quite confident in advising others how to decorate their home, something she herself would never undertake without the guidance of a top decorator.

She leaned back in the Chippendale chair, frowning. ''Explain this better. You give advice. You tell people where they should eat and arrange it for them, then you tell them what they should be buying?'' Arabella nodded happily. ''And you know what they need? You don't get scared that you're directing them wrong?''

''No, of course not. It's usually perfectly plain what they should be getting. They just don't seem to see it like I do.'' She shrugged. ''Odd, isn't it? If I ever have a *really* grown-up home myself, I'd know *exactly* how I'd want to decorate it.''

''You mean you wouldn't hire a decorator?''

''Good God, no. It wouldn't be my own place anymore.''

''Incredible!'' Sylvia shook her head in amazement. ''I'm afraid I'm just like your friends. I wouldn't know where to start decorating an apartment, much less a house. Sounds like you've got talent.''

"Not really, I just like to make places look nice, find odds and ends that give character. For example, when I tackled this place for Jeremy, it was so easy. There was so much great stuff here already, and finding new things was a terrific adventure.''

"You're the one who decorated Warmouth?'' Sylvia tried to keep her jaw from dropping. "But this place is so huge, and everything about it is magnificent. There's not a thing I'd change.''

Arabella grinned broadly. "Well, thank you kindly. And do tell Jer that you approve, won't you? Occasionally he needs to be reminded that I'm not a *complete* fribble— I saved him a boatload of money and a ton of time.''

Sylvia straightened in her chair, her mind running down a new track. "Tell me honestly, please, what you think of what we've done at Harcourts. I'd really welcome your opinion.''

Arabella leaned forward, her voice excited. "I love your new line, truly. It's got lots of super items, and all the accessories give it a ton of flexibility. Jeremy's put together a great design team and, frankly, they've pulled Harcourts out of the artistic rut it started to hit a few years back.''

"I agree, he's done a tremendous job turning things around.'' She studied Arabella intently, deciding it was time to voice the idea that had taken hold as the girl was talking. "You know, sounds to me like you could start a business of your own.''

"Me? A business?" Arabella threw back her head and gurgled.

"Why not?"

"Doing what? Making reservations and telling people what they need to stick on their coffee tables? I don't think so." She brandished the butter knife in a dismissive gesture reminiscent of Jeremy.

"I wouldn't be so quick to drop the idea. Your friends seem happy enough to take your advice for free, don't they?"

"I know, but that's different."

"What's so different?"

"Well—" Arabella cocked her head and dangled a piece of toast as she thought the matter over "—if I make a mistake it doesn't matter because they're friends. But if they were paying me, well…I don't know—" She cut off, popped the toast in her mouth and concentrated on folding her napkin with fanatical precision.

"Maybe that's just lack of confidence," Sylvia insisted. "All it takes is the courage to try. You like what you're doing and people are coming back for more, aren't they?" Suddenly it became important to convince Arabella to delve into the potential she sensed lay just below the surface.

"Ye-es," Arabella bit her lip. "Actually, there's this friend of a friend who's sent me *all* her friends and the list does keep getting longer." A tentative glint hovered as what had seemed an impossibility seconds earlier, began to take shape.

Sylvia watched Arabella lay her cup carefully down in the saucer. The lip-biting transformed into a speculative smile. Her cautious eyes glistened with a new hope, replacing the self-doubt of moments earlier.

"Are you serious, Sylvia?" she asked carefully. "Do you really think an idea like this could work? You're not just trying to be nice, are you? I don't think I could bear it if..." Tears welled and her voice trailed off.

Sylvia wanted to reach out and reassure. Instead, she spread the jam matter-of-factly and pretended she hadn't noticed. "Let's go through a checklist and see."

"All right." Arabella sniffed, rubbed her nose with a shriveled Kleenex and paid close attention.

"One—a number of people of your acquaintance have asked you to perform certain services for them out of friendship, right?"

"Right." Arabella folded her hands neatly on the table before her and listened attentively.

"They are pleased with what you've done for them and have returned for more. Correct?"

"Right."

"They've even recommended you to their friends, who in turn have sent you more potential clients."

"Right." A slow smile hovered around the girl's full mouth.

"Even your stubborn, perfectionist brother gave you free rein with his home."

She answered with a wide grin.

"So what are you waiting for?"

"I don't know," she exclaimed. "You make it sound so simple, so...but it's *me* were talking about. Anything I've ever done has been half-assed. Jeremy can tell you," she added dolefully.

"That may very well be true. In the past. But how about rewriting the script? Who says you have to go on doing things in a half-assed manner?" she queried, gauging Arabella's reaction. "You have all the right connections and potential clients are lining up. You could create a company of your own and charge, let's say, a nominal yearly fee. It would be a kind of super-deluxe concierge service, but mostly for women and their needs."

"My God!" Arabella whispered, gripping the tablecloth. "It's absolutely, totally and utterly brilliant!" she squeaked, letting out a long breath. "But a business— I don't know the first thing about running a business, I..." She picked up her knife, then twiddled it nervously as a picture formed in her mind. She could already envisage the office, the touches, who she would take where, what shops and boutiques she would contact. At the sound of the door opening she whirled around and, seeing her brother enter, pounced. "Jer!" she exclaimed. "Listen to this *marvellous* plan Sylvia's come up with. I believe it might actually work. Oh God." She wrung her hands in anguished excitement. Jeremy, still clad in his riding clothes, turned an inquiring brow toward Sylvia and walked across the room.

"Good morning," he said, dropping his riding crop on a chair before sitting down between the two women. The sight of his sister and Sylvia seated at the breakfast table framed by the bay window, sun glinting through the floral blinds behind them, one so blond and bold, the other so burnished and ethereal had, for a moment, taken his breath away.

"Listen, Jer, you simply must pay attention." Arabella leaned over and clasped his hand. "Sylvia thinks I should start a business."

"A business?" He tilted his head doubtfully and reached for the rolls.

"Don't sound so skeptical." She withdrew her hand, offended. "Why on earth not?"

"For one thing, you've no skills," he replied bluntly. "And secondly, you're not qualified."

"What a beastly thing to say!" She stared at him down her small straight nose, mustering dignity, then sought support. "Go on, Sylvia. *You* tell him."

"Well," Sylvia murmured, already regretting her bright idea and wishing she'd kept her mouth shut. "It merely struck me that if Arabella spends the better part of her time calling up restaurants, clubs, visiting decorators and advising people what they should buy out of friendship, perhaps she might consider putting those same skills and contacts to good use." She glanced at him apologetically.

"You see?" Arabella pounced again. "It's brilliant, absolutely fucking brilliant. But trust you to be negative!"

"I'm not being negative. I'm being realistic. Let's face it, Ara, your track record isn't exactly steady—"

"Oh, do shut up! What about here? The house? Sylvia, don't listen to him, he's being a jerk. God, I don't know how you stand him," she added with a look fit to wither an angry rattlesnake. "I'd have given him the sack ages ago." She turned her back on her brother. "Anyway, women must stick together. You could be my partner, Sylvia, we could—"

Ignoring the onslaught of insults, Jeremy buttered his roll thoughtfully. Despite her grand words, Arabella seemed to be sincerely interested in his reaction. Even now she was peering up at him through her lashes, hoping he didn't notice.

"Well?" she said finally, unable to disguise her excitement. "Isn't it brilliant? *Please,* Jer," she begged, changing tactics, "don't just sit there, say something!" She nudged his arm impatiently.

"I didn't say it was a bad idea," he answered warily, "but—"

"There. I knew it. You're the best brother on the planet!" Nearly sending Lady Margaret's favorite Wedgwood flying, Arabella leaned across the table and embraced him.

"Ara, look what you've done to my shirt, damn it." Jeremy gave the butter and jam splattered on his shirtfront a couple of ineffectual dabs and sighed.

"Sorry." She smiled penitently and dipped her napkin into the hot-water jug.

"I hope you don't feel I've been interfering in an area that's none of my business," Sylvia murmured.

"Not at all." His smile made her draw in her breath. "It might be the very thing. Pretty nifty of you to come up with an idea like this," he added, trying to disguise how impressed he was. In the brief moments she'd spent with Arabella, Sylvia had summed her up better than her own family and zeroed in on her true potential.

"You know, there's no reason why we couldn't brainstorm this idea with Reggie and the crew," Sylvia said, encouraged by his reaction. "Maybe we could incorporate Arabella into the Harcourts group, create an international personalized service for our VIP clients," she added, the idea growing as she spoke. "You could direct the creative, hands-on part," she stated, meeting the girl's popping eyes full on, "and we could find someone to take care of the business side."

"Did I hear my name mentioned?" Reggie entered through the French doors, balding head glistening.

"Oh, Reggie!" Arabella exclaimed. "Just the man we need." She jumped up, grabbed his hand and dragged him to the table.

"What's all this about?" he asked, bewildered. "Aren't you supposed to be out there entertaining the matador? I saw him practicing his golf swing on the lawn a few minutes ago. Looked rather down at the mouth."

"Never mind him." She waved a dismissive hand. "We have far more important matters to discuss." Arabella plunked Reggie into a chair on Sylvia's left.

"I suppose if the man can handle a bull—"

"Oh, shut up, Reg, forget Alfonso and listen."

"How can I forget him when he keeps trying to ask me questions and I don't understand a bloody word the man's saying? He should learn to speak the king's English if he plans to stick around here."

"Reggie, don't try my patience any further," Arabella pronounced in a tone so similar to Lady Margaret's that both Sylvia and Jeremy smothered laughter. "Sylvia's come up with the most *brilliant* notion. We're all going to be partners and make tons of lolly and—"

"Hey, wait a minute," Jeremy raised a forestalling hand. "Slow down, we've barely begun thinking about it, let alone made any concrete plans."

"Do stop being a wet blanket, Jer," Arabella admonished, slipping onto the Hepplewhite chair next to Reggie and plying him determinedly with toast, butter and jam. "Would you like eggs, Reggie darling?" She batted her lashes. "I'll get you bacon, *and* sausage, too, if you like?" She smiled sweetly, jumped up and headed for the sideboard. "The works?"

"Sounds like I may need them," he muttered, letting out a resigned sigh. "Would somebody kindly explain what this is all about?"

"I'll take all your VIP clients to shop and choose Harcourts designs and wine, and dine them when they come to town. It was Sylvia's idea. Isn't it clever?" Arabella dropped an extra slice of crisp dark bacon temptingly next to the eggs.

"Now, Ara, for goodness' sake, calm down," Jeremy spoke deliberately. "It's still just an idea." He sent Sylvia an uneasy glance. "I don't want you to feel in any way obliged," he said, lowering his voice. "Ara can get easily carried away."

"Oh, Jer, stop *spoiling* everything." Arabella turned on him, eggs sliding dangerously close to Reggie's shoulder. "It'll be marvelous. Isn't it a wonderful idea, Reggie?"

"Don't know. Still haven't clicked what it's all about. Refuse to think about it before I've eaten." He shifted so she could lay the plate down in front of him.

"What shall we call it?" Arabella placed the overflowing plate down askew, ignored his last comment and clasped her hands over her small breast dreamily.

Jeremy raised a rueful eyebrow at Sylvia. "You're

the one who set this ball rolling, Syl. It's your call.'' He grinned across the table.

''I think it could work,'' she answered slowly. ''I have the feeling she could do it. In fact, I'm almost certain of it. It strikes me she's never had a chance to find her feet.'' Sylvia smiled reassuringly. ''I wouldn't have let her get her hopes up unless I really thought the idea was workable, you know.''

He'd called her Syl again, albeit unwittingly, but it had popped out as naturally as— She pulled herself up sharply and concentrated. ''We'll need to toss some numbers around, but if they're feasible, there's no reason why Arabella's business shouldn't be an asset for Harcourts,'' she finished reasonably.

''Oh, Sylvia, darling—*thank* you.'' Arabella swooped down and embraced her in a scented hug.

Clarissa chose that precise moment to open the dining-room door. She stood taking in the scene, recognizing at once that things were going horribly wrong. This wasn't at all how she'd imagined things. Arabella and Sylvia were embracing in a most inappropriate manner, Jeremy was grinning from ear to ear like a bloody Cheshire cat, and Reggie Rathbone, of all people, was steadily plying himself with large amounts of crisp bacon, fried egg and sausage.

''Have I missed something?'' she asked, forcing a smile that barely disguised her anger.

''No,'' they answered in unison.

The room went silent, the exuberance of moments earlier fading before her formidable glare.

''Dearest Clarissa, you had to come in now and spoil it, didn't you?'' Arabella flounced crossly into

the nearest chair, pouting, while Clarissa stood transfixed and furious on the threshold, trying to make up
her mind whether to sail in majestically and ignore
the comment, or make a regal exit.

13

As she had every Monday morning for the better part of her adult life, Harriet Hunter alighted from the tube station at Green Park and made her way steadily down St. James's.

But today her steps lagged and as she turned the corner into St. James's Place a weary sigh escaped her. She fumbled in her ancient handbag for the heavy set of keys, inserting first the top one, then the lower, into the locks before turning the brass handle of the glossy black door. The polished plaque beside the door read Harcourts Enterprises U.K.

Heaving the door open, Harriet made her way across the dark entrance hall and switched on the lights, then climbed up the first flight of carpeted stairs—on principle she never took the lift—and let herself into the reception area of the main office.

Peering at the dial of the bulky mahogany grand-father clock that dominated the room, she satisfied herself that she'd made it to the minute. It was seven fifty-seven, precisely. This gave her just under an hour before Finch and the others turned up for work.

Hanging her shabby beige raincoat in the cupboard, Harriet peeked automatically into the bevelled-glass mirror and patted the strict bun, which she liked to think of as a *chignon,* approvingly. Not a wisp of hair had dared to wander. Her glasses sat perched halfway down what had developed, over the years, into a beaky nose. Harriet rarely indulged any personal feelings about her appearance, but today she took a closer look at herself and sighed. There had been a time when bright gray eyes and a blooming complexion had stared back at her from this very same mirror, when dreams and hopes had brightened her future.

Those days seemed a long, long time ago. Today she saw only bleakness, and a set of new, not-so-subtle creases furrowing deeper into her grooved cheeks.

Not that it made much difference at her age whether she had more wrinkles or less. Who cared what an old woman like herself looked like? Or anything else about her for that matter.

Muffling a sigh, she moved away and switched on the desk lamp. Indulgence and self-pity led nowhere. But today she felt more depressed than she had in a while. Her horse had lost at Goodwood and the phone call she'd been awaiting so desperately hadn't materialized. The kitchen ceiling of her little basement flat in Clapham had several leaks that the landlord claimed were her responsibility to repair. And there was no one, simply no one, she could talk to anymore, particularly about her present misgivings, which, despite her desire to ignore them, increasingly crept up on her.

She sat down wearily and closed her eyes, thinking

of the child in whom she'd invested so much of her love. Now it all seemed rather futile and unrewarding and distant. At the time when the problem had occurred, she'd been stimulated by a sense of purpose. She could help him, save him, do something worthwhile, despite the price to be paid or the doubts she carried. Now she felt empty and betrayed.

Her mind wandered and she thought of her old friends. Once there had been *real* friends, like Dexter Ward, who'd trusted and confided in her. All gone now. Only she remained. Her racing cronies were just that: cronies. To them she was Harriet, the funny old lady with the good tips, the quaint jokes and the eccentric hats. In the office she transformed into a severe, know-it-all exemplary figure, the bastion of Harcourts. How could she possibly admit to weakness, to needing anybody or anything, when *she* ran their lives?

It was unthinkable.

This realization brought her a certain measure of satisfaction. Without her they would all flounder. Major Whitehead depended on her for his every whim—why, even Sylvia Hansen, whom she secretly admired, had asked her advice on several occasions about what theater to attend and so on.

The rush of pride improved her mood considerably. She straightened her shoulders, pulled her moss-green cardigan closer about her and puttered through the dark hall to the kitchen where she turned on the old kettle with the frayed electric cord. Some idiot from the design department had implied that the appliance was a health hazard, that someone might be electrocuted and Harcourts sued for millions. Health hazard, indeed! What rubbish. These young people were forever throwing away perfectly good items and replacing them with newfangled fripperies that usually broke after a short period of use.

But she'd stood firm on the kettle issue. She'd be damned if she would permit one of those white plastic affairs into what she thought of as *her* kitchen. Like her, the kettle still had life in it. And all this superfluous replacing of perfectly good articles was the sort of unnecessary expense that broke companies in the long run, she reckoned, filling up the kettle at the kitchen sink.

With a despondent shake of disapproval she turned on the old radio that for years had sat in exactly the same position on the linoleum counter, next to the faded cake tin that had once sported a picture of Edinburgh Castle. She muttered, irritated, when a rap tune blared forth, instead of the BBC. Someone had been fiddling with the knob again. She twiddled the used button crossly back and forth until it settled in its customary spot, then glanced at the numerical clock that Major Whitehead had given Finch last Christmas. She had no time to waste. Finch would be here at eight fifty-six sharp, as was his manner. The bus dropped him at eight-fifty at Piccadilly Circus and it took him exactly six minutes to reach the office from the bus stop.

While the kettle hissed, she opened the cupboard door above the sink and removed a dented tin of Cadbury's chocolate fingers, carefully placing three biscuits on a china plate. Waiting patiently for the kettle to boil, she calculated the time difference between London and South America. It was still the middle of the night there, she reflected. But under the circumstances this might be the best time to ring. For a while she stared blindly at the steam wheezing out of the spout.

Then she blinked and picked up the blue china teapot. Methodically she preheated it, then, emptying out the hot water, added two precise teaspoons of Twinning's Earl Grey. When the kettle gave a shrill whistle she topped up the pot with boiling water, then placed it on a solid wooden tray with the cup, milk and biscuits. Carrying it toward the reception area, she swallowed hard. This wasn't going to be an easy task, however she chose to think about it.

A strident ring from the front doorbell made her jump. She nearly lost her balance as tea slurped. Hands trembling, she laid the tray nervously on her desk. Hurrying across the faded Isfahan rug, she dabbed ineffectually at the damp stain on her blouse and spoke into the intercom.

"Who is it?" she demanded in a querulous voice that sounded as unsteady as she felt. No one had any business disturbing her before opening hours. Particularly not today.

"UPS, madam, special delivery."

For a moment Harriet Hunter remained completely silent. Then, bracing herself, she pressed the button and let the messenger in.

At nine o'clock sharp Sylvia breezed into the office, still basking in a glow of weekend cheer.

"Good morning, Miss Hansen."

"Good morning," she called as she passed through the reception area where Miss Hunter sat, perched behind the large mahogany desk, white-veined hands magnified by the muted pool of light peeking stealthily from beneath a green lamp shade. She reminded Sylvia of a medieval scribe. How, Sylvia wondered, was she able to see what she was doing? A good set of fluorescents or perhaps just lightening up the color scheme would do the job nicely, but she knew better than to comment. It was a waste of time.

Smiling, she entered her office, dropped her briefcase next to the desk and slipped into her chair. Even the dim office seemed different. Not so dingy or old any longer, rather friendly and familiar, instead; a place she was getting used to and might even regret leaving. A persistent sunbeam had even sneaked past the heavy gray drapes, brightening the place up considerably.

Sylvia leaned back and let out a contented sigh. Except for Clarissa's relentless barbs, which had become less restrained as the weekend progressed, the time had flown delightfully. Arabella, full of professional zeal, had sent Alfonso packing to the local golf course with a reluctant Reggie, and dug into her laptop.

On Sunday, Lady Margaret had insisted Sylvia join the rest of the party in the family pew at church. Sylvia had sung hymns, listened to a sermon on "loving one's enemy"—which she did not plan to take into account when dealing with Thackeray—and had been formally introduced to the sparse-haired, bespectacled vicar and his jolly rotund wife, who joined them for sherry and Sunday roast at the manor. It was as English as could be, yet it hadn't driven her nuts. And although there were no more moments spent alone,

Jeremy was constantly at her side, cracking jokes, making her laugh, seeing to her every whim and acting the perfect host.

After her initial moment of overwhelmed wonder, she'd relaxed and enjoyed herself. Not for a moment had she felt left out or uncomfortable. And, to Clarissa's obvious regret and Jeremy's insistence, she'd driven back to town in the comfort of Reggie's Aston Martin, instead of the cramped back seat of the Jag.

Things were looking up, she decided, flipping on her laptop to check her e-mail. Even Thackeray and the stolen design collection seemed less daunting after days spent in such agreeable surroundings. This was her first taste of an English country house weekend and, to her own amazement, she'd enjoyed every minute of it.

She'd used some of the downtime to sort out her thoughts regarding Harcourts and the problems they were facing, even tried to broach the subject to Jeremy. But he'd refused to talk to about it, saying that once they began, the weekend would end up in a brainstorming session, instead of a much-needed rest. And he'd been right again. It had allowed her the distance she'd required to get a game plan going, to rally her thoughts and her brainpower. She'd let go the unease that she'd sensed of late, able now to face the problem head-on. No way would she let a bully like Thackeray intimidate her. And, if necessary, she planned to confront him.

Let him come. Let him try his tricks and see what lay in store for him. Maybe she had a few tricks up her own sleeve. Her face set in a determined expression, Sylvia donned her glasses and set to work, all the negativity and doubt of the previous week behind her. Thackeray, she reflected grimly, making a quick note to have Aaron track down all his deals dating back five years, was in for a major surprise if he didn't back down. He had never been charged or indicted, but she'd heard rumors. It was certainly worth investigating his past. If he wanted to play hardball, then they could play hardball, too.

A knock sounded on the door.

"Come in," she called, already logged on to her e-mail.

The door opened and she looked up. Miss Hunter stood in the doorway, holding a package.

"This arrived earlier. A United Parcel Services delivery."

"Thanks. Just put it on the table over there. I'll get to it in a minute." It took her several seconds to realize Miss Hunter was referring to UPS.

"Lord Warmouth would like to see you in his office immediately."

"Fine. Tell him I'll be right over." She threw Miss Hunter a quick smile.

"He looked worried," Miss Hunter confided, clasping her hands over her corseted breast. "Mr. Rathbone is already with him."

"Very well." She sighed and logged off, aware that once Miss Hunter had decided on pursuing her she would have no peace until she went. Sylvia rose, stared for a moment at the package on the coffee table and hesitated. Then, realizing it must be something from New York, she dismissed the idea of opening it immediately and followed Miss Hunter's dipping tweed skirt out the door.

"What's up?" she asked, entering Jeremy's office, both men's expressions leaving her with a sharp sense of foreboding.

"I got an e-mail and a phone call from Colombia," Reggie said, clearing his throat.

"And?" She changed gears and moved quickly toward the chair next to him and sat down.

"Bernardo's been kidnapped," Jeremy announced grimly.

"No! That's impossible." She gave a horrified gasp.

"Not in Colombia it isn't." He was standing by the window, his expression grim.

Sylvia sank back in the chair. "But how? When did this happen?"

"Sometime late last night, I believe."

"Oh my God, you don't think that bastard Thackeray could have…" Her voice trailed off as multiple scenarios presented themselves.

"It did occur to me," Jeremy agreed slowly. "But quite honestly, I don't see the link. Even if the leak came out of one of the Colombian factories, presumably he would have *bought* the information. I can see no reason for him to dirty his hands in something of this nature. It doesn't make sense. Which makes me think the kidnapping is unrelated," he reassured her, mouth set in a forbidding line.

"What did they say happened? Who called?" she asked, aware that Jeremy seemed very much in control. "If Thackeray isn't the kidnapper, then who is?"

"Bernardo's brother called half an hour ago. Someone—they presumed terrorists—captured Bernardo as he was driving home from a dinner party at his mother's. They're waiting to know what the kidnapper's demands are."

"This is terrible," Sylvia muttered, controlling her distress.

"It is. I can't think who would want to kidnap one of our directors, which makes Bernardo's brother's theory all the more plausible."

"You're sure Thackeray couldn't be behind this?" Sylvia insisted, the same uneasiness of the past week overwhelming her once more.

"I doubt he'd get involved in anything of this nature. As you said, he wants to keep his reputation lily white. Arousing suspicions would be the last thing he'd need."

"True," she agreed. It made sense. "Not that I don't think he's past resorting to kidnapping, mind you."

"Agreed, but in this particular instance I don't see how it would suit his purpose." Jeremy's fingers drummed the back of a chair absently, eyes narrowed.

"We must remember too that kidnapping is an everyday occurrence in Colombia. Bernardo's brother didn't sound in the least surprised. Bloody daunting, if you ask me," Reggie murmured, his head shaking compassionately. "What a way to live."

"Poor Bernardo. Jeremy, we must do something immediately," she said, rallying. "Inform his family that we'll help at once," she added, horrified by the prospect of Bernardo, possibly gagged and blindfolded, and being hurt by a bunch of thugs.

"That's something we need to discuss very thoroughly," Jeremy said deliberately. His eyes held hers for a long moment.

"What do you mean?" She sat up straight and looked at him in surprise.

"That we mustn't be too hasty."

"What do you mean too hasty?" she retorted hotly. "He's our responsibility. We must offer help at once."

"Not necessarily."

"Jeremy, I don't understand." Sylvia rose, unbelieving. "Why wouldn't you want to help the man? It's ridiculous, inhumane."

"Hold on." Jeremy moved from the window and laid an appeasing hand on her arm. "*A*, we don't know if the kidnapping's company related, and *B*, we mustn't show our hand too soon or we'll do more harm than good. Reggie told Bernardo's brother to get back in touch as soon as the target has been established."

"God, it sounds so—" She could barely find the words to describe all she was feeling.

"There may be some tough decisions up ahead, and substantial costs involved," Jeremy continued in a measured tone, taking a step back and eyeing her.

"I don't care what it costs, we have to save the man's life," she said. "The decision is already made."

"Not so fast," he countered. "It's not quite that simple."

"Jeremy, I wish you'd stop talking in riddles and get to the point," Sylvia exclaimed, irritated. He wore that same studied expression as when he'd told her about the phone call the other day at Warmouth, and she wondered suddenly what he might be holding back.

"Do you know something I don't? Because it's plain enough to me, Jeremy. Maybe terms can be negotiated—as long as we don't risk Bernardo's life—but that's all."

"What you're not getting is that it may not be just Bernardo who's being held hostage," he replied dryly, "but Harcourts."

"Bernardo's is a part of Harcourts."

"Precisely. And if we give in, we may be opening the door to continual future harassment. In other words, this may require some strong action." His eyes bored into hers.

"And you think I'm not tough enough to stand up to these sons of bitches, don't you?" She moved to the fireplace and sent him a jeering, humorless smile over her shoulder.

"I didn't say that."

"You'd be surprised at the types I've had to deal with," she said. "Though I guess someone of your background would find that difficult to believe."

"You think so?" he said, shoulders squared, hands shoved into his suit pockets.

"For God's sake, Jeremy! This is no time to be quibbling. The man must be going through hell!" Right now, all she could picture was Clara, Bernardo's lovely young wife, and those three gorgeous dark-eyed children fearing for their father's life. "How can you be so unfeeling?" she cried, facing him. "This isn't about money. A man's life is at stake, not a fucking stock option."

"I wish you'd calm down and stop being hysterical."

"I'm not—" She loosened her fists, took a deep

breath and regained control. He was right. She must not let emotion override good sense. She must stay focused or she'd screw up. "Why don't we contact the police?" she said at last.

"That's out of the question."

"Why?"

"Because this is Colombia we're talking about, not the U.S. I'm very well aware of all your concerns," Jeremy said in a calmer tone, "but unless we deal with the kidnappers in the appropriate manner, there may be serious consequences for Harcourts."

"'Appropriate manner'? Do you have a British code for that, too?" she demanded, anger resurfacing at his apparent indifference. "What do you know about kidnappings and ransoms anyway? How would someone from your world have the first idea of how to go about negotiating with Colombian terrorists—" She broke off, hot with anger at the callous way in which he was treating the whole matter.

Reggie cleared his throat once more. "Don't mean to intrude, Sylvia, but if anyone can deal appropriately with this sort of situation, Jeremy's your man."

"Yeah, right," she sneered. "Hunting with hounds in a red coat—"

"Pink."

"Oh, shut up. Who gives a damn what color it is." She rounded on him.

"A hunting coat is referred to as pink, not red."

"Oh well, gee, thanks for enlightening my poor ignorant American mind. Like I really give a damn right now! At this very moment, Bernardo may be undergoing some sort of ghastly torture, but who gives a fuck? We're worried about the color of riding coats. And *you* think he can deal appropriately with this situation,'' she added, turning on Reggie.

The phone rang shrilly and Jeremy pounced over the desk and pressed the speaker button. Sylvia stood impatiently next to the desk and waited, clasping her hands nervously. Jeremy removed his jacket, sat down and set his shirtsleeved elbows on the leather and mahogany surface and waited, eyes narrowed. Each second inched painfully by as they waited for the connection.

''Put him through,'' he instructed Miss Hunter at last. Sylvia swallowed.

''Pablo?''

''Yes.'' Pablo Villalba's crackling voice came over the speakerphone.

''What's the news?'' Jeremy glanced at Sylvia.

''Not good, I'm afraid,'' Bernardo's brother said. ''We got a call ten minutes ago. It was too short to trace. They want five million U.S. in cash. One-hundred-dollar bills over two years old only.'' Sylvia drew in her breath. Five million was more than she'd expected, and the ransom confirmed Jeremy's theory. Maybe they were holding up Harcourts, after all. She saw a muscle twitch in Jeremy's cheek and his fingers clench and unclench.

''Tell him we'll—'' she began.

Jeremy held up his right hand abruptly, stopping her in her tracks.

''Pablo may not be alone,'' Reggie whispered, leaving her feeling foolish. The call was likely being monitored.

''We'll need some time to raise the funds,'' Jeremy countered. ''There may be a delivery problem.''

"We have seventy-two hours," Pablo informed them.

"Tell them I need more time. I'll have to talk to the CEO. She's on vacation right now and may take several days to locate."

"I'll transmit the message."

"I'll be dealing out of Miami," Jeremy said slowly, looking straight through Sylvia. "We'll need at least a week to raise the funds."

"I don't know if they'll accept. They—"

"Believe me, Pablo, they'll accept. They know they're wasting their time if they don't. Any idea what group is involved? Is it FARC rebels?"

"I don't think so. No one has claimed direct responsibility as yet." Pablo's voice sounded uncertain, as though he was loath to commit over the phone. Sylvia frowned, trying to catch every innuendo.

"Keep me updated, day or night. You have my mobile number?"

"Of course."

"Goodbye and good luck."

The phone clicked and Jeremy straightened thoughtfully. "That line was bugged," he declared.

"How do you know?" she queried.

"You can always tell," he muttered, rising. "I'd better get going to Miami. Tell Miss Hunter to have the plane readied for 2:00 p.m. I should be able to make it by then." He scooped his briefcase off the floor. "You can both hold the fort while I'm away. I'll keep you posted." He slipped his cell phone into his breast pocket and came out from behind the desk.

"Hey, not so fast." Sylvia stood smack in his path and faced him. In the past few minutes he'd commandeered the room, but that didn't mean she'd let him get away with it.

"Sylvia, there's no time to discuss this, I'm afraid. I'm heading out immediately. My gut says we can't leave it any longer."

"Your gut?" she challenged.

"Yes, my gut." Their eyes locked.

"I thought you didn't consider that good business practice."

"Well I'm afraid that's what we've got to go on right now," he said through gritted teeth. "If you'd kindly step out of my way, I'll get going."

"Oh, no, you don't." Sylvia shook her head and jutted out her chin. "You ain't going nowhere, buddy. Not without me, that is," she added, raising her eyebrows when he started to protest. "I'm going over to the Stafford to pack, and I'll join you back here in twenty," she said, spinning on her high heel.

"I don't think that's a good idea," Jeremy declared, surprised. "Miami's not a suitable place for you to be involved in—"

"Not suitable? Since when do you decide what's suitable for me?"

"Look, Sylvia, I wish you'd be reasonable." He ran frustrated fingers through his hair and turned to Reggie for support. "I don't like the idea of her being directly involved. It could be very risky."

"Well, *her* is going along, however unsuitable. So get used to it."

"But you're a woman."

"That is the most pathetic comment I've yet to hear you utter," she said over her shoulder. "I'm coming along, whether you like it or not, and you have ex-

actly twenty minutes to get used to the idea.'' She
flashed him a look that dared him to query her decision, then turned and headed quickly out the door.

Ten minutes later she was pulling out clothes from
the closet, deciding what to take on the trip. The gall
of the man. He'd intended to walk out of there and
not even tell her what he was doing, she raged, throwing her cosmetics into her makeup kit and dashing to
grab her toothbrush.

Five minutes later the bellboy was carrying her bag
back over to the office, where the company Mercedes
was waiting on the curb.

She was about to enter the vehicle, when she remembered. ''Oh, shit!'' she exclaimed, recalling the
unopened package that had arrived earlier in the day.
She hesitated. Should she quickly run up and see if it
was anything important?

As she was making up her mind Jeremy descended
the stairs, a garment bag thrown loosely over his arm,
ear glued to his cell phone. It would just have to wait,
she decided. They'd only be gone three or four days
and anything else important could be retrieved on her
laptop, which was tucked safely under her right arm.

Several minutes later the car glided onto St
James's. ''Sorry about that,'' Jeremy apologized, finishing his call. ''Just sorting out a couple of things
before we go. You all right?'' he asked, peering
across at her from the opposite corner of the back
seat. She looked pale, worried and strained. Stretching
his hand across the black leather, he covered hers.
''We'll deal with this, Syl. Just trust me.''

She was about to ask him why on earth she should
trust him, then changed her mind, loath to admit that

she was out of her depth in this horrible, unprecedented situation. "I'm fine," she muttered, removing her hand. "This whole thing got to me, that's all."

"Don't worry," he said reassuringly.

"My God, Jeremy—" she asked, lips trembling "—how do we know they haven't already killed him?"

"I should know by tonight," he answered grimly, staring out the window at the midday traffic.

"How can you be so cool about it? And how can you be so sure that you'll know?" she queried, irritated by the assertiveness in his manner. He was too damn self-assured, as though he'd entered another world and become someone else. It was disturbing. "Well?" she prodded.

"I've put out feelers."

"What kind of feelers?" she asked, eyeing him suspiciously. "You seem very sure of your facts all of a sudden."

He turned, looked her straight in the eye, then glanced at the window separating them from the driver.

"When I asked you to trust me, I meant it. I would never have taken this on if I didn't know what I was doing."

"But how can you possibly know anything about Colombian kidnappings?" she argued with a contemptuous laugh and a dismissive gesture.

"I may not know the Colombian brand but I'm pretty familiar with terrorists. I'd be willing to bet they follow a similar pattern worldwide."

"What are you talking about?" Sylvia's mouth dropped open.

"I've dealt with a few terrorists in my time."

"You?" She threw her head back and let out a guffaw. "The earl of Warmouth doesn't deal with terrorists."

"You're absolutely right," he agreed. "The earl of Warmouth does not deal with terrorists. He leaves that to special agent Peter Field."

"Peter Field?" Sylvia's confused brows met in a straight line over the bridge of her nose. "Who's he?"

"My code name. MI-6 at your service." Jeremy inclined his head.

"You? MI-6? You're kidding," she whispered, flabbergasted.

"You thought only well-seasoned commoners entered the Secret Service?" He quirked a brow. "Sorry to disappoint you."

"You're not serious." She recognized that same mischievous glint lurking and drew in her breath. "You? A special agent?"

"I was...still keep in touch." He grinned apologetically. "I'm sorry to have kept you in the dark. It is, of course, rather confidential."

Sylvia simply stared at him. A thousand questions came to mind but she could voice none of them. Quietly he took her hand and held it firmly in his as the car mingled with the cabs and airport buses circling the roundabout and headed to the terminal at Heathrow airport.

14

Sylvia boarded the plane in a daze, sipped Perrier in rigid silence until they were airborne, and tried to picture Jeremy in the new role he'd described. So that's why he'd been so in control in Scotland, why he'd taken charge automatically earlier in the office, why he'd remained sublimely calm and unruffled despite the tension. Still watching him, laid-back and annoyingly at ease half hidden behind the *Financial Times,* it was hard to imagine him playing at James Bond.

She gave an irritated start. *Playing.* Was that what this was all about? Why else would someone of his wealth and background bother to dirty his hands with covert operations if not to seek thrills? On the other hand, she reflected, peering at him thoughtfully, maybe this had been his manner of justifying his existence—like his job at Harcourts. She flipped through a memo, the increasingly complicated elements of Jeremy's persona leaving her disturbed and restless. Just as she'd thought she was beginning to know the man better, he'd thrown her for another loop.

After several minutes Jeremy laid down the paper. She could feel his eyes on her, and was annoyed that she wanted to turn toward him. She continued to look out the window, not certain yet how to react. Staring down beyond the wisps of cloud, she identified a group of identical houses in identical lots. Only the miniature swimming pools varied in shape. Then rural England disappeared as the plane picked up altitude, the cloud cover thickened and Sylvia did her best to get a grip on her confused emotions.

"Something the matter?" Jeremy asked innocently.

"Is something the... Like you don't know," she burst out, despite her resolve to stay calm. "I just love not knowing that the head of my European division is an operative."

"Was."

"Okay, *was*. I don't suppose you felt it important enough to mention?"

"No. Why should I? Brad knew, which was all that mattered." He gave an arrogant shrug.

"Well, gee! Thanks both of you for keeping me so well briefed." She crossed her arms petulantly and let annoyance rule.

"I fail to see why you should be so upset. My contacts may come in extremely handy," he said mildly.

"You mean you've solved the problem of the designs being leaked to Thackeray?" she asked sweetly, voice dripping with sarcasm. "Tell me about it."

"No," he replied, mortified. "You know very well I haven't. I was referring to the kidnapping situation."

"In future, try and be more precise," she snapped.

"For Christ's sake, Sylvia, knock that chip off your shoulder and grow up." Irritated, Jeremy eyed her over the rim of his whiskey tumbler, wondering whether she'd realize someday that the world wouldn't crumble if she ceded a little control.

"Chip on my—" she burst out, astonished.

"That's exactly what it is." Jeremy looked her straight in the eye. "You seem intent on believing everyone is out to undermine you. I won't say I haven't taken a whack at it," he added humbly, "but the truth is, you're about as aggravated at having to deal with me as I've been at having to deal with you."

"Just because I'm a woman," she retorted darkly.

"In part. I admit it." He nodded, and reached for his blazer on the far seat, rummaging through the breast pocket for a cigar.

"Well, that's progress. I suppose that just because we've been getting along better, you think it's time for you—being a man, of course—to dive in and take charge."

"Rubbish."

"Oh, so you didn't give the flight orders without asking my opinion? Or unilaterally decide how we're going to deal with the kidnappers?" she goaded.

"What earthly difference does it make which of us decides when we fly?" He rolled his eyes and neatly sidestepping the second part of her taunt. "Unless it hurts your ego?"

"How dare you!" she spluttered.

"It's a travel arrangement, Syl, not a major event, for goodness' sake. Stop making an issue out of every damn thing. You were busy, I wasn't. I merely moved things along faster for our convenience.''

"Like hell you did." She eyed him witheringly.

"Don't these arrangements suit you?" he asked solicitously.

"I don't know. I have no idea what your plans are," she retorted, eyes blazing.

"Pablo has kindly offered us his flat in Grove Isle. It's a staffed three-bedroom and it's vac—''

"Oh, so you talked to Pablo again and didn't bother to advise me?"

"He called on my mobile while you were at the hotel," Jeremy answered patiently. "And no, there's no other news. Unfortunately. He was calling from a safe line, so I was able to tell him I'd be in Miami tonight. Of course if you'd prefer to go to a hotel, that can be arranged. But frankly, our current plans would be a lot more discreet. We don't exactly want to announce our presence in the area. But if you insist," he added gallantly, "your word would be my command.''

"Like hell it would."

Jeremy leaned back in the wide leather seat and threw up his hands in mock despair. He couldn't help but enjoy her furious face, and felt sorely tempted to lean across the seat and kiss away her anger, but knew that would not be a good idea. Not now. Instead, he handed her the copy of the *Financial Times*. "I've stayed in the apartment before," he said reasonably. "It's a lovely spot. I honestly think you'll like it. But it's up to you, of course," he added with a noncommittal shrug.

Out of habit Sylvia opened her mouth to protest,

then, realizing once again that he was annoyingly right, she closed it. The lower profile they kept, the better. Also, to her amazement, she realized she would much prefer to stay at Bernardo's brother's apartment than alone in a strange hotel. In the old days she'd loved the buzz and rush of five-star luxury, businessmen and well-dressed women circulating in gleaming marble-floored lobbies, but lately the experience had lost its sheen. Finding herself alone every night in London was getting to her in a way it never had in the past, even during her long engagement to Brad, when she'd spent the better part of her time shacking up in five-star anonymity. Now, for whatever reason, that anonymity not only bothered her but left a void. As though a fundamental element she hadn't defined yet was missing in her life.

"Well?"

She shrugged indifferently.

"You know very well the whole thing suits you down to the ground, so stop acting like a ten-year-old and making such a bloody fuss," Jeremy declared.

"I'm not making a fuss," she retorted. "I'm objecting to you saying that I have a chip on my shoulder when I don't."

"Okay, I'm sorry." He cast his eyes heavenward. "I never mentioned the word *chip,* okay? Although I wouldn't mind eating one. I'm hungry." He pressed the button on the side of the armrest.

"Chip, my ass," she muttered, crossing her arms protectively across her chest.

"I'm sorry I pissed you off."

"I don't have any chips." Sylvia stared stonily out

the window. "Not one single, teensy-weensy, itsy-bitsy one."

"Fine."

"Understand that you and I are not the same." She pointed a manicured finger straight at him and leaned forward. "I fought for every goddamn thing I own, everything I am. Anything you did, you chose. You probably thought playing at James Bond was fun. You don't know what it is to fight for every square inch of terrain, to know that if you make one single mistake, just one, that's it." She paused and took a long breath while he watched her intently, taken aback by the sudden intensity of her words. "You can't know," she added in a milder tone, "because there's always been a cushion waiting right underneath you if you fell. People of your background have no idea what it's like to be judged, considered inferior and incompetent just because your parents—" She broke off and stared at her lap. He frowned.

"You're awfully good at judging other people yourself, you know." There was an edge to his voice and his fingers flexed.

"If there's one thing I know about, it's being judged."

"So I've accomplished less, simply because I was born with more?" he asked. "Why do you think I went into the Secret Service?"

"I have no idea. For kicks? Why else would you bother to put your life in danger? I guess it was a way of passing the time."

"Don't give me much credit, do you?"

"Why should I? With all your fancy inside contacts, we're no closer to finding out how Thackeray operated than we were three weeks ago. I would have thought it would be child's play to someone from MI-6— God,'' she muttered, raising her hands crossly. ''This is a ridiculous discussion that's getting us nowhere.''

''I agree entirely,'' he murmured dryly. ''I thought we'd covered some ground, but apparently I was wrong. I thought we'd become less adversarial.''

Sylvia faced him, eyes kindling. ''Why? Because you fed me on the weekend? Or because by some misbegotten chance we landed in the middle of nowhere, and I melted in your arms? You think you can wind me around your little finger like you do everyone else, don't you?'' She looked at him askance.

''Are you annoyed with yourself because you think I might?'' he taunted, placing a cigar carefully in his mouth.

''Don't you *dare* light that thing,'' she exclaimed, reaching over and flicking it neatly from between his lips. ''This is a nonsmoking flight.''

Jeremy glanced from right to left. ''I don't see any signs—''

''Jeremy, shut up.''

''Yes, ma'am,'' he responded meekly, with a disarming glint.

For a moment she battled, then gave way. ''You are *the* most frustrating man I've ever met,'' she exclaimed roundly, letting out a huff and a laugh. ''And this discussion is pointless.''

''Isn't it?'' he agreed sympathetically. ''I never quite got the gist of it, either.''

''You're impossible.''

''So I've been told.''

"By your aunt, no doubt."

"Yes," he conceded, painfully eyeing the Cohiba being viciously massacred between her thumb and index finger. "And by my sister as well. You do realize, by the way, that's a rather expensive cigar you're destroying?"

"Good riddance." She gave it a last squish and tipped it into the ashtray.

Jeremy cast it a fond glance, then sighed and leaned back thoughtfully. There was something deeply flawed in Sylvia's approach to life. It was disturbing to realize that the outer, polished person, harbored an insecure, frightened soul. Listening to her, he'd experienced a sudden rush of compassion, realizing all at once how hard she must work to maintain that appearance of total confidence and control. All the sharp cynical retorts hovering on the tip of his tongue had died and he saw only the fragile creature he remembered curled in front of the fire at the inn in Scotland. Why, he wondered, did he feel so strongly drawn to this incredibly complex, enigmatic woman? She was the last person he should feel attracted to, yet all he wanted was to get closer to the real woman he knew lay beneath the armor. But until she accepted whatever haunted her, she would never be at peace, he realized.

"I still haven't thanked you for helping Arabella," he said, getting up and stretching.

"Don't try and change the subject. Anyway, there's no need to thank me."

He sighed. "Haven't we beaten the other subject to death, old girl? Surely I can say thank-you without getting your back up. I'm grateful that Arabella's having a chance to do something worthwhile for once.''

Sylvia eyed him warily. "Arabella's doing more than that. She's trying to be her own person. Over the past few days she's come up with some very interesting and well-formulated ideas. Maybe that seems weird to someone like you.''

"What exactly do you mean? That's the second time today that you've painted me as some kind of jackass.'' He eyed her and Sylvia looked away, a sudden knot forming in her throat.

"I didn't mean to be rude.'' She shook her head and murmured, half to herself, wishing she didn't feel the nervous tension that preceded tears. She held on to her last thread of control and waited for it to subside. "I'm sorry if I've been judgmental,'' she whispered at last, desperately trying to keep her voice steady. "It's just that I see you and realize that you've never had to face the real world. Maybe I'm just jealous.'' She attempted a watery smile. "You can't begin to imagine what it's like to live in a small backwater town where you're constantly humiliated, assumed to be worthless because that's all your family has ever been, where you're called a—'' She shuddered, swung her head around and pulled herself up short. What on earth was she doing? Why was she talking to him like this? Her past was nobody's business. The images that flashed before her eyes had no business being aired. She caught Jeremy's green eyes gazing at her, filled with a new, unrecognizable quality, and shifted hers. Much good all those long, painful hours of therapy had been.

Jeremy noted how her arms hugged her body protectively and frowned. "What has this got to do with Arabella?" he asked, guiding the conversation back onto neutral terrain.

Sylvia shrugged, taking a quick sip of water. "I couldn't understand at first why Arabella is the way she is. Why anyone with the privileged life she's led could be so...unsure of herself, so vulnerable. Then I realized that she's been crippled by all that privilege. She needs to build something for herself, something she can feel empowered by, that she'll be able to give herself credit for."

"And the same couldn't have applied to me?" he asked quietly, sitting down once more and crossing his ankles.

Sylvia frowned. "Why are we discussing this, anyway?"

"Why, indeed. I was merely thanking you for helping my sister. It was damn generous of you to come up with the idea of incorporating her into Harcourts, and I'm grateful to you for making the effort."

"It wasn't purely altruistic," she said, unbending, "I honestly think it'll be good for the company."

"So do I," he responded in a warmer tone. "Still, it was dashed nice of you. Under all that armor you're rather a generous, kind bird, aren't you?" He grinned now, back to his old self, unable to resist the gentle taunt.

"The politically correct term is *person,* Jeremy, not bird," she responded, smothering her own grin.

"Very well, *person,* if it keeps you happy." Then, to her utter surprise, he leaned over, lifted her hand to his lips and dropped a fleeting kiss on her palm.

"You rang, my lord?"

Sylvia sat hastily back as the flight attendant entered the cabin, and wished she weren't blushing.

"Yes, Katie. I think we could use another round of drinks here, and do you still have those chips? The ones with the paprika on them? Or did I hog them all on the last trip?"

"I'll see if there are any left." Katie smiled. "Would you like a glass of champagne, Miss Hansen?" she asked, swinging her pretty, auburn head in Sylvia's direction.

"That would be great. Thanks." At this rate, she'd end up an alcoholic, but right now, she could use the drink.

15

A blast of sticky humid heat hit as they exited the terminal at Miami International, the sweltering South Florida temperatures cruising in the upper nineties.

"Thank God for AC," Sylvia gasped as they climbed into the limo after making it through international arrivals, where three Haitian porters had all vied desperately to carry their bags. Jeremy had finally located their Cuban limo driver, who'd nipped around the corner for a *cortadito*—a lethal, syrupy black coffee with a dash of milk.

"Don't mind if I take off my tie, do you?" Jeremy asked, loosening the knot.

"Go ahead. I feel like stripping right here."

"Be my guest," he responded, wiggling his eyebrows suggestively.

"I can't win, can I?" she laughed, sinking back in the corner.

Then, as the car swerved out of the airport, past the exit to Coral Gables and on toward downtown, Jeremy switched his mobile phone back on, reminding her of just why they were here.

"Any messages?"

"No." He checked again and shook his head. "I wasn't expecting anything so soon. We need to make some decisions, Syl."

"I already told you. We pay."

"We'll discuss it when we reach the apartment," he murmured, indicating the driver's wide, black-suited back.

The trip had passed extraordinarily quickly, she reflected, allowing herself a few minutes of relaxation, grateful for the temperature-controlled luxury of the limousine. After the chips and drinks had appeared, they'd discussed the matter most on their minds: Bernardo and the tactics to be used.

Sylvia glanced out the window at the oncoming traffic. She wished she hadn't let her emotions get the better of her. She'd let slip more than she'd meant to in the conversation on the jet.

She took a fleeting side look at Jeremy. Hopefully he hadn't given much credence to her ramblings. He was probably too worried about the kidnapping to have paid much attention. She leaned back into the corner of the limo, relieved to be back in America—although Miami was so very different from the rest of the States it almost seemed like another country. Still, she felt better knowing they were going to deal with the rebels from home base.

The driver turned left onto Bay Shore Drive, past a park where track-suited joggers and kids on bikes moved briskly by the sea, then turned right, into a pretty street bordered by attractive homes and crossed a small causeway onto Grove Isle. Sylvia watched the boats bobbing in the marina to her left, the yachts and motorboats sporting colorful canvas awnings. Straight ahead, three buildings rose diagonally in the center of the tiny island.

"Nice," she remarked.

"Isn't it? Great clubhouse, too. There are three pools, two for the buildings and one for the hotel and club. The restaurant, Baline, is excellent."

"Good. Maybe we can dine there tonight. Save having to go out."

"You mean you don't want to hit the clubs on South Beach with me? I'm dreadfully disappointed," Jeremy teased as they reached the security gate and an attractive African-American attendant with an elaborate hairdo and very long, bright-pink sequined nails cleared them in. "Have a nice stay," she said with a smile and a slow Southern drawl as she waved them through.

"Instead of a nightclub, maybe we should take in a game of tennis."

"Are you kidding? In this heat?" Jeremy responded as the car drove smoothly up the ramp of Building Two.

"You know, we shouldn't be kidding around when Bernardo's in such danger," she murmured as they glided between tall palm trees, past a number of courts to their left.

"Just a way of keeping the tension level bearable," he responded mildly. "No use in us getting so wired we can't think."

Several minutes later they stepped into the cool lobby. It was decorated with Asian touches and a waterfall. A glorious Ikebana flower arrangement graced the center table.

"Not bad," she remarked as they stepped into the elevator and Jeremy pressed the penthouse button.

An hour later they were showered and changed, and had let go of some of the inevitable tension caused by the circumstances of their journey. Sylvia spent fifteen minutes on the phone with Aaron in New York determining how the funds should be delivered when the moment came, first to Miami and then onward. It would not be an easy task but Aaron seemed confident he could manage.

It gave Sylvia a measure of relief to know the money could be made available if necessary. She'd have to get Brad's ultimate consent but knew that wouldn't be a problem. He would be the last to quibble at paying to save a man's life. She slipped on a light sleeveless dress. Contrary to her first impression, she realized that Jeremy wasn't reticent about helping Bernardo. He simply knew how to play the game right, she conceded, pressing in her earrings and dabbing on a touch of lip gloss. If the operation wasn't handled in the correct manner, it would open the door for Harcourts to become an easy victim of other attacks of this order.

It struck her as heartless to be thinking in this manner, when it was hard not to constantly obsess about Bernardo's situation, to wonder if he was being badly treated—or worse, if he were still alive. But Jeremy was right. Again Sylvia admitted to feeling relieved that she had someone next to her who knew how to handle such a situation.

Similar thoughts drifted through Jeremy's mind as he stood behind the granite counter of the apartment's ultramodern open kitchen and concentrated on the preparation of the *mojitos*. Three calls to London had rendered little, but his contacts were digging, seeing what they could come up with. As he swirled the ice in the drinks, Jeremy wondered if there could be a connection with Thackeray. Somewhere in the back of his mind remained the name that he was certain he'd heard before but was unable to identify. And it troubled him, as though some link in the chain was hanging there, obviously loose, and he was unable to connect it.

Then, aware there was little use in pursuing the matter until he had concrete information to work on, he allowed his thoughts to turn to Sylvia. Today on the plane she'd inadvertently revealed more about her past in two sentences than in all the time he'd known her. But she remained a conundrum, albeit an utterly enticing one, under whose spell he was seriously in danger of succumbing. He slipped a sprig of mint into each tall glass. How could he get her to open up? To trust him? He smiled as she emerged from her room, walked across the spacious living room and stopped by the window.

"It's fabulous." She exclaimed, pointing outside. Moving the sliding door, she ventured onto the balcony.

"Did you get Aaron?"

"Yes. He'll be in touch. We have an account in Aruba, as you know. He…" She hesitated, then went ahead. "He agrees with your policy, says we must negotiate carefully or we'll be opening ourselves up to any number of unforeseen demands."

Jeremy nodded but didn't answer. He didn't want to spend the evening going over and over what was on their minds. He was certain Pablo would call later and things would heat up. But for now they needed to try and relax.

Sylvia moved out to the balcony. After carefully adding an exact measure of white rum to the drinks, Jeremy followed her lithe figure onto the penthouse's wraparound terrace. Again the powerful need to understand her better, to discover what lay hidden inside that high-powered, tense body, that quick, intelligent mind, recurred.

It was cooler now that evening had come. Taking a deep breath, Sylvia gazed at the one-hundred-and-eighty-degree panoramic view encompassing Coral Gables, its town hall's tower discernible in the twilight, spreading past Mercy Hospital and over the downtown area to the right. She could see a tall tiered building illuminated in blue, green and violet laser lights.

Jeremy joined her, handed her the *mojito* and leaned on the railing. He wondered if she was at all aware of just how lovely she looked in the short silk dress, her hair sleeked back after her shower. Absently he checked the mobile in his right pocket, making sure reception was okay, then glanced at her, face tilted up toward the perfect crescent moon shimmering in the bay. Together they lingered, sipping the *mojitos,* and looked past the floodlit tennis courts, where a game of doubles was in progress, to the masts bobbing and tinkling merrily in the marina. The scent of her freshly washed skin and a whiff of light perfume wafted his way on the evening breeze and he swallowed. This was no time to be romantic. They had priorities, he reminded himself. How could he forget that the weight of decision and the manner in which this operation was to be conducted lay primarily in his hands. For a while they listened in companionable silence to the strains of laughter and light music floating up from the decks. But despite all the tension surrounding them tonight, Jeremy couldn't help thinking how wonderful it would feel to dig his hands into her silky hair and pull her close.

Instead, he shoved them into his pockets, ashamed, wishing there was no kidnapping to deal with, no business commitments to interfere in their lives, no company to run; just he and Syl together, here in the moonlight, with nothing but themselves to consider.

"The maid left a note," he said, redirecting his thoughts with an effort. "She'll be in tomorrow morning." He dipped his index finger in his glass, swirling the ice, lemon and rum. "How do you like my *mojito?*"

"Strong," she remarked, taking another sip.

"Treacherous."

"But decidedly delicious." She raised her glass.

"Frighteningly so," he said with a bantering grin, determined to keep the evening as carefree as possible.

"Right." Sylvia shifted. The gleam in his eyes was too intimate for comfort. "What are we going to do now, Jeremy? I gather Pablo hasn't called your cell phone yet?"

"I don't think he'll phone till much later tonight. I'm hoping when he does he'll have some answers that will give us a clue about the best way to go."

"It doesn't seem right to be sipping cocktails in

the sunset when Bernardo and his family are going through such hell, does it?''

"No, I suppose it doesn't." He glanced at his glass. "But right now there's absolutely nothing we can do but wait. You've set the process in motion with Aaron. I assure you that I have every Tom, Dick and Harry I know working on the case around the clock. We'd do better to relax a little while we can. We may not get another chance until all this is over," he added dryly. "Now, how about a bite of dinner at the club and a walk around the island? I'll take the mobile with me." He gave his right pocket a reassuring pat.

"I guess you're right. It just seems so callous, so…" She let her hand drop.

"I know." He laid a hand gently but firmly on her arm. "But worrying ourselves sick isn't going to help. It'll only drain us mentally and we'll be much less able to deal with business when the phone finally rings. Remember what you said at Warmouth about leaving the office *at* the office, not packing it in the luggage?" His eyes glowed warm and understanding, leaving her breathless.

"I remember," she said, nodding.

"Well, you were right. Until that phone rings, we relax. It doesn't mean we're unfeeling, it's simply that we need to be as calm and prepared as we can when the time comes."

"Okay." She let out a short breath and smiled brightly at him, wishing his presence didn't have this intoxicating effect on her. "Let's dine and be back quickly." She moved inside the contemporary living room, needing some distance. She could not, she reflected, glimpsing the stark colors of the halogen-lit abstracts gracing the white walls, allow *anything* to occur between them. It would merely muddy the waters. It was unprofessional and in the long run it could only become a hazard.

Their lives were so different, she argued silently, flinging a thin white sweater over her shoulders. They had nothing whatsoever in common. And the only plausible result of any passion would be embarrassment, once the fire that smoldered white-hot between them was extinguished. Extreme embarrassment, she admonished herself, heading for the door. Not to mention the awkwardness of having to face one another at Harcourts, every day at present, and later, at least several times a year. It was unthinkable, she concluded with a regretful sigh as he opened the front door for her and she passed through with a smile. But terribly tempting nevertheless.

Downstairs they made their way through the breezy tropical gardens. They walked in silence, side by side along the path that hugged the tiny island. The bright lights of downtown shimmered in the gleaming dark waters as they approached the clubhouse through the veranda.

Jeremy led her inside in that usual masterful yet gentlemanly manner, which for some reason didn't annoy her any longer. He'd reserved a table at Baline, the club restaurant, and they were graciously led by the maître d' to the covered terrace overlooking the bay. The tables were lit with tiny votive candles and spaced agreeably apart, creating a luxurious, tropical yet intimate ambience. Soon they were seated in a secluded corner and studying the menu.

It was only as they were finishing their appetizers that Sylvia sensed she was being observed.

At first she dismissed the notion. Then an icy chill crawled up her spine and instinctively she turned.

And saw him.

He smiled mockingly from across the room in the opposite corner, a cruel, satisfied smile framed by exotic palm trees and sea that left her paralyzed. For a moment she stared back, unbelieving.

"Something wrong?" Jeremy turned, following her gaze.

"It's him," she whispered hoarsely. "That's Thackeray, right there with those two men."

"Are you talking about the man in the blazer next to the potted plant?"

"Yes. I'm damned if I'm going to sit here and let him get away with this." She jerked her chair back.

"Sylvia, be careful, this is a restaurant. Don't make a scene." Jeremy rose and caught her arm, eyes narrowed.

"I don't intend to. I just plan to introduce you," she retorted, voice hard as she whisked the napkin briskly from her knee and rose. "Don't you think it's a hell of a coincidence that he's here?"

"Perhaps," he muttered, following suit. "It looks as if we're about to find out."

16

Sylvia snaked between diners and potted palms, with Jeremy following hard on her heels, until they reached Thackeray's corner table.

"Good evening, Aimon," she purred. "What a strange coincidence meeting you here, of all people."

"Sure is." Thackeray half rose and flashed her what Jeremy considered a wolfish, too intimate, smile.

"May I introduce the head of Harcourts European operations—Jeremy Warmouth?"

Did she intend a showdown among the potted palms? Jeremy wondered. He must avoid that at all cost. If Thackeray did happen to be involved in Bernardo's kidnapping, then he needed him confident and unsuspecting, not on his guard.

Thackeray reached across the table to shake hands. "This is my attorney, Manny Hernandez," he said, introducing a heavily overweight balding man in his mid-forties. "And this is Ricky Rico," he muttered dismissively. Jeremy nodded, acknowledged the introductions and kept a close eye on Sylvia, mapping out ways of removing her from the restaurant before she caused any major damage.

He studied the man Thackeray had introduced as Ricky Rico. He looked like a rap singer, with his gold rings and black Lycra clothes. A heavy chain and diamond cross hung on the chest of a shiny black T-shirt. He'd slip Rico's name by his contact in London later. You never knew what might come up. Thackeray, he observed, did not look pleased at their sudden descent upon his table—though he was doing a good job of disguising his feelings. Apparently Sylvia confronting him had not been on the agenda.

Jeremy frowned. Surely after her walk-out performance at Aureole, Thackeray would expect her to have the upper hand? Then why did he seem so confident, so very full of himself? Could it just be the coup he'd carried off or was there more? Had Jeremy missed something staring him in the face?

He paused, registering each minute detail, each facial expression, and thought suddenly of Bernardo. On the surface, they still had no link connecting Thackeray and the occurrences in Colombia, despite the disappearance of the designs. While Sylvia continued her cat-and-mouse dialogue with Thackeray, his gaze fell again on Ricky Rico. What could have induced Thackeray to invite someone like Rico to a first-class restaurant? This was clearly the muscle guy, the one who did the dirty work behind the scenes so that Thackeray could keep his nose clean. Hernandez was likely a henchman in his own way, too, he decided, eyeing the fat, pompous, whiskey-sipping lawyer. No doubt Thackeray used him to launder money.

Jumbled thoughts lined up like soldiers in his head. Despite his suave and debonair attitude, Thackeray was so ill at ease, one could slice the air with a knife. Only Ricky Rico went on munching, apparently oblivious to the artificial atmosphere.

"Syl, we'd better get moving," he said, touching Sylvia's arm and smiling perfunctorily to the table at large.

"Right," Sylvia agreed, nodding a cold goodbye. Ricky Rico chewed on blithely.

"By the way, in case you're interested, my last offer still stands. My yacht's anchored in St. Barthes, and I'd love to show you around the Caribbean." Thackeray sent her a suggestive smile that made Jeremy's fingers twitch. Instead, he took a firm grip of her arm, restraining the impulse to smash those white-capped teeth straight down Thackeray's filthy throat.

"Thanks, but I'm not here on vacation." Her voice throbbed with unspoken anger and Jeremy waited on tenterhooks, begging her not to give herself away. He tightened his grip on her biceps.

"Pity. Could've been fun. Sales doing well these days?" Thackeray ventured, not quite able to conceal his curiosity.

"Excellent. We had a worldwide blow-out sale. I'm sure you can't possibly have missed the advertising. It's been everywhere." Sylvia raised a supercilious brow, allowing her eyes to rest contemptuously on Ricky Rico, enjoying Thackeray's growing discomfort.

Rico laid down his fork, looked up from his half-finished plate and stopped eating. The diamond cross swung to a halt on the pumped pectoral muscles etched under the tight black Lycra T-shirt. Thackeray's mouth twitched involuntarily. Jeremy caught the surreptitious exchange of eye contact with Hernandez and his thoughts went into overdrive.

Perhaps Sylvia had hit a bull's-eye. Maybe they were involved in Bernardo's disappearance. Clearly Sylvia's presence in Miami had not been part of Thackeray's plans. Up until this moment Jeremy had been floundering in the dark. But now his gut told him he was onto something. There was more going on here than met the eye. For the first time in this whole investigation, he sniffed a breakthrough. Disguising his elation, he said good-night, determined to investigate Ricky Rico. Dropping a few bills on their table, Jeremy indicated to their waiter that they were leaving. They passed through to the lobby and continued toward the garden.

"God, I can't believe that bastard had the nerve to chat casually with us when I'm sure he's planning another setback for Harcourts," Sylvia muttered furiously. She flexed her tense fingers. "It's unbelievable."

"Forget him. Just keep quiet and walk."

Jeremy directed her quick, nervous steps toward the pool area. He'd have to find a way of sending Sylvia back to New York tomorrow and head down to Colombia on his own. Whether she liked it or not, he refused to have her exposed to unnecessary danger. The less involved she was, the better.

"Are you all right?" Jeremy still held her as they stepped onto the deck by the pool.

"Of course I'm all right," she snapped. "I can't believe Thackeray has the nerve to act in that presumptuous manner. Did you hear what he said? Inviting me to his goddamn yacht in St. Barthes? I think the man's crazy. God, I wish I could strangle him. It makes me so frustrated.''

He rubbed her back gently. "Don't get upset, Syl. It's not worth it. We'll get to the bottom of the Harcourts mess and he'll back down.''

"Jeremy, you sound like a broken record. *Everything'll be okay, Syl,*" she mimicked crossly. "I don't want him backed down, I want him liquidated, finished, obliterated.'' Her hands clenched and she spun away. "There's something so…evil about him.'' She shivered.

"I don't know what that bastard's up to—probably no good, but right now we have other priorities. There's Bernardo to think about.'' He must divert her. If she thought for one minute Thackeray was behind Bernardo's kidnapping, she'd insist on joining him on the trip to Colombia. He recognized that could be fatal. She could endanger the entire operation, and more importantly, herself. He had no doubt she was right. Thackeray was evil and ruthless, although just how far the man would be willing to go to acquire Harcourts remained to be seen. In the meanwhile, he didn't intend to put Sylvia in danger.

"I have this strange…this really bad feeling,'' she said, turning and facing him. "My gut tells me he's involved in Bernardo's kidnapping. I can't explain why. Call it a hunch. Maybe it was that weird sleazy little pockmarked guy with the gold chain. He gave me the creeps,'' she added. "Plus, it's too damn pat, Thackeray being here in Miami with those two sleaze-balls.''

"Maybe. There are lots of possibilities right now. Thackeray isn't necessarily involved," he replied reasonably, determined to calm her frayed nerves and persuade her to let him go to Colombia alone. He continued stroking her back, soothing her, glad she was venting her pent-up anxiety.

"If he knows we're not scared of him, that may push him into making a move, a mistake, something that will help us expose him," she insisted hopefully.

"Perhaps. But I doubt he'd be foolish enough to invite any kind of scrutiny from the authorities right now." He shrugged, his powerful shoulders etched in the night shadows, and wrapped his arm around her, walking her gently along the winding path above the sea. "By tomorrow I should have news from London."

Sylvia allowed herself to be led down the shallow steps toward the towpath. Thackeray's triumphant smile and the face-to-face confrontation had left her weak. She wished she could rid herself of the growing suspicion that his smirk held more than mere elation; it was a smile of awareness.

He knew something she didn't. He was sending her a subliminal message, but she hadn't the first clue what that message might be. She hated feeling anxious and powerless. She glanced at Jeremy, then thought better of confiding further in him. He obviously didn't take Thackeray's possible involvement with Bernardo's kidnapping seriously. All at once she frowned.

"You're not keeping anything from me?" she asked in a belligerent tone.

"Calm down, Syl. I know no more than you do.

So Thackeray is aware we're here, and we let him know we're not taking any shit, right?'' Jeremy appeased, holding on to her despite her sudden effort to break free.

"Do *not* patronize me,'' she muttered through clenched teeth.

"Look, I'm not claiming the man's a Boy Scout,'' he answered. "But be reasonable. He probably has any number of business dealings and interests that have nothing to do with either Marchand or Harcourts. It's very possible that he's here for some unrelated reason.''

"On the same night, in the same restaurant?'' she retorted scornfully. "Give me a break.''

"I still think you're assuming too much. Thackeray may want Harcourts, but kidnapping one of our employees and putting himself in a vulnerable position is hardly the way to achieve that, is it?''

Sylvia tried to steady herself, let his words sink in and take them to heart. His reasonable answers might well hold a kernel of truth. She could not let herself be blinded by paranoia. "Okay. But if that man shows up in Colombia, so help me God, I'll wipe that smirk from his face myself. And then I'll get to work on you.''

"Yes, ma'am.'' He smiled through the darkness, tweaked a strand of hair that had fallen into her face and pushed it gently behind her ear. Then he slipped his arm around her in a friendly manner and they continued in slow silence, past the pool, the cabanas, the bar and the wrought-iron chaise lounges lined up for tomorrow's sunbathers.

They stood for a while above the rocks. A soft

night breeze blew inland from the bay, mingling with the whisper of lapping waves, the tide rising above the watermark. He was probably right. Sylvia knew it was stupid to let anger cripple her. But for some reason, Thackeray affected her that way. He was sinister and dirty and would stop at nothing to achieve his goal. She shuddered, felt Jeremy's arm squeeze tighter and, with a sigh, gave in to the overpowering need to rest her head on his shoulder. When his fingers gently caressed her neck, she didn't stop him. She wanted more, could feel the restrained power in him and the shaft of desire that automatically speared through her. She hadn't meant for this to happen, but to resist seemed useless, as though tonight fate was determined to bring them together on more planes than one. The tingle that always caught her unaware crept deliciously over her as his hands came down her shoulders.

Thackeray faded and another shiver coursed through her—this time, not of fear, but of longing. She remembered their passionate kiss in Clachnabrochan, then on the terrace at Warmouth Manor, and experienced an intense need for more. He did something to her, made her want to let down her guard, let him explore that part of her being she'd never been aware existed until lately. The part—if she was truthful with herself—she'd never dared expose.

It was a risk. In the morning they'd wake up and life would go back to normal. It would be up to her to set the ground rules, as much for her own sake as his. But tonight, just this one time, she wanted to know what it felt like to relinquish herself to a man she was fast coming to believe she loved.

As though guessing her troubled thoughts, Jeremy slipped his arms about her and held her close.

God, how he wanted to kiss her again, feel the soft yet intense movement of her lips under his, her vibrant body melting against him as it had before. He remembered her face earlier, when she'd recognized Thackeray, the sudden flash of fear. There was so much, he was sure, hidden under the bright polished veneer; he knew he should ask, wanted to help her learn to trust him with her secrets, but right now he could think of nothing beyond his desire for her.

Through the haze Sylvia sensed him battling, recognized the moment in which he decided not to press her verbally but to love her, instead. She sighed and raised her mouth to his. When at last their lips touched, all logic vanished and a wave of blinding pleasure gripped her.

Right now, she realized, feeling his mouth gently graze hers, she would have given anything to lower her armor once and for all, pour out her story and lift the iron shackles that for years had held her captive. She wanted to be free to love him, without secrets, with no restraints or regrets. But that was wishful thinking.

The wind picked up, blowing silky strands of hair off her face. Around her the palm trees rustled and lights twinkled like magic lanterns, shimmering in the inky waters of Biscayne Bay. At any other time this would have been the most romantic of settings. But suddenly his warm lips and roaming hands seemed like the pathway to purgatory and her heart ached with a new pain, for he was teaching her to need him; to want more than he had to give.

Before she could think further, Jeremy pressed her to him. A blazing shaft ripped her from head to toe. At least for now, he wanted her—needed her—as much as she did him. It made no sense that this could be more than a simple satisfying of the ever-growing desire that had been bubbling between them for so many weeks. Nevertheless, as the kiss deepened and the night air cooled, they moved smoothly against one another, unable to resist, finally giving in to the pull of the magnet that had dragged them toward each other for longer than either of them knew.

Rico sipped his espresso and registered every single thing going on around him. The Gringo was obviously not happy that the beautiful blond woman and the English dude had come up to his table. She seemed almost aggressive, as though she hated him, he reflected, wishing he could pick at his gold tooth where food had wedged. But Manny Hernandez would give him a lecture on manners if he did, so he resisted the temptation and listened, instead.

Hernandez got on his nerves with all his high-flying airs and *Old Cubano* bullshit. He could put on all the fancy airs he wanted, Rico reminded himself, smothering a grin. Maybe his family had been some big deal back in the old country. But here in Miami, Rico knew very well that Manny's dad lived a block down from his own grandmother in a not-too-fancy suburb and shopped at the same Nica supermarket for the same brands of rice and black beans. Still, there was no use getting Manny pissed off unnecessarily. Manny had big clients like Thackeray, knew how to act gringo when he needed to act gringo, and Ricky was clever enough to be aware of his own limitations. He knew that, whether he liked it or not, he needed the Mannys of this world.

This evening's events had proved *very* interesting and cheered him up immensely. Thackeray had barely been able to hide his anger. He liked seeing the Gringo lose it. Watching him realize he was just a man like the rest of them, that his shit smelled the same, made Ricky feel better.

Gringos—and Old Cubans, too, for that matter— liked to consider themselves superior to the likes of him. Well, fuck 'em and let 'em believe it, if it made them happy. He'd still screw them in the end if the opportunity arose. He listened patiently as Thackeray quizzed Hernandez on the latest shipment of goods, knowing the more information he got out of them, the better. You never knew when it might come in handy, or how much other gringos might be willing to pay for it.

Ricky drank the espresso—disgustingly weak compared to his *colada* at the local cafeteria—then accepted eagerly Thackeray's offer of an after-dinner drink. There was nothing like expensive cognac to help remind him of how far he'd come from Calle Ocho. Plus, he was getting a kick out of watching Manny suck up to the Gringo; fucking brown-nose couldn't be more obvious if he got on his knees and reached for the guy's crotch.

Qué gran mierda, they all were. But a profitable *mierda.* A necessary *mierda* to his continuing well-being. The thing to do, he realized as the waitress laid down the snifter of vintage VSOP, was to take charge without them knowing it. They wanted him to go deal with the imbecile who'd fucked up and kidnapped the hotshot in Colombia. Half an hour ago he'd considered turning them down. Now the proposal was growing more attractive by the minute, especially after Thackeray's and Manny's worried comments and their concern that the other two gringos might be on their way down there, too. So they were all connected in some way. What luck, he reflected, picking up the snifter in his gold-and-diamond ringed hand. Maybe, just maybe, a number of other *avenidas* might open up once he got a better look at the whole picture.

Enjoying this new train of thought, Ricky stared past the potted palms and gazed out into the darkness. All at once his eyes narrowed. He rubbed his hands gleefully and took a closer look, spying a couple kissing passionately on the path.

"Hey, *mira*, guys." He pointed excitedly out the window at the couple etched by the crescent moon, still locked in an endless embrace. "She must be *caliente,* the blonde, huh?" He grinned, still rubbing his hands excitely.

Thackeray stretched past him, then smothered a string of oaths. The minute he recognized the pair, he tensed. His knuckles turned white and the stem of his wineglass snapped. A puddle of dark red liquid seeped over the white cloth and Thackeray turned abruptly.

"Let's get the fuck out of here," he muttered, cleaning his hand with a napkin and signaling the waiter for the check.

Ricky pretended not to notice, just winked at Manny, shrugged and got up, adjusting his chain and jacket. So Thackeray was hot for her, too, and damn pissed she'd chosen the other gringo. Well, well. Little by little he was identifying everybody's weaknesses. Like the Greek guy with the heel and the arrows—Achilles, that was his name. Maybe this gringa was Thackeray's Achilles' heel. You never knew, he reflected with satisfaction as they walked out of the restaurant, when that might come in useful.

17

They didn't bother turning on lights or locking the front door. Instead, they stumbled between kisses to the bedroom at the far end of the passage. Sylvia dropped her purse and kicked off her pumps. Jeremy tugged relentlessly at the zipper of her dress and she tugged just as hard at the buttons of his untucked shirt. They popped open at the same instant her zipper gave and together they pulled off the rest of each other's garments amid laughter and Jeremy's determination to not leave her mouth alone for a second.

Then they were tumbling onto the huge king-size bed, sprawled recklessly over the covers, moonlight slithering over their taut, needy bodies. Sylvia purred like a contented kitten when Jeremy slowed the rhythm, kissed her softly, lips lingering on her throat, her breasts, then ventured farther, his thumb gently grazing her anxious nipples.

God, how she wanted this, how badly she needed him.

Her hands traveled greedily over his firm chest, down the flat, muscled surface of his stomach, then farther. When she finally reached and took him in her hand, feeling a shiver run through him. This was more than she'd ever dreamed of, more than she'd ever had. Sex had never been something spontaneous in her life. Instead, it had been a well-orchestrated symphony that she'd thought of as an integral part of a balanced adult relationship. But this! God, nothing had ever compared to this. His hands roamed, too, fingers parting her thighs, drawing responses she could not control, did not know she possessed. When after only a few intimate caresses she came, letting out a cry as much of surprise as delight, tears of joy touched her cheeks.

She'd never come like this in her life before.

It had always required time, the skill and patience of her partner and concentration on her part. Now she poured into his hand, aching with pure, unadulterated pleasure as again he brought her to peak. Her eyes opened, met his. She read the delighted satisfaction Jeremy was deriving from giving her pleasure, and her pulse beat even faster.

He cared. Truly cared.

This, too, was a new and unexpected wonder. With Brad, there had been great sex but of a different sort—studied, well-coordinated sex guaranteed to give mutual satisfaction. This was entirely different, she realized, breath catching as she clung to him. This was savage, instinctive and earthy. The need to feel him deep within her came as much from her soul as from her body.

As though guessing her need, Jeremy lay her back among the rumpled covers, where she arched as at last he entered her.

He thrust hard, unable to contain the need for her, sinking deep inside her where he knew he wanted to be. He couldn't define what it was about her that drew him as no other woman ever had. Yet here he was, secure in the knowledge that his feelings were deeper than any he'd ever experienced, that the vise strangling him since Clachnabrochan was loosening at last. It was here, deep within her, that he belonged, and here he intended to stay.

All at once life seemed crystal clear: Sylvia was the woman he'd been searching for all these years. It made no sense but he didn't care. He'd tried so hard to refute her, had hated her self-confidence, her power, her strength and attitude. Now he knew without question that she was everything he desperately wanted. Their bodies moved in natural sync with something akin to familiarity, as though they'd been making love for years, knew each other's deepest secrets, joyfully accepted each one's strengths and weaknesses.

Jeremy made love to her slowly and thoroughly. And as they climaxed within each other, he held her so tight he thought she'd break, until there was no room left for anything but the strong beat of their pounding hearts reaching for one another.

At 3:00 a.m. they were abruptly woken by the lilting jingle of the mobile. Disentangling himself from Sylvia's arms and the bedsheets, Jeremy reached for it, sat on the edge of the bed and rubbed his eyes.

"Hello."

"It's Pablo."

Jeremy sat up straighter. The voice sounded different and he frowned. "Go ahead," he said warily, signaling to Sylvia to come closer. Pulling the sheet about her, she leaned over and switched on the bedside lamp. Jeremy mouthed to her and she tried to understand what he meant, then handed him a pen and paper. He began to jot down notes. She peered over his shoulder.

Doesn't sound like the same voice. I think it's a scam.

My God. She looked at him, horrified. Could they have kidnapped Pablo, too? What on earth was going on? She waited impatiently, listening to his monosyllabic responses, then pounced when he finally hung up.

"What happened? What did he say? Why didn't you think it was Pablo?"

"I got Reggie to phone Pablo's wife and give him a code. He didn't mention what he was supposed to. His voice sounded different from the voice yesterday morning."

"Maybe his wife wasn't able to transmit the message."

"You may be right, but Reggie said she'd assured him she could."

"What was the code?" she asked, sinking next to him.

"He was supposed to say, 'I tried to call but the answering machine was on.'"

"I see." In a natural gesture she slipped her hand to his neck and massaged, kneading his shoulders. He closed his eyes and sighed.

"God, that feels divine. Don't stop," he murmured, enjoying her fingers, liking the fact their presence on his neck felt so right. Never before had making love felt quite as it had tonight. He sighed and tried to focus on matters at hand. There was so much he wanted to say to her, so much to express. But it would have to wait. Right now he must get down to Cartagena first thing. And Sylvia, he vowed, would not be with him on that plane, however much she might protest to the contrary.

"Syl, I'm going to have to leave in a few hours." He sat up straighter and took her hand.

"You mean *we*."

"No, I mean *I*." He dropped a kiss on her shoulder. "There's no use both of us going. And frankly, after what happened in the restaurant last night, I think you should stay put. We still have Harcourts to run. You need to get back to New York and keep an eye on what Thackeray may be up to. Both of us going down to Colombia is silly and will only attract attention."

This last was true. The everyday running of the company had to be taken into serious consideration. "I suppose you're right." She sighed unwillingly. It seemed wrong to allow him to leave.

She was suddenly scared. Now that she'd found him, would he be taken from her? Something might happen to him. He might be kidnapped too or killed or—she closed her eyes and stopped herself. He had to go because that was the right thing to do.

"All right," she muttered at last. "You go. I hope you can straighten this mess out. Just promise me you'll come back in one piece."

"It would take the heck of a lot more than this to

get rid of me, now that I've found you," he murmured, laughing softly and pulling her back in his arms.

She woke in the darkness, reveling in Jeremy's warmth at her side, remembering the wondrous things he'd done to and with her body. She didn't want him to go, she wanted to wake him right now and argue that two minds were better than one, but she also knew she was merely giving in to her own desires, not their best interest. Tonight she'd granted herself this one indulgence and made love with him, but that didn't mean the world had turned head over heels. She tried to convince herself that she was in control. But the thought of losing him seemed too great to bear and all the arguments that earlier had seemed overwhelmingly reasonable now floundered. Was it just the meeting with Thackeray that had left her so wanting, so desperate for Jeremy's touch and his lovemaking? Or was there another overwhelming need tugging at her heart? If only she could forget everything, give and be taken.

But the price for that was too high and she knew it. Worse than the pain of knowing this could be nothing but a fling would be to see all that care and concern in his eyes turn to polite pity and disgust if she revealed to him who and what she truly was.

She rose from the bed, trailing the sheet behind her, entered the marble bathroom and switched on the lights. She would just have to accept that what had happened was a blissful moment in time, nothing more. Her real concern right now must be Bernardo.

She poured water from the Evian bottle by the sink and took a few sips before returning to the room. In a few hours it would all be over. They would each be flying in opposite directions, severing the tentative bonds that had formed.

"Come here," he murmured from the bed.

Slowly she crossed the room and settled in bed with her back to him. They must try to get a few hours' rest, though sleep would probably be impossible. She twisted the pillows and tried to settle, then felt him draw her against him. Unable to resist, she snuggled her butt up against his stomach and sighed when his arms encircled her. For a while they lay in companionable silence.

If only they could stay like this forever, Sylvia thought dreamily, cocoon themselves in this quiet room and forget the outside world. A voice told her these were not wise dreams. Oh, to hell with always following the careful, cautious path, she thought—she would throw caution to the wind any day if she believed this feeling could last forever.

Snuggling closer, she felt his hand cover her breast and let out a sigh of satisfaction. She never even realized when sleep finally hit.

18

Exiting the plane at JFK airport, Sylvia knew that the decision, although it had been hard to agree to, was also the right one. Jeremy had wanted her to fly with the company plane but she'd insisted he take it down to Colombia. After all, he might need to make a quick getaway.

Ramon, the chauffeur who'd been working with Harcourts for fifteen years, was waiting for her on the curb. Sylvia sank into the smooth leather seat as she had so many times before, aware that something radical had changed.

She was no longer the same woman.

There had been little time to talk, little time to express the overpowering emotions that had gripped them both so unexpectedly. But she didn't need words to know that what they'd discovered in one another was wonderful and unique. As the car merged onto the Van Wyck Expressway, she closed her eyes for a brief moment, experiencing the thrill of discovering for the first time that she could feel this intensely. Did this only happen once in a lifetime? Probably.

Suddenly, despite the kidnapping, Jeremy's phone calls to London investigating Ricky Rico and her own fears that Thackeray might be involved, she wanted to laugh. If she'd been told a month ago that this sentiment existed outside the covers of a romance novel, she would have scorned the idea as ridiculous. Yet here she was, as the car headed over the Triborough Bridge and on toward Manhattan, sure as she knew her own name that she'd fallen head over heels in love.

Warm happiness such as she'd never known soared through her. She could almost see the new light reflected in her own eyes. Her face glowed and her body felt energized and vibrant, as though she'd received a shot of some magical elixir straight in the vein. This must be what the expression *walking on a cloud* meant, she thought, feeling giddy with joy. Everything, from Jeremy himself to the unlikely circumstances surrounding their newfound relationship glistened. Instead of Colombia and rebels, she dreamed of Warmouth, of Arabella and Lady Margaret, and sighed. Would they one day become the family she'd never had? It was absurd to dream impossible dreams, she cautioned herself, and yet…she couldn't marshal her customary cynicism. She thought of Jeremy's expression and his parting words: "Now that I've found you, I'll never let you go." Weren't those enough to make any girl dream a little?

Feet on the ground, she commanded herself, knowing she must stay focused and trying to recall all the perfectly good reasons why a long-term relationship with Jeremy would never work. But they seemed vague, part of a distant mirror that no longer reflected her present. Would he ask her to marry him? She bit her lip, watching the shoppers on Madison Avenue filing by, and tried not to react like an excited teenager. But the next step in this extraordinary whirlwind of events might indeed be marriage. She closed her eyes and allowed herself a few more moments in paradise: marriage to a man she most definitely loved. Could this truly be happening to her?

On arrival at the office building on Park Avenue, she sent Ramon a grateful smile, then leaped from the limo with a new spring in her step, walked through the entrance and cruised happily into the chrome-and-glass elevator, saying bright hellos to anyone she knew and to some she didn't. When she reached the fifty-second floor she tried to sober up, smother some of the glorious elation bubbling like vintage champagne just below the surface as she sailed through the reception area.

After several moments of greeting staff, hugging Ira and Ham and dropping off the toffees she'd promised Anita, the Nicaraguan cleaning lady, she entered the sanctum of her private office, aware that she must meet with Aaron immediately.

For a minute she stopped on the threshold and gazed at it. For years it had been the focus of all her hopes and dreams. Yet now that her wings had spread far beyond its walls, she realized with amazement, how small a world it had been. She thought again of Warmouth, of the cultured conversation, the reverence for music and art, Jeremy's wonderful gallery filled with his family's age-old passions, and realized suddenly that an existence fueled solely by work could only be empty. Even the challenge of managing

Harcourts seemed relatively inconsequential. Jeremy had opened a door to a whole new existence, she realized as she approached the desk, one she was dying to embrace.

She dropped into her chair, spinning it around like a child and laughing in delight. Then her phone rang and she came back to earth with a jolt. A brief conversation confirmed her meeting with Aaron in twenty minutes.

Pulling herself together, Sylvia banished her dreams to the back of her mind and forced herself to focus. Right now she needed to raise a ransom to save one of her employee's life. The sooner she got a grip, the better. Jeremy and her romantic fantasies would simply have to be put on hold.

A quick knock on the door followed by her ever-efficient assistant, Marcia, made her raise her head and smile.

"The mailbag from London is here. Miss Hunter sent everything you left behind on through, including the rest of your luggage. I had that delivered to your apartment." She laid a package and a pile of envelopes on the desk. "I've sifted through the main stack. There are a couple of personal notes, and the rest I've dealt with as usual. How was the trip?" she asked, cocking her head.

"Great. I mean, we're still in the dark about the designs," she added quickly, suddenly recalling why she'd been in London in the first place. "But Jeremy is on his way to Colombia to investigate."

"Great. You look like you're in good shape," Marcia remarked, still quizzing her. The two women had developed a strong working relationship over the past year. Now Marcia was her closest ally, along with Ira and Ham. Her small circle of confidants made Sylvia aware of all she'd relinquished for the sake of a brilliant business career. Like having a close girlfriend that she could confide in, someone you went to lunch with and told your deepest secrets to over Caesar salad and a glass of Chardonnay. All at once she felt a deep, unprecedented need to let her hair down, to find pleasure in the little things she'd scorned in the past and that now seemed so alluring. For a moment she was tempted to invite Marcia to lunch and confide in her, but common sense asserted itself just in time. She could not suddenly let all the dictums of corporate hierarchy go, merely because she was in love. That was absurd.

With an effort she pulled herself together, regretfully watching Marcia leave. Then reluctantly she slipped on her reading glasses, determined to descend from cloud nine to the real world and get through the mail before Aaron arrived. There were many pressing issues that needed her attention. She thought for a moment of Jeremy on his way to Cartagena. To her amazement, she felt sure he would deal with business and everything would be fine. Was she being over-confident? Blinded by her feelings? Or was Jeremy truly the man she believed him to be, the first person she'd ever trusted enough to delegate to?

With a sigh she pulled the pile of letters and the package toward her, ready to dig in. She flipped through some of the mail then reached for the package. It seemed strangely familiar. Of course. The day of their departure, Miss Hunter had brought it into her office, announcing in that prim manner of hers that it

was from United Parcel Services. It had taken Sylvia
several minutes to realize she meant UPS.

Smiling at Miss Hunter's antiquated manners, she
took the ivory-handled paper knife Major Whitehead
had offered her last Christmas and slit open the top.
An object wrapped in tissue paper lay nestled within.
She glanced again at the big bubble envelope post-
marked from Houston, Texas, then began unwrapping
the item, curious as to what it could be.

Peeling off the last layer of paper, Sylvia held up
an extraordinary object: a stuffed bird on a wooden
stand with a pink rubber pacifier hanging from its
beak. She tilted her head. Who could have sent her
such a bizarre object?

Then recognition dawned. She dropped the bird on
the desk and recoiled, stumbling as she rose in horror
from her chair and backed against the wall.

"Oh my God!" she whispered, clamping her hand
over her mouth, staring at the hideous thing lying
sideways on the desk. She gripped the back of the
office chair, and swallowed in shocked revulsion,
gripped by a deathly chill. There was something un-
cannily, grotesquely familiar about the bird. What
made it even more repugnant was the pink rubber
pacifier hanging from its mouth, as if the bird had just
devoured its young. The bird's message hit her like a
punch to the gut, and icy fingers clawed her spine as
she gazed, transfixed, into its eerie glass-bead eyes.

Panic seized her and her hands shook uncontrolla-
bly. It was a mockingbird, the state bird of Arkansas
and the mascot of her old high school. Whoever had
sent this knew about her past, and meant to terrorize
her. And the pacifier—oh my God, the pacifier.

Her hands on the chair stopped dead and she let out a ragged sigh. In all her fantasies of Warmouth and marriage there was one subject she'd left out: Jeremy would want children. A chill crept up her spine. Oh God, how could she have let herself get carried away when she knew perfectly well it was all a dream. She must stop immediately before she allowed herself to travel down an impossible road. Trembling, she reached for her bag and removed her wallet. As she had several weeks ago at the Stafford, she removed a tiny photograph, sent all those years ago by Sister Bertha, from beneath the credit card. Her eyes filled with tears and her heart with longing. Her hand trembled as she gazed at the precious photo. What wouldn't she give to know what had happened all those years ago?

She replaced the photograph and, staring at the strewn paper and the bird, made a decision. She would do what she should have done years ago and find out the consequences of her selfish actions. Whatever they were, whatever she found, it would be better than not knowing.

Obliging her scattered brain to focus, Sylvia blew her nose and forced herself to think. Somebody had discovered the secret—the truth about who she was, where she came from, and what had happened to her twenty years ago. Someone was telling her loud and clear that the nightmare she'd buried so carefully, layer by layer, year by year, could surface, reach out and destroy her.

Staring into the bird's beady eyes, she recalled Thackeray's mocking smile in the restaurant the night before and caught her breath.

It was him. Had to be him. She just knew it. That was why he'd been surprised to see her march so confidently across the room to confront him; he must have thought she'd already received this package and had been waiting to see her crack.

Sylvia sat down, unable to control her shivering, and tried desperately to regroup. She must think, must take action, must counter whatever plan Thackeray had set in motion. She stretched out her hand to the bird, determined to rid her desk of it before Aaron arrived, but recoiled, unable to touch it. Thackeray was going to pursue her, hound her until she had no more strength left to fight. She should have realized that he wouldn't give up so easily. How naive she'd been all this time, how blind and stupid. Beyond his desire to acquire Harcourts, there was his personal need to humiliate her, to avenge her embarrassing rejection at Aureole, an invitation she never should have accepted in the first place. She should have known the man was up to no good. It just proved how overconfident she'd become.

And she'd publicly humiliated him.

She should have realized immediately that he would seek his pound of flesh. He would never forgive her. His whole profile was as clear as crystal now. The man wasn't just ruthless and ambitious, he was psychotic. Acquiring Harcourts and bringing her to her knees had turned into an obsession. She'd read that in his expression last night. By sending her a sinister message, more menacing than any words, he'd achieved his objective of leaving her paralyzed with fear. But how had he found out? she wondered, panic taking hold. Who had told him about her baby?

Sylvia closed her eyes and wished desperately that Jeremy were here. Not that there was anything he could do, but at least she'd feel better knowing he was close at hand. Then her fingers clenched. If Jeremy knew about her past, knew what kind of creature she was, it would put an end to any future. She let out a tiny moan.

A wave of debilitating nausea washed over her, leaving her limp and dizzy. Thackeray must have dug deep into the past she'd so carefully hidden, found out her real name, discovered everything about her from the time she was born. But who remembered? More accurately, who still cared? Angry tears poured down her cheeks. She squeezed her eyes tight shut and clenched her fists, body racked by sobs. She couldn't let him win, couldn't let him send her back across the tracks. She tried to stop the tears but failed. They simply wouldn't cease, as though a dam had burst within her and every repressed feeling for the past twenty years was gushing out.

She'd wanted so much to believe that Thackeray had backed off, she realized, chastising herself, that a relationship with Jeremy was possible, that a magical future with the man she'd finally found and loved lay ahead. But it was only a dream. A silly, stupid adolescent illusion. She should have known life would catch up with her in the end, that there was no reprieve. She'd allowed herself to be fooled into the stupidest illusion of all: thinking she could give herself a new start.

The tears came harder. What an idiot she was. She'd acquired a position of power that she'd believed could protect her, when in fact it had made her more vulnerable than ever before. She'd let down her guard and let love in, only to discover, just when she'd learned how wonderful and fulfilling it could be, that it would never be hers. Slamming her fist on the desk she groaned, beset by physical and mental anguish. Jeremy would never want her now.

Suddenly she swiped her hand over the desk, sending the bird and the torn envelope and several other items flying across the floor. Then she sank back in the chair, tears streaming, and didn't even try to stop the flow of wet mascara dribbling onto her blouse. She felt drained, sapped of every ounce of strength. The incredible empowering energy of moments earlier had disappeared, swept away in a hurricane of fear and insecurity. She, who over the years had fought, scrapped and brawled tooth and nail, weathered every storm and borne each festering wound so valiantly, she who had vanquished every challenge presented to her with determined resilience, could bear no more.

She was tired, she realized, wondering how she would deal with the upcoming meeting, hands drooping into her lap. Tired of fighting for every square inch she had, tired of peering over her shoulder—subconsciously perhaps, but peering nevertheless. Tired of wearing blinders, pretending that what she had was enough, when now she knew what she wanted out of life was something far different from anything she'd ever imagined—and yet still, as ever, beyond her reach.

Exhausted, she lifted the phone and dialed. "Aaron? Look, I'm sorry, I'll have to see you later. I'm not feeling great right now."

"But we have to make some immediate decisions and I—"

"Not now," she snapped, voice cracking, suddenly unable to handle any more. "I'll call you."

Placing the receiver back in the cradle, Sylvia sank back in her chair and wept.

19

It was bad luck crossing those two in the restaurant last night, Thackeray decided as he walked through the dark, phantasmagoric lobby of the Delano Hotel, with its panoply of wall sconces, the Salvador Dali chair and weird fur ottoman, the sophisticated dressed-down actors and the wannabes sipping cocktails and eyeing each other, careful not to miss a beat.

Usually this amused him, gave him a power rush. But today all he wanted was to have this meeting with Hernandez over and done with, and get the show on the road. He had to be in London in two days for Marchand business and had no time to lose. Rico better get his ass down to Colombia today and fucking well deal with business. If he wasn't careful, everything would be shot to hell.

And last night was still a mystery. Why was Sylvia still so damn cocky when she should have been scared shitless by now? Hell, the woman should be quaking in her goddamn Prada pumps, not giving him that sassy know-it-all attitude. Maybe she hadn't received the package yet. Or had it simply not had the desired effect?

The thought made him pause. He stood at the bar and ordered a double scotch on the rocks. Surely the bitch couldn't be *that* sure of herself? He'd been banking on the fact she was still haunted by her past. He frowned darkly. No, he was sure his initial assessment had been correct. He'd just have to confirm via London whether the package had arrived.

He tipped the barman and, taking the scotch, sat down to wait for Hernandez in one of the uncomfortable chairs next to a backgammon set. He needed to press his advantage now, strike while the iron was hot. His eyes narrowed as he thought of what he could do to reinforce the message, bring down the final blow that would make her crumble. But first he had to get the Colombian business settled.

Problem was, he couldn't get the image of Sylvia in the arms of that English bastard out of his head. Was he fucking her? Jeremy Warmouth didn't look like the kind of guy who'd mess around, especially with his lady boss. On the other hand, the dossier on him said he had a steady girlfriend, some English aristocrat he'd dated for years. A sudden thought crossed his mind and he grinned, making a mental note to read everything he had on the girlfriend. She might prove useful. As for Warmouth, he apparently came from one of the oldest and wealthiest families in England, was some kind of duke or lord or whatever. Big fucking deal. The prick probably couldn't even put his pants on without ringing for assistance from his bootlicking lackeys.

He thought a moment and smiled grimly as alternatives began to take shape. If Sylvia was fucking Warmouth, she might be willing to play ball just so he didn't find out about her past. Or, if it wasn't serious and *His Lordship* was merely playing around, he might not like seeing Thackeray moving in on his steady girl. The grin broadened. He'd call his friend James Murray, the art dealer. James knew everybody and was never against anything that would make him a few extra pounds.

He thought again of Sylvia and took a long sip of scotch. The pleasure of watching her writhe would make up for a lot. Seeing her last night, he'd realized she wasn't really his type anyway—too put-together, too sure of herself. Even if he broke her will, she'd still have that uppity look about her, that challenge in her eyes. And he liked his women submissive and adoring and weak.

As the scotch seeped in, the tension eased. All was not lost. In fact, if he played his cards right, things might turn out doubly to his advantage. Even though he'd decided Sylvia Hansen wasn't his type, he'd be happy to fuck her if she asked him extra nicely.

The thought made him grin. It wouldn't hurt, he reflected, watching Manny hurrying through the lobby in his direction, to get his cake and eat it, too.

Armed with the interesting pieces of knowledge that Ricky Rico worked indirectly for Thackeray and had been seen in Cartagena several times with a member of factory staff, Jeremy stood in line at Customs and wondered how to proceed. The name Ronaldo had fallen into place as his contact in London was speaking. Ronaldo was the name of Harriet Hunter's nephew, whom she'd asked to have placed in the factory a couple of years ago. Nothing made sense but he intended to get on the phone to her and ask for the man's address as soon as he got out of the Cartagena airport.

Then Jeremy noticed a familiar face and frowned. The man turned away and he wondered if he'd seen right. Then, when he leaned forward again, Jeremy caught sight of the heavy chain and diamond gold cross swinging ostentatiously. *Bingo.* It was Ricky Rico, presenting his passport.

An elderly lady with dyed blond hair, wearing a bright-pink T-shirt and sneakers, stood blocking the line between them. Should he say he was in a desperate hurry and ask the woman to let him go next? The unyielding set of her shoulders and the bursting string bag filled with a variety of packages discouraged him. Jeremy could easily envisage her taking a swing in his direction if she thought he was queue barging.

The place swarmed with officials and armed guards with dogs. The last thing he needed was to draw undue attention to himself. He waited, drumming his passport impatiently while the customs officer carefully examined Ricky Rico's documents and asked him a number of questions. Ricky seemed very much at ease, answering in a confident bored manner. Ricky Rico must be well connected down here to be this comfortable, he concluded.

Jeremy prayed Ricky would have baggage; then there'd be less of a chance he'd slip through Jeremy's fingers into the crowd. Ricky glanced in his direction and Jeremy half turned, pretending to study a group of tourists with cameras slung over their shoulders, sporting baggy shorts, baseball caps and University of Wisconsin T-shirts. Out of the corner of his eye, he watched Ricky stride away, slipping his passport into his back pocket with a self-assured swagger. This was obviously not the first time Ricky Rico had landed in Colombia. His instincts told him they were here on the same errand.

When it was his turn, Jeremy moved up to the window and presented his passport, eyes trained on the exit through which Rico had passed.

"You have a visa?" the man asked.

Jeremy smiled and pointed to the page.

"Why you come to Colombia?"

"Business and pleasure."

"What kind business you do in Colombia?" The man flicked the pages of the passport and sent him a penetrating look through thick glass.

"Manufacturing." Come on, man, Jeremy begged silently, move it along, for Christ's sake. He watched as the officer flipped through his passport once more, then finally stamped a blank page. He'd lost sight of Rico but that wasn't surprising, since most of the passengers had headed to the arrivals lounge and would be waiting for their luggage. For the first time in memory Jeremy begged for a delay in the luggage retrieval, buying him enough time to catch up with his quarry.

The officer handed him back his passport and Jeremy made his way quickly down the corridor and into the arrivals hall, scanning the crowd. There were several belts, all piled with the luggage of incoming flights, but there was no sign of Rico.

"Damn," Jeremy exclaimed under his breath while a wiry bronzed porter came up to him.

"You 'ave luggage?" He smiled hopefully.

"One case. Your people insisted it come in via the luggage belt."

"Okay. *Muy bien*. Over here."

Jeremy followed the white-shirted porter and examined the group of passengers squeezing close to the luggage belts, attempting to retrieve their belongings. A woman holding two small, brightly clad children bustled in front of him, stopping them from climbing onto the luggage belt. To his left, an obviously American businessman tried but failed to blend in with the crowd. To his right, a woman in leopard-print pants and glinting designer glasses complained in loud French to an uncomprehending official that her luggage had been damaged in transit. A smattering of tourists hovered, reaching over their shoulders, fearing their bags might be lost.

But there was no sign of Ricky Rico.

Jeremy smothered his disappointment. He was certain now that Bernardo's kidnapping had brought Ricky to Colombia—in what capacity, he couldn't yet tell, but his presence here, the link with Thackeray and the information from London all coincided. The important thing now was to somehow make contact with the man without scaring him off, he reflected grimly. He was willing to bet that if Ricky Rico could be persuaded to talk, a hell of a lot would start falling into place.

The luggage belt jolted into action and Jeremy watched as cases and nylon bags bounced out. Just as he sighted the weathered Harrods suitcase that accompanied him everywhere and had belonged for many years to the former Lord Warmouth, a flash of gold at his side made him turn and catch his breath. Ricky Rico was standing next to him, pointing authoritatively at a glossy Louis Vuitton suitcase.

Jeremy spun around, a wide smile in place. He could not miss this chance.

"Excuse me, but weren't we introduced last night? Mr. Rico, isn't it?" He thrust out his hand before the other man could make any pretence of avoiding him.

"Sure." Ricky nodded, eyed him uncertainly, and then grinned. The gold tooth gleamed and his eyes shifted. The porter heaved the three Vuitton suitcases from the belt.

"*Cuidado, hombre,*" he exclaimed as the man hauled the heavy cases onto the trolley. Jeremy wondered what they contained to cause the porter to sweat so profusely.

"Have a nice stay in Colombia." Ricky smiled at Jeremy once more, and then turned to leave.

"I'm sure I will," Jeremy said quickly, his mind in overdrive. "You down here for pleasure?"

Ricky's eyes narrowed. "Maybe."

The two men sized one another up. Although Rico was definitely a henchman of some sort, he had a swagger, too, as if he sensed the value of the secrets he carried, knew they gave him a certain measure of power. He also enjoyed an expensive lifestyle, Jeremy noted, wondering if that could be exploited. He knew he had to try.

"How about a drink later on?" he asked, looking the other man straight in the eye, seeking his reaction.

Ricky's eyes narrowed. Jeremy recognized doubt and greed battling for precedence.

"Why not join in me in my suite at the Santa Clara Hotel, say, around eight?" He made no pretense that this was a social call. They both knew it was business. Jeremy held his breath. This was make-it or break-it time. The man knew something, of that he was certain. The question was how much?

"How about eight-thirty?" Ricky said finally.

"That would be fine," he murmured, careful to hide his elation.

"Great."

"Look forward to it." Jeremy nodded pleasantly and watched as Rico sent him a curious glance, then grinned.

"I'll be there, *viejo*. Don't worry."

Ricky turned on his heel and followed the porter smartly out into the arrivals area. Jeremy watched as two men in dark suits and Ray-Bans approached Rico. One paid off the porter while the other pushed the trolley. Then they disappeared through the throng and out into the street.

Turning, Jeremy spotted his own bag and the porter removed it from the carousel. Nothing to do now but wait and see if Rico took the bait. In the meantime he'd try to reach Pablo on the mobile number he'd received from his sources.

Jeremy settled in the back of the hotel limo, grateful that he finally had a quiet moment to think of Sylvia and all that had transpired between them. Their rushed departure had left little time for more than a quick kiss and hug. Still, he'd managed to get a few parting words in, and hoped she'd reflect upon them.

Furthermore, he hoped that she'd take them to heart. Extraordinary though it was, he'd meant it when he'd said he never wanted to let her go. She'd probably thought him crazy. It was the sort of thing an adolescent might say to an older woman after a first affair. But he'd meant it. Knew it to be true.

Jeremy lit a cigar and wondered how it was possible to be so sure that this woman—the one whose presence at Harcourts he'd deplored and whom for months he'd done his best to avoid—was the one person he wanted to spend the rest of his days with. Cupping his hand to protect the flame, he smiled. It was totally unlike either of them to act in the spontaneous, crazy manner they had. Yet for reasons stronger than anything they could define, he and Sylvia had known instinctively that they belonged to one another. What had occurred between them was so special, so unique and wonderful, that the truth simply couldn't be denied.

He must have been blind not to see in her what he did now. Last night had been so much more than he'd imagined, yet it had confirmed what he'd known since Scotland: that under Sylvia's tough outer shell, there hid another woman whose feelings and desires ran so deep and passionate they left him dizzy. There was something poignant about her, too, something raw and needy that made him ache to hold her tight and promise he'd never let anything hurt her again.

A rush of tenderness overwhelmed him and he wished he could jump back on the plane to New York, take her in his arms and get her to tell him everything he was dying to know about her. It was clear she carried a heavy burden, and he wanted to share it. Not that he could rush matters, he realized. Sylvia had been alone too long and protected herself too carefully to easily shed her painstakingly erected wall of protection. It might take months, even years to pry it all out of her, whatever it was that had marked her. But he didn't care. He knew he was prepared to invest whatever time and patience it took to help her emerge from the cocoon she huddled in, and evolve fully into the woman he saw waiting in the wings.

She was smart and intelligent, beautiful and bright. But beyond that, she was sensitive and giving. For some unknown reason she had chosen to stunt that sensibility, lock it under a heavy slab of sarcasm and sophisticated polish. Occasionally, like last night and in Scotland and on the terrace at Warmouth, she'd allowed him a glimpse of the other woman. Now he was determined to discover her wholly, and make her his.

What would the family say when he told them he wanted to marry his American boss? he wondered ruefully. They'd all expected him to end up with a well-born British socialite, someone like Clarissa, someone who knew the ropes of English society and would understand all the demands that Warmouth inevitably imposed. Yet now he came to think about it, it was Aunt Margaret who'd insisted on Sylvia coming to Warmouth for the weekend.

His eyebrows met over the bridge of his nose. Aunt Margaret was no fool. Had she sensed something between them? Had the invitation to Warmouth been her way of prodding things in that direction? Arabella was besotted and thought Sylvia was the best thing since Christ walked the Sea of Galilee. Clarissa, he realized reluctantly—because he didn't want his daydream spoiled—was an issue that would have to be dealt with now anyway, Sylvia or no Sylvia. He would try to be as kind as possible.

The car swerved, barely avoiding a man in a straw hat on a wobbly bicycle pulling a rickety cart filled with coconuts. Jeremy grabbed the door handle and wondered whether Sylvia would hold Warmouth against him. Brad had implied that Strathaird Castle and its obligations had been part of what had brought his relationship with Sylvia to an end. Although that hadn't been the full story, of course, for in truth Charlotte and Brad had been in love with one another since they were teenagers. They just hadn't known it. Still, he remembered Brad saying Sylvia had detested the Scottish castle and the rural way of life. A weekend trip to Warmouth was one thing, but how, he wondered uneasily, would she feel about living in Sussex?

He let out a puff of cigar smoke, enjoyed the warm sea breeze and listened to the merry salsa on the car radio. There was little use conjecturing. He had no doubt Sylvia would need some persuading before she agreed to the Warmouth situation. But maybe she could be brought around. He grinned, shrugged, and, stubbing out the cigar, gave free rein to his imagination.

By the time the car reached the hotel entrance, Jeremy had formulated a happy scenario whereby Sylvia commuted to London and New York during the week and came home—home being Warmouth—on the weekend. He practically had their schedules worked out. With a sigh he stopped himself, aware that he was letting his imagination run riot. For all he knew, Sylvia might refuse his proposal outright. What to Clarissa represented a major inducement—his title, wealth and position—might actually prove a disincentive to Sylvia. The challenge struck him as titillating and he grinned.

As the driver walked around the car and opened his door, Jeremy switched modes, aware that his focus needed to be on finding out whether Harriet Hunter's nephew and the Ronaldo mentioned as being in contact with Ricky Rico were one and the same. The thought left him uneasy. God, he hoped it wasn't the case. Poor old Harriet would be devastated if she thought her precious nephew was up to no good.

But as he alighted he was still grinning. Sylvia had better be prepared, for he had every intention of keeping her by his side—despite England, tea and rain.

There were two ways to go, Ricky Rico decided, making his way thoughtfully down the wide corridor of the Santa Clara Hotel to the suite Jeremy Warmouth occupied. He'd known the meeting at the airport was no fluke. The gringo was here because of Ronaldo's stupidity, of that he was certain. Just thinking about the *idiota* made his blood pressure peak. What a *come mierda*. Ronaldo had proved useful in the past but had messed up this time around and couldn't be counted on in the future. This latest act of idiocy had blown the cover off the Harcourts operation that had been shaping up so nicely—*muchas gracias*, asshole. Worse, it had put his own position at risk. Thackeray was pissed as hell. He'd asked him how he could have let Ronaldo do such a fucking stupid thing—like it was *his* fault the *idiota* had decided to kidnap his boss. Probably thought Thackeray would admire his *cojones,* reward him with a higher place in the operation. Ha! The only place the stupid bastard had won himself was a trip to the bottom of the Caribbean.

And now he, Ricky Rico, had been sent on this shit job. Thackeray was treating him like a fucking dog, despite the dinners and the show. He had no respect. *Nada.*

Ricky's face contorted into a snarl. If this thing blew up, he had no doubt it was *his* ass that would be hung out to dry. And that, he acknowledged with a grin, was why he'd agreed to meet the *inglés.*

He'd learned from Ronaldo that the guy was an English lord. That was surprising. He'd imagined an English lord would be a worse prick than Thackeray. But Warmouth was different, polite. Not at all stuck up like Thackeray and Hernandez. He flicked an imaginary speck of dust from the lapel of his three-thousand-dollar black Armani blazer and pulled himself up to his full five foot five. This man had shaken his hand like an equal. Still, he mustn't forget that it was he, Ricky Rico from Little Havana, who was in control here. *He* was the one with the information that the gringo so clearly wanted to buy.

He walked very slowly and weighed his options. He could pretend he knew nothing and try to find out what the gringo was up to, then he could sell that news to Thackeray and get back in his good, very lucrative graces. On the other hand, he could, for a price, furnish the gringo with some very useful information, with Thackeray none the wiser.

Of course, the best plan was one where he could screw them both.

He'd had a productive afternoon, he thought with a grin, one that left all his options open. He'd discovered Ronaldo had hidden the Harcourts director in the shed behind his grandfather's hut in a nearby village. Ricky had told him to keep him there until they decided on the next step. Of course, it was Ricky Rico who would do the deciding. But he hadn't yet made up his mind: should he quietly get rid of both Ronaldo and the director, as Thackeray had ordered? Or perhaps work with Ronaldo, negotiate a ransom deal, cut himself a piece of the action and *then* send the *idiota* swimming?

As he strutted down the corridor of the ancient cloister, now transformed into the Sofitel hotel chain's first entry into the South American market, Ricky knew he'd need to be careful. Thackeray wasn't a guy to mess with, but neither, clearly, was this guy Warmouth. He paused, drumming his fingers a moment on his gold cigarette case. With the Colombian operation pretty much blown, thanks to Ronaldo, his chances for making a little money on the side were severely curtailed. And since Ronaldo would be fired the minute this gringo learned the truth about him—assuming Ronaldo lived that long—there was the distinct possibility that Thackeray would rework his Colombian operations and try to renege on their original deal.

So, he was back to his first question: did he stick with Thackeray, who might fuck him over, or cast his lot with the British dude?

A quick grin flashed as he congratulated himself on

his coolheaded analysis of his options. He'd learned that from the gringos—that you had to keep a cool head, not let emotions get in the way of making the right decision. That was what made his Latin cohorts so vulnerable. They always let their feelings get in the way. He prided himself on being different—for him, it was all about the money.

He reached the double-paneled door of the suite and shrugged. So be it. He would feel out this new gringo, then make up his mind where it would be wisest to throw in his lot. Suddenly he remembered Thackeray's reaction when he'd seen the blonde locked in this guy's arms. He'd pretended he didn't care, but Ricky could see he'd gone ballistic. He grinned again and prepared his entrance. Destiny had placed this new gringo in his path and nothing, he knew, happened by chance.

Making three little signs in his palm he lifted the diamond cross quickly to his lips and kissed it fervently.

Then he reached out and pressed the buzzer.

20

Crouched on her knees, Sylvia picked up the debris—scattered memos, three pens and the remains of a shattered vase of freesia—caused by her moment's rage. She placed the stuffed bird gingerly in her large handbag, resolved not to let it daunt her. The damage lay in what it implied, not what it was.

After making sure she'd eradicated all traces of her momentary weakness, Sylvia rose stiffly from the floor. She entered the bathroom and quickly wiped her face as best she could, donned her largest pair of black sunglasses and prepared to leave her office. In the reception area she passed Marcia, tottering down the corridor in her high heels, arms piled with memos.

"Sylvia, do you have a moment? I need you to sign some of these."

"Can they wait till tomorrow? I'm not feeling great. Jet lag, I guess. I'm going home."

"You? Jet lag?" Marcia's eyes widened, unbelieving.

"Yeah. Bad headache. I'll see you tomorrow."

"But—"

"Just put the documents on my desk," she said, trying to control her irritation. "I'll deal with them in the morning."

Marcia's mouth sagged in wonder.

Sylvia bolted for the elevator she'd entered so happily only an hour earlier. The effort of staving off her inner agitation was almost too much to bear. As she descended in the crowded elevator, she clenched her fingers, gulping in deep quick breaths she hoped no one would notice, trying to look bright and composed. She finally reached the lobby, barely able to drag her elegantly shod feet across the gleaming marble, out to the curb and the car beyond.

Only once the front door of the apartment closed firmly behind her did Sylvia let out a long, shaky sigh. She entered the bright, airy living room, threw her purse down on the huge ecru sectional that had so delighted her when she'd had the apartment newly decorated, then flopped next to her bag and kicked off her shoes. The apartment, the office, all the cornerstones of her life that until now had provided the sturdy framework of her existence seemed suddenly illusory and transient. She could lose the apartment tomorrow if she didn't pay her mortgage. Right now she could afford to pay, no problem. But what if she was obliged to leave Harcourts?

She froze. That was impossible.

She shook her head. She mustn't think like this. She must fight, not let the fear sidetrack her. She had a good stash set by, didn't she? But not enough to maintain the high standard of living she'd set for herself, and which meant so much to her. Her eyes settled for a moment on her prized collection of pre-

Columbian pottery, chosen so carefully with her decorator to fill that precise niche in the dining-room wall. Her eyes filled with unshed tears. She could not, would not, allow Thackeray to deprive her of all she'd battled for so diligently. She would not let him send her back to the humiliating existence she'd once known.

Bereft and frightened, Sylvia huddled fearfully in the sea of ecru canvas. What could she do about Thackeray? Who could she turn to? How could she counterattack?

Nobody knew the truth. Not even Brad, whom she'd almost married, knew that she'd so callously given her baby up for adoption out of fear and shame. She also knew that she could not have given her unwanted baby a better life than she herself had known, that together she and the child would have faced nothing but a grim future, which neither would have ever escaped. But what if she'd kept it? What if she'd fled and taken the baby with her? What then?

Now people only knew her as what she'd so carefully become: the beautiful, intelligent, efficient Sylvia Hansen, CEO of one of the world's top-tier corporations, a woman with no flaws, a woman other women envied and aped. There had been a lifestyle article on her in *W* magazine; heck, she'd even been interviewed by Regis and Kelly. Surely all that should protect her from the Thackerays of this world.

Yet it was precisely that fame and attention that made her vulnerable. God knows what would happen if the circle she moved in now learned the truth about her origins—that she was nothing but trailer-park trash. It would be all over. Her carefully acquired class, all the veneer, the knowledge and culture she'd accumulated so arduously, the contacts she'd cultivated and cherished because they exemplified who she was and what she represented. The friends she'd made—or were they merely acquaintances?—would shed her like snakeskin if Thackeray dropped his bomb, leaving her exposed, defenseless and susceptible, prey to every jeering critic.

As the horrifying picture emerged, she shivered. She'd be run out of town. The boards on which she sat so proudly would request her resignation. Before a week was over, the word would be out and she wouldn't be able to show her face in a restaurant or a store, let alone a party.

Her lip trembled. She bit it hard and drew blood. And for the first time in years, her thumb slipped surreptitiously into her mouth.

She sucked it fervently, fighting off the increasing dread. She curled farther into the deep corner of the monstrous couch, her prized piece of furniture that had cost a fortune and that now seemed cold and anonymous and offered her little or no comfort. All at once the entire apartment struck her as impersonal and alien, as though she were no more a part of it. The only photographs were several flawless glossy studio shots of herself. She had no family mementos, no knickknacks, nothing that hinted at the real woman. Nothing was out of place. If she walked out of here with her personal belongings tomorrow, a mere half hour of packing would eradicate her presence.

She sucked her thumb assiduously, fingered her ear, and thought of Jeremy, of his loving words and gentle smile when he'd left, and her own excited and breathless reaction. Of Warmouth, with its wealth of memories reaching back generations, of Lady Margaret and Arabella, the dogs and the funny topiary plants, pruned like animals, bordering the gravel paths. They would all be part of the past if Thackeray exposed her. For she could never bear to face any of them knowing that they were receiving her only out of good breeding and courtesy. Certainly any respect they might have had for her would be wiped out the minute they learned the truth.

Desperation rose inside her like a tidal wave. She wanted to be wanted, to be loved by Jeremy, by them, by everybody. Perhaps, Jeremy being Jeremy, he would feel obliged to stick by his insinuation that their relationship was for keeps. That, she reflected, blinking away the tears seeping onto her cheeks, would be worse than anything.

She let out a sigh that ended up in a groan. This couldn't be happening. It had to be a nightmare. Perhaps she could talk to Thackeray, find out what it was he wanted, negotiate with him and cut some sort of deal. But what? What would it take? What would he want? How high would the price be?

Very high.

But wouldn't anything be preferable to this, to the possibility of losing her life, having to face a past she'd striven so hard to forget? She could not allow it to wound her again.

She twitched the two-tone beige cushions with her toe and played out a couple of optimistic scenarios whereby she was able to negotiate a reasonable deal with Thackeray. But logic defied her. He wanted Harcourts. What he had in mind was surely unethical, perhaps even illegal. But shameful though it was to admit, even compromising the company might be better than suffering the type of humiliation he was clearly willing to mete out.

Horrified at the path her mind was following, Sylvia forced herself to regroup. Maybe she was letting matters get out of proportion. Maybe this situation wasn't as bleak as it seemed.

She sat up straighter and pulled her thumb out of her mouth. The first step was to locate Thackeray and find out exactly what he was planning, see if they could find a common ground. Perhaps, if she was very wily, she could still turn things around, somehow.

Of course, Thackeray would know she was afraid. That was why he'd smiled at her in that horrible, overconfident, knowing manner at the restaurant in Miami. He wasn't stupid. He knew he'd hit on her one true vulnerability. The idea of the stuffed bird was cunning and gross and showed just how far he was prepared to go. She wondered again who could have told him the truth.

All at once a face that she'd refused to allow on her radar screen for the last twenty years surfaced. Fighting a wave of nausea, arms coming close about her, she let out a moan.

It couldn't be.

Surely that monster could not still be alive and out there, stalking, ready to harm her again after all this time. Hadn't he done enough damage for one lifetime?

Her fingers clawed the cushions, nearly ripping the soft fabric as the old panic set in. She sensed the overpowering shadows lurking, trailing relentlessly, haunting her as they had for longer than she liked to remember. Of course, it had to have been Don who had exposed her to Thackeray. It could only have been her vile stepfather, the man who'd branded her in the first place. She wanted to wrench the cushions, scream. Why hadn't she kept tabs on him?

Because she'd wanted to stay as far away from him as possible, pretend he didn't exist, that none of what happened had happened, scared that even knowing his whereabouts would somehow make her vulnerable. Now she wished desperately that she had followed his movements after her mother died, made sure she knew exactly what he was up to.

Instead, she'd blanked him out.

Only he would be filthy enough, vengeful enough, plain mean enough to stoop to this. Thackeray must have rooted him out of whatever rock he was living under and offered him an irresistible opportunity.

A bitter cry ripped from her throat as she scrambled, shivering, to her stocking feet. She paced the vast minimalist living room, staring at the view of Manhattan but seeing only the flat prairie fields of Middle America. She moaned, saw herself creeping up the unkempt path to the wooden house—a shack, almost—that for all her adolescence had spelled home. The rancid smell of the neighbors' trash, the black plastic bags ripped open by raccoons, rotting food remains and garbage boldly scattered behind the broken chain-link fence that separated the two run-down properties on a street of shoddy dwellings that had once formed a lower-middle-class neighborhood, filled her nostrils. Her throat tightened as it always had every time she'd approached the overgrown porch covered in junk, a broken lawn mower and an eaten-away hose that Don never bothered to move, ready to be tripped over, her mother's whining voice reaching out from behind the grimy panes of the kitchen window.

Whenever she'd tried to get close, to confide or share any of her adolescent dreams or needs with her mother, she'd known nothing but bitter disappointment. Her mother was too beset by her own problems, having married a man who'd turned out to be no good, a drunk loser with a mean nature who so frightened her that she'd succumbed to his every whim. Sylvia hated him as much for that as for himself. Seeing her mother groveling before him had made her sick. She'd vowed to get her mom out of there. But the one time she'd made the suggestion, she'd received a ringing slap across the cheek that had sent her reeling into the kitchen cupboard.

Her mother had told Don, of course. She'd expected a beating, had dreaded his belt, but amazingly, he'd told her that if she wanted to leave, he'd take her wherever she wanted to go. Just fourteen years old, she'd packed her bags, gathering up the money she'd managed to save, and naively crawled into the chopper he'd borrowed from a friend.

Sylvia gazed out of the huge apartment window, hearing the dreary drone of a chopper's engines, Don's horrible hysterical laugh next to her as he swooped into the Ozarks pretending to crash, only to rise up moments later when she'd completely lost all belief that she'd live. When they finally landed, she'd grabbed her bag in a blind panic and thrust herself out of the chopper, only to realize they were back in the field they'd set out from.

That's when she knew he'd never let her go.

She swallowed nervously as the memories enveloped her. Closing her eyes tight, she tried desperately to blot out the terrifying sound of creaking floorboards in the dead of night, coming closer and closer. Then the terrifying squeak of the door handle turning and Don's alcohol-filled breath pouring over her as she strove desperately to fake sleep.

She let out an anguished moan, the same cry of misery she'd let rip when she'd discovered that the key to her bedroom was missing. When she'd tried to hint to her mother that she was afraid, she'd been given another harsh slap. Her mother had called her a filthy-minded slut. After that, the only escape had been school. She took every extra class, joined every club, studied as hard as she could and made herself as scarce as possible, slipping in and out of the house like a ghost, barely seen or heard.

Then one day she'd returned home early after school to an empty house. Even though she hated the place, it felt good to have it to herself, if only for a few hours. She'd taken a bottle of Coke from the refrigerator, kicked her sneakers off, curled onto the sagging ripped couch and fallen fast asleep.

Sylvia crouched, numb, by the vast panoramic window and stared blindly at the high-rise buildings and the Hudson as she relieved the scene. Don's hand clamping down on her mouth, and the ensuing panic. Her limbs became paralyzed as the awful nightmare replayed itself step by step: the helpless realization that nothing was going to save her, that all her efforts to fight him were in vain, his raucous laugh when he'd ripped off her skirt, torn her panties, bitten her breasts and forced himself inside her.

She let out a muffled scream, rocked now by crippling, indescribable pain. She sank to her knees, clenched her fists against her mouth, trying to flee the agony of the violation, not just of her body but of her mind, heart and soul. It was as if he were again ramming his filthy organ inside her virginal body, the one she'd vowed would never be vulnerable again.

And now, by a freak set of circumstances, she was at his mercy once more. She would never escape him. However far she ran, however convinced she was that she'd succeeded in escaping him, he would stalk her, ruin her again and again until at last she broke.

She focused on the potted plants that even yesterday had made the apartment seem so attractive and special. Rising painfully like a weary old woman, she fumbled with the catch on the glass door. It slid smoothly open and she staggered out, face contorted, hands reaching blindly for the parapet. She gazed down sixty-three floors at the traffic, people and cars moving like toys in the street below.

Then something registered past the pain in her heart and her aching body and soul, and she heard the sharp ring of the telephone. Blinking a moment, she stared horrified at her raised, unshod foot. With a gasp she staggered away from the edge, aware of what she'd been about to do. With a piercing scream she backed away, hurtled inside the living room and stumbled over the rug. Reaching the phone, she grabbed it like the lifeline it was. When Jeremy's deep soothing voice poured down the line, she smothered a moan and collapsed in a cold sweat onto the nearest chair. She couldn't speak, but it was enough to hear his voice, asking repeatedly if she was there, if she was okay.

The next two days were hell. She tried desperately to function in her normal manner, to follow the negotiations going on in Colombia without letting Jeremy sense her pain, or her lack of interest. At the same time, she knew she must be available for Ham and Ira, ready to address all the current matters at Harcourts requiring her immediate attention.

But after three days of undiminished pressure, little or no sleep and the ever-mounting fear that at any moment Thackeray might lose patience and expose her, Sylvia could bear it no more. Living like this was making her sick. After a fourth night of wandering, sleepless, around the apartment in her pajamas, desperately seeking a solution that would get her off the hook, she gave in, as frightened and vulnerable as the terrified sixteen-year-old who, desperate and alone, had left her newborn baby in the care of the nuns at the convent of St. Theresa and never looked back.

But now the memory of her baby, whom she'd only glimpsed once for a few short moments, obsessed her every moment. All she could think of were tiny crumpled red fingers, a puckered face and that wail, that tiny heart-rending wail.

Five days after she'd opened Thackeray's awful gift, Sylvia sat pale and determined behind her desk and sipped the coffee Marcia had solicitously laid beside her. She was vaguely conscious that Jeremy seemed to be coping well with the situation down south, that he had set certain plans in motion. And the leak at the factory remained a question. But frankly, she was finding it hard to show even minimal interest in the problems at the factory. It all seemed so insignificant next to her present plight.

At times she stopped obsessing and tried to take charge, shades of her old self seeping through the depression. Hadn't she risen from the ashes once already and quite literally conquered her place in the world? Then she'd remember that was the very place she was on the verge of losing if she didn't take immediate action.

She had to do *something*. She could not allow fear and regret to paralyze her. She'd begun cowering again like a hunted animal, jumping when a door banged. That would only serve to undermine what little strength she had left. Wherever Thackeray was, she must find him and reach some sort of agreement before he destroyed her completely.

She got up and moved about the office nervously, feeling a bit better now that she'd decided on a course of action.

For a moment she stared wistfully out into the rainy morning. In all these years she'd never allowed herself to think of the past. Now it haunted her day and night. She had to know, she realized, panicked, had to find out what had actually happened to her child. She'd been a coward, she realized, despising herself more by the moment. But she'd been too afraid, too weak to muster the courage to go back, to know and face the truth. Now, it was all she could do to face herself, the shame was so great.

What kind of woman, however young and desperate, abandoned her child? Not that she'd wanted to. But what choice had she had? She'd had to get away; she was in no position to care for a baby. God knew how often she'd been on the brink of returning during those first terrible months. Once, she'd even gone to the bus station, bought a ticket and nearly boarded the Greyhound. But something, not just fear, but something else, had stopped her.

And now justice, in the shape of Thackeray, had come knocking at her door. She'd committed a terrible sin and would have to pay. There was a little girl out there—surely a woman now—who had grown up without her, who'd never even known her mother's name. She'd provided for her, certainly, sending donations to the convent regularly, increasing the amount as her own success had grown, but money didn't equal commitment, nor did good intentions wipe out the stain. Every single night, Sylvia prayed that her little girl was happy, that she'd found a good home and a loving family, persuading herself that it was for the best. But what if her prayers had been ignored? What if her daughter had fallen into the hands of someone like Don?

She whimpered and dropped her forehead against the glass pane. It was only right that now she would pay. Her life was nothing but a fabricated illusion. Jeremy and her newfound feelings were all a dream. She didn't deserve to share a life with a man she loved. Maybe this was God's way of punishing her. Like Moses, she'd been shown the Promised Land but was being denied entry. She was a fraud, a piece of soiled goods. No matter how she tried to dress herself up, the stain on her soul would always show through.

No man in his right mind, once he knew the truth, would want a woman who'd abandoned her own child.

She closed her eyes tight and held on to the back of the chair, fighting the nausea. Jeremy had fallen in love with a lie. Given a chance, she'd have gladly married him and continued the lie. Oh God! What had she become?

Sylvia collapsed onto the thick-piled carpet, buried her face in her hands and wept bitter tears. Even if Thackeray and his threats magically disappeared, she would still have to live with herself.

After several minutes she managed to calm down sufficiently to lean on the arm of the chair and rise, trembling, to her feet. She glanced at her gold Panthère Cartier watch, another symbol of what she'd become, and forced herself to reason.

It would not be hard to locate Thackeray. In fact, he was probably expecting her to find him.

Sylvia let out a long, shuddering sigh and swallowed. She was playing right into his hands but she had no other choice. Whatever else happened, she must at least try to save Harcourts from a dreadful scandal that could send the company into a tailspin.

Dropping once more into the office chair, Sylvia straightened her aching back, took a long deep breath, then picked up the phone.

21

"How much?"

It was a deliberate, plainly stated question that Ricky Rico could not ignore. He could extricate himself from any number of wily, sinuous situations, but straightforwardness was a trait he found hard to handle.

It did not come naturally to him to respond. Instead, he hesitated, thrown by the directness of the question. How much was his information worth? He hadn't labeled it with a price. Now, gazing at the handsome furniture, the ample sofas and lush tropical plants dominating the stone-walled room, he panicked. What if he priced himself too low? He could hardly retract. By the same token, if he went too high he could screw up and lose the onetime opportunity that he sensed had come his way.

Taking a long sip of whiskey, he shifted in the wide armchair and tried to look as comfortable and at ease as his host: a smooth operator who knew the ropes, Ricky reflected. The man was in no hurry.

Or so he wanted Ricky to believe.

It hadn't taken long to sum Ricky Rico up, Jeremy reflected, eyeing him askance without appearing to do so. A brief conversation related to last night's dinner, and the story had told itself: Ricky loathed Thackeray. Jeremy didn't need to be a rocket scientist to deduce that if the right buttons were pressed, information would follow. With that in mind, he had set out to woo his quarry. An hour and a few Blue Labels later, Jeremy was confident that Ricky Rico would, for a price, be prepared to sell Thackeray out.

It was too good an opportunity to pass, and however immoral Sylvia might consider it to be, Jeremy had every intention of pursuing what he knew to be his only choice. Bernardo was out of danger, of that he was now certain. A couple of Rico's comments had alleviated the fear that for hours had haunted him. Bernardo was alive and well, and when the time came, Ricky would reveal his whereabouts. What Jeremy needed to get to the bottom of was the role Harriet Hunter's nephew, Ronaldo, had played in all this. He was beginning to think it was more prominent than at first believed.

So he waited patiently, knowing time was on his side.

It might require a little prodding. Rico was reluctant to disclose his information without a secure deal. How much he was prepared to pay would depend on what Rico had to proffer. There would be a slow and cautious negotiation. Jeremy knew better than to precipitate the moment. It was all in the timing. So he lit another cigar and half closed his eyes. *La Bohème* echoed softly from the wraparound speakers.

Through the open windows and beyond the wide

stone terrace he could see a vast expanse of clear indigo-blue night. He thought of Francis Drake and Captain Morgan, who had frequented the area and whose pirates had left their marks carved in the heavy wooden beams of many of the local residences. They, too, had had tricky deals to negotiate.

Jeremy glanced sideways at Rico seated in the half light, still unsure of Thackeray's involvement. It seemed odd that he would risk exposing himself in such a crude manner. Jeremy frowned and pondered. What if this hadn't been in Thackeray's plans? What if things weren't running quite as smoothly as he wanted them, too. Perhaps his phone call to London later that night would shed light on the situation. Now he needed to stay absolutely calm. He'd already taken a huge risk playing his hand so soon. If he didn't get it absolutely right, it could backfire on him.

On the other hand, he needed answers now. He'd give Rico exactly another thirty seconds to decide. If nothing happened, he'd apply some pressure.

Finding a plausible excuse to return to London had not been altogether easy. Still, Sylvia had managed it without too many questions asked. Now, several days later, she was glad of Lady Margaret's invitation to join her and Arabella at an auction at Sotheby's. Anything to keep her mind off the business that had brought her here. Business she still needed to confront.

The last person she'd expected to see when she stepped into Sotheby's auction was the man she was desperately deciding how to deal with. At first she wondered if she was mistaken. Maybe she was so obsessed with the problem and how she was going to handle it, she was seeing double.

But the bronzed aquiline profile did not lie. It was Thackeray, all right. Sylvia's pulse leaped and something akin to nausea swept over her. She held frantically to her jittery poise and, swallowing the bitterness, mustered her dignity, and followed Lady Margaret and Arabella down the center aisle, bordered on either side by rows of chairs for the bidders. *Lord, please don't let him know how scared I am.*

She hadn't prepared herself for facing him in public. Since arriving in London, she'd been scouring her brain, desperate to solve the problem of how to approach Thackeray. And now here he was, not three steps away, cool as a cucumber.

At that moment Sylvia knew the meaning of hate.

It ripped through her like a blazing angry arrow. She had to dig her nails into her palms and restrain the urge to rush forward and attack him physically. The worst thing in the world would be to let her tumultuous feelings show. She couldn't, mustn't. This was the endgame and she must stay calm.

Thackeray didn't raise his head when Lady Margaret eased her lime silk-clad bulk into the aisle opposite. Sylvia drew a long breath. He seemed intent on studying the catalog. It was a silver and enamel sale and Sotheby's auction rooms were filling fast. Perhaps he was filching ideas to copy for his new Marchand line, Sylvia reasoned savagely. With an effort she smiled at her companions.

"Such a crowd," Lady Margaret commented, looking around her. "Arabella, don't stare, dear, but is that Damian Antsworth over there? If it is, he looks considerably older than when I last saw him. And why on earth is Sarah James here? She's never seen at these events. Sylvia, have you heard from Jeremy?''

''Not for a couple of days,'' she responded, glad of the distraction. She kept her eyes fixed on her own catalog, listening to Arabella and Lady Margaret's prattle, and flipped through silver salvers, eighteenth-century epergnes, candelabras, enamel snuff boxes and other items in which she had little interest. She'd accepted the invitation as a means of getting away, taking a break—if such a thing existed—from the havoc ravaging her since she'd received Thackeray's little package back in New York. But obviously, she thought, the vise of hysteria gripping her, she'd gone from the frying pan into the fire. Thackeray was here, no more than ten feet from her. And, she realized, swallowing hard, she needed to come up with an immediate game plan or she'd be destroyed.

It wouldn't be long before he'd raise his head, turn and see her. What would she do then? She stared again at a Paul de Lamarie silver mug, trying not to give in to panic. Had he known she'd be here tonight? Was this just another step in his plan to intensify the pressure? Nothing scared her more than the prospect of a public showdown. Should she leave while there was still a chance, or brazen it out?

''So sorry I'm late.''

In a daze, Sylvia raised her head, startled to see Clarissa looming over her. She gave the woman a perfunctory smile as she squeezed impatiently past her, apparently determined to sit on Lady Margaret's left. Clarissa wore one of her usual shapeless outfits.

Her voluminous bag hit Sylvia on the temple as she pushed past, creating a stir.

That's when Thackeray noticed her.

When she turned, he was staring straight at her.

Controlling her rising anguish, Sylvia smiled and waved, hating herself but unable to think what else she could do. Jesus, how she loathed that smarmy grin, those odious flashing teeth, so like a hyena's, that symbolized everything he stood for: a scavenger.

"Who is that devastatingly good-looking man waving at you?" Lady Margaret asked in a loud whisper, green silk rustling as she leaned across Sylvia to get a better look. Thackeray obliged her with a nod and another Hollywood-style grin.

"A guy I know from business in New York. Actually, he's our biggest rival," Sylvia murmured.

"*Well,*" Lady Margaret sat back, impressed. "He doesn't lack for looks."

Clarissa peered past her and Arabella poked her in the ribs.

"Don't stare, Clarissa. He'll notice."

"Who cares? He's just a thick-skinned Yank."

"Shut up," Arabella snapped bitingly, sending Sylvia a quick embarrassed glance. The two women had become fast friends since Sylvia's trip to Warmouth. In fact, Sylvia realized, spending time in Arabella's company was one of the few activities that seemed to hold her demons at bay.

The auctioneer stepped onto the podium.

"My lords, ladies and gentlemen, we are here this evening…"

Sylvia shut out the auctioneer and tried to focus on her plight. She only had half an hour, forty-five minutes at most, before she would have to face him. Being with Lady Margaret and the others put her at a disadvantage. She would have to keep up appearances at whatever cost and Thackeray would realize that she was loath to expose herself in front of them. *Shit.* Why had it happened like this? All the cards seemed stacked against her. She watched, numb, from the corner of her eye as Thackeray bid discreetly on several items. How, she wondered for the umpteenth time, could she turn this situation to her advantage?

Her chest ached. She felt weighed down and heavy, all her usual energy sapped by the past days' strain. Since receiving the stuffed mockingbird, she'd functioned in overdrive. Now, when she most desperately needed all her faculties at their sharpest, her mind was as blank as a white page. She could think of no words, no tactics, no strategy, no game plan. She was toast.

''…And here we have an exceptional set of hallmarked late-seventeenth-century platters…''

Unfortunately, they sold quickly.

The auction was over all too soon.

Lady Margaret, who'd been especially keen on a certain enamel box, had been outbid by a Russian antique dealer in a charcoal suit, black shirt and purple silk tie.

''Dreadful little man,'' she murmured as he walked cockily before them while they filed toward the exit.

Sylvia barely heard. Murmuring assent, she guided Lady Margaret's elbow and kept a sharp eye on Thackeray. Her pulse rate was up in the three digits. Stay calm, she ordered. She could not lose her grip. When he eased closer and was nearly beside her, she

realized the bastard had calculated his exit to coincide
with hers.

This was it.

Her heart quailed.

Surely he wouldn't dare have a public showdown?

For a moment she trembled inwardly. Her world
was tottering on the edge of a deep ravine and only
she could save it from crashing into the hollow.

Then he came alongside her. In a flash, she knew
he would not expose her here. He was still stalking.
Rather, he would ingratiate himself, seek to enter the
good graces of whoever he thought might be useful
to him.

Sure enough, seconds later Thackeray greeted her
with a broad, friendly smile.

"Sylvia, we meet again. Another coincidence.
How's Arkansas doing these days? Great to see you.
And just as I was beginning to feel lonely in ol' London town." He reached out a hand that she could
hardly refuse. She murmured, dazed, then reluctantly
introduced a curious Lady Margaret and watched,
frustrated, as Thackeray turned on the charm full
blast. Instead of the brief greeting she'd hoped for, a
full-blown conversation was getting under way.

By the time they reached the exit, she knew with
a sinking heart that Thackeray had no intention of
letting her slip through his fingers.

This was turning out exactly as he'd hoped, Thackeray gloated. It had taken one phone call to learn
where she would be tonight, another to ensure his
presence in the right spot at the right time. Despite
her fixed smile, it had been clear she'd barely been

able to manage her fear. The ploy had worked and the ensuing agony he'd successfully inflicted was about to produce its effect.

While listening with seeming interest to Lady Margaret's ramblings, he watched Sylvia carefully, noted each gesture, each step, each move. As a child, he'd derived immeasurable satisfaction from capturing animals and devising contorted ways of making them suffer. Observing her gave him a similar rush. Seeing Sylvia squirm beneath that polished front she was trying so hard to keep in place thrilled him.

He would get what he wanted.

Did he really want to fuck her, he asked himself absently, or was that merely part of the ultimate humiliation?

Lady Margaret moved onto the steps, followed by the pretty young brunette and the thin hoity-toity woman, just as Thackeray was envisioning Sylvia standing naked before him, ready to perform his every whim. He would taunt her, humiliate her in ways she couldn't begin to imagine, remind her of what had happened to her in adolescence. Don Murphy had not told him the full version, but it was easy to deduce what must have happened all those years ago. Rape victims never got over it, he'd heard. So much the better. If he could take her back to that same state of anguish and guilt, inducing her to hand over Harcourts on a platter would be a breeze.

Satisfied that he'd finally put his finger on how to break her, Thackeray concentrated on chatting up the other women around him. Forget the young one. But what about the other bitch to her right. He looked at her a moment and smiled. This must be Warmouth's steady. She smiled back archly.

"Would it be presumptuous of me to ask you ladies to join me for dinner?" he asked, his twinkling eyes and rakish smile encompassing Lady Margaret, Arabella and Clarissa.

"We really shouldn't," Lady Margaret replied in a voice that had every intention of accepting.

"Sounds super," Clarissa waxed. "Dreadfully decent of you to drag us all along. Are you sure you wouldn't prefer to have Sylvia to yourself?" she added sweetly. "I know if Jeremy were here, I'd much rather be with him on our own."

"Jeremy?" Thackeray pretended to frown and Sylvia's heart sank a notch lower. "That wouldn't be Jeremy Warmouth, would it?" Sylvia caught the glint and cursed Clarissa's blabbering mouth. She had just handed him another bullet to fire.

"Yes," Clarissa fluttered. "My boyfriend."

"This is amazing." Thackeray shook his head, helped Lady Margaret walk down the steps and turned to Clarissa over his shoulder. "I saw Jeremy just the other day in Miami. In fact—" He broke off, glanced at Sylvia, who cringed.

"You all right?" Arabella sent her a curious look and grabbed her arm.

"Fine. Just hungry, I guess. I didn't eat lunch."

"Sylvia, weren't you just in Miami, too?" Clarissa purred, eyes icy as she came alongside Thackeray, who was waving to the driver of a silver Bentley waiting on the curb. "Gosh. Do you think we'll all squish in there?" she continued, distracted by the glistening vehicle gliding toward them.

"You could always sit on my knee if there's not enough room," Thackeray murmured playfully and Clarissa laughed back.

Sylvia swallowed. This could not be happening. Their eyes met and she froze, wondering what Thackeray's latest intent might be. She was beside herself, desperately searching for an excuse that would get them out of the dinner invitation, but could think of none. In silent horror, she watched Lady Margaret's large form being assisted into the car, fox stole and all.

Sylvia sat squeezed between Arabella and Clarissa, barely able to control her feelings. It had all gone awry. She tried to focus, but Clarissa and Thackeray kept up an incessant trail of conversation that left her more edgy than she already was.

"Maybe we could palm her off onto him," Arabella whispered into Sylvia's ear as the car turned into Berkeley Square, then on toward Charles Street, where it stopped in front of the unassuming door of Mark's Club. Sylvia wondered, surprised, how he had managed to secure a table at this exclusive, member's-only establishment.

"Good evening, Lady Margaret," Bruno, the urbane headwaiter greeted her with a bow, then nodded and smiled to Sylvia and the others. Sylvia had been here several times with Jeremy and Reggie. A sudden tug of nostalgia gripped her. How she wished Jeremy were not miles away, and perhaps in danger himself at this very moment, but here by her side.

Sylvia reluctantly climbed the narrow stairs flanked by a wall full of paintings, prints and etchings, trying desperately to think how she could counter Thackeray's offensive. She felt bereft, alone and afraid, like a recently captured prisoner walking toward her fate, not knowing whether she would live to tell the tale.

At the top of the stairs facing the bar she watched a medium-size, very British-looking, balding man with reddish cheeks dressed in a dark gray suit and bright-pink tie rise from the window embrasure.

"Good Lord, James," she heard Clarissa exclaim, in her high-pitched staccato. "Is that really you? I haven't seen you for ages."

"Hello, hello. It's been awhile, hasn't it?" The man smiled, pecked Clarissa on the cheek, then greeted Lady Margaret, whom he also appeared to be acquainted with. This was getting worse and worse, Sylvia realized, nonplussed, as though she was on-stage in a play in which she didn't know her part. Thackeray introduced her, taking her stiff arm in his as the group moved through the narrow bar into the main room.

"Well, well. Life is fraught with surprises, isn't it? Who would have thought the likes of you and I would be dining at Mark's Club. Bet you didn't even know it existed back then in Arkansas, did you?" he taunted. "Must've been quite a thrill hitting New York City and making it big. Quite an achievement for a girl with your, uh, checkered background?"

"What do you want?" she muttered in a low whisper, unable to contain herself. "Why don't you come straight out and say it?"

"Not so fast," he murmured, squeezing her biceps.

Sylvia stared stolidly at the room. A warm glow from the table lamps and picture lights shrouded English rural scenes. It seemed unreal that only weeks before she'd sat in this very room with Jeremy, sipping champagne, discussing the house specialty, a scooped-out eggshell filled with scrambled egg and topped with caviar. But all that seemed a distant vision as Thackeray guided her, amid soft, well-bred British voices, to the sofa, hand still firmly gripping her upper arm.

She sat down like a robot next to him, glanced at a handsome couple, seated in one of the corner niches covered in ancient throws, conversing animatedly, and watched Lady Margaret accommodate her skirt over her knees, babbling merrily, a picture of English elegance in this most elegant of English decors. What was he going to do? she wondered desperately. Was he about to expose her publicly? The realization of all she was about to lose hit her hard in the gut and she swallowed a gasp.

Thackeray appeared relaxed but she knew that was only a front. Every so often his eyes narrowed and strayed in her direction. Her only satisfaction was the realization that however much he paid, he would never be accepted, never blend into a place like this. He was as out of place as a penguin on a tropical beach. He played the part, knew the moves, but this would never be his world.

Yet neither was it hers, she reminded herself glumly. As he'd just reminded her, she was no better than him.

This was Jeremy's world.

Sylvia took a nervous sip of champagne and hoped she was disguising her fear. It tasted bitter.

"You're awfully silent," Arabella commented. "A penny for your thoughts?"

"Sorry." Sylvia tried to laugh. "Just daydreaming. This place is so English," she scrambled for something to say. "Kind of like a private home."

"Bet you'd like a place like this, Sylvia," Thackeray interjected.

"Really? I thought Sylvia's taste ran more to the modern," Clarissa murmured slyly. "At least, that's what you've had me believe."

She sipped absently, bereft of words, and smiled weakly, feeling all the world like a wet, wrung-out cloth. She was helpless, putty in his hands. My God, she could use a triple scotch, neat, to get through what was shaping into one of the strangest, most nerve-racking evenings of her life. She half listened to the conversation, aware that she was answering like an automaton. She peered at the softly lit paintings, the classical mantelpiece, the huge vase of flowers. No one around her could begin to imagine the inner drama she was living. The man sitting next to her knew her deepest secrets. He could smash her, crush her, send her back to the depths of oblivion in the blink of an eyelid, if he so wished. And would have no compulsion in doing so, if and when it suited him.

A steady, nearly blinding headache worked its way up behind her eyes, making it hard to concentrate.

"My, my, you're quiet tonight, aren't you?" he said. The last time we were in a restaurant together, you were a lot more vocal."

"I'm tired," she hissed through gritted teeth.

"I'll bet," he muttered so softly only she could hear. "Why not throw in the towel while you've still got the chance, baby? Who knows, I might just change my mind. And next time I'll be sending you a hell of a lot more than a bird." He turned back to Clarissa, oozing charm.

"Seems rather taken with Clarissa, doesn't he?" Arabella remarked. "Wouldn't it be hilarious if she fell for him and went off to America? Good riddance. At least Jer wouldn't have her hanging on his sleeve all the time."

Sylvia nodded, too shaken to answer. This was outright blackmail.

"Your life sounds perfectly *fascinating,*" Clarissa purred, eyes pinned on Thackeray. Perhaps, she reflected craftily, she'd at last found a way of capturing Jeremy's waning attention. If she could secure this man's interest, then Jeremy might sit up and take notice. For this man was obviously no lightweight. He was certainly powerful and wealthy. And he had enough discernment not to be swept off his feet by Sylvia's razzamatazz or by Arabella's ethereal beauty. She, on the other hand, considered herself attractive and mature, the kind of woman a wealthy man like Thackeray might be interested in considering as a wife. Americans loved titles and anything aristocratic. Perhaps if she could bring him to the point of proposing and let Jeremy know…well, there was a fine possibility he might wake up and realize what a dreadful fool he was making of himself with Sylvia.

She listened to Thackeray's description of his one-hundred-and-twenty-foot yacht, at present anchored off St. Barthes, and cooed, suitably impressed. By the end of dinner she'd make sure she'd secured an invitation and that the whole table knew about it. With this in mind, she set out on a full-fledged campaign to captivate him.

Watching Clarissa flirt with Thackeray, Sylvia fumbled painfully through the different courses, trying desperately to find a loophole she knew didn't exist. She longed to extricate not only herself, but Harcourts, from the mess she'd landed them in. And Thackeray looked so damn pleased with himself she ached to slap him. This must be truly as good as it got for a man like him, she concluded bitterly, one woman out to get him, the other wondering desperately how she could escape his clutches.

Worse was knowing that soon she would be forced to make a decision that would change her future forever.

22

Ricky Rico's shocking revelations had rocked Jeremy's well-entrenched faith in all of Harcourts's time-tested institutions and would require his immediate action when he reached London. As he looked down from the plane window at the colonial city of Cartagena, he felt relieved and somewhat satisfied. Bernardo had been released without Harcourts disbursing a penny and was now safe and sound and back at home. The only cost involved had been Rico, who hadn't come cheap but was worth every cent. He did not plan to mention that he'd bribed the man, Jeremy reflected, knowing Sylvia's moral stand on such matters. Plus, he still needed Rico.

It felt good to be homeward bound. He'd barely spoken to Sylvia, who seemed oddly distracted, strangely unconcerned in Bernardo's fate and almost uninterested when he'd finally told her that the man was out of danger, her lack of concern bordering on the indifferent. He tried not to feel miffed. After all, he might have been in danger himself, for all she knew.

Knowing it was silly to presume things—the phone could be a treacherous instrument of communication—Jeremy leaned back in his seat and concentrated on how he was going to resolve his more immediate problem. Of all the members of Harcourts's huge staff, he never would have believed that the traitor could be the one person he'd always considered above suspicion. Yet the truth had proved otherwise. And he would have to take the painful step of seeing that justice was done.

She'd chosen to meet him in the park because she could breathe outside. Now, as they walked next to the pond, ducks gliding on the still waters, Sylvia realized that it mattered little where she met the man, the horror was the same. She forced herself to remain calm and listen.

"Thought you'd come around, as soon as you knew you had nowhere to run," Thackeray gloated. He wore a fine tweed jacket, gray flannels and carried an air of wealth and power.

"Get on with it," she muttered, determined to listen to whatever his ignoble proposal was with an outward appearance of composure. If she knew where he was coming from, perhaps she could counter him. There had to be a way, she told herself over and over. Just had to be.

"Forthcoming this morning, aren't we?" he remarked in the same taunting voice she'd come to hate. "Mighty impatient to know the scoop now that you're in, huh?"

"We're just wasting time. I have to be back in the

office in half an hour," she said, barely registering the cutting edge to his words, the sneer in his voice.

"Okay, here it is in a nutshell. It's dead simple. You have the confidence of the board, right?"

"I guess."

"You know you do, so shut up and don't play games." His eyes narrowed and he kicked a tuft of grass at the edge of the path they were walking down. "I want you to begin pitching the idea of a merger. Make 'em understand that by merging Marchand and Harcourts we'd become the most formidable corporation in the business."

She had to admit, it was ingenuous: blackmail her into using her influence with the Harcourts board to engineer a merger with Marchand, creating a corporation of truly global reach. She knew what would happen next: he'd force her to rubber-stamp changes to the company's structure that would allow him to funnel money from drug sales and God knew what else through Harcourts's far-flung entities. She swallowed and listened as he expounded on the theme. The merger would look like her idea; it wouldn't even be a hard sell, she reflected, listening to the projected numbers as she watched the ducks sailing smoothly in single file under the bridge while Thackeray walked next to her, businesslike and efficient. And with Harcourts's impeccable reputation, the likelihood of the feds being interested in monitoring the company's activities was minute, leaving Thackeray to expand his illicit empire at will.

She eyed him reluctantly. If the idea wasn't so monstrous, it would be brilliant. But then, he'd chosen his target well, hadn't he? She'd already done so

many horrible things in her life. In a way, it was normal he'd assume that, with pressure, she'd cave in
and help him implement his monstrous plan.

"And what if I don't agree?" she asked at last,
stopping by two faded striped deck chairs under an
oak tree, as though waiting for passersby to sink
thankfully into them and enjoy a few rays of morning
sun.

"The whole of New York and London gets to
know what a fucking little white-trash whore you are.
Just be glad I've decided you're not worth fucking,"
he responded without hesitation.

Seeing the harsh gleam in his eye, she believed
him. There would be no reprieve, no escape. She
swallowed hard and thought fast. "I guess you've
won, then. I'll need a few days to think this all out,
see how best to implement the scheme. It's inspired,
of course, and should work." She heard herself ut-
tering the words as though someone else was speaking. She sounded as cold and efficient as him.

"Just don't take too long and don't try to mess with
me or I'll screw you so bad you'll have nowhere to
run. Is that clear? I want this to be a wrap before the
end of the year. That doesn't give you too much time.
You'll need to start working on the board right away.
Guess Warmouth won't be a problem, huh? You're
good at fucking your way out of problems," he added
venomously.

She barely heard him, and gave a cursory nod. "I
want some guarantees. How do I know you won't
fuck me over after the deal's closed?"

"The only guarantee you've got, baby, is that
you're useful to me. Without you I can't do the deal.

Just make sure you go on being useful and you won't have to worry, will you?'' His mouth took on a cruel sardonic twist and he stepped closer, reached for her shoulder.

"Don't.'' She pulled back and stood rigid under the tree. "Don't come near me. Don't touch me. I've agreed to your scheme but that's the end of it.''

He took a speculative step forward and involuntarily she cringed. "Still afraid of the Big Bad Wolf? I thought you'd gotten over that a while back. From what I heard you'd done pretty much all of Arkansas before you dropped your kid off and ran away.''

"Get out of here,'' she hissed, tripping on the tree's roots as she backed away. "I've agreed, haven't I? So leave me alone.''

"Not so fast, Miss Upper East Side. You may discover I don't look so bad when you're out there all by your little self,'' he murmured with a harsh laugh.

"I said I'd go along with the plan. I can't think when you bug me.''

He reacted immediately, as she'd known he would. "Fine. Forget it. Just think hard and come up with answers. And fast.''

She nodded, unable to speak, his figure looming over her more than she could stand. She let out the breath she was holding when he suddenly spun on his heel and marched across the grass back onto the path, then out the gates and off toward Buckingham Palace, without a backward glance.

She watched until his tall, tweed-clad figure disappeared, then sank, legs trembling, into a deck chair. She was wet to the skin, shivering, soaked in sweat. Sylvia stared at her surroundings, the old ladies walking dogs, brisk businessmen taking the shortcut through the park, a young couple sitting cuddled on a rug holding hands, and tried to assimilate the enormity of what she'd just agreed to do.

She'd just sold out Harcourts.

How could she? For a moment she thought of running after him, telling him she didn't care what he did to her, she refused to do his bidding. But her legs wouldn't move or her body follow the wishes of her tormented mind. Tears seeped shamefully down her cheeks and her shoulders slumped: she'd sold her soul to the devil and now there was no turning back.

The car veered into St. James's Place and a bemused Jeremy prepared to alight. He wondered anxiously if Sylvia would be in. He hoped so. He wanted to see her, touch her, then share with her the disturbing knowledge that had kept him awake most of the night pondering how best to resolve the issue, while causing the least possible damage.

He jumped out of the car and bounded up the stairs, stopping short in the reception hall when he saw Miss Hunter.

"Good morning, Lord Warmouth," she said in her usual placid tone. "What a pleasure to have you back."

"Good morning," he muttered automatically, trying to associate this innocuous little old lady with the traitor who'd arranged for the theft of Harcourts's designs and calmly handed them over to her nephew to be sold to Marchand. She had betrayed Harcourts, him, Dexter Ward, who had hired her years earlier, and all they stood for. How could she? He hesitated, about to speak, then changed his mind. It couldn't be quite that simple. There must be a deeper motive than mere gain for her to have betrayed a life's dedication. Frowning, he entered his office, some of his righteous anger dissipating. Miss Hunter must be deeply troubled to have stooped to such an act. He knew her and didn't question her loyalty to Harcourts and Dexter Ward. It was impossible, he argued, that she could have done this without pressure. Could Ronaldo have been threatening her? He had no doubt that sleazeball wouldn't hesitate to put pressure on his old aunt. He'd had few regrets when the Colombian police had taken Ronaldo into custody. Still, she'd left him with no choice but to confront her.

He stepped behind his desk, ran his agitated fingers through his hair, then pressed the intercom.

"Is Miss Hansen around?" he asked.

"I'm afraid not, my lord. She hasn't been in yet this morning."

"Thank you." *Damn.* Jeremy experienced a moment's disappointment. Surely she must have known he was returning this morning? Couldn't she have made the effort to be here to greet him?

He opened his briefcase, feeling peeved and somewhat anxious. Could Sylvia have changed her mind about him? He removed his papers and sifted through them, determined not to let her absence faze him. But a meeting with Reggie and Sylvia regarding Miss Hunter must be held at once. His feelings and their personal lives would have to stay on hold until they'd dealt with the immediate concerns besetting Harcourts. At least they'd found the leak. Unfortunately there was not enough evidence to pin it directly on

Thackeray. Ronaldo hadn't had direct contact with him—he only dealt through third parties—and frankly, if what his contacts were discovering proved to be real, he might need Ricky Rico to testify in an American court. His most pressing concern was how on earth they would deal with Miss Hunter.

For a moment he reviewed what he knew about her and realized, mortified, that it wasn't much. He'd just taken her for granted all these years, as they all had. She was simply Miss Hunter, the dull, staid, perfectly respectable and slightly comical figure he'd portrayed to Sylvia that night in Scotland, a sort of mascot, who never showed any emotion, never changed, just carried on staunchly, year after year, her hair going from blond to snow white, her racing habits her only noticeable eccentricity.

He felt troubled, too, by the picture her nephew, Ronaldo—who'd finally broken down and confessed the truth—had portrayed. At the time, he'd dismissed Ronaldo's story as the man's way of covering his back. But all at once Jeremy wondered. Leaning on the desk, fingers steepled, he reviewed the conversation with Ronaldo, recalling the description of a highly emotional woman, so intense in her loves and hates that she had put her life and reputation on the line for the sake of a long-dead passion. He had never dreamed that she could have had an affair in her youth and that Ronaldo was the product of that affair, her illegitimate son, brought up by her sister, who'd married a Colombian. In fact, he'd taken Ronald's dramatic, tearful story as a decoy and hadn't believed a word. Now he wondered. Could the subdued, sedate figure sitting behind the large oak desk in the hall be the desperate victim of ancient passion? The notion was hard to reconcile. Was this why Dexter Ward had insisted so vehemently to his grandson Brad that Miss Hunter be preserved in the company, despite her age?

He let out a long huff. The problem was becoming increasingly tricky by the moment. He leaned and pressed Reggie's button on the intercom. As he was about to speak, a knock on the door interrupted him.

''Good morning and welcome back.'' Reggie bustled in. Jeremy felt a rush of relief, glad of the support.

''Morning. Good to see you.'' The two men shook hands. Jeremy moved from behind the desk and they sat on opposite sofas.

''Told Finch to heat up the espresso machine.'' Reggie laid a file on the glass coffee table and flung an ankle over his knee.

''Espresso machine?'' Jeremy's eyebrow shot up in amused surprise.

''Yep. One of Sylvia's innovations. Wish you could have seen Finch and old Hardy Hunter's faces when she told them it was being installed. It was worth every minute of the diatribe I had to listen to afterward.''

''Good God. I can well imagine. Rather you than me.''

Reggie laughed good-naturedly, then turned serious. ''Now, tell me everything that happened. I gather you've identified the culprit?''

''I have.''

''Thank God.'' Reggie moved expectantly to the edge of the sofa.

''Let Sylvia arrive first.''

"Isn't she in?" Reggie frowned, surprised. "That's odd. She's usually here right after Miss Hunter. Even beats Finch to it some days."

"Apparently not today," Jeremy replied dryly.

Finch's knock and tight-lipped entrance put an end to further conversation.

"Good to see you, Finch. Tried the new coffee?" Jeremy queried.

"I have not, my lord. Neither is it my intention to do so," Finch sniffed disdainfully. He held the pot far from his person and poured as though the delicious aroma of fresh espresso permeating the office might contaminate him. Despite his concern about Sylvia's whereabouts, Jeremy smothered a grin.

Jesus, it was already eleven o'clock, Sylvia realized, emerging from a troubled daze as a clock chimed somewhere in the distance.

She rotated her stiff neck and waited for her numb mind and limbs to come back to life. Jeremy must already be back in the office, she reflected, a deep enduring sadness taking hold. If she could only run back up St. James's and throw herself into his strong, welcoming arms as she longed to. Instead, she must play the game, pretend she'd changed her mind, make him believe that all that had transpired between them was nothing but a fling, a one-night stand that she might have had with any man.

She closed her eyes again in a desperate attempt to obliterate the pain. What well was she going to dip into? From where was she going to muster the strength, the resilience to go on? How was she going to simulate indifference when all she wanted was the feel of his body wrapped around hers, the warmth of his deep, soothing voice whispering sweet nothings, and the heat of his kisses? What price was God prepared to extract from her this time around? Sylvia experienced a sudden rush of anger. How much would she be expected to pay for the debt to be canceled?

Dragging herself up she did a yoga stretch and after a few deep breaths started walking, formulating a hazy survival plan. Coffee. She would go somewhere—anywhere—and have a strong cup of coffee. The thought of food made her want to throw up but she must eat, must build up mental stamina and physical strength to face what was up ahead. Then there was her appearance. Reaching the gates of the park, she fumbled in her purse for her compact, stopped next to the ice-cream vendor and stared at her tear-stained reflection. She couldn't appear like this in the office. Turning to a booth selling mugs and T-shirts for tourists, she bought a pack of tissues. It was essential to get cleaned up before facing Jeremy.

She waited while a group of schoolgirls in gray flannel uniforms, long socks, dark red felt hats and school ties passed in a line, singing a happy tune. For a moment she watched them, a knot in her throat. Jeremy had told her he knew who the culprit was, but frankly, right now she didn't give a damn. All she could picture was her own little girl whom she'd never seen leave for school, never pushed on a swing, never taken care of when the child had the flu, or dried her tears after a fall.

And now it was too late. Too goddamn late. She'd

messed it all up, in the name of what? Success? Security? Power?

That all seemed so trivial now, she reflected, crossing the road, oblivious of the oncoming traffic. She walked up the street, weighed down by more pain and sorrow than she'd ever believed possible.

What child, she asked herself as she entered the corner door of Fortnum & Mason's café, would want anything to do with a mother who'd abandoned her at birth?

In the ladies' room Sylvia removed her sunglasses, blew her nose and cleaned up. She stared at herself in the mirror and let out a heavy sigh. She'd made her choice then, as she had now. And there was no other option but to get on with it.

Arabella pressed the send button of her e-mail with flourish. In her short time at Harcourts she'd sent all her boyfriends packing—including the toreador—and had spent hours on the phone, rushing to every club, restaurant, boutique and hairdresser in London she considered worthy of her list. Now she felt ready to implement her plans. Her only worry was Sylvia, who'd seemed uninterested and distracted since her return.

Perhaps she missed Jer, Arabella reasoned. After all, it didn't take an Oxford degree to realize something was up between those two. With any luck, Arabella hoped gleefully, they'd soon be rid of the Clarissa threat once and for all. She seemed very taken with Sylvia's rich American. But what about Sylvia and her brother? Would Sylvia want to marry him? she wondered, taking her nail varnish out of the top drawer of her desk and unscrewing the cap, liking the idea. The Warmouths could stand some new blood, she decided, carefully touching up an offending nail, and she, Arabella, faithful loving sister that she was, would do everything she could to bring it about.

It was most fortunate that Clarissa had taken to flirting madly with that Thackeray creature. Probably just trying to make Jeremy jealous, but maybe they'd all get lucky and she'd run off with the vile man— who, she'd told Aunt M. quite firmly, knowing her proclivity for handsome men—was *not* under *any* circumstances to be allowed within a mile of Warmouth. It wasn't any of her business, she sighed, but since she loved Jeremy, thought the world of Sylvia, and loathed Clarissa with a passion, she wasn't above a little interference.

Arabella cocked her head to one side and waved her hand to help the nail dry, wondering why Sylvia had been so reticent about voicing an opinion about the dreadful Thackeray. Could he have something to do with the way Sylvia was reacting? She frowned, suddenly thoughtful. Perhaps she should put a little bug in Jeremy's ear—have him do some digging into the man's background. Couldn't hurt, she decided.

Realizing her brother must now be back in the office, Arabella straightened the jacket of her new Armani pantsuit and checked her nail. Armed with a bulging file, she headed out of her office and into the hall. She waved brightly at Miss Hunter and hurried toward Jeremy's door, anxious to pour out her news. She was sure he'd be pleased with the way she'd managed the new department, and that made her immeasurably proud.

She peeked around the door and jumped inside. "Surprise!" When silence reigned and nobody budged, Arabella's grin turned into a grimace. She looked from her solemn brother to Reggie's deep frown and Sylvia's tired face, shocked.

"What on earth's the matter?" she asked in an awed whisper, closing the door carefully and coming farther into the room. She saw them exchange quick hesitant glances and flushed.

"Okay, don't tell me if you don't trust me. I thought I was part of the team now, but if that's not the case, fine."

"Oh, take a damper," Jeremy said wearily. "This is serious. Sit down," he added, motioning the free armchair.

"What's wrong?" Arabella sat clutching her file, aware that she'd stepped into drama.

"Well, you remember I told you we were dealing with a serious internal matter regarding some missing designs?"

"Yes?" Arabella sat breathless.

"Miss Hunter is the traitor."

"No!"

"I'm afraid so. She sold the designs—indirectly— to Thackeray."

"That dreadful American chap whose—" She slapped her hand over her mouth, stared at Sylvia wide-eyed and gulped. What on earth was going on? Jeremy looked pale and angry, Sylvia seemed retired and distant and Reggie looked damn uncomfortable. Arabella wavered on the verge of blurting out what she thought. Then, realizing she'd only make matters worse, she sat in expectant silence, determined to find out exactly what was going on.

Harriet Hunter sat in her flat, hand resting on the receiver of the old black telephone that she'd just hung up. She stared at the peeling plaster, the dull curtains whose faded pattern could no longer be distinguished. All these years she'd loved him. All these years she'd done all she could, the possible and the impossible, to improve his life.

And now it was over.

She thought of Harcourts, of all it had meant over the years, of the lengths she'd gone to give her beloved Ronaldo all he ever wanted. She'd believed him when he'd said he was being threatened. Those things happened in Colombia all the time. One heard about them on the six o'clock news every day. But that he, her own blood, should have betrayed her, gone to these lengths to…she was just a silly old fool who hadn't kept up with the times and had been taken for a ride.

She rose and stared into the empty grate, remembering Jeremy's face when he'd entered the office this morning. She'd been quick to read the barely masked confusion, the bewildered sadness, the disappointment. When he'd closed his office door, calling for Reggie and Sylvia, without asking her to come and take the meeting's minutes, she'd known.

He knew.

They all knew.

For the first time in her fifty-odd years with the company, she'd gone home early, unable to bear the shame, seeing the inevitable disgust in their eyes.

What would happen to her now? she wondered dully. What would she do and where would she go? They would never allow her to stay on after this. That was out of the question. She herself wouldn't hear of it. Fifty-one years of her life seemed suddenly pointless. She'd given Harcourts her life and in the end she'd betrayed it.

She sat down with a bang in the nearest springless armchair. Perhaps she should talk to someone, try to make them see the sense of it all. But there was no point and no one anymore to talk *to*. She'd allowed Ronaldo to blind her to the truth, had handed over Harcourts's precious designs without the least qualm or thought of what her action meant, considering them merely the price for saving his life. She hadn't even really been worried about what she'd done.

Now, as she sat in the chilly basement flat, the enormity of her act sank in. She must be stark raving mad to have gone to such lengths. Perhaps she was. Maybe she'd lost her perspective on life. Maybe she just wasn't meant for today's world.

Clutching the threadbare arms of the armchair, she closed her eyes. Her mind drifted, to Dex, to the old days, to those happy carefree times during the war when life was simple and she'd driven an ambulance during the blitz and life held so much purpose. Every hour had seemed worth living. She'd loved having a worthy task to perform, a goal to achieve, knowing she was needed. In a way, she supposed sadly, she'd tried to replace that feeling by investing all she had emotionally and financially in Ronaldo.

But that was over, gone. She could see clearly now that, despite her efforts, Ronaldo had grown up into a good-for-nothing scoundrel who'd used her. He had no love for her. He'd even been harsh and cruel on the phone just now, telling her she was no longer of any use to him. All along she'd been nothing but a pawn in his game.

Wiping the single tear from her powdered lined cheek, Harriet breathed deeply. She must not allow weakness to dictate. Perhaps she'd have a cup of tea. Tea always made her feel better.

With an effort she got up, moved slowly across the sitting room and entered the diminutive kitchen. She switched on the kettle and placed the faded china cup next to it. Then she went through her usual ritual of warming the teapot before scooping in the tea leaves. All the while her mind drifted back to the war, to the long nights on call, the tense waiting and wondering, the wailing sirens, people rushing through the streets to reach the nearest bomb shelter while she walked calmly to her vehicle, in control.

She'd never been afraid, she reflected proudly, pouring the boiling water carefully into the pot. She'd never once thought about dying. Yet now, as she placed the lid on the old brown teapot, she felt afraid of life. There was nothing left. Those who had mattered to her were all gone, even Ronaldo. There was nothing much left to live for except the odd horse race.

Reaching to the cupboard above the sink, she pulled out a prescription bottle. The doctor had given her some strong sleeping pills and warned her not to take more than one because of her heart. Placing the bottle carefully on the tray, she returned to the sitting room and set it on the small side table next to the armchair. Then she leaned over and switched on her radio set. It too was a relic of the old days when the BBC had begun their programs with an inspiring rendition of "Billy Bolero." It all seemed very far away in this new world of cell phones, computers, people moving from place to place in a fast-paced rush she could barely follow. For a while she fiddled with the broken knob of the radio until at last she located her favorite station that played the old forgotten tunes she loved, the ones she'd danced to half a century earlier.

Settling in the armchair, she hummed along to the static-filled version of "It Had to Be You" and leaned back, letting the tea steep a while. Five minutes later, she sat up straight and meticulously poured herself a cup. She added a dash of milk. No sugar. That too was an old wartime habit born of rationing. When the tea had cooled sufficiently, she took a tentative sip and sighed. Ah! It was just as she liked it, strong, hot and reassuring.

The radio was now playing "Smoke Gets in Your Eyes." And all at once her own eyes turned bleary as she remembered a certain evening, dancing in the town hall in Clapham, with the young man whom she'd loved once upon a time and who'd left for France the very next day, never to return.

Her hand reached for the bottle of pills. She unscrewed the top absently and dropped a handful into her palm. For a moment she stared at them dreamily. Then, as the music changed once more, she popped them in her mouth and took a long draft of tea.

When her head fell back against the cushion she smiled, as the radio crackled out her favorite version of "The Sunny Side of the Street."

23

"What do you mean Miss Hunter hasn't shown up for work?" Reggie looked up from his desk, filled with sudden foreboding, while Finch stood opposite. "Damn," he exclaimed.

"Miss Hunter *never* misses a day, sir," Finch continued in his lugubrious monotone. "Perhaps we should investigate."

"You're right. She may be ill. Did you phone her flat?"

"There's no answer, sir."

"Perhaps I should pop around and take a look," Reggie muttered, an uneasy shiver gripping him. "Just make sure she's all right." He got up, then hesitated. "Uh, why don't you come along, Finch," he said, straightening the knot of his tie.

"Me, sir?"

"Yes. I—"

"Very well, sir. I'll get my coat."

Finch never questioned anything, just did as he was ordered, and for once Reggie was glad. He didn't want to explain, or talk about his rising fear. Had she found out that they knew the truth? Had she guessed?

In the hall he grabbed his jacket and umbrella and popped his head into Arabella's office. "Ara, hold the fort, will you? I'll be back in an hour," he said through the open door.

"What's going on?" she exclaimed, curious. "I've just had Clarissa whining down the phone for the past twenty minutes—she really is such a bore—and—"

"Sorry, old girl, later."

He was about to step into the outer hallway, when Lady Margaret marched out of the caged lift, followed by two of her dogs snuffling along behind her.

"Ah! Reginald. Just the man I wanted to see." She smiled, cheeks crinkling like soft parchment. "Have you any idea, dear boy, what is going on between Jeremy and Sylvia? This whole business strikes me as very odd. Something has to be done at once." She frowned and pursed her lips. "He's been quite distracted since his return, and I was so hoping that the two of them would get together. I suppose I'm just an inveterate old meddler, but now that Clarissa's involved with that dreadful American, it seems such a great opportunity to foster—"

"Lady Margaret, I'm sorry, but I'm afraid I have a crisis on my hands," Reggie interrupted. "I have to leave at once."

Finch stepped into the hall behind him and Lady Margaret's eyes widened. "My goodness. You both look like death masks. What on earth is going on?" she asked in a very different tone.

"It's Miss Hunter, madam," Finch answered lugubriously. "She didn't turn up for work and there is no answer at her flat."

"But that's absurd. She always turns up," Lady Margaret exclaimed, cheeks furrowing.

"Quite so, madam. Which is why we are concerned."

"And so you should be." She nodded firmly. "I presume you're off to find out what's wrong?"

"Yes, madam."

"Very well," she answered briskly. "I shall accompany you. Arabella," she announced, seeing her niece hovering in the background, "you can make yourself useful for once and take care of Daffy and Flaffy." She shoved the leashes into Arabella's reluctant hands and headed for the stairs. "Now come along you two, no dawdling." She beckoned to Reggie and Finch, now in full charge of the operation. "My car's waiting outside. We'll drive straight to Clapham, and on the way, *you*," she said, addressing Reggie with a look that spoke volumes, "can explain to me exactly what has been going on here," she admonished. "I loathe that wretched lift," she added. "I felt quite claustrophobic coming up. It really ought to be changed for something more modern, Reggie. Kindly make a note of it."

"Yes, of course," Reggie murmured, outgunned.

"What impractical stairs," Lady Margaret huffed as they reached the ground floor where her large form took up most of the passage. "Now come along, hurry up," she ordered, taking full control of the mission. "There's no time to be lost. Let's just hope we don't get bogged down by morning traffic."

24

The New York day was as drizzling and gray as her mood.

Leaving her apartment with a heavy heart, Sylvia stepped into the waiting car, aware that she was about to take the final step in her well-laid strategy. The closer she got to Park Avenue, the darker her mood turned.

After Harriet Hunter's suicide—a sad shock to them all—and the ensuing funeral, she'd jumped on a plane back to New York, unable to face the inevitable confrontation with Jeremy. Each time they met, he had sought opportunities for private conversation. He'd made calls she didn't return, left notes she didn't answer. But avoiding him had become impossible. She couldn't look him in the eye or bear his closeness, knowing they had no future. Worse was the knowledge that she was about to betray those who most trusted her.

Entering the Harcourts building, her tension grew. A sense of calm order had returned to Harcourts's offices now that the mystery had been solved and the culprit identified. Everyone was working enthusiastically on the next line, believing it would take Harcourts to new heights. No one could begin to suspect that the real menace to the company's fortunes was sitting at its helm.

Sitting in Sylvia's office, Jeremy stared at her, shocked at the transformation she'd undergone in such a short time. She was pale, her cheeks hollow. Christ, she must have lost ten pounds. Even her usually lustrous hair looked dull.

"Thanks for coming." She smiled perfunctorily. "I have a proposition from an unbelievable source."

"Oh?" Jeremy eyed her, betraying none of the tumultuous emotions assailing him.

"Yes. I was pretty amazed. In fact, at first I thought it took a lot of balls for him to even suggest it but then—"

"Him?"

"Thackeray."

Her jaw clenched and he frowned. "What has he come up with?" he asked suspiciously. Thanks to his contacts at MI-6 and their counterparts in the FBI, he was in the midst of getting together a nice thick file on the man that he hoped would send him behind bars for a while, if they played their cards right.

"I know, it's amazing." She shrugged and slid a file across her desk. "Take a look. I felt that it was my obligation not to dismiss it outright. After all, whether we like it or not, Marchand is the biggest outfit next to ours, and what he's suggesting makes perfect business sense."

"I shouldn't have thought anything to do with a

character like that made sense, except possibly the sight of him decked out in orange and in handcuffs," he muttered, picking up the file reluctantly.

"I know. But read it anyway. I think you'll see what I mean."

Jeremy flipped through the pages. Despite his aversion, he could not help but admire the complex proposal. After a quick review he laid it down. "Interesting. A pity the idea doesn't come from another source. We might have considered it." He gave a short laugh, wondering if now was the time to channel conversation onto more personal ground.

"Hmm. That was my initial reaction, too," she replied, shifting her glasses. "Then I took a closer look. You know, we never proved Thackeray was to blame for the Colombian business."

"Like hell we didn't. Okay, we don't have his fingerprints on it but that's about all that's lacking."

"So? This is business, Jeremy, and all that's water under the bridge. Harcourts has survived, even prospered. And right now he's presented us with a unique business proposal. By merging, we could become the most powerful company in our industry. I'd be an irresponsible CEO if I didn't bring that to the board's attention."

"I don't believe this." Jeremy rose and faced her. "How can you even think of allowing that man any credence. He's a thief and a scumbag."

"We haven't got proof beyond a reasonable doubt," she demurred.

"You sound like a bloody lawyer, for Christ's sake." He moved across the office and eyed her from his position by the window. It was as though she'd transformed into another being. When he'd tried to approach her, to kiss her hello and touch her cheek, she'd recoiled from him as though disgusted. Now she was calmly suggesting that Harcourts should merge with the enemy. It was unbelievable. Jeremy pinched the bridge of his nose and tried to keep his thoughts straight. He knew he was tired, but every instinct told him something was seriously wrong and he needed to identify what that something was. Arabella had mentioned that Thackeray had been flirting with Clarissa. Nothing about this made any sense. Not Thackeray's sudden arrival in London, or this proposal, or Sylvia's baffling reactions.

He looked at her seated aloof behind her desk, her black suit neat and trim, legs and arms crossed as though protecting herself from some unknown entity, the antithesis of the soft pliant creature who'd writhed so passionately in his arms in the moonlight. Different, too, to the businesswoman he'd known previously and whose manner had always been annoyingly straightforward and brash. Now she seemed distant, unwilling to give an inch.

"Don't tell me you're considering this proposal seriously?" he said with a bitter laugh.

"Actually, yes. I'm planning to present it to the board this afternoon. I've already sounded out several of the members and had favorable responses."

"You're joking." He was dead serious now. *What the hell had happened to her?*

"Not at all." She swung her chair around, tweaked her hair neatly behind her ear and picked up the file he'd discarded. "If I'm right in my assessment, this should pass pretty unanimously. I thought you'd want to know before.''

''Thanks.'' He threw her a cynical laugh. ''You might as well tell me you're setting up shop with the devil himself. Why bother to advise me?'' he added, returning to the desk and leaning his hands on it.

''It's a courtesy I feel I owe you,'' she said carefully.

''Another time don't go to all that trouble,'' he snapped, straightening. ''If that's all you have on your agenda, I'll take my leave. I'd better warn you that I'll veto this project.''

Sylvia shrugged, leaving him as hurt as he was angry. ''It's just sensible corporate practice, Jeremy. Nothing to get so upset about.''

''I'll make my own decision on that one,'' he replied. Then, spinning on his heel, he walked smartly out of the office, flabbergasted. He recognized nothing about her, neither her manner nor these dealings with Thackeray, which she seemed to take in stride.

As he walked toward the elevator, he wondered for a brief second if his feelings for her had clouded his instincts and he'd misjudged her completely. But he didn't think so.

For a minute Jeremy floundered, powerless. Unless he got his ducks in a row very fast, Thackeray was going to win the round. And he had no intention of letting that occur. Making sure the case against Thackeray was watertight and would not fall to pieces in court was essential. As he descended the fifty-two floors to the lobby, Jeremy shifted into battle mode. Again his personal feeling would have to go on hold. Right now, Harcourts's future was at stake. He relived his recent meeting, eyes narrowed. She'd been nervous. Extremely nervous, now he came to think of it. Oh, she did a good job of dissimulating, but he'd worked in close quarters with Sylvia long enough to tell. That and her diminished appearance gave him food for thought. Was it possible, he wondered, that Thackeray was forcing the issue? If only he could reach her, get her to trust him sufficiently to open up and tell him her inner misgivings. But that was an unlikely scenario. Right now she was holding him at arm's length. Still, he was not about to give her up. Maybe things had changed and she'd decided he wasn't the man for her, but, hell, he'd go down fighting.

"Okay, when do I move in?" Thackeray's harsh voice on the line made Sylvia squirm. "Did they buy it?"

"Yes. The board's agreed to your proposal."

"Good girl. Go on keeping your ass in line and I may just leave you there to run things. But no fucking around, understood? You toe the line or I'll kick your ass right back to Arkansas where you belong."

"Stop talking to me like that," she muttered, sudden anger gripping her. She'd done all he wanted, hadn't she?

"Don't you get frisky with me, bitch, or I'll serve your past up as entrée at Aureole."

"How dare you," she retorted. "Why don't you leave me alone? I got you the deal, didn't I? What more do you want?" Desperation and anger collided as a rush of tears ran down her face. She could bear this no longer.

"I'll say and do whatever the hell I like and you'll sit there and take whatever shit I deal out, so shut the fuck up and listen. I want this thing signed, sealed and cemented within the week. No messing around, d'ya hear?" His refined accent had deteriorated into an uncouth slur.

Sylvia recoiled. She was in the apartment staring out the window. She'd done such a good job at convincing the board that Thackeray and Marchand were the way to go that now they were all on her side. She'd even persuaded them to give Thackeray a board position, and to her horror they'd agreed unanimously. Only Jeremy had abstained.

She'd lost ten pounds in the two weeks and felt as though she'd gained ten years. She'd allowed herself no respite, no time to think of her own personal plight. Each night she popped a handful of sleeping pills, slept fitfully, then dragged herself into the shower in the morning. By the time she got to the office she was awake once more and plunged into her work, where she remained there till eleven at night, never letting up.

And now, all at once, she knew she couldn't go through with it. No matter what he did to her, she couldn't live with herself. She glanced at her reflection in the huge beveled mirror, horrified at what she saw: a traitor, a heinous, repulsive, weak-minded piece of trash. Was she really all the things she'd so vehemently rejected all her life? Was this what she was destined to end up as?

"Hey, I'm talking to you." Thackeray's twang grated in her ears and she pulled up with a jolt.

Stretching her hand out, she stared at the cell phone. The voice was still blabbering as she switched off.

She knew now what she had to do. Fingers trembling, she dialed Marcia's line. Better to lose it all, turn her back on all her achievements, than live the hell of the past few days. She would not, could not, survive knowing she'd sold herself and all she stood for. For years she'd subconsciously thought of herself as a whore because she'd been raped, when in fact she'd been nothing but a victim. Now she had a choice: facing the truth and who she really was, or prostituting her soul and turning into what she most despised.

"Hi, it's me," she said when Marcia picked up. "I want you to call an emergency board meeting at three this afternoon. Oh, and try to reach Jeremy at the Lowell. I want him to be there." She hung up and dropped onto the sofa, engulfed in a rush of relief.

She hadn't allowed herself to think of Jeremy, but the pain in his eyes haunted her as badly as all the rest. It was finished now and any thought of resuming their relationship would be over once he heard what she had to say later in the day. She let out a trembling sigh. How could she have allowed Thackeray to terrorize her to this point, when she knew his intentions, his plans for expanding Harcourts's Colombian arm, making it into a hub for the trafficking of drugs and stolen goods. She shook her head and wiped her eyes. It was as though she'd suddenly woken from a horrible nightmare. But it still wasn't over, she reminded herself. First she must face the board and hand in her resignation. Then there would be the agony of seeing Jeremy's eyes filled with horror and disgust—and that

was just the beginning. She swallowed hard and
touched the canvas sofa fleetingly. Once again she'd
be on the run, fleeing Thackeray and his certain desire
for revenge.

At two-fifteen the car turned onto Fifth Avenue.
Sylvia let out a sigh and closed her eyes. In less than
an hour, she would hand over her resignation and
nominate Jeremy as CEO. She had a bag packed with
her essential belongings stacked in the trunk, a plane
ticket for Rio de Janeiro tucked in her purse, a number
of credit cards and a wad of cash. Earlier in the day
she'd transferred the bulk of her money to an account
in the Caymans, then in a second transaction she'd
closed that account and transferred the lot to Switzerland. At least that would provide her with some
financial security while she found her feet and lay
low. Her stomach lurched as the car stopped on the
curb.

For the last time.

Tears burned, but she couldn't afford to chicken
out. It was this or die.

Minutes later she was riding the elevator, nodding
to staff as though this were a day like any other. She
reached her office and stepped inside, feeling as
though it already belonged to someone else. Dropping
her head in her hands, she smothered an anguished
sob.

Reaching her desk, she opened the top drawer. So
much to clear out and no time to do it. She sat down
and slumped in the chair. Her chair. The one that
she'd acceded to with so much pride.

Then all at once she looked up and saw him sitting

in the shadows, fingers steepled on his knee. Gasping, Sylvia dropped her briefcase in fright.

"Who let you in here?" she almost screamed as Jeremy rose and approached her.

"Marcia."

"What…why are you here? The meeting was called for three." Hands trembling, she crouched and picked up the scattered belongings from her briefcase, avoiding his eyes. *Oh God, why had he come? It only made the situation ten times worse.*

"I came for the emergency board meeting, and because you are about to hand over this company to Thackeray. I want to know why."

He hadn't tried to help her, she noticed, rising. He'd just stood there watching her like a hawk. She pulled herself together.

"Why, Syl? Why are you doing it? What is it this man has said or done to make you do this?" he said quietly.

Sylvia flinched. Her eyes shot to his, then away, the wonderful gentle expression that had conquered her heart too much to bear. Suddenly she collapsed into the soft leather chair and her hands fell to the desk.

"Why are you doing this, Sylvia? What's pushing you? For God's sake, Syl," he said, leaning across the desk and reaching for her hand, "surely you trust me enough to tell me."

She felt the pressure of his fingers and trembled. God, his warmth felt so good, that steady firm grip on her hand. All at once she could stand it no longer. A flood of hot tears burst forth, pouring down her cheeks and onto their joined hands. The next thing, she was in his arms, tenderly cradled, face buried in the lapel of his blazer, trying desperately to regain her armor.

"It's all a...a l-lie," she sobbed.

"What's a lie?" He'd managed to maneuver them into the chair and place her on his knee.

"M-me, I'm a l-lie," she whispered, shuddering, unable to stop the flow of tears. "I—I'm n-not what you think I am. You don't know, w-wouldn't w-want to—to know the person I t-truly am."

"Nonsense, darling. Whatever you've done, or think you've done, I'll still love you," he murmured, stroking her hair, tweaking it behind her ear and kissing her temple tenderly.

"No." She shook her head vigorously. "You've no idea, you couldn't have. In your world p-people don't experience th-this k-kind of thing."

"Why don't you tell me about it?" he murmured softly.

"I—I c-can't."

"Yes, you can."

Despite her panic, the note of determination behind his tenderness reached her. She leaned against him and shuddered. Slipping a finger under her chin, Jeremy wiped her eyes carefully with his large white handkerchief while she sat, perched on his knee like a child. It was warm, comforting and wonderful. And too good to be true, she realized, wriggling regretfully from his knee. She stood next to the desk and looked at him sadly. He thought he would be able to surmount the odds, but she knew better. This was the last time she would enjoy that unique smile that left her melting inside, feel those eyes she loved so dearly upon her, lavishing her with love. Even as she schooled herself to speak, Sylvia knew a last minute's hesitation.

"Go on," Jeremy urged, reaching again for her hand. "Tell me."

It was too late to retract. She'd blown it, the life she'd so carefully constructed and the chance she might have had at happiness if things had worked out differently. Sylvia thought of the ticket in her purse. At least she'd have her honor to keep her company wherever she ended up.

"I'm not what you think I am," she began hesitantly.

"So you've already remarked," he replied in a matter-of-fact tone that divested the speech of its initial drama.

"Yes, but you must understand," she insisted, removing her hand from his and stepping back. "I'm nothing but white trash."

He frowned and she smiled, despite her anguish. "You don't even know what that is, do you? Where you come from it doesn't exist. Well, let me explain, it's poor white people who live in pathetic, trashed-out homes and trailer parks, who have nowhere to go, nothing to care about, and who can't even stir themselves to change their miserable lives. They drink beer all day, don't bother to clean up the garbage rotting outside their houses, beat their wives and live like animals."

"Don't—" He half rose.

"No!" She raised her palm. "You wanted to know, so I'm telling you. I was born in a small town in Arkansas. When I was seven, my father died and my mother remarried. My stepfather was a drunk helicopter mechanic who never got over the fact that he wasn't a pilot. He went to Vietnam. There they let him pilot whatever he wanted. He was miserable when the war ended and he had to come home. When he got really upset he'd hit my mother, and when that wasn't enough he beat me. Then I started growing up."

She turned and stared out the window at the rain scurrying down the huge panoramic panes, watching the Staten Island ferry in the distance. "I knew I wouldn't escape him in the end," she murmured absently. "I think deep down I knew that one day it would happen. Maybe in a way it was my own fault." She tilted her head as though debating the matter.

Horrified at what he was hearing, Jeremy rose, then restrained himself. He wanted to go to her, hold her tight and tell her nothing would ever hurt her again, but something in her manner told him she needed to vent this, get it all out.

"One day I came home from school early and I thought the house was empty," she continued, as though recounting someone else's story. "It was my own fault for not being on my guard. I should have checked, made sure there was no one around. But I didn't. I relaxed, fell asleep on the couch. That's when it happened. I tried. I really tried to stop him," she insisted, hands waving wildly. "I tried to fight him, I really did, but he was so strong. It was useless. I know you'll think I consented, people always do. Think the girl's to blame, I mean," she added in an explanatory aside. "It's hard to explain rape unless it's actually happened to you. There's a point where

you can't go on. He smelled of beer and…oh God—''
Her voice cracked. She stopped, closed her eyes, and
again Jeremy forced himself to stay silently put,
aware that a single word might break the flow.

''I got pregnant,'' she continued conversationally.
''I knew I couldn't keep the baby. He beat me all the
time I was pregnant, he was so angry. Said it was my
fault, that I was a whore and a slut. He told my
mother I'd undressed in front of him, seduced him in
his own home. And she believed him because she
couldn't face the ugly truth. A few weeks before the
baby was born, I went to the nuns at the convent
where I'd gone to school when I was little. It was an
orphanage as well. They told me they'd care for the
baby and find her a good home. I only heard her cry
once,'' she ended in a small voice. ''Just that one,
tiny cry. Then they took her away and I—'' She
reached her hand out as though trying to rediscover
something she'd lost.

''Syl. Syl?'' Jeremy's voice and his arms hugging
her brought her back to earth. She tried to step out of
his embrace but he held her close

''You see now why I'm a lie, why you couldn't
possibly be associated with a woman like me, don't
you?'' she asked, searching his face. ''All my life I've
tried to hide my past. Even from myself. I was prepared to sell this company down the drain because I
was too ashamed to admit who I am. In a way, I'm
no better than my mother was when she believed him,
instead of me. Thackeray found out. He tracked down
my stepfather. He said he would bury me if I didn't
do as he told me.'' The words tumbled out and she
shuddered, swallowed a sob. ''That alone should tell

you what kind of person I am. I didn't even have the guts to recognize that it's all my fault, that I've been living a dream, an illusion. One day it had to catch up with me. I'm only sorry that you had to be the one to suffer because of my—''

''Shut up!''

''What?'' She blinked up at him.

''Stop that immediately.''

The sight of his eyes brimming with anger made her stiffen. She tried to pull away, afraid he might hit her. She didn't think she could bear that humiliation.

''You must stop this nonsense immediately, do you hear?'' Jeremy's voice was low and intense. ''How dare you talk about yourself in this manner? What happened to you is dreadful, but it only makes me love you more. I don't give a damn where you come from, Syl, and neither should you. You should be proud of yourself, not ashamed, because who you are—all any of us really are—are who we *make* ourselves.'' He touched her cheek and his eyes softened. ''Oh, Syl,'' he said, drawing her close, ''my poor, poor darling. What a dreadful time you've had. You deserved so much better. I only wish I'd been there to protect you.''

Sylvia lay against his chest in limp amazement. All she registered was that he hadn't rejected her.

''As you rightly say,'' Jeremy continued, ''I probably can't begin to imagine how awful it must have been for you, but God knows I'll never let anything or anyone touch you or hurt you ever again.''

''But—'' she protested.

''Will you stop arguing and listen? Don't you understand that I love and admire you? My God, how many other women would have managed as you have? Been as courageous as you and turned their lives around, as you've done?''

''Admiration?'' she whispered, wide-eyed, searching his face.

''The deepest admiration, my darling. I hope one day you will come to understand what an amazing woman you are.''

''I don't think *you* understand.'' She shook her head and tried to free herself from his grasp. ''Jeremy, I've just told you I let myself be raped by my stepfather. My own mother thought of me as a whore.'' She pulled away roughly and stepped back. ''I abandoned my baby. I don't deserve you. You're a gentleman—an English lord, for Christ's sake. You need a woman who you can be proud of, not someone you'd be ashamed to introduce to your friends. Get real, Jeremy. You're just trying to fool yourself into thinking what I've told you doesn't matter. But it does. It matters a lot.'' She wrapped her arms around herself and retreated once more to the window.

Jeremy pondered a moment, then said in a measured tone, ''Would you do me a favor?''

''Sure. If I can.'' She brushed the hair off her cheeks and waited.

''I want you to take a close hard look at yourself and tell me who you see.''

She gave a short, harsh laugh. ''Don't. The psychotherapy stuff doesn't work. Believe me, I've been that route.''

''Then let me tell what I see.'' He tilted his head, crossed his arms and studied her. ''I see a beautiful, intelligent, classy, powerful but hurt woman who, coming from nowhere, has climbed to the top.''

''Yeah, right—and it's going to be a pretty painful fall.'' She let out another desperate laugh. His words, she knew, were merely bandages.

''Look at me,'' he continued, oblivious. ''I happen, by a stroke of good fortune, to have been born into wealth and privilege. I try not to take it for granted. Hearing your story makes me realize just how lucky I am. Neither does privilege make me perfect. I screw up as much as anyone. Why do you think I joined Military Intelligence? Or I came on board at Harcourts? You yourself said I didn't need to.''

She turned slowly. ''You never really told me why, did you?''

''I needed to prove myself. I wanted to know who I really was.''

''But you don't need to prove anything.''

''Of course I needed to. Just as now I need you in my life.''

''You *definitely* don't need me.'' She shook her head firmly. ''I know right now you think you do, but believe me—'' she nodded sagely ''—once you've thought it over you'll realize I'm right. It just wouldn't work out, Jeremy. Our worlds are too far apart. I could never fit into the Warmouth scene and your family and...and all that...'' She waved her hands vaguely, unable to hold back the tears.

''My family,'' he said, drawing closer, ''adores you. My aunt thinks you're terrific and Arabella has turned into an awful bore singing your praises. They'd like nothing better than to have you as part of our family.''

"Right," she muttered. "Wait till they hear the truth. I'd be willing to bet your aunt would bow out gracefully. And she'd be right." She nodded again emphatically and folded her arms protectively around her. "I'm entirely wrong for you, however much you try to justify a relationship, and she of all people would be the first to tell you."

A sharp knock fell on the door and Marcia popped her head around. "The meeting begins in ten."

"Oh God, the meeting. I'd forgotten. What am I going to do?" Sylvia asked helplessly, fisting her hands into tight balls and turning toward Jeremy.

"Tell them the truth."

Slowly Sylvia nodded and swallowed. "That's what I intended to do."

"Good girl." He gripped her shoulder reassuringly, knowing the only way to get her past her blind spot was if she faced the truth once and for all so that it no longer loomed over her like a spook. "I'm proud of you. Proud that you've seen what's right and that you're doing the honorable thing."

She nodded absently. "That's why I called the meeting. I can't go on pretending. It's the end of the line, but at least I'll be honest with the board and with myself. And at least I'll save Harcourts from Thackeray."

Sylvia straightened her shoulders, took a deep breath and faced the door that connected her office to the boardroom.

Jeremy restrained himself from touching her, realizing she must do this alone. It was now or never. If she got through it, then just maybe they'd have a chance. He held his breath, read the determination written in her eyes and watched as she wiped away the smudged mascara, passed her fingers through her hair, then, with a trembling hand, dabbed on some lipstick. My God, she was brave, and how very much he loved her. After all she'd been through, all she'd suffered, she still had it in her to stand tall. He smiled. This was not, he realized, the time to tell her what he'd been up to all morning and the agreeable surprise that had awaited him back at the hotel. She'd find out soon enough. "Shall we go?" she said with a brave little smile.

Inclining his head, he stepped forward and opened the door.

Sylvia stopped on the threshold. This was the last time she would step over it. She took another deep breath and looked around the room. All the board members were present, some chitchatting in low voices, others doodling. Thackeray sat to the right of her chair with the air of a contented lion who'd just gulped down a lamb.

The sight of him, so confident and full of himself, gave her strength, and she advanced firmly into the room, head high. Jeremy followed close behind her. Thackeray didn't even blink at his presence. Neither did he rise. Sylvia sat down and silently prayed for the words to go forward.

"I called for this emergency board meeting because I am handing in my resignation." A shocked murmur permeated the room. "I know this comes as a surprise after our last meeting."

"What the hell—" Thackeray jolted to attention.

"I'm ashamed to say that then I allowed myself

to be blackmailed,'' Sylvia barreled on, ''and I omitted to tell you that Mr. Thackeray has other plans for Harcourts than those outlined in the proposal.'' A hush came over the room.

Thackeray scraped back his chair, his face flushed and furious. ''The woman's nuts!''

''Unfortunately, I'm perfectly sane, which in this instance is no credit to me. This whole misunderstanding is entirely my fault and I take full responsibility,'' she continued in a determined, calm tone that belied her inner turmoil. ''I'm ashamed to say that I have misled you. I should have had the courage to tell you from the start, but I didn't.''

''She's completely crazy,'' Thackeray snapped, seeking support around the table.

''No, she isn't.'' Jeremy's voice rang loud and clear through the boardroom. ''Ladies and gentlemen,'' he said, ''please listen to what Miss Hansen has to say. It is extremely important.''

''Thank you, Jeremy. Sadly, it is.'' She stopped, took a deep breath, then continued. ''Recently, I was sought out by Mr. Thackeray, who threatened to reveal my sordid past to you and the press if I didn't comply with his demands.''

Horrified exclamations ensued. ''I'm sorry to say that I was a coward and didn't react as I should.'' She clasped her hands tightly in front of her. ''I went along with his demands because I didn't have enough courage to face who I am.''

''She's nothing but a white-trash whore,'' Thackeray spat, furious. ''You double-crossing, two-faced—''

Sylvia faced him. ''Not quite, but close. I'm a

white-trash kid from Arkansas who was abused and
made a lot of mistakes and—''

"You fucking bitch, how dare you?" Thackeray
rose and swung his arm at her. But before he could
strike her, Jeremy's right fist slammed into his face,
sending him reeling across the room. "Don't you dare
touch her, you bastard," he hissed. Then, turning
back to the amazed board, he straightened his tie.
"Perhaps you'd be interested to know that the IRS
and the FBI are extremely curious about Mr. Thackeray's present and past activities. I believe," he added
dryly, "that there's a long list to choose from."

Sylvia watched in amazed silence as Jeremy moved
briskly toward the door and opened it. "You can
come in now, gentlemen."

Four men in almost identical gray suits entered and
went straight over to where Thackeray lay nursing his
jaw on the floor. One of them presented a badge.
"FBI," he announced. Then, heaving him up, they
marched the bewildered Thackeray out the door without a backward glance.

"Well, my goodness," Barry Granger, one of Harcourts longest-standing board members, exclaimed,
rubbing his forehead. "I shall never cease to marvel
at how dramatic these Harcourts board meetings can
be. Sylvia, let's get this straightened out. What is this
about your past? And why didn't you tell us?"

"It's not a pretty tale. I came from a poor trailer
home in Arkansas. I was raped by my stepfather, got
pregnant—'' She broke off and bit her lip. "I'm
sorry. I thought if you knew, you'd all despise me.
I've tried so hard to become something else."

"Hell and damnation," Granger exclaimed, shaking his thick shock of white hair and eyeing her askance. "Where the heck do you think I started out? In the Astor mansion?"

His bushy white eyebrows furrowed. "And whatever happened, it's over. But you shouldn't have let that bastard get the better of you, shouldn't have gone through this all on your own. Don't you know who your friends are?"

"Thank you, Granger. I appreciate it. But I'm tendering my resignation right now," she said in a small, tight voice, handing him an envelope.

"Like hell you are. I don't accept it, and I'll vouch I'm speaking for the rest of the board when I say that. I can see that you may need a break, after all that's happened, and we can appoint someone meantime to take care of things while you go on vacation. But after that, we want you right back here at the helm, young lady, and no mistake about it." He rapped the table firmly. "I'm sure my colleagues will agree when I say you're the best CEO Harcourts could wish for."

"Hear, hear…" resounded unanimously throughout the room.

As Jeremy moved to her side, hand gripping her shoulder, Sylvia tried to assimilate everything that had happened. Was it possible that they still wanted her? She thought of the plane ticket in her purse, the money transfers and the bag in the car. She'd been so certain of rejection, she'd gone to extremes. All at once, relief and exhaustion hit and she wondered if she'd make it to the end of the meeting.

"I want to put forward the following motion," Granger continued, clearing his throat. "I say we ask Warmouth here to step in while Sylvia takes the time

she needs to get over this harrowing experience. I feel
like a fool for not having seen the light earlier, and
can only say I wish I'd been there for you, Sylvia.
You are not the only one to blame for allowing
Thackeray to get as far as he did. If we'd been less
greedy and paid a little more attention to detail, this
whole thing could have been avoided. And next time
anything big comes down, you come straight to me.''
He wagged his finger at her. ''Not that it will,'' he
added. ''There aren't too many Thackerays about,
thank God, and by the looks of it, he'll be away for
a few years.''

The board took only a few moments to deliberate
while Jeremy stood with Sylvia, hands firmly planted
on her shoulders.

She still could not believe they hadn't rejected her.
Maybe they hadn't understood right. Maybe she
hadn't been clear and should make them understand.
They didn't seem in the least fazed by all the dreadful
sins she'd committed. But that was surely because
they didn't know the full extent of her wickedness.
She turned to Jeremy, about to protest.

''No,'' he murmured in a low peremptory voice,
guessing her thoughts. ''It wouldn't make any difference. They don't need a graphic description to guess
what you went through. The point is, they don't care.
If anything, they'd be even more shocked and sorry
for the little girl who suffered so. But the truth is, it's
the corporate officer you are today that they're interested in.''

''But—''

''We'll deal with the rest together,'' he said softly,
sitting in the chair vacated by Thackeray and letting

his hand slip over hers. "There's nothing to be afraid of anymore."

Granger cleared his throat again.

"All in favor of Warmouth substituting for Sylvia say aye."

"Aye." The vote passed unanimously.

Jeremy nodded, then glanced around the table. "Thanks for bestowing your confidence in me. I'll try and do as good a job as Sylvia, though that won't be easy." He smiled tenderly in her direction.

Sylvia smiled back despite the pain. She had not lost her friends after all. They didn't value just her corporate skills, they actually cared about Sylvia, the person. It all seemed unreal, almost too much to bear. If she didn't get out of here fast, she'd burst into tears. With a wobbly "Excuse me," she got up and walked with as much dignity as possible from the room.

"You go after her, young man," Granger urged Jeremy. "And make sure she doesn't slip through your fingers," he added with a wink.

"Damn right," Jeremy concurred. With a quick nod to the board, he bolted through the connecting door after the woman he loved.

25

The facade of the convent hadn't changed. It was the same old gray stone, and the ancient wooden door with the creaking hinges, brought from an Italian cathedral over one hundred and fifty years ago, still stood in place just as it always had.

Now as she rang the bell, Sylvia traveled back in time. She should have done this years ago, she realized. She felt more in control, now that she'd started seeing Dr. Hetherington, a therapist in her mid-fifties who specialized in teenage abuse and was kind, firm and competent. At first, it had been virtually impossible to speak of her ordeal, but little by little she'd opened up. Although each session left her drained, she felt more able to see clearly.

Jeremy had stayed with her in New York and was going in to the office every day. They had put Reggie in charge in London, and to everyone's surprise, Arabella had stepped up to the plate and was doing an amazing job of seconding him.

But the trip back to Arkansas was something she'd insisted on doing alone. Jeremy had supported her decision, as though he understood that she needed to come to terms with this on her own. He'd moved them out of the apartment, insisting they needed to be somewhere else, a different atmosphere where she could let go of some of her pain and simply relax, and they'd checked into a large suite at the SoHo Grand.

Jeremy hadn't mentioned the future and she was thankful. Right now, it was all she could do to cope with her past, let alone plan for tomorrow.

She heard footsteps approaching, down the convent's stone corridor she knew so well, and stiffened. The door opened and a nun peered out.

"Hi, I'm Sylvia Hansen," she said nervously. "I made an appointment with the Mother Superior."

"Come in, dear. I'm sister Anne." The nun gave her a broad, pink-cheeked smile. She spoke in the Irish brogue that Sylvia recalled so well from early childhood, realizing she'd never questioned how an order of Irish nuns had found its way to rural Arkansas. She stepped inside and sniffed, the familiar aroma of Irish stew reaching her nostrils. She looked about her. She'd played in this corridor as a small child, recalled the laughter and warmth the nuns had shown her. A glimpse of her dad, picking her up in his arms after school and carrying her toward the door, flashed.

She stopped and closed her eyes, cherishing the lost sensation, the security and warmth it gave her. Then suddenly her father's face was replaced by Jeremy's and she wanted to weep. At last she'd discovered the feeling again, one she hadn't known since she'd lost the only man who'd truly loved her and whom she'd lost too soon. She rubbed her eyes and followed Sister Anne to the Mother Superior's office.

"Come in," a voice called.

Sylvia entered with the same respect and slight trepidation she'd felt years ago. "May I?"

"Come in, come in." The elderly Mother Superior, who introduced herself as Sister Clara, smiled and indicated one of the simple wooden chairs.

"Thank you." Sylvia sat and took stock of the familiar office plastered with bright crayon drawings, miscellaneous objects from art class, file cabinets and a hodgepodge of papers on the desk. "I'm sorry to bother you when you're obviously busy," she began hesitantly.

"Not at all, not at all," she said, the Irish lilt flowing once more. As though guessing this was not an easy encounter, Sister Clara leaned back in the chair, her wise eyes filled with understanding, and folded her hands carefully on her dark brown habit. "Now, what can I do for you, child?"

"Well, I...I don't quite know how to tell you this." Sylvia pressed her hands together, mouth dry. Perhaps this woman knew where her daughter was. The thought both thrilled and terrified her. What if—

"Why don't you just tell me, dear?" Sister Clara said in a kindly voice. "There's nothing the good Lord can't take care of," she encouraged.

Sylvia swallowed and nodded. "When I was sixteen I came here to have a baby," she said in a rush. Sister Clara nodded with no sign of disapproval. Sylvia picked up courage. "I...all these years I've sent donations. Sister Burser knows, but she's not sure who they come from. I...you see, I couldn't keep the baby and I didn't know what to do, because my step-father—'' She broke down in tears and dropped her face in her hands.

"Now, now, there's no need to get upset. We've all had our trials and tribulations. I'm sure you did what was right at the time and you couldn't have chosen a better place for the baby.''

"But I don't know what's become of her," she wailed, hands shaking. "I abandoned my child, Sister, and never looked back. I just sent money. What does that make me?''

"Human, my dear. Maybe you couldn't look back. Maybe you weren't meant to," the other woman replied softly. "Now, when you told me you were coming to visit today, I figured it was something important, so I made a few inquiries.''

Sylvia stiffened. She leaned forward anxiously. "Do you know where my little girl is?''

"I do.''

"Where?'' Her knuckles went white, she was clenching her hands so hard.

"She's up in heaven with the good Lord, my dear," Sister Clara said softly. "I looked up the records. I'm afraid the wee thing was sick. She lived for only three days, then passed from this earth in the arms of Sister Mary, who went to God herself just three years ago.''

"My child is dead?'' Sylvia whispered, white as a sheet, wondering how the knowledge could hurt so much when she'd never even held her baby in her arms.

"Yes, child. But don't question the good Lord's wishes. There was damage. And from what I read in

the report, you were in rather disastrous shape yourself. They wanted to keep you in the hospital longer,
but you insisted on leaving. You had suffered enough,
and the child would only have suffered too had she
survived. She had brain damage, you see.''

"He killed her,'' Sylvia whispered savagely. "He
beat me and in the process he killed her. That bastard
killed my child.'' Anger overwhelmed her. Somehow
she would see justice was done. But not now. Now
she wanted to see her baby's grave, to mourn. "Did
you bury her, Sister?''

"Of course. We christened her Mary, after the
Holy Mother, and she received a Christian burial, as
was her due. If you would like, I'll show you her wee
grave. Sister Mirta, who does the gardens, always
mentions how well the flowers grow just there. Maybe
there's a reason.'' She smiled kindly.

Sylvia rose shakily and followed Sister Clara
through the glass doors into the garden. They walked
in silence under the cloister, through the quiet gardens
of the convent and on through a wicket gate to the
graveyard. At the end of a row of small graves, in the
shade of a laden chestnut tree, she spied the little slab.
The inscription read Mary, the date of birth and death,
and quoted the Bible: "What the Lord giveth, the
Lord taketh. May you rest in peace in His arms.''

She kneeled down on the grass and touched the
stone. "God forgive me for abandoning you,'' she
whispered, tears bathing her cheeks as she gazed at
the bright marigolds covering her child's tiny grave.

"He already has.'' Sister Clara smiled tenderly
down at her. "You did everything you could for her,
and all you've done for the orphanage these past years

has helped many others who survived but had no one. We were able to build a new nursery with the funds you provided. Would you like to see it?'' Gently she helped Sylvia rise and drew her arm through hers, guiding her away from the grave.

At the end of the path, Sylvia stopped and turned back. ''Goodbye for now, Mary,'' she whispered. ''You'll always be with me wherever I go.''

Then she turned and followed Sister Clara back into the building, straightening her shoulders and preparing herself for the future she now knew she could face.

Eyes half-closed, Sylvia let Jeremy knead the kinks out of her shoulders as they lay on the sofa, her head in his lap, watching television. For the past few days she'd done nothing but lounge around the suite, too tired to do anything but watch TV and try to let go of some of the stress. Years of it, she realized, letting out a little moan of delight when he touched a sensitive spot.

Jeremy's hands wandered to her shoulders, then slipped to the open zipper of her plush velvet tracksuit. She stiffened. They hadn't made love since Miami.

During the past days she'd refused to think about the future, hadn't allowed herself to do more than take one day at a time. Now as his fingers moved to her breasts and desire speared, she realized how much she'd missed him. She also knew it was time to talk.

Removing his hand gently, she turned in his lap. ''Jeremy, we need to talk.''

''About what,'' he murmured, kissing her ear.

"About us. We can't just...get involved again and—"

"Again? I thought we *were* involved." He continued nibbling her ear, let his hand slip back to exactly where it was before she'd removed it and continued stroking, making it hard to concentrate.

"Jeremy, you must realize that I'm not a suitable companion for you, that this will never work out for—oh my God—" She let out a low moan as he taunted her breast and his other hand slipped inside her before she had time to protest. Unable to think straight, she succumbed to delight when he found that magic spot she'd never known existed. He sensed her, touched her in a way she'd never been touched before. Unable to resist, she arched, arms encircling his neck as they accommodated themselves into a comfortable position on the couch. Her lips met his. She could feel his tongue playing, driving her as crazy as his fingers. Something tense loosened inside, uncoiling, a sudden delicious release that left her soft, moist and ready. She brought her hand down and reached for him, stroking him, feeling how much he wanted her. Then all at once she fell back as an unexpected orgasm ripped through her. It went on and on and he didn't stop caressing. She wanted to beg, for him to stop, to go on, to—

Sylvia sank back in his arms saturated, delighting in everything about him, his scent, his body muscles, the feel of him. Next thing she knew he was moving inside her, pressing the small of her back against him as their bodies met in a frenzy of unleashed desire. She looked into his eyes, nearly wept with joy at what she read there, each thrust a message of love and possession she knew she could never live without. She didn't even try to resist or take over, just let him guide her wherever he wanted, until at last they came together, bursting into one another, their love and passion sealed by a commitment deeper than any words.

26

At 6:00 a.m. Don Murphy stepped bleary-eyed off the Greyhound bus at the Port Authority in New York City. He held an old army duffel bag in one hand and stared, yawning, at the address on a piece of grubby paper in the other.

Park Avenue. Even he'd heard of that. Mighty fancy address. Good. If she could afford a place on a street like that, she could afford to pay him to keep his mouth shut.

Pushing through the crowd of early-morning travelers, he headed for the nearest bus stop. After several inquiries he boarded a bus heading for the Upper East Side and stared out the window. This sure was a long step away from where she'd started out. Maybe it was time to remind her.

Don rubbed his unshaved chin and absorbed the city. The last time he'd been anywhere as big as this was when he'd traveled to Little Rock to board the plane to go to 'Nam. He sucked in his cheeks and stared at the pavement crawling with busy shoppers, people hurrying along carrying briefcases, files stashed under their arms, cell phones glued to their ears. Life had changed, he realized suddenly. Back then, things hadn't seemed as frantic as they did now.

A rush of unease spread over him. Maybe this wasn't such a great idea after all. Then he leaned back, glanced at the fat Latino lady in the red coat next to him and shrugged. He was here now, so what the hell. He had nothing to lose. He'd kept the wolves at bay for a while with the money Thackeray had given him, but that was about to run out. What he needed was security, a nice little nest egg to see him through his old age. And Sylvia was his ticket. The thought of frightening the shit out of her gave him a little thrill, too, he admitted. It had been a while since he'd intimidated anyone, and he liked feeling that he was still in charge.

The bus stopped a little way down from the address Thackeray had given him. He got off and stood on the sidewalk, staring up at the high-rise structures. When he reached the huge entrance of the building, he found it hard to quell his growing anxiety. He hadn't expected it to be quite like this. The buildings hadn't seemed so tall or so flashy when he'd imagined this scene back in Smokey's. Now, for the first time in many years, he felt insignificant. Still, he masked his discomfort and walked across the gleaming marble toward the elevator, determined to reach his goal.

The shiny doors opened like magic and people poured forth. He moved out of their way, afraid he'd be tramped on, they moved so fast. Then he caught sight of a familiar blond head. It wasn't long and straight anymore, like the hair he'd lusted after, but he'd know it anywhere. Hadn't he dreamed of it night after night until he'd finally had her?

Quickly he pulled himself together and followed the elegantly dressed woman back toward the main entrance. He quickened his pace, afraid he might lose her in the crowd if she got to the street before him. His heart beat faster. It was her, all right. He recognized that determined, uppity walk of hers. He remembered the way she'd writhed under him, how she'd fought, and wished he could do it all over again. The memory emboldened him. He quickened his pace, pushed a passerby aside, then reached out and laid a hand firmly on her shoulder.

She spun around. Don watched, delighted, as horrified recognition hit. A slow, cruel smile of satisfaction spread over his face. She was still afraid of him. Sweet.

"You!" she whispered in a cracked voice.

"Yeah, baby, it's me a'right. Didn't think I'd let you miss me forever, did ya?" Then he gripped her arm and steered her out into the street, walking fast up the sidewalk before she could pull away.

Sylvia trembled. She wanted to scream but no sound came. Ramon was sitting in the car waiting for her, looking in the opposite direction. Don steered her off the sidewalk and into the busy street. Her knees wobbled and her legs felt like jelly, as though they would crumble beneath her. This couldn't be happening.

"So you've made it in the big leagues." Don maneuvered them into a side street. Sylvia looked around her like a terrified rabbit. A woman passed and glanced their way. She willed herself to call out.

Again she opened her mouth but no sound emerged. Her hands shook and fear paralyzed her. She stared at him, wide-eyed and unbelieving. What could he be doing here? How had he managed to locate her? Usually she wasn't even in the office these days.

Slowly she forced herself to calm down and take a look at him. He was older. Much older. His once-handsome face looked craggy and gray. The cruel lines around his mouth were more pronounced and though she could still feel his strength in the iron grip on her arm, something had changed there, too.

"What do you want?" she croaked, once she was able to breathe. They were standing in the doorway of an old Eastside building. It was windy and she turned, shielding her face, giving herself time to think straight. If he was here, it was because he wanted something. He wouldn't have come just to violate her again, she reasoned, despite her terror. "What do you want?" she repeated, eyeing him again warily.

"I can think of several things I wouldn't mind having," he drawled chattily. "First I'd like to get out of this damn wind. Maybe we could go to a restaurant. You got money, you can pay."

"There's a diner farther up the street."

"Good. Then that's where we'll go. Wouldn't want any of your fine friends seeing us together in some fancy joint, would we?" He sent her another knowing grin.

"What else do you want?" she repeated, walking stonily ahead. He'd removed his hand from her arm, as though he knew he had her nailed. Lord, she was sick of everyone believing they could blackmail her.

"Oh, not much by your present standards. Just

enough to keep me in comfort for the rest of my days. How about a monthly stipend? We cut a deal. You send me money and I leave you alone.''

"You want me to support you?" She stared at him, wondering if he'd lost his mind.

They reached the diner. It was in the basement of a building and they walked down a few shallow steps. Inside, the ambience was warm, bright and friendly, a retro sixties makeover with a jukebox, lots of plastic and Formica. It made Don seem even more out of place than he already did.

They sat at one of the turquoise-Formica tables. A pretty, blond waitress, not over twenty, brought them plastic menus and stared at Don as if she'd seen a Martian. Sylvia found herself looking at him again. She'd spent a lifetime hating this man with a vengeance, yet now she felt nothing. He'd raped her, killed her child—she never thought of it as *theirs*— and now he was trying to shake her down for money. But for some reason she'd gone blank inside. Not numb from fear like moments earlier, not ravaged by loathing for all he'd done to her, just plain blank.

She stared at him hard, at his old bomber jacket and jeans, same as he always dressed, his faded T-shirt and tobacco-riddled teeth, and knew she wasn't afraid any longer. That was nothing but a first reaction to which her mind and body had become conditioned. Now that had passed and she could suddenly see clearly, knew she had nothing left to lose. After all, she'd faced herself and the past. What else was there for him to blackmail her with?

Nothing.

Suddenly she wanted to laugh, it was so obvious. All at once she felt light as a feather.

They ordered two coffees and Don lit a Lucky Strike. He watched her speculatively across the wiped table. She was a beaut, all right. Always had been, always would be. He wondered for a second if he could still get her into bed, but didn't think so. Nah. Not worth it. Plus, he was tired and didn't really care about fucking broads anymore. It was the cash he cared about. And she was good for it.

He cleared his throat, leaned back and tried to look at ease. Sylvia didn't seem as frightened as she had when he'd first accosted her. In fact, she looked too damn confident by half. He wished he could do what had always worked in the past—take off his belt, throw her over the couch and beat her good and proper. It had always left him feeling real good to see her cowering.

But unfortunately that wasn't an option anymore. He shifted, took a long drag and wondered why she wasn't blabbering nervously, asking him what he wanted. Instead, she sat, hands neatly folded on the table, and appeared extraordinarily calm. Well, that was about to change.

"I had a visit from a friend of yours," he said in the same taunting manner of old.

"You mean Thackeray?"

"That's the man. Seen him lately?" he said, smirking.

"Well, that'd be kinda hard." She drew her eyebrows together.

"And why is that?" His mouth twitched irritably. He didn't like it when women played games.

"Because he's in the slammer, that's why. Let me see, fraud, drug trafficking, money laundering," she listed. "You name it. They pretty much pinned everything on him. So I guess he won't be around for a while, if ever."

"You mean he's in the clapper?" *Shit.* He hadn't counted on anything like this.

"Oh, yeah," she assured him. "And one other charge I forgot to mention—*blackmail.* Ring a bell?"

Don was starting to feel mighty uncomfortable. This was not going as he'd imagined it would when he'd come up with his bright idea back in Smokey's Hole.

"You're bullshitting me," he muttered with false bravado.

"Oh, no, I'm not. I'm surprised you didn't know. It's been in all the papers. Maybe it missed Fayette-ville. That's where you hang out these days, isn't it? Still hankering after that chopper, Don?"

"I didn't come here to talk about choppers," he snarled.

"No," she said deliberately. "You came here to see what you could get out of me. By the way, how much did you take Thackeray for?" she asked sweetly, tilting her blond head, an innocent, questioning look on her face that didn't deceive him for a second.

"None of your damn business," he growled as the pretty waitress laid two cups of steaming coffee on the table.

"Oh, but I think it is," Sylvia said softly. She leaned forward. "You told Thackeray about what happened all those years ago and you know what? It almost worked. Except for one minor detail.'' She crossed her arms on the table and stared straight into his face. ''I'm not afraid of you anymore.''

''Oh yes you are,'' he hissed, showing his rotten teeth. ''You were scared out of your fucking mind back there in the street, remember?'' He leaned quickly over and grabbed her wrist in a sharp, burning twist.

''Not so fast,'' she hissed, holding the stare despite the pain. ''Take your hands off me right now or I'll have you arrested for harassment, you bastard.''

''I'll tell them everything,'' he taunted triumphantly.

''Go ahead. I'll sue you for rape, assault and battery, and I'll put you behind bars for the rest of your worthless fucking life.''

The hand loosened and his eyes widened. ''You're bluffing. If anyone knew the truth about you, you'd lose all you've got,'' he said knowingly.

''Not anymore.'' She rubbed her wrist.

''Stop playing games, Sylvia. You always played games. Played too damn many with me. That's why you got what you deserved. You should have just let me fuck you the first time around. You might have enjoyed it. I could have shown you a thing or two. All I want is a decent retirement, something to live on, enough not to worry. You could help me.'' His voice dwindled into a whine.

''You're pathetic,'' she said, disgusted, pulling out her wallet. ''Here.'' She slammed a copy of the baby's picture on the table and picked up the check. ''That's all you'll get out of me, Don Murphy. Take a good look at it. Maybe it'll keep you warm on a cold winter's night. Now get the hell out of town before I call the cops on you. If I catch you anywhere within a hundred yards of me, I'll slap you with a restraining order.''

Rising, she marched to the cashier, paid for the coffee, stepped back out into the windy street and never looked back.

Sylvia walked into the hotel suite, surprised to see the lights low and candles lit everywhere. She'd spent the afternoon walking in the park, ridding herself of any last vestiges of anger, then had gone on a shopping spree at Bergdorf's, feeling lighter and happier than she had in years. Don Murphy's presence and the realization that he was not a huge, terrifying monster but a pathetic old pervert had liberated her. If she remembered him at all, it would be as the wretched, wizened man sitting opposite her in the diner. The only thing from the past she couldn't eradicate was that she was unable to bear children due to his ill-treatment of her. She stopped a moment, looked around her at the lovely scene and sighed. Jeremy must have prepared this, she realized, tears melting in her eyes, overwhelmed by a wave of tenderness. Wonderful, dearest Jeremy, the man she loved but could never have.

''Darling? Is that you?'' He came out of the bedroom in his shirtsleeves, brows creased. ''God, I've been so worried. Where were you? I called you on the mobile and there was no answer.'' He wrapped his arms around her and she snuggled close. It felt so wonderful to be worried over, to have someone care about where she went and what she did. For so long she'd lived alone. Even with Brad, the relationship had been terribly adult, modern and efficient, taking care of their own personal issues and sharing quality time. But this was different. So gentle, so loving, so simple and caring. She reached up and touched his face, then dropped a kiss on his lips. Was this what being married to the right guy felt like? Someone you could dream of sharing the rest of your life with?

"What's all this?" Swallowing the rising knot in her throat, she stepped out of his arms and let him help her remove her coat. Another sigh tugged at her heart. He was so kind and polite. That was something she'd always appreciated in him, even back in the days they'd been doing battle. He invariably rose when she entered the room or sat down at the table, always made sure she was comfortable. It wasn't an act as it was with some men, a ploy to impress. It was simply second nature to him. He would do the same with his aunt, his sister or the cleaning lady, she realized fondly, loving him all the more.

"I thought we'd dine in tonight, if that's all right with you. I have a bottle of champagne on ice."

"Oh? What are we celebrating?"

"That," Jeremy said deliberately, "will depend on you." He moved toward the open kitchen and she swallowed hard.

This was it. Oh God. How was she going to tell him?

Jeremy pulled the bottle from the ice bucket and carefully popped the cork. Then he poured two glasses of crisp, bubbling Cristal and handed her one across the counter.

"Come, let's relax a little." He drew her by the

hand toward the soft, cushioned couch, leaned over and turned down the volume of the Vivaldi CD, then pulled her head onto his shoulder and slipped his arm around her. They sat for a while in silence, enjoying each other.

Sylvia took a long gulp of champagne and basked in the warmth of his arm. It felt so darn good—heavenly, she reflected, heart aching. God, how she wished she could do this forever. But she could not allow him to make that mistake, for she felt sure he would regret it for the rest of his life. His role demanded that he have a wife who could bear him children. He needed an heir, someone to continue the long, noble lineage that was his birthright.

And she couldn't come through.

Shifting in his arms, she let out a bitter sigh of regret. Why was there always a price to pay for any happiness that came her way?

"You sound weary, darling. Everything okay?"

"Everything's fine." She would not spoil the magic moment by telling him about Don Murphy. Perhaps she never would. It was part of the past and the visit would only anger him. Still, it had brought closure for her. She was free now and ready to look toward the future, with no murky secrets ready to jump out of the closet and pounce on her.

"Shall we light the fire?" she said suddenly, wanting the atmosphere to be perfect. Whatever time they still spent together had to be flawless, she realized, getting up and crouching by the grate.

"Let me. I'll do that. You'll get those lovely hands dirty."

"I think I almost liked you better when you treated me as a human," she teased. "I won't break."

"No, you won't." He crouched next to her and cradled her face. "You're a very strong and wonderful woman, Syl, but inside you're lovable and tender. And that's why I love you."

"Don't." She pulled away and rose abruptly.

"Why?" He rose too and stood over her, green eyes searching hers. "Look, there's no use putting this off any longer," he said at last. "I want to marry you, you know that."

"Please don't." She backed away.

"Don't what? Ask you to marry me? Of course I'll ask you to marry me." He frowned and shook his head. "For goodness' sakes, you can't expect us to live together for years and years. We're getting a bit past it if we plan to have a family, don't you think?" he said with a touch of humor.

"Jeremy, darling, I..." She moved farther away, wishing she didn't have to say the words that would seal their future.

"Tell me. Whatever it is, just tell me." He stood, back straight before the fireplace, and waited.

She would always think of him just like this, Sylvia reflected, in his gray flannels, blue shirt, silk tie and pale yellow cashmere sweater. Other men probably wore exactly the same thing, but to her it was Jeremy.

"Jeremy...I can't have children."

"What do you mean?" He frowned, uncomprehending.

"When I was raped, there was permanent damage."

"But surely—"

"No. I don't think anything can be done. The doctor told me after the birth. Look, we need to face the facts. You need to have children to bear your name and carry on the Warmouth line. You could never have a wife who was infertile," she pleaded, coming toward him and gently touching the knot of his tie.

"I don't see that it's *that* important," he countered mildly. "We could always adopt." He didn't look nearly as fazed as she'd expected him to.

"But that wouldn't be right. Besides, your family might object."

"It has nothing to do with my family. Sylvia, darling, let's get one thing straight. I'm a man in my own right." He gestured with the glass and let out a frustrated laugh. "I don't lead my entire existence worrying whether or not my family will approve or disapprove of what I do or don't do. They'll just have to like it or lump it."

"That's what you say now," she countered, "but maybe someday you'd come to regret your decision, wish you had your own blood following in your footsteps."

"Good Lord, this isn't the Middle Ages."

"I don't know—" Sylvia cocked her head doubtfully "—Warmouth seems kind of Middle-Agey to me. I'm sure it would expect a proper heir."

"Okay." Jeremy sent her a quick questioning glance, then sipping thoughtfully, he made up his mind. There was no use insisting when she was in one of her stubborn moods. He'd just have to wear her down until she saw things his way. "We won't go on discussing it now," he said mildly. "Besides, we've got to get ready for our trip to London tomorrow. Reggie called to say the designs for the latest collection are ready. Given all the problems we had with the last ones, I thought we'd better take a look at them in person—minimize the chance of any more mistakes.''

"Good idea," she agreed, somewhat taken aback by his sudden change of attitude. "I can be packed in fifteen minutes."

"I knew you'd agree. I told the captain to have the plane ready by nine tomorrow morning. I hope that suits you?"

"Jeremy, you are the most autocratic—"

"Now, now," he laughed, dropping a kiss on her protesting lips.

"Jerk," she said, laughing. "*Suit me,* indeed. You haven't the least intention of changing your plans," she exclaimed, tossing a cushion at him.

"Just acting with the best possible intent," he murmured.

"Right. Who do you think you're fooling? Remember when we last quarreled about travel arrangements?" she added with a pang of regret.

"We?" He quirked a brow and grinned. "*I* never quarreled. You had some misguided notion, and as far as I recall, I acted as a perfect gentleman and let you have your way—astounding, really, since at the time all I could think of was how much I wanted to make love to you on the jet's conference table."

"Jeremy!"

Without further ado, he reached over, locked her in his arms and, before she could protest further, kissed her thoroughly.

27

Two days later Sylvia lifted her head groggily from the bathroom sink. She felt terrible and wanted to disappear into a hole in the ground. That's what drinking too much champagne on the flight and eating potted-shrimp sandwiches at Fortnum & Mason had led to. But she'd felt extraordinarily hungry. Fish had been on her mind all day long. And when she'd seen the shrimp sandwiches on the menu, she'd pounced as though there was nothing left on the planet to eat. Now, she reflected grimly, she was paying the price for her greed.

She raised her head and groaned. Jeremy was to blame for having plied her with all that champagne during the flight, she reflected dolefully. But as she straightened her stiff back and prayed the nausea wouldn't return, a smile escaped her as she recalled other moments of their return flight to London. Then as she was about to leave the bathroom, another wave of nausea had her leaning over the basin once more.

"You okay?" Arabella asked, expression worried

as Sylvia emerged, pallid from the executive ladies' bathroom.

"Fine. It must be those potted-shrimp sandwiches, I guess."

"God, you look green." Arabella eyed her askance. "Are you sure you shouldn't go back to the hotel and rest, see a doctor or something?"

"I'm fine." Sylvia gulped, then her stomach heaved once more and she spun around. After several minutes of retching, with Arabella soothing her worriedly, she sank back on her heels, relieved. "I think it's passed, thank God."

"You look a little better." Arabella glanced at her curiously.

"This is the second time it's happened. I thought yesterday morning it was something I'd eaten on the plane. But then it began all over again."

Arabella frowned. "That's odd. Only in the morning, you say?"

"Yeah. Really weird. I guess it could be a virus, and not the shrimp."

"You're not preggers, are you?" Arabella asked, hand poised on the slim hip of her skinny jeans as she handed Sylvia a glass of water.

"Pregnant?" Sylvia squeaked. "Good Lord, no." She shook her head and laughed. "That's impossible." She gulped down some Evian and felt immediately better.

"Why not? Lots of people get pregnant. Sounds like morning sickness to me. My friend Sophie is having her first baby and she was exactly like this for the first three months. Enough to put one off the whole idea forever, I might add,'' she said with a disdainful sniff.

"But that's just totally impossible," Sylvia repeated regretfully.

"Why?" Arabella asked as she and Sylvia walked down the corridor and back across the hall. She reached for a biscuit from the tray Finch was carefully carrying and followed Sylvia into her office.

"Because—look, it's a long story. Something that happened to me when I was a teenager. I can't have kids." She rotated her neck and did a yoga stretch.

"Ah." Arabella nodded. "Still, you never know. Doctors can make mistakes." She shrugged and munched.

Sylvia looked the other way, afraid the sight of the cookie might make her want to throw up again. Then suddenly, as she sat down, Arabella's words sank in and she began counting. Goodness, she realized, pulse missing a beat. With all that had happened, she hadn't even noticed that she'd missed a period. Was it possible that the doctors had been wrong...?

"What is it, Syl?" Arabella asked, eyes narrowing. "Come on, tell me. What is it?"

"It's just that—no..." She shook her head. "That's crazy."

"You're not making any sense," Arabella complained.

"Wait. Let me think." She leaned back in Major Whitehead's chair, too excited to focus. It couldn't be. Surely it wasn't possible. Yet the fact remained that she'd missed her period and was feeling like hell. "Arabella, do me a favor," she said in an excited rush. "Is there a pharmacy around here?"

"There must be a Boots in Piccadilly, I should think. Why? Do you want Finch to get you something? I'll ring for him." She leaned across the desk to the phone.

"No!" Sylvia grabbed her hand, panicked. "No, not Finch—you. Please do me a favor, Ara. Go over there and buy me a pregnancy test, will you?"

"Aha!" Arabella jumped up gleefully. "I knew it. I'll be back in a jiffy. Don't budge." She pointed at Sylvia severely and left the room.

Ten agonizing minutes turned into fifteen and then twenty. Sylvia fiddled impatiently, doodled on her pad, got up and sat down several times, unable to get on with her work. What if it was true and she was pregnant? What then?

Finally the door burst open and Arabella rushed in, breathless. "Here. I'm sorry it took so long but there was a queue at the cashier's. Some wretched woman wanted drops for her eyes and couldn't decide which ones to choose. Anyway, here you are." She laid the white-paper package on the desk.

Sylvia stared at it and swallowed. Her future lay inside that bag. If the test read negative, well, then it was no more than she'd expected. But what if it read positive? A deep longing took root, although she did her best to squelch it. Instinctively she touched her belly then took a deep breath. "Thanks. I guess this is it."

"Wait." Arabella went to the door and peeked out, then turning, she beckoned conspiratorially. "Go now, while there's no one about. Promise you'll tell me at once, won't you?" she pleaded, fidgeting like an excited child and pushing Sylvia out the door.

She was crossing the hall when Jeremy walked in.

"Hello, darling." He dropped a kiss on her forehead and took off his coat, which he hung up on the ancient bronze coat stand. "Feeling better?"

"Fine." She tried to sound normal. If only he knew what was in the works.

"You still look rather off-color," he murmured solicitously, touching her cheek. "You shouldn't be in the office when you're ill."

"I'm not ill," she muttered impatiently. "Just a little queasy."

"That doesn't sound very promising." He lingered, slipping his hand over her hair. "Hadn't you better see a doctor if it doesn't get better? There are all sorts of bugs about. You must be careful." He took her arm and led her toward his office.

"Look, I'll join you in a minute," she said, unable to curb her anxiety. "If you'll excuse me, I was just on my way to the ladies' room." She smiled, a tight bright smile that left him wondering what on earth was the matter with her, and he watched as she disappeared down the corridor.

It was the longest five minutes she'd ever spent, Sylvia concluded, staring at the vial and willing it to change color. When the test finally turned blue, her hand clapped over her mouth and she smothered a cry of joy. Then doubt gripped her. What if the results were faulty? After all, it wasn't a laboratory test. A pharmacy one might not be reliable. Hadn't she read somewhere a high percentage of these tests were defective? Leaning against the wall, Sylvia let out a ragged sigh. Perhaps she shouldn't believe it. Maybe she should go to a doctor first and have a real test before getting her hopes up. Still, as she sank onto the toilet seat, a new and extraordinary sensation overwhelmed her.

And suddenly she knew with absolute certainty that she was expecting Jeremy's child. It was ridiculous to be so sure and she experienced a moment's hesitation. Then, after throwing the test tube in the trash can, she washed her hands and prepared to leave.

Arabella stood hovering impatiently outside, face wreathed in expectant excitement. "Well?"

"It went blue. I guess that means—"

"Positive. Yippee! You're pregnant!" she exclaimed loudly, jumping up and down. Then she threw her arms around Sylvia and began dancing a jig.

"Ara, stop, please, it may be wrong," Sylvia begged, laughing. "It may be a mistake, for all we know, the test could be completely unreliable. Oh God." Tears rushed to her eyes and Arabella stopped. "I don't think I could bear it if it turns out to be wrong," she whispered.

"It won't." Arabella assured her. "I'm absolutely, one hundred percent sure you're really pregnant."

"Who is pregnant?"

Lady Margaret's loud voice echoed down the passage and the two women turned in openmouthed unison.

"Aunt Margaret," Arabella muttered, shocked. The two women watched as she descended upon them, a chartreuse dressed and coated figure trailed by the corgis.

"I was on my way to the Ritz for lunch but had

an urgent call, and thought I'd dash up to the loo here first. Did I hear you say someone was pregnant, Arabella?''

"Uh, not really."

"I'm not deaf—not yet, anyway—and as far as I know, one either *is* or *isn't* pregnant." Lady Margaret drew herself up and eyed them both with suspicious humor, drawing her own conclusions. Arabella looked about to burst with news and Sylvia's face was covered in a dazed, dreamy smile that told its own tale. "Well" she exclaimed, delighted, "this is a lovely surprise. I gather I'm to be a great-aunt. Quite right and about time, too, after all the goings-on. Does Jeremy know yet?" she asked in a conspiratorial undertone.

"Not yet." Arabella shook her head.

"Well, what on earth are you waiting for, child?" Lady Margaret turned to Sylvia. "Bustle about, girls, this is no time for dawdling. God knows it's taken him long enough. About time the family grew. The loo will just have to wait, I'm afraid. Fiiiinch," she called in a singsong staccato. "Where are you?"

As always, Finch materialized out of nowhere and inclined his head.

"You called, my lady?"

"I did. Kindly produce a bottle of the best vintage champagne in the house and take it to Jeremy's office immediately. Oh, and Finch—" she smiled benignly "—bring glasses for everyone, if you please, including that creature with the purple lipstick at the front desk. This is an occasion."

"Very well, madam." Finch remained impassive.

With another little bow he retreated, displaying neither surprise nor emotion at the unusual request.

"Now," Lady Margaret said, taking matters in hand, "you, Sylvia dear, had better run along to Jeremy and tell him the good news before we all descend upon him. And you, young lady," she continued, addressing Arabella, "shall come with me and wait in the other office while she makes her announcement. Quite something for Warmouth to finally have a new heir," she murmured, a sudden tear trickling down her powdered cheek. "I must say, Sylvia dear, I'm dreadfully pleased that you're going to marry Jeremy. I always knew you had it in you." Her cheeks quivered and she dabbed her eyes with a lavender-scented hankie, before enveloping Sylvia in a fond embrace.

"But we're not certain yet, Lady Margaret. What if it's a mistake? It would be too terrible to get everyone's hopes up, especially Jeremy's, and then—"

"Oh, twaddle!" Lady Margaret dismissed, straightening the ruby and diamond fern on her lapel. "One just has to look at you to know, my dear. Now hurry along and stop worrying. It's not good for the baby."

Taking a deep breath, Sylvia headed across the hall toward the door of Jeremy's office. She hesitated a moment, containing all her emotion and excitement. Then, mustering her courage, she knocked.

"Come in," he called, looking up as she entered. "Everything okay?" The phone rang and he picked up. "Yes...yes, of course. No, that'll be fine...okay, we'll close on that one. Perfect." He placed the phone back in its cradle and smiled. "That was about the Chinese platters we talked about the other day. We're all missing poor Miss Hunter. That new temp spends her time yaking on the phone. I'm missing three files and—''

"Jeremy—" She clasped her hands in front of her and swallowed.

"Yes?" He frowned, and rose quickly and came around the desk. "Is something the matter, Syl?"

"I think I made a mistake."

"A mistake," he repeated in a hollow tone.

"Yes."

"What sort of mistake?" he asked anxiously. Had she decided she didn't love him anymore? He gripped the desk and waited. She looked distinctly odd, almost dreamy, not like Sylvia at all. He moved forward and gently grasped her arm. "Maybe you should sit down. I think that potted shrimp affected you more than we thought."

"It's not the potted shrimp."

"Not the potted shrimp?" He frowned, mystified.

"No." She shook her head and a slow smile broke on her lips.

"Then what is it?" he asked, flummoxed.

"It's a baby."

"A what?" His eyes nearly popped out of his head.

"A baby. I made a mistake." She grinned. "I thought I couldn't get pregnant, but I've missed my period and the test is positive." She flung her arms around his neck and he hugged her so tight she thought she'd burst.

At that moment the door flew open. Finch marched in, carrying the champagne bucket and balancing a tray arrayed with flutes, followed by Lady Margaret, Arabella, Reggie, the new secretary, and the doorman, who had already found time to wager a bet with Lady

Margaret's chauffeur that the future Warmouth heir would be a boy.

"It'll be the first wedding at Warmouth since your parents', Jeremy," Lady Margaret exclaimed, handing around glasses.

"Aunt Margaret, we haven't asked Sylvia if she wants a Warmouth wedding," Jeremy murmured, looked down at Sylvia fondly, barely able to contain his joy. He smiled at her and she grinned back, utterly content. She didn't care where they were married.

"Not want to get married at Warmouth?" Lady Margaret exclaimed. "What nonsense, Jeremy. Of course she wants to get married at Warmouth. Now, Finch, pop that champagne and let's celebrate."

"Aunt Margaret, give poor Syl a chance to make up her own mind," Jeremy laughed. "She'll be put off before she's had a chance to get used to the family."

"No, she won't." Arabella smiled happily and raised her glass. "You two are meant for each other. Nothing can stop you from being together."

"I'll drink to that," Reggie seconded.

Sylvia's hand slipped into Jeremy's. For a moment her life flashed before her: the good, the bad, the important and the insignificant. Then she turned and Jeremy took her in his arms.

"This has all got onto an awfully fast track." He grinned. "I still haven't had the chance to ask you to marry me properly."

"Go right ahead," she whispered, grinning back, happier than she'd ever believed possible.

"Very well." He took a step back and raised her

hand close to his lips. "Will you do me the honor of becoming the next countess of Warmouth?"

The room hushed in silent expectation, glasses hovered in midair, and everyone held their breath.

"I will," she replied. And meant it.

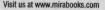

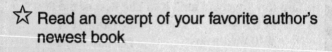

FIONA HOOD-STEWART

66670	THE LOST DREAMS	___ $6.50 U.S.	___ $7.99 CAN.
66833	THE STOLEN YEARS	___ $5.99 U.S.	___ $6.99 CAN.
66606	THE JOURNEY HOME	___ $5.99 U.S.	___ $6.99 CAN.

(limited quantities available)

TOTAL AMOUNT	$_____
POSTAGE & HANDLING	$_____
($1.00 for one book; 50¢ for each additional)	
APPLICABLE TAXES*	$_____
TOTAL PAYABLE	$_____

(check or money order—please do not send cash)

To order, complete this form and send it, along with a check or money order for the total above, payable to MIRA Books®, to: **In the U.S.:** 3010 Walden Avenue, P.O. Box 9077, Buffalo, NY 14269-9077; **In Canada:** P.O. Box 636, Fort Erie, Ontario L2A 5X3.

Name:_____

Address:_____ City:_____

State/Prov.:_____ Zip/Postal Code:_____

Account Number (if applicable):_____

075 CSAS

　*New York residents remit applicable sales taxes.
　　Canadian residents remit applicable GST and provincial taxes.

MIRA®

MFHS0903BL